CH00926628

Zanzibar Uhuru

by Anne M Chappel

a revolution, two women and the challenge of survival

Copyright © 2015 by Anne M Chappel

All rights reserved. This book or any portion thereof may not be reproduced or used in any manner whatsoever without the express written permission of the publisher except for the use of brief quotations in a book review.

Cover design and illustrations: copyright © 2015 Anne M Chappel

For further information contact: zanzibaruhuru@gmail.com and zanzibar-stories.blogspot.com.au/

Disclaimer:

This book is a work of fiction. Any similarity between the characters and situations within its pages and places or persons, living or dead, is unintentional and co-incidental.

ISBN-13: 978-1505511840

ISBN-10: 1505511844

Contents

Acknowledgements

Writing this book has taken me on a journey. It has not been entirely alone. Thanks go to the many people that have helped me along the way with practical help and encouragement. Thanks to Adelaide's Kensington & Norwood Writers' Group members for constant support; to my editor, Valerie Williams for her thoroughness; to my husband, Mervyn, for his editing and patience; to my Zanzibari friends for their stories and help; to my daughter for her advice, it was always valuable, and to my son for being there. My children make it all worthwhile.

This story is a story but it is also based on facts as remembered and recorded.

Anne M Chappel, Adelaide, Australia, 12 January 2015.

Introduction

Zanzibar is an enigma. Therein lies its charm and its tragedy. It is part of Africa and at the same time deeply connected to Arabia and the monsoon lands fringing the Indian Ocean. The main islands of the archipelago are Zanzibar, locally called Unguja, and Pemba. Over the centuries, they were settled by those seeking a haven, and yet became places renowned for slavery and genocide. They have endured a turbulent history that continues to divide their people. It is a history far more bloodthirsty than suggested by their tiny size.

For more than two thousand years, travellers have come to Zanzibar. The Phoenicians, Chinese, Greeks and Portuguese left artefacts and the ruins of fortresses. Amongst those who stayed were the Persians; Yemeni and Omani Arabs; Sinhalese from Ceylon; Parsees, Bohras, Ithnashri and Ismaili Khojas, Kutchis from India; Pakistanis; Comorians; and Goans. It is believed that seafaring Indonesians visited and left behind the skills of making outrigger canoes called *ngalawa*.

Zanzibar Town, also called Stone Town, was built on a triangular parcel of land pointing out into the sea facing Tanganyika. If you look west past the smaller islands and sandbanks fringing the harbour, you can imagine the coast of mainland Africa over the horizon.

Over time, Zanzibar grew steadily in influence and wealth. You need a protected harbour to be a trading post, safe from storms rising with the monsoon winds. You need fresh water to supply passing ships. Some claim the water in Zanzibar filters down through ancient aquifers from the melting snows of distant Mount Kilimanjaro.

Stone Town is the commercial capital of the islands. Solid two to four-storey buildings of coral limestone line the wandering maze of streets right down to the seafront. There, modest palaces and official buildings gleam whitely in the sun, taking pride of place, with the right to have the healthier sea air and views of the arriving dhows and inter-island steamers.

The city took on its present form in the days of the great Sayyid Said bin Sultan, Sultan of Oman and Zanzibar, over one hundred and eighty years ago. The Arabs from Oman built large homes to house their families, followers and slaves.

Local history tells the story, more like a parable, of three of Sultan Said's wealthy sheikhs and their argument as to how to create a lasting memorial to their position and power. One elected to build two magnificent trading dhows but they were wrecked in a terrible storm. The other chose to build a palace on the seashore but it burnt down. The third, Sheikh Bushiri Al-Harthi, built an enormous home on the northern side of Ras Shangani, the apex of Stone Town's triangle, arguably the best site along the seashore. He called the house Mambo Msiige, translated as 'do not imitate'.

The story of Mambo Msiige continues with the detail of Sheikh Bushiri's determination that his house should endure. For extra strength, he ordered eggs to be mixed into the limestone plaster covering the blocks of coral rocks that formed the three-storey high perimeter walls. Perhaps this house is a symbol of Zanzibar; crumbled and weathered, it has endured the vicissitudes of time.

His house survived but his ownership did not. In 1859, after the death of Sultan Said, his sons manoeuvred to become the next Sultan. Sheikh Bushiri unwisely supported Sayyid Barghash whose challenge failed. Sayyid Majid bin Said Al-Busaidi became Sultan, and he sent his defeated brother into exile in Bombay, India. Sheikh Bushiri's punishment was to forfeit the magnificent rambling building overlooking the harbour. Hubris is not confined to kings and sultans.

Sayyid Barghash bin Said Al-Busaidi had his turn but he had to be patient for eleven years. In 1870, he became Sultan. Sultan Barghash was a builder, a visionary who put his faith in the British Empire to protect his interests, and in doing so, lost his own empire. The islands were never again free from interference by Western powers. The Scramble for Africa was on: Zanzibar was important for its position protecting the sea route to India. In 1890, partly to block German imperial intentions, Zanzibar became a British Protectorate. It would remain so for seventy-three years.

Zanzibar is famous in history for three industries: slaves, ivory and cloves. They were interrelated. The islands became a plantation economy and workers were needed for the clove harvest. The slave trade would have been more modest but for the added demand coming from the French colonies of Mauritius and Réunion, and the western coast of the Americas for cheap labour. Ivory too played its part in encouraging slavery, for slaves were burdened with the pale curved tusks on their journey to the coast. The demand for ivory came from across the globe, including the cutlery producers in Birmingham, the German reliquary carvers and the billiard ball makers of Boston.

Britain's Colonial Office controlled her Empire. White colonial administrators arrived and dominated the Sultanate. The British Resident lived in a palace and controlled all the major decisions of the islands, even to the extent of having the final word on the appointment of new Sultans.

Reporting to Zanzibar's British Resident were the administrators heading every government department. During the late 1950s and early 1960s, colonial staff regarded a posting to Zanzibar as the end of their colonial careers. The rush towards independence in all British colonies meant there was nowhere else to be sent, no other titles of seniority to which to aspire.

Uhuru! was the cry across Africa after the Second World War. The demand for freedom from the colonial yoke gathered in intensity. It could not come quickly enough for Africans and optimism prevailed. Joyful enthusiasm greeted the granting of independence to the Gold Coast in West Africa, renamed Ghana. President Dr Kwame Nkrumah represented a shining example of a free Africa.

After the due process of negotiation and democratic elections, Zanzibar was declared independent on 10 December 1963. Prince Philip, the fresh-faced Sultan Jamshid bin Abdullah al-Said and the recently elected government watched the lowering of the union jack at midnight on Cooper's Fields outside Stone Town. A new flag was unfurled; a new country was born and immediately accepted into the United Nations.

There it was, democratically elected, modelled politically on Britain, with a bill of rights and the division of powers entrenched in its constitution. It was a formula for governing these islands or the whole of India.

Sadly, the people of Zanzibar were deeply traumatised by the political process.

The monsoon winds were moderate on the eleventh of January 1964. This year seemed no different to other years down the stretches of time. The variable days of November were past and the sea wind blew steadily out of the north-east. The fastest dhows had arrived in Zanzibar Harbour and were resting at anchor, their cargos unpacked. The rest of the fleet were out in the Indian Ocean, their sails filled with the *kaskazi* blowing from India and the Arabian Gulf.

This was a year when it was better to arrive late in Zanzibar Harbour.

Regional Map of East Africa

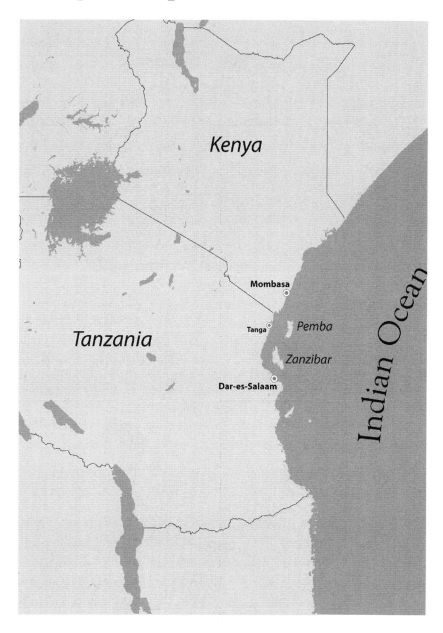

Greater Zanzibar Town Area in 1961

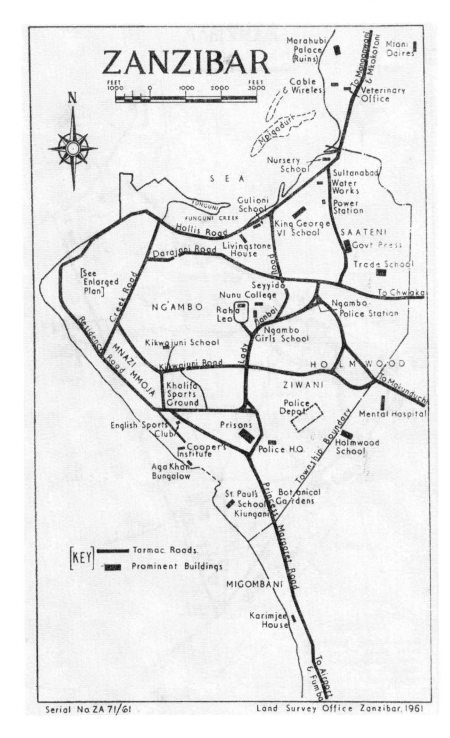

Detail of Stone Town Area in 1961

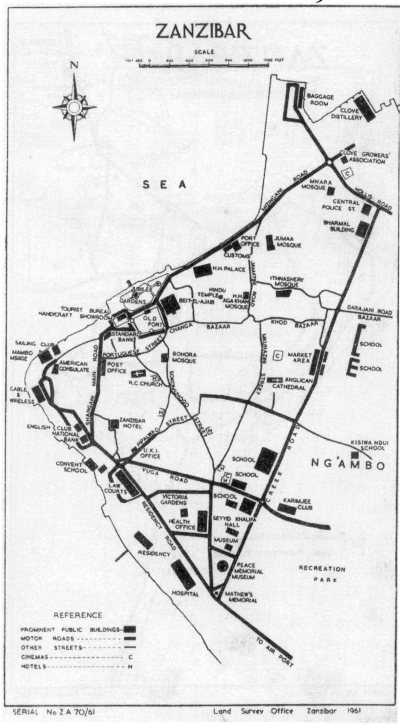

Section 1. 1964. The Revolution

1. Fatima. My Family, My Life

Liandikwalo halifutiki   What is written cannot be rubbed out

Zanzibar

'Wait, wait for me. Don't go! I am coming!'

I am running as fast as I can. I am the youngest and my call carries across to the beach where the sun shines on the sand between the coconut palms. There are no shadows. I hitch up my skirt. Sweat is running down my back; my hair is free. I am laughing and my heart is hammering. I see the tall outlines of my brother and sister against the brightness. Taha and Basilah turn and wave.

They are faster than me, and together they run along the beach where the sea rushes gently onto the sand. I follow and see how with one wave their footsteps are washed away.

This is a dream that rises in my sleep, a vision I cherish. It is many months since I lost all that was precious to me.

*****

During the school holidays of December 1963, my parents decided I would be allowed to continue on to high school. I was keen on my studies and did well, taking exams seriously. There was a place for me at the Aga Khan Girls' School if my grades were acceptable. However, I needed to improve my English marks. At home, we spoke KiSwahili and did our Qur'an lessons in Arabic. Babu, my grandfather, spoke and wrote Arabic well. He was a religious scholar.

My Baba, my father, Ahmed bin Khaleed al-Ibrahim, spoke English fluently and made speeches in that language. I had been preparing for half-year exams for standard six, and Baba came to help me with English grammar. I was practising on old exam papers.

'Say it aloud in your head and it will come to you, Fatima. Examiners will give you a verb, for example, "to run" and ask you to make up a sentence in various tenses. I will do one for you. Present tense is—I run to the beach. What is the future tense? It is—I will run to the beach, past tense is—I ran to the beach. Note the change in spelling. Sometimes a verb adds "ed" to get the past tense. The more you read English books, the easier you will find it.'

My Mama, who could not speak fluent English, was listening.

'London Bridge is fallin' down, fallin' down,' she sang. 'London Bridge is fallin' down. My fair lady.'

'Mama, what is that? Why is London Bridge falling down?'

'I don't know,' she laughed. 'That was taught to me by our English teacher. She said nursery rhymes would help us learn!'

'Maybe, Mama, if I learn well, I too can become a teacher.'

I have these memories. In the journey of my dreams, I am again with them, listening to my Baba talk. It is so real that when I wake, I have to discover where I am. Over and over again I relive the heartache and the painful journey that brought me here.

I was born on Unguja Island, Zanzibar, late in 1951 during the years of the Sultan, Sayyid Khalifa bin Harub. Our Sultan died the year I turned nine. My Baba was sad for he was well loved in our islands. We were all his subjects. I listened to stories about our leaders.

'One of our ancestors was a *wazir*,' Mama said, 'a minister to Sultan Barghash when he became Sultan a hundred years ago. He travelled to England with his Sultan when they met the British Queen.'

Mama's name was Amal bint Yusuf and she was distantly related to the Sultan, of the al-Busaidi family, who long ago came from Muscat in Oman to rule in Zanzibar.

The present Sultan was Sayyid Jamshid bin Abdullah al-Said, Sayyid Khalifa's grandson. Most Fridays, after prayers, my Baba attended a *baraza* meeting at the Sultan's country palace at Kibweni or at his Stone Town palace on the waterfront. During the *baraza*, the men would talk about political matters, about our clove harvest or the arrival of the dhow fleet on the monsoon winds. You could bring your problems to the Sultan for his help and understanding. We were safe in his care for he was a just man. This is what I heard from my Baba.

There are times I think I see Mama in the street. A laugh or a faint perfume takes me back. A pain shoots through my heart. These memories are like a vision you have of another life. They walk with me. I do not have photographs, nothing to remember the dead. I fear my memories will fade, like dreams when daylight comes, and then who will remember them? The Prophet Muhammad (Peace be upon Him) said we should honour our parents. He guides and comforts me in the ways of Allah.

Recently, they celebrated another anniversary of the Revolution, with speeches about the victory over what they call the 'wicked ways of imperialism and colonialism' from which we have escaped. Yet the dead have no voice, and the life we lead is not filled with freedom and has little joy.

The people are too scared to complain about how little food there is in Darajani Market. For hours we wait in sun and rain, lining up for our hungry families while the leaders live well. Young men cannot get jobs except in the police or army. Fear has sealed everyone's lips.

I was only twelve in January 1964, neither child nor woman. My sister, Basilah, the brave one, was to be married after Ramadan in six weeks' time. She was eighteen and beautiful: to me she was grown up and I was a child. Her black hair hung shining to her waist. I wanted to be like her.

I followed Basilah around from the day I first walked. One of my delights was to bring her presents to show her how completely I adored her. I collected flowers from our garden and shells from the beach and she would gently accept them, crouch down and thank me earnestly.

'How pretty, Fatima, thank you. This is the loveliest shell I've ever seen.'

My parents had approved a suitable match for Basilah with a distant cousin. She had met her future husband when they were children and she liked him and his family. When his father approached my father, and our Baba asked her, she gave her consent. Of course, once she was a woman, she could not be with any man unless she had a companion so she knew little of men's ways.

Mama said love would grow with the passing of the years. Mama's aunt visited Basilah to talk to her and be her *somo*, or marriage guide, to teach Basilah the duties of a wife. I would wait by the door to listen to their secret talk.

Mama chased me away. 'Go child! You are not yet a woman; this is private business. Your turn will come.'

The wedding was to be a grand occasion, for Basilah was the first child of our family to be married. It would be a gathering of local families where connections went back many generations. My brother, Taha bin Ahmed, was two years older than Basilah. He was helping my Baba with the clove trees and coconuts on our *shamba*, and did not yet plan his marriage. I asked him if he was in love with Basilah's best friend, Jannah, but he told me to go and play in the garden. You could tell love by little things, a longer glance as she passed by with her family, the way he said her name.

I would tease him with a saying, *japo kidogo chatosha kwa wapendanao*, 'a little is enough for those in love!' It made him mad and he would chase me out of the house while I ran shouting to my *ayah*, Paka, for help.

My Baba was a wealthy man. I only realised that later. Our family had a home in town in Shangani where the old houses were, and clove groves in the *shamba* around our country home. The name of our farm was *Salama Daima,* which in English means 'Peace Forever'. The clove harvest had brought us wealth in the past. Every year, workers came to pick the cloves before they burst. I helped spread out the red buds on the woven mats to dry after the harvest. How sweet they smelt to me! It is the smell of my country.

We travelled between our big house in the Shangani area of Stone Town, capital of our islands, and the country house beyond Bububu. We had a black car and I would sit in the back with the window open and wave to everyone. Donkey cart drivers would wave back from behind their loads of coconut husks and call out, '*Hujambo! Kidogo* Missus!'

How grand and proud I felt!

The road to the *shamba* was narrow, winding through the mango trees. Our house was near the beach and it was large and full of family and servants. Basilah and I each had a maid, an *ayah*, to care for us. My *ayah* was called Paka because she was so small. She had been with me all my life, and I loved her.

It was a carefree time, for surely childhood should be without fear, and I was dearly cherished. When visitors came to call, I would sit within Baba's arms as he spoke with his friends. I would listen to the men talk. They spoke about the clove price, the coconut harvest or politics.

My Baba was involved in this politics. Sometimes men would speak urgently and argue and Baba would shoo me away.

'Go, Fatima, little one, do not worry, go and help Mama and Paka.' I was always chased away!

Uhuru, independence or freedom, was on everyone's lips. Zanzibar's second election to decide which party would run the country had already taken place. In December 1963, our Independence Day had been celebrated at midnight with the lowering of the British flag and the raising of our own flag. Taha and Baba had gone to the ceremony where a Prince of Britain stood with our Sultan and our new Prime Minister. Next day, Taha showed me our flag.

'See Fatima, here are the clove buds that made our island wealthy,' he said, 'so they are golden, and the red background shows us the colour of the

Sultan's flag.'

Taha told me in his serious, listen-to-me-I-am-your-older-brother voice. 'Baba is an advisor in one of the parties forming the new government, the ZNP, and will be important now the British people are leaving.'

'Why are they leaving?' I asked, for I was used to seeing the *wazungu*, the white people, in town driving around with their families and playing and swimming on our beaches. Some evenings we went to listen to the Police Band playing in front of the English Club in Shangani, and the European bandmaster in his white uniform conducted music from their country. Their strange ways were talked about, for they ate pigs and worshipped in the Christian Church in Mkunazini Road.

'This is our country,' Taha said. 'It is time for us to take it back from overseas rulers and our flag will stand alone! All over Africa this is happening. It is a new dawn for Zanzibar. It is *Uhuru*.'

They were happy the ZNP had won the last election organised by the British Government. The first one had been a draw to everyone's surprise and even more talk and more loud arguments went on.

When I was nine, in 1961, there had been fighting and many deaths. Many people feared what would happen if the African party won. These matters did not concern me. It was for men to deal with. I was safe then: all I wondered about were our plans for Basilah's wedding.

Mama had been buying Basilah new clothes for many months. Bright silks and *kangas* for everyday wear covered her bedroom. New furniture was chosen for life in her husband's home, including a camphor chest for storing clothes and bed linen. We thought of little else besides the business of planning for the wedding feast. Advice was given by my aunts and Mama's friends who gathered to discuss wedding organisation and family matters. I even heard talk about who they might consider for my husband one day. Laughter filled our house and through it all Basilah smiled in gentle happiness.

The ceremony would take three days. Baba and the bridegroom would do the *nikah*, the marriage agreement, at the mosque, after the agreement of the *mahr*, or bride settlement, according to our custom. The bride could not appear unveiled before any men except her new husband so the bridal feast would be brought out to men and women separately. I was to have special dresses, and Mama said I must hand round sweets to the women guests, special sweets I loved, like the warm honey cake, *bint-al-sahn*.

The wedding had been postponed until after the fasting and family time of our month of Ramadan. A cousin had passed away unexpectedly in November and, out of respect, Baba changed the date.

Basilah's wedding day would never be, for now came the Revolution which ended my life as a child and ended so much on our islands. That time is cast in darkness forever. This is what I remember.

2. Revolution

12 January 1964. Mambo Msiige, Stone Town, Zanzibar

03.10. Angela shook her husband's shoulder. 'The phone, the phone.'

Mark Hamilton leapt up. Moonlight, reflected from the sea, glowed in ripples on the ceiling.

'What's the time?'

'A little after three.'

Their bedroom, on the second floor of the house south of the main Mambo Msiige building, faced west over the sea, past the buoy marking the point of Ras Shangani.

He reached the phone in the hallway before it rang out.

'Yes? Hamilton.'

'Sorry Mark. Shamte. I can hear firing. Direction of Ziwani Barracks.'

'Right, sir, I'll get hold of the Commissioner. Call you back.'

Angela turned on the light and shrugged on her dressing gown. She ran her fingers through her hair.

'Trouble? Is it bad?'

'Could be. That was the PM. There's shooting at Ziwani Police Barracks.'

He dialled Paul Sinclair, Commissioner of Police.

'Paul, what's up?'

'Yes. Just heard. There's a mob at Ziwani. I can hear shots. Might need the Mobile Force. They should get it under control. I'm going to check it out. Will let you know.'

Mark rang Mohammed Shamte back. 'Sir? It's not good. Ziwani is under attack. The Commissioner is going in with police. Will need the Mobile Force at Mtoni Barracks. He hopes he can sort it out.'

'You had better notify everyone on the Security Plan.'

Mark sat down. By the phone was his leather briefcase. The folder he removed had a red cover unlike the other standard manila folders of government business. On its cover was the label, 'Mr M Hamilton, Permanent Secretary, Prime Minister Mohd Shamte', and underneath in capitals, 'SECRET'. It contained his prepared phone list and itemised emergency procedure. His hand was steady.

'Angela. Go to the Kelele Square verandah. Let me know if you can hear or see anything.'

He started: Duty Officer, Ministers, Attorney General, Administrative

Officers, Permanent Secretary Finance—Henry Small. All reports of security issues were to be sent to him. He hoped each man remembered what to do.

Angela came back. 'I think I hear firing, but it's a long way away. What news?'

'Don't know yet. Let's hope Mtoni Barracks holds and the Mobile Unit can get moving. Could be a long night. We have the Prison and Malindi Police Station to fall back on. I don't hold any hope of securing Ng'ambo Police Station.'

03.40. The hospital was next. He rang the Medical Superintendent.

'Dr Hughes. Mark here, sorry to wake you. We've got a developing situation at Ziwani Barracks. Expect casualties. Can you prepare the hospital for emergencies?'

The doctor sounded half asleep. 'I'm in town, but most of my staff live in Mazizini. Do you want me to call them in?'

'Yes, remember 1961. Get them all in. Establish full emergency status.'

Next on the list, Cable and Wireless. It was their communication centre with the outside world, with Britain. He rang the manager.

'Sorry, Michael. It's about twenty to four. We have an emergency. Problems at Ziwani, maybe elsewhere. There's a mob attacking. Can you open communication channels with Dar-es-Salaam, Aden and Nairobi? I'll ring you back shortly.'

The British. He needed to contact them. Zanzibar might need military help. Angela was back.

'I can distinctly hear firing now.'

'I'm waiting on Sinclair.' His finger was on the next phone number. 'We need to get hold of the British. Let's hope it doesn't come down to depending on their help.'

'Why not?'

'Well, they refused to sign the defence pact we asked for. Said Zanzibar was to become an independent country. Not a good reason.'

03.55. The phone rang.

'It's Sinclair.' Mark could hear the agitation in his voice. 'Been to Ziwani. It's lost, overrun. I'm taking more men back to attack but they've got into the armoury. I saw a group handing out weapons, maybe forty or more men.'

'What about Officer Derwent?'

'His men were overwhelmed. Managed to turn on the alarms and he escaped.'

'What arms have the rebels got? Any idea who they are?'

'All of them. A hundred and fifty rifles at least. Two Bren guns. No. No idea but they're organised. I suspect it's the UMMA Party. We'll mount a counter-attack shortly. I've got a few men. I can't get through to Mtoni and the Mobile Force. I'm sending Smith to get them. Asked him to contact you if he can't get me.'

'Right. I'll inform His Majesty and Ministers. Hospital's on standby.'

'It's not looking good. Losing those arms. Will ring you as soon as possible.'

04.10. Mark phoned Reginald Cross, the British High Commissioner. His First Secretary answered after a single ring.

'You're up. You've heard,' Mark said. 'Can you let Cross know we're opening up Cable and Wireless? It's serious. We'll need to contact the British in Aden. Evacuations might be in order. We don't have a full picture at the moment. We'll keep you informed.'

'Thanks, Mark. Will prepare communications.'

As he put the phone down, Angela put her hand gently over his on the receiver. She had changed out of her pyjamas. The hall light enclosed their two figures. He wiped the sweat from his upper lip.

'We need to talk. What about the kids? Where's this all going?'

'It's in the balance, my dear,' Mark replied. 'We don't know who we're dealing with. How they'll act if they take full control. Already they have arms. They might attack us here. We can't discount that. There are the Afro-Shirazi Youth gangs to consider. They were the bad influence in '61. Also we've had recent security reports of mainlanders coming over here to join anti-government movements. They may have organised this or merely aided and abetted it.'

'What do you want me to do? It's happened so soon, only a month after independence.'

'But it's happened. Can you get me some clothes? Get the girls up. Keep them calm. Better dress them. Make it black. Mary can stay down here with us. Show Elizabeth where you were keeping watch. We must keep a close eye on the square. It's important. Keep behind the wall. If she sees any mobs, people in a group, come and tell us. Keep the dog down here, don't want her barking.'

'Right. What about our neighbours? The Reynolds are in the Cable and

Wireless flat this month. They're meant to be leaving next week for the UK.' Angela said. She had gathered her hair behind her and to Mark she looked pale in the light from the single bulb. She's doing well, he thought. How lucky he was to have her beside him. Panicking would get them nowhere.

'I'd forgotten they were next door. Before you wake the kids, get across to Heidi and Jack. Use the sea-side doors. Ask them to join us. He should know the situation already. And see if the big launch that arrived last night is still moored offshore.'

The phone rang once and Mark picked it up. It was Smith.

'Mark. Glad to get you. Terrible. Just escaped.'

'Take a breath. Are you hurt?'

'No. I'm north of the town, in Beit-el-Ras. It was close. Drove to Mtoni with one police *askari* to check on the status of the Mobile Force. Didn't expect it. Ran into a roadblock. Made a mistake thinking it was our chaps. A mob came for us, smashed my windscreen. I got out my revolver and shot at them. Some fell. We ran into the bush. I came back along the beach. The buggers will soon have the rifles, the automatics and submachine guns.'

'Smith, make your way into town. Get to Malindi Police Station if you can. Be careful and check it's still in our hands. Ring when you get there. I'll give Sinclair your news. It's not over yet.'

The Reynolds had arrived from the Cable and Wireless flat. Jack, the Attorney General, looked battered. He was puffing, smoothing down pale strands of wispy hair over his almost bald head. His shirt was misbuttoned. Heidi, a head taller than her husband, was standing to attention in a midnight-blue silk dress with her gold bangles and a large black handbag. It was as if she was turning up for evening drinks. Her chubby arms were folded over her chest.

'It's happening, isn't it? Like we said it might? I think I need a double G&T,' said Heidi.

Jack put his arm around his wife's waist. It accentuated their height discrepancy. 'We'll be all right, my dear. Glad our boys have left for school. We would've been off home in a week. It's the Arabs I'm worried about.'

'I told you we shouldn't delay after independence. Now this,' said Heidi.

'Yes, well,' Jack said. 'What's to do Mark?'

Mark looked at his wife. In two days, their girls would have left for their boarding schools in Nairobi and been safe. Their suitcases were half-packed with their new school uniforms.

'Can Heidi help Angela? Make us tea. Get the girls up. Can you stay here? I'll put you in the picture after I've spoken to Sinclair.'

Sinclair answered immediately and Mark relayed Smith's story about his futile attempt to reach the Police Mobile Force.

'So we've lost them. More arms for them. If they open that armoury, that's another two hundred and fifty rifles lost to us,' Sinclair said. 'It's looking worse. Fighting is ongoing at Ziwani but we don't have enough firepower. All we can probably do is buy ourselves a little time. We need help, and fast.'

'Looks like it,' Mark answered. 'The AG's with me. I suggest I contact the PM and get a message to President Kenyatta in Nairobi and President Nyerere in Dar. One of them must support us.'

'That could be our only hope. It's a concerted attack. I want to check on Ng'ambo Police. Malindi should be all right. Let's hope they're holding out.'

04.35. Mark rang the Prime Minister.

'Sir, we've losing Ziwani and the Mobile Force is overwhelmed. Commissioner Sinclair doesn't hold much hope for Ng'ambo considering its position in the native township. Cable and Wireless is operational. Do you think you should contact President Kenyatta and President Nyerere and ask for reinforcements? The airport is open at the moment. Even if it falls, either of their forces could retake it.'

'Ali Muhsin is here with me.' Shamte replied. 'He knows the Kenyan Minister of State, Joseph Murumbi. He will ring him. Can you put in a formal request to both governments? We must declare a State of Emergency and twenty-four hour curfew forthwith. Can you get through to the radio station at Raha Leo?'

'Sir, I asked Yahya not to open the station. He can do a broadcast but keep it shut as we cannot protect it at this stage. I've put our Internal Security scheme in place.'

'Good. Do we know what force we are dealing with, Mark? Who are these people attacking our country in the days before Ramadan? How will violence solve anything?'

Mark felt a pang of regret. If the administration had pushed through funds to secure the armoury, they would not have been so vulnerable. He felt like saying sorry. The fledgling government was critically exposed. Their enemies knew and had taken advantage.

'I don't know sir. They seem to be in considerable numbers and well organised. I suspect it's the UMMA Party behind it. We all know they've had Chinese training.'

05.00. No sooner had Mark replaced the handset than it rang again. It was Sinclair.

'Mark. Ng'ambo Station is under attack. We'll retreat to Malindi. I've got some Special Forces and Arab irregulars. Few arms but might get some more. Will ring you from there. We can protect the harbour entrance to roads to the palace. Any response from the mainland?'

'Not yet. We've contacted them. State of Emergency has been declared and twenty-four hour curfew.'

He put down the phone.

Heidi, Angela and Jack were talking quietly in the hall.

'Is Elizabeth all right, Angela?' Mark said.

'Yes. Wants Mary with her so they're both there. I'll keep checking on them. What's our plan?'

Mark stood up to face them. Heidi was hugging herself.

'If we get confirmation that Kenya or Tanganyika will send their army, we can announce this on the radio and that will change the game. Otherwise? It's serious. Trouble is, once it's light and word's out, all hell's likely to break loose. Everyone will get into the act. You know what happened in '61. Mob violence and madness take over. Looting is the least of the worries. It's the Arabs. The women will suffer.'

They all knew what that meant.

'And our kids? Can we take the risk they won't attack the British?' Angela asked. 'We don't know who these people are. Even if we did ...'

The phone rang. Mark answered.

It was David Snelling, the Permanent Secretary, Education and Information. 'Strange. Just heard, the radio's on. Not us. Wasn't it meant to be off air?'

'Yes. It must be closed down. We don't want the rebels to get it.'

'Will do.'

Mark faced them again. 'Our plan? It'll be dawn soon and it'll get more complicated. At least the phones are working. Angela, is that launch offshore?'

His wife nodded. 'It is.'

'The safe option is to wait offshore,' said Mark. 'You'll need to get out before dawn. Jack can help.'

'What about you?' said Angela.

'I must stay for the moment. Too much going on. Get our Zodiac dinghy down to the beach. Make sure the rowlocks are secure. It'll take five people.'

The phone rang.

'Mark. David here. Spoke to Frigout at the radio station. He sounded odd. Couldn't do anything. I reckon he had a gun at his back. What do you suggest?'

'Isn't our radio signal relayed somewhere else? Through Marahubi? Could you break something there?'

'Yes, that's right. I'll raise the engineer out there and disable something. Bye.'

Mark stayed sitting. It was getting worse. Ideas spun through his head and he placed a firm hand on his knee to stop its nervous jiggling. He had to keep calm, had to think. He took deep breaths.

Elizabeth stood in the doorway, her arm round her younger sister. 'Dad? What's happening?'

Black clothing emphasised their pale faces, their youth. Elizabeth, at almost fourteen, was in-between child and woman, long straight hair and a slim serious face. At twelve, Mary was the baby, eyes wide, pale hair dishevelled, half asleep. Yet a sweetness graced her features and heralded the beauty she would become. Around her neck was wound a pink silk scarf with spotlights of glitter. On her arms, pale spots of calamine lotion showed where mosquito bites had been treated.

I have to protect them, thought Mark.

'Hello, Mrs Reynolds, Mr Reynolds,' said Elizabeth. 'Mum, we're hungry.'

'Good idea,' said Mark. 'Get some food, but we need someone on watch. Heidi, can you take over?'

'I'm wearing the Christmas scarf you gave me, Mrs Reynolds,' said Mary, arranging the material round her neck. Mary was nudging her sister and giggling. Both were looking at Jack Reynolds's bare feet. Jack had huge flat feet and walked with them splayed outwards. Mark knew that his girls called him 'Mr Duck'. Angela glared at her daughters.

The phone rang.

'It's done,' said David. 'We broke the connection at Marahubi. Frigout phoned Cable and Wireless and asked them why the station had gone off air and could they fix it. So Raha Leo is overrun. But Mark, it won't last once they work it out.'

'Keep me informed.'

05.30. Mark put down the phone. It rang. This time it was the British High Commission.

'Cross here, Mark. Not looking good. I've informed Aden. They'll keep in touch. They want to know the status of British subjects.'

Mark interrupted. 'Any chance of support from them?'

'Shamte asked but you know the situation. Independent country. This is now an internal affair. There's no attack from outside. HMG doesn't consider it appropriate for UK troops to intervene.'

'How do you know that?'

'What?'

'That it's not aided and organised from outside.'

'Who would that be?'

'You know as well as I do. And they might attack British civilians.'

'I've requested *HMS Owen*, it's a marine survey ship, to come here from Mombasa on standby. Only about two hundred British are left here.'

'What about the Indians, Arabs and others who until a month ago held valid UK passports?'

Jack leant close to Mark to listen.

'The question now arises as to the legal government.' Cross's voice was low.

'What in the hell does that mean?'

'Well they're a minority government.'

'So what! They're the legal government we put in place with democratic elections.' Mark was shouting. 'We attended the handover. We set the rules. No such question arises. You don't hand over to rebels attempting a coup d'état! We're waiting for troops to arrive from Nairobi and sort this out. Sooner the better.'

He almost smashed the phone down.

'Amazing,' said Jack. 'What's he thinking?'

Elizabeth and Mary arrived back with their mother. Angela carried a tray of tea and biscuits.

'Thanks,' said Mark. 'While we've got a moment, let me help you get the dinghy ready.'

'I can do that,' said Jack standing up. Mark looked at him. Jack was pushing fifty and his shirt barely connected across his stomach.

'I know where it's kept. Can you man the phone?' Mark said. 'Come on, Angela. Kids, wait here and hold the dog.'

They went downstairs into the storeroom. The basement air was cool with the salt sea smell he loved. Together they slid their black rubber dinghy through the seaward doors. The craft was a sturdy army surplus unit. Angela fetched the oars and Mark inserted and secured the rowlocks, threading pins in the base on each side.

Mark removed two lifejackets. 'No space for these if you are taking five. I'll leave the lifejackets for the kids here. Luckily, the sea's calm.' They hauled the boat out onto the narrow way between the house and the sea wall. 'Let's take it onto the beach in case.'

'In case we have to leave in a hurry?'

'Yes,' Mark answered. 'It's best. I don't want to risk you and the girls. Wait offshore. Kenya's army unit might arrive in a few hours and this will be sorted but it's not a done thing. Can you row out to the launch?' They stood shoulder to shoulder and looked out to sea. It was a warm night, a tropical night, like so many others before. Lights from Stone Town played onto the black waves and the white hull of the launch at anchor. Green starboard lights shone in duplicate, winking on the water.

'It's not far. Hope the captain is on board. Explain the situation and tell him we are commandeering his boat. It's a State of Emergency. He must wait there and, if need be, Jack and I'll join you. Maybe Jack will go with you. If the rebellion is sorted, we'll wave to you to come back in.'

Together they continued to haul out the dinghy and it bumped heavily down the sea wall steps. They pushed it into the shadows. The tide was out, exposing the pale beach which was taking on the first faint glow of dawn. They returned to the others around the telephone.

'What shall I take with us?' said Angela.

'No time,' Mark said. 'It's getting light.'

Jack was on the phone. He waved for Mark to come closer.

'Mark's back. I'll tell him. That's good news.' He put the receiver down. 'That was Sinclair. He's in Malindi Police Station. No action there yet but they are guarding the entrance to the harbour and palace. The good news is he has confirmation a Kenyan General Service Unit will be here at midday. They're assembling at the airport now. Murumbi appears to be onside but he's waiting on a final sign-off from President Kenyatta.'

'Well, that not a sure thing but he should support us after those negotiations with the Sultan for the coastal strip last year.'

'Sinclair says the Sultan is ready to fight,' said Jack, 'but it would be better that His Highness and his family were safe offshore. The steamer, *Salama*, is in harbour. His advisors are trying to get him to go aboard but he's refusing to leave.'

06.15. Mark tried to take stock. Who was behind this? Most likely the UMMA Party, formed by the charismatic Mohamed Babu and his young firebrand followers, trained in revolutionary techniques in Cuba and China. They didn't call themselves the 'Masses' party for nothing. It was a well-tried political process—fire up the masses, the lumpen proletariat, and give them direction. They may not encourage mob violence but the crowds would be hard to control. Chaos would work in their favour.

'Its decision time,' Mark said. 'It'll be light in a few minutes and news will spread fast. What we do know is we're dealing with a lot of rebels in several groups and they are organised. They've taken over our two arms stores and soon they'll have a mob behind them. Unless the Kenyans or British come in, we're in deep trouble. On our personal front, we can't take that chance with you and the kids here.'

'What will you do?' Angela said.

'I must stay here to work with the PM and help Sinclair in his situation. Jack, I suggest you go with Heidi, Angela and the kids. It might be easier to commandeer that boat with you there.'

The phone rang. It was Sinclair. 'We've done a count,' he said. 'We have over a hundred men here but few rifles. Any chance of supply from Pemba? There's that little De Havilland in Pemba, goes to Tanga in the morning. It could be filled with reinforcements. Can you organise it?'

'Will try,' said Mark.

'Good, and by the way, turn the radio on. I fear they'll get control there. We are dealing with an organised mob. They've had training.'

Jack turned from talking to Heidi. 'Mark, I'd like to stay. Help you. That's if Angela and Heidi can make it out to the launch on their own.'

'Of course we can,' said Heidi standing taller and putting an arm around Angela. 'We can do it. You'll be able to watch from the beach. Let's go now and that's us and the children safely out of the way. How will you get out?'

'We'll swim! It's not far. I'll see them off,' Jack said. 'You need to organise the arms from Pemba.'

Mark hugged his wife and daughters all together. Mary hung on longest, wrapping thin arms round his waist, her pink scarf encircling him.

'I'll be fine, Angela,' he said. 'It may not be long before you can come back. If by midday we haven't come out, you must consider asking the captain to take you to the mainland or to the *Salama*, if it's still in the harbour. We can hold the fort here. But don't come back without a clear message from us.'

They took nothing with them. Elizabeth and Mary ran down the beach ahead of the adults who dragged the dinghy. The beach was striped with shadow and deserted, the sand cool as their feet sank in. Offshore, two fishing craft, *ngalawa*, passed silently by in the early light, lateen sails billowing above tiny hulls. It was the time of *tangabili*, the time of two sails or light winds, and tiny waves splashed the low tidemark. Tendrils of clouds suffused with crimson were spreading over the town.

The girls jumped in first, scrambling into the craft's bow. It bounced lightly on the water. Heidi and Angela sat side by side, each taking an oar. Jack waded in holding the stern steady.

'Good luck,' he said. 'I'll wait here. Wave when you're there.'

It took a little while for the women to coordinate their strokes and get under way. Jack could hear them counting, 'One and two, one and two,' as the oars rose and fell, spray rising as the blades hit the waves.

Jack was proud of them. He waited in the lee of the steps and listened. Yes, he could hear shots, not regular, but definitely shots. The dinghy moved quickly from the shore. The women seemed to be rowing well but struggling with direction. Jack realised a strong current flowing around Ras Shangani was pushing them off course. Heidi was pulling more effectively, and they paused and corrected with extra strokes from Angela. They arrived at the launch and he listened for their call.

'Hello, anyone on board? Hello there.'

A figure appeared on deck. Jack couldn't hear the ensuing conversation but saw the girls climbing aboard followed by Angela and Heidi. He returned their waves before he climbed the steps back into Mambo Msiige.

3. Field Marshall John Okello. The Attack

12 January 1964. Raha Leo Revolutionary Headquarters, Ng'ambo, Zanzibar

Field Marshall John Okello is my name, Field Marshall of the new Zanzibar Republic. I am the soldier who today leads the Revolution against the imperialists! My strength is that of ninety-nine men.

The world will hear of me for all Zanzibar will hail me as their saviour. On this day, I was created Field Marshall, for I am conquering the invaders and ending the domination of my brothers and sisters.

The weak-hearted were not there when I cut the wire fence into the grounds of Ziwani Police Barracks in the dark hours of this morning. Many of my men had run away in fear. I had no fear. I led the remaining soldiers of my battalion into the police compound. We crawled towards the armoury knowing that before this day was gone, we would either be rulers or corpses. My men had trained for weeks in the coconut and clove plantations. They had practised with sticks, stones, bows and arrows, hammers and even tyre-levers.

We rushed the building. Our only hope was to seize their weapons in a surprise attack. An imperialist sentry saw us and opened fire killing two of my men. I overpowered him and took the rifle. I killed him with the bayonet. The police had been sleeping upstairs because of the heat of the January night. They were now fully awake and hurried down the stairs to get their weapons. My men struggled with them. A siren went off and the police trumpeter blew an alarm. I fired, shooting the man dead and his trumpet fell. I rushed to cut the siren wire.

We had overwhelmed them. Our attack was an absolute victory. Those we did not kill, I persuaded to surrender. We smashed open the doors to the armoury and I handed out rifles, Bren guns and automatic weapons. Our firepower was now secured and the Revolution had started. We raised the flag of my revolutionary army and my flag of Field Marshall over the Ziwani Police Barracks. The great day has arrived!

4. Fatima. The Call

Vita havina macho   War is blind

12 January 1964. Shamba – Salama Daima. Zanzibar

Some things are clear in my mind, as if I saw them in this morning's light; other things, you thought you saw disappear. Memories twist your life into little pieces and will not go away. What I remember too well is the smell of burning.

The phone rang at our *shamba* early Sunday morning before light moved against my bedroom shutters. My Baba spoke loudly and then went quiet. I lay there listening and wondering. I heard another two phone calls. Then Baba came into my room and woke up my *ayah*, Paka, for my maid slept on a mat next to my bed.

'Paka. Wake up. You must rise. Get Fatima dressed. Be quick. You have to leave immediately. There is trouble in town.'

I did not understand. Was this not a day for celebration before Ramadan. What trouble could there be? But Paka heard the urgency in my Baba's voice for she dressed me in dark clothes and took Basilah's black *bui-bui*. It dragged on the floor a little for I was shorter than my sister, and I had to hold the cloth up with one hand. We went out to the verandah where Baba and Taha were talking and looking down the road as if they were expecting someone to arrive.

'It is better if we send Mosi and Amina away,' Baba said to Taha. 'No need for them to be here in danger.'

'I will wake them and send them to the village,' Taha replied.

Mosi and Amina were an old couple who had always lived with us, and they cared for our house at the *shamba* when we were in town. Amina was like a grandmother to me. She would sit under the trees telling stories of my Baba as a little boy. Amina taught me to weave a fruit basket out of coconut leaves, what we call *pakacha*. I used it to collect mangoes from our trees. Mosi was poorly and struggled to walk, his legs bent like an old coconut palm.

Baba turned to us. 'Listen carefully, Paka, I want you to take Fatima to your brother Ali's house in Ng'ambo. You will have to walk. As quickly as you can. There is trouble around our *mjini* town. Do not go near the police stations. Be careful on the roads. Hide if you have to. Stay there inside with Fatima till we come for you. Do not go to our house in Shangani. Be patient.

Stay there till we call you. Take this packet and look after it: you may need to use it for Fatima. Go quickly now, and may Allah be your protector! *Ma'salaam!*'

I started to cry for I did not understand. 'Baba, let me stay here and wait for Mama. I will be good. I will be quiet. I do not want to leave with Paka. Please!'

He held me firmly by my shoulders.

'Fatima, be still and listen carefully. Now is the time to be brave, little one! Do as I say. We will come for you as soon as we can. You must obey Paka. She loves you and will take care of you. May Allah's peace and blessings always be upon you and guide you, my precious daughter.'

His face was kind and wise and I loved him, so I turned to Paka and took her hand. I wondered why this seemed like a farewell. As we walked away down the path towards the town road, I stopped and looked back.

I saw Baba and Taha standing together, tall in their white *kanzus* on the verandah in the dark. All seemed so peaceful, so normal, the clove trees dark behind the house and beyond, the outline of the palm trees waving against the pale sky. They raised their hands, and with one hand I waved back, before I turned and followed Paka. This is how I remember them, together, my Baba and my brother.

I would never see them again.

I cried that day; sometimes Paka cried but never did she let me go. She held my hand tightly until my arm ached. We were bound together on that journey into town, to Ng'ambo near Stone Town, where her family lived in the native township. At the beginning, it was easy for we had been warned early. Some people had no warning but terror travels on wings and, before we were half way to town, our world was upside down.

Paka walked fast, talking to me, to herself, repeating, 'Surely, *inshallah*, all will be well.'

We journeyed down forest paths running close to the main town road under coconut palms and clove trees. Nothing seemed different at first. We walked past Kibweni Village and all was quiet but for cockerel calls and a stray dog's barking. Paka stopped to listen and wait. All was as it should be as we walked past quiet huts from which early risers called friendly greetings.

We were two small figures wrapped in black *bui-bui* covering, like shadows in the bush. Daylight came and Paka became anxious, crying and talking to herself. I knew this route so well, but I had not walked it before.

We passed the road to the ruins of the Beit-el-Ras Palace and the Sheriff Musa Mosque. Once I had prayed at this shrine with Mama, for she said it was a special place for mamas to pray for their children.

After three hours, we were close to the Marahubi Palace ruins, not far from town, and my legs were aching from walking and running. Paka stopped. She pulled me off the path, down behind a mud wall. Trucks were coming down the road filled with men shouting and singing. As they passed us, I saw the men were carrying guns and shining *pangas*, the large knives our workers use for bush clearing. Green branches were stuck into the front of the truck. Paka was shivering and praying to Allah for His protection. We did not move until the road was empty.

The last miles from Saateni Village into town were the nightmare that has never left me. Paka covered me in my shawl so only my eyes were visible and we crept along the path. Soon we met people fleeing, pushing past us on the road and out into the forest. Most were women and children: Arab, Indian and African. Why were we going into town if so many were leaving? More vehicles passed us, cars and trucks filled with men shouting and waving weapons.

'*Mapinduzi*!' they were shouting, 'Revolution!'

'What does that mean?' I asked Paka. 'Where are the people going? Why are they running?'

She looked at me, saying nothing and I saw the terror in her eyes. Paka led me away from the road and I collapsed behind a cage holding chickens. Maybe Paka was wondering what to do, which way to flee, but Baba's voice was strong in her ears and her actions saved my life.

Once more she took hold of me. 'Fatima, rise up! We must be strong and do as your Baba wishes.'

We came closer to the native town on the edge of Stone Town: smoke was rising in clouds making dark shadows in the sky. I thought of Mama, Basilah and Babu, my grandfather, in our family's house in the Shangani area not far from us. Baba told us not to go to them. I believed then they would be safe, far from this craziness.

People were rushing past us shouting. 'Flee, run, run, they are shooting and burning.'

They were open-mouthed words shouted by strangers. Half-running, half-dragged, I stumbled along. We could not hide in the bush as the road was now lined by houses. All we could do was seek safety in shadows when our strength left us. Fear consumed me, the fear of something beyond, round the corner, the next bend, where it was filled with noise and smoke rose in a dark column.

The horror was everywhere in the chaos of shouting and screaming. I saw a man carrying an old lady, her thin arms waving, holding her tight to him as he tried to keep up with others. Mamas carried babies, looking over their shoulders as older children came behind. Some families tried to take bundles of their possessions with them as they fled. There were wheelbarrows, *hamali* carts and pick-up trucks with furniture in the back. All were rushing out of our town. I knew then that they were fleeing to seek a place of safety and a deep horror came to sit in my chest. What of my Baba and Taha who we had left behind?

We came to Creek Road which led towards Paka's family house. A line of shops were burning and Paka cried but she hurried me past the heat and flames. We passed a cart filled with coconut husks, the thin donkey standing still, patiently, its head down as people ran round it, this way and that. I looked up and saw the driver was sitting in front of his load, bare brown legs hanging down, bent over as if resting like his donkey. On his chest down his white robe, his *kanzu*, there was a red stain. His *kofia* cap had fallen forward over his face.

The light was sharp over everything, the strands of the coconut palms that hung over the edge of the cart, the donkey's bent hind leg with a thin river of blood running onto the black road, the red sandals left behind, looking so used up, and the fallen husks spilt across the road. Nothing was right.

Paka tugged my arm. 'Do not look, Fatima! May Allah have mercy on him.'

She pulled me behind a mud wall to wait for trucks to pass. Paka rose up again, holding me close, her hand digging into my arm. The smell of burning was bitter in my throat. We heard screaming, shouting and sharp bangs close by. Young men ran past us carrying things over their shoulders: chairs, bags, rolls of cloth. Madness had been let loose, as if people had become wild animals. As I ran behind Paka, I stumbled and fell face forward over shoes left on the road. A sharp pain shot through my right arm and I cried out.

Paka pulled me. 'Hurry, my child. We are almost there.'

We were amongst the lucky ones on that day of the Revolution, so I can tell this story and have these memories I do not want.

I could not see properly and yet I saw and I remember. Creek Road was filled with cars and trucks loaded with men with honking horns. Bodies in white robes lay on the black road outside burning shops. The air was shimmering. Everyone ran, somewhere, anywhere.

We arrived at Paka's family house down the dirt road, a tin-roofed, brick house with a mud-walled room on each side.

She banged at the door, crying. '*Hodi, Hodi*, my brother, help!'

The door opened and we were let into a darkness filled with silent people. I was safe, home in their home. When I sat down panting, shaking and wet with sweat, I noticed blood was dripping down my arm over my green bracelet. The day before, while we were playing in the garden, Amina had woven strips of palm leaves into a broad bracelet round my right wrist.

'To bring you good luck in your studies,' Amina had said.

I held out my arm to show Paka the bleeding. She cried out. I had cut myself when I fell on Creek Road. Paka fetched a bowl of water, washed my arm and bound it with a piece of torn *kanga* cloth. The wound throbbed beneath the bandage.

We waited. That wait became a lifetime of waiting. Not knowing was the worst—hoping day after day that Baba would come here, down between the huts, calling my name. Perhaps my bright-eyed sister would be with him, coming to fetch me, laughing at my tears, wiping them away with the edge of her pretty *kanga*.

They would tell me it had all been a short madness, order was restored, and everything would be back to life as it was: that the wedding plans were under way, and soon I would return to school. And one day, I might be a teacher.

But normal was about to change, and maybe it was better not to know.

5. Waiting

12 January 1964. Mambo Msiige, Stone Town, Zanzibar

07.30. Mark Hamilton was talking to a police officer in Pemba. 'Right, don't delay. As soon as you can. Take out all the seats. Time is critical. Our airport is secure at the moment. We don't know how long that will last. Can you get here within an hour?'

He put the phone down and turned to Jack.

'They're fine,' Jack said. 'They'll be fine. Waved when they got there.'

'Phone's playing up,' Mark said. 'I couldn't get a line. I think there's a flood of calls going out at the same time; it's getting jammed. We've organised the steamer *Salama* to sit offshore, about five hundred yards from the quayside, out of firing range. It will be a safe haven if the situation deteriorates further.'

'What about His Majesty?'

'He's fully informed,' said Mark. 'It's not far from the Palace to the harbour. Rebels could get there without going past Malindi Police Station, so it's a worry. He's got guns but he has to consider the safety of the women and children with him. Sinclair phoned again. He managed to shoot up a truckload of rebels going past. They ran away and he got another seventeen rifles. Nowhere near enough.'

'And the Ministers?'

'They seem to be moving about still. Ali Muhsin is with Sinclair at Malindi. He's trying to get others to join them to put up a fight. I'm sorry now we stopped their permits.'

'What do you mean?' said Jack.

'We discouraged them from getting permission to have guns.'

'They'll be defenceless.' They both paused, fully aware of the implications.

'I'd better go and check out the square,' Jack said.

08.00. As Jack turned away, the radio made a few clicks and a strange voice spoke in Swahili.

'Wake up! I am Field Marshall Okello! Wake up you imperialists! There is no longer an imperialist government on this island. Now I lead the government of freedom fighters. Wake up, you black men! Let everyone of you take a gun and ammunition and start to fight against remnants of imperialism on this island. Never, never relent if you want this island to be yours.'

The voice stopped. They could hear panting and the man breathing deeply.

'I tell the people. All arrested imperialists must be brought to my headquarters at Raha Leo. If they resist, they must be shot. Now, I go to fight enemy forces at the prison. If resistance continues, there will be a terrible hail of bullets from which no creature will emerge alive. I want all men with guns to report to me now. We are going now to defeat the imperialists. I am going now.'

It was hypnotic, a high chanting lilt to the cadences. The voice of a man who took pleasure in making people fear him.

'Who is that?' said Jack.

'No idea. Okello? Never heard of him. That accent, it's not local. He's from the mainland and I don't think from the coast.'

A different voice came on. Excited too but Mark recognised the tones of a local man.

'All freedom fighters are to remain alert. This is Aboud Jumbe. All fighters are to search enemy properties for arms. Come to our headquarters at Raha Leo for instructions.'

'This is worse than I feared,' said Mark.

'It's full daylight. I'll keep watch upstairs.'

Mark rang Sinclair at Malindi Police Station.

'Did you hear that broadcast?'

'Yes. Okello? Sounded mad but Jumbe is with him so we know the Afro-Shirazi Party is involved. I'm afraid the situation is close to desperate. We can't guarantee safety on the streets. Mobs will get going soon. The Sultan and Ministers are in danger. We'll hold out here at Malindi for as long as we can. Ali Muhsin wants to fight, brave man, but few supporters have come to join him.'

'Right, I'll inform the Cabinet.'

Prime Minister Shamte sounded exhausted.

'Yes, I heard the radio,' Shamte said. 'Who is this man that says such things?'

'We don't know,' Mark said. 'I recommend that His Majesty and family, Cabinet, all Ministers and Cabinet Secretary go as quickly as they can to the *Salama*. We have launches to ferry them to the steamer. If you all collect there, we can have discussions and take action.'

'Yes. That's best. His Majesty is in immediate danger. He has said he will die fighting in the palace. What about his family? There are women and children with him. Mark, how will you come?'

'I can get there by boat. I'll see you there. First, I will get the Duty Officer to contact everyone and tell them to proceed to the ship.'

Mark phoned Henry Small, the British official, his second in command, who was also the Permanent Secretary for Finance. Mark told him that all Cabinet members were to proceed immediately to the *Salama*. If they could keep the legitimate government intact, they would have a bargaining position.

As he put down the phone, there was a rapid knocking on the front door. He called up to Jack. 'Did you see anyone arrive?'

'No. Shall I go down?'

'Stay there. I'll check before I open.'

They seldom locked their doors in Zanzibar. It was a Muslim society and theft was unknown. Everyone knew everyone else and within the streets of Stone Town, someone was always watching you from the windows, verandahs and roofs overlooking the streets. As Mark approached the door, the knocking began again.

'*Hodi*, Mark. It is me, Khaleed al-Ibrahim.'

Mark opened the door. An elderly Muslim man dressed in a simple white *kanzu*, his feet in sandals, stood before him. His neat beard was mottled grey and his *kofia* cap with its intricate design was pushed back. He was bowed over a large package wrapped in a cream *kikoi*. He held it out to Mark.

'*Karibu*, my friend. Come in.' With one hand, Mark bolted the door behind Khaleed. 'Let us go upstairs. I must be by the telephone.'

'Thank you, Mark. I have come to you for help. These are dangerous times. *Inshallah*, God willing, they will pass.'

They went upstairs. Mark put the package down. 'Khaleed. Please sit. We can talk.'

'I have heard this and that,' said Khaleed. 'Bad things. I knew you would know how serious it is. I am old. What can I do?'

Mark quickly explained the situation as Khaleed bowed his head.

'I fear there is little hope unless we get help from our neighbours,' Khaleed said. 'They should help for we are the legitimate government. We would help them if need be. It is a pity our defence was not better prepared.

For we knew this could happen soon, did we not? Did you and I not discuss this?'

'A few more weeks,' said Mark, 'and it would not have been so easy to overrun the armoury. Now it is hard for us to fight back.'

'True. Did you investigate those stories I told you about?'

'We have received many rumours,' said Mark.

'These ones seemed more serious. Strangers have been coming in from the mainland up north near Muwanda during the last month. Locals noticed.'

'Sorry, it was not checked yet.'

'Well, it's too late now. I must not be long, Mark. My daughter-in-law and granddaughter are at home. I ask a favour of you. Can you care for these things for me?'

'Of course,' replied Mark. 'I have a safe place for them.' He knew then how negative Khaleed was about their chances of winning back control.

'My son, grandson and younger granddaughter are at the *shamba* near Bububu. I spoke to them once but now cannot get through. I must care for my daughter-in-law and her elder daughter. My son and I may be marked men for they know we have worked for the ZNP.'

'Try phoning from here,' Mark suggested.

'My daughter-in-law is trying to get through at home. What I need to ask, do you have a gun I can borrow?'

Mark looked at the calm old man who had been so generous in his friendship over the six years of his posting in Zanzibar.

'Khaleed. I do not. If I had, I would give it to you. I'm sorry. Can you bring the women here? Come back with them. You'll be safer with us. We've been watching. No gangs have come through the square yet. Maybe I can leave Jack Reynolds here and take you in the car and fetch them?'

'No, no,' said the old man rising. 'You must organise what you can for peace to return to us. This madness must end. I will hurry home. I will pray for mercy for the people. We must leave it in Allah's hands. We are His servants.'

Mark felt a deep pang of guilt. Arab families would now be waking to this news, to the voice of the man Okello shouting hatred and violence into their homes. How they must fear for their women and children. He himself had secured his family offshore. How many could do that?

Mark called to Jack. 'Is it all clear from there?'

'Yes,' said Jack coming in from the verandah. 'A few people hurrying past. No armed groups. It's hard to see with the trees but I can see across the square.' Jack greeted Khaleed.

'Khaleed is leaving now. I'll walk with him to the end of the square. Can you stay by the phone?'

08.30. As they walked outside, Mark felt it could have been the start of a normal day, so little had apparently changed. They walked together to where the square narrowed under the spreading mango tree at the end of Mambo Msiige. He took both of Khaleed's hands in his own. 'Go well, my friend. May Allah protect you and your family.'

'That is all I ask for,' Khaleed replied before hurrying away. Mark watched until his bowed figure disappeared into a narrow lane. Godspeed, he thought.

Mark bolted the front door and joined Jack who was holding the receiver. 'It's the PM for you.'

He took the phone. 'Sir,' he said into the receiver. 'One moment.'

'Jack, can you keep watch again?' and then to the PM. 'Sorry, sir. Are you going to the *Salama*?'

'A little later,' he replied. 'Ali Muhsin is going to join me at the British High Commission. From there, we can talk to the British. It is Cross's suggestion.'

'Don't delay too long,' Mark said. 'And His Majesty?'

'I sent Sheikh Barwani to him to try to persuade him to leave for the *Salama* immediately. For the sake of his family. He has about twenty family members in the palace. But he refused. He has a rifle and pistol and says he will stay and fight. You know he is good with guns. That is the answer he sent back. Barwani says he has the motor cars standing by.'

'It would be much better if he left now, before things got worse. Did you hear the radio broadcast?'

'Yes. I have never heard of this man Okello. He is not a local. Perhaps a man of the moment and no more. I must go. We are leaving for the British office.'

'I'll meet you on the *Salama*.'

Mark put the receiver down. At his feet was Khaleed's package. It was heavy, wrapped tightly in a cream linen *kikoi* with its border of green and red lines. There would be enough room for it in their own safe hiding place which they'd discovered amongst the nooks and crannies of the old house.

He sat looking at his desk, a mess of notes. Above the desk hung his dress sword, used for those formal colonial occasions when full whites were worn with white pith helmet and all military medals. The sword was of no use now, a mere symbol of a weapon, a pretence, a shameful reminder of what their force once was. We are now toothless, he thought.

When Mark returned from storing Khaleed's possessions, Jack was hurrying back from the front verandah.

'Mark. Come see. Quietly. There's a group in the square. Six of them, armed.'

Mark went down on his knees and crawled to the balustrade. Light was shining between the uprights. Through the flamboyant tree's branches, he could see men moving nervously towards Mambo Msiige. They were hugging the walls along the further edge of the square. They paused, two looking back, the rest pointing their rifles forward. The rear guard carried raised *pangas*. They were dressed in a motley range of shirts and long pants. One with a cap appeared to be the leader, beckoning them on across gaps between the buildings. Mark and Jack watched for a few minutes until the group disappeared north out of the square.

They looked at one another. 'Hell,' said Mark. 'What about Khaleed?'

'He should be well away,' said Jack.

They returned to the phone. Mark could feel a pressure rising in his throat. This was the reality of their situation. Mobs were on their way.

'I think it's time to leave. On the *Salama,* we can organise with the Cabinet,' Mark said. 'I still hope the British will come. It's their responsibility. So soon after independence.'

'Perhaps,' said Jack. 'But it might depend on what the British High Commissioner tells them. Cross might be the key to this. I agree we must go. No use to anyone if we're caught. We can't defend ourselves.'

'I must let Small, the Commissioner and the PM know. Can you keep watch?'

The PM had not left the British High Commission.

'We are trying to contact Karume to negotiate,' Mohammed Shamte said. 'Cross and Small are here and Ali Muhsin. It seems best.'

'Sir, we've seen an armed group passing us in Kelele Square. I suggest you can operate from the safety of the *Salama.*'

'That is our plan. We are expecting help from the mainland.'

'I'm going to the *Salama* now.'

Small came on the line. Mark told him his plans and their sighting of the first group of rebels.

'I'm safe here in the High Commission,' Small said. 'We're trying to get hold of Abeid Karume. We can't locate him.'

'That's not the major issue at the moment,' said Mark. 'Arms from Pemba should arrive in a couple of hours. Look, I have to swim out to a launch. If, for some reason, I don't arrive at the steamer and contact you, can you take over?'

'Sure thing.' Small sounded delighted.

'The Cabinet members should leave now. Their lives are in danger.'

'They're safe while they're with us. We're trying to negotiate.'

'Negotiate? With whom? With rebels, with a mob? For how long is it safe? The *Salama* will give them protection.'

'I'll tell them what you say.'

Mark put down the phone. He was angry. Small was prevaricating. Delaying the Ministers. Where was his loyalty, he wondered? How could you make deals at this stage, with an unknown thug called Okello? Did the two Ministers hope the British Commissioner was working to get the British to send in troops? He was starting to doubt that.

He rang the Commissioner of Police.

'We're going to run out of ammunition at some point,' said Sinclair. Mark could hear he was rattled. 'Being careful with each shot. A few rebels around, shooting all over the place. Thing is we don't have a water supply inside. I've asked the hospital to send an ambulance with water but they're flat out. We'll have to survive on what we've got.'

'Jack Reynolds and I are leaving for the *Salama*. I've requested the Ministers to meet me there. His Majesty is still in the palace. How desperate is it?'

'I'll keep in touch with him. He shouldn't leave it till the last moment. At this stage, we can provide an escort for His Majesty. Might not be for long.'

He called Jack who left the verandah.

'Two more rebel-looking louts have come through.'

'Let's go.'

6. Field Marshall John Okello. My Victory

12 January 1964. Raha Leo Community Centre, Ng'ambo, Zanzibar

My victory is assured. For my freedom fighters took a secret oath of allegiance to me, promising to fight to the death without fear or reluctance. This vision was received by me in dreams over two nights. I was told to enter the Mtoni River and on a bank I would find a black, red and white stone. From this stone I was told to crush a little sand of each colour and place it into a large bottle. This I did and I hid the magic stone by the river.

During the second night I received further directions which I followed. I killed a pure black cat and pure black dog and took their blood and brains. I mixed these in the bottle with the sand. I spread this mixture on the road where my soldiers passed on the way to battle. They jumped across the magic mixture three times. The stone I found was our source of courage, and the brains our source of bravery.

With this, how could we lose?

Two hours ago, I took over the broadcasting station at Raha Leo Community Centre and broadcast my victory on *Sauti Ya Unguja,* Zanzibar Radio Station.

'Wake up, you imperialists!' I said, 'Wake up, you black men!' I announced that anyone resisting my revolutionary forces faced complete extermination.

I made the Raha Leo Community Centre my headquarters and from here we will overthrow the remaining pockets of resistance. I ordered all imperialists to be brought to my headquarters. If they showed any opposition, they should be shot. I instructed my fighters to go to imperialist properties and collect food and weapons.

My men hailed me, 'Father of the common people'. I have told my story many times today to all those who were not present to witness my victory. The imperialist government of Zanzibar had no army but they had two more police strongholds we needed to capture—the Prison Headquarters and the police station at Malindi near the harbour in Stone Town.

With our superior forces, we overwhelmed the Prison Headquarters, but Malindi Police Station held out against two attacks. I will next deal boldly with the Sultan and my remaining enemies but without capturing this last major station, we could not capture the Sultan's Palace. I made a radio broadcast to the Commissioner of Police at Malindi and to the Sultan.

I warned the Commissioner if he did not surrender, I would come to the station and then things would be worse than any living creature could bear. I gave them twenty minutes to surrender.

When I arrived outside Malindi Police Station to take command of the attack, we opened fire with our automatic weapons. Parts of the building began to burn. Many people were killed and when we went in, there was no one. They had run away from the rear.

I gave Sultan Jamshid many ultimatums on the radio.

'I give you twenty minutes to kill your wives and your children yourself. I do not want to see your face. You must save me from this unpleasant duty. If I find you, I shall kill you and all your dependants.'

After overpowering Malindi Police Station, I led my men to the Sultan's Palace on the seafront at Forodhani, and we sprayed the building with bullets. We found no one there.

I appointed myself Leader of the Revolutionary Government and Minister of Defence and Broadcasting. As Leader and Field Marshall, I proclaimed that all weapons belonging to the opposition must be handed in—or a thousand of their youths would be shot. If these people proved stubborn and my orders were disobeyed, I said, 'I will take measures eighty-eight times stronger than at present.'

I took control of Stone Town and organised my men from my headquarters. Sections of the town were given to groups to do house-to-house searches for weapons and opposition. All confiscated goods were brought back to Raha Leo. My men were told to break down locked doors and check everything for opposition to my orders. These search parties hardly stopped to eat. I ordered some men to go to Karimjee Hospital to make sure none of our enemies were hiding there.

I instructed my freedom fighters to make sure no Europeans were touched or threatened. I said I had given cameras to the Europeans so they could take photographs of anyone disobeying me. If anyone disobeyed my orders, they would be jailed for thirty-five years or hanged.

This island's government is now mine. All the imperialist possessions will soon be under my control. This is the story of my victory.

7. To the Salama

12 January 1964. At sea off Stone Town, Zanzibar

08.55. They went out the sea-side doors. Sunlight was bright upon the beach.

'Can't lock this entrance.' Mark said. He closed the door and thought, I'll never come back.

'What about your dog?'

Their family spaniel sat at his feet, tail busy, brown eyes attentive, pleased at the prospect of a beach walk.

'Good lord. Totally forgot. We can't leave her. She'll have to swim.' The launch was moored about three hundred yards offshore. He could see waving from its stern. 'Jack, can you swim that distance? I could bring the dinghy back.'

Jack patted his stomach. 'I can do it. Might not look like it, but I won the hundred yards backstroke in my final year at Winchester. Now, I might be a tad slow.'

On the beach, a Zanzibari woman and a young girl were walking along as if the day was but a normal day. They were barefoot, wearing bright matching *kangas*. A baby was tied to the mother's back. The child was swinging a *kikapu* and dancing round her mother on the sand.

Mark greeted the woman and she reciprocated. He told her about the rebellion.

'*Hatari*! You must go home quickly. Bad men are in the streets. Be careful!'

The mother uttered a low scream. She grabbed her daughter's hand, turned and ran back towards Forodhani using one hand to support the baby behind her. The girl's feet slipped in the soft sand. She dropped the *kikapu*.

The tide was coming in. Jack and Mark kicked off their shoes and entered the water: it was pleasantly cool.

'Jack, head to the left of the boat. The current will take us back this way. Come, good dog. Come, Sally.'

Mark took it slowly, waiting for Jack who was doing a measured breaststroke. The waves were choppy, hitting him in the face. Slowly, they drew closer to the launch and he could see their families lined up in the stern. The dog was panting behind him. He kept speaking to her, turning to swim on his back. There behind them was the long seafront of Stone Town, sparkling white beneath the sky, from Mambo Msiige on the point of Ras Shangani, past the English Sailing Club to the old wharf at Forodhani. The House of Wonders shone high over the waterfront, its spire topped by the Zanzibari flag of independence, only a month old. It was where he worked, his office near that of the Prime Minister.

Beyond the trees stretched the long building of the Sultan's Palace with its crenellated walls where he imagined the Sultan was facing an impossible choice. Should he leave the palace his great-grandfather built, the Beit-el-Serkal, or should he stay and fight, and face the possibility of his family being slaughtered?

Beyond the palace on the outskirts of Stone Town, Police Commissioner Sinclair was holed up in Malindi Police Station with his *askaris* and ring-ins. It was their last outpost, waiting on the possible delivery of arms from Pemba and help from Kenya. Behind Stone Town, at the Raha Leo Centre in Ng'ambo, the rebel, Okello, had his headquarters from where he called on the mobs in his mainland-accented Swahili.

Jack was tiring and the dog was struggling with the waves splashing into her open muzzle. Lying on his back, Mark held the panting animal on his chest as Jack pulled closer.

Jack's bald head was shining pink and he groaned with effort. 'Keep going, I can make it!'

By the time they reached the launch and clung to the ladder, they were both exhausted. Mark lifted the dog up to waiting arms. He noted the boat's name stencilled across the stern *Pluton* and its origin, *Tanga, Tanganyika*.

The dog was shaking herself to the delight of his children.

'Thank you Daddy. We forgot her,' said Mary as she hugged the dog and waved her pink scarf around, as if it was playtime. 'Lizzy said you would remember. Sally is so clever to swim all that way!'

The captain stepped forward after Angela and Heidi had greeted them.

'Yes,' he said. 'The husbands are here now. That makes the wives happy. Ferdinand Lascalle. I am the captain. This is my boat. Your news is not good. I hear the fighting.'

'That's right, Captain Lascalle,' replied Mark and introducing Jack and himself. 'The situation is serious.'

The captain was taller than Mark, bulky and heavily tanned. He was a hirsute man sporting an uneven beard, wearing only an old cap, once white, and a pair of low-slung red shorts.

'You see, I do not have my full crew on board. Only one here. My pilot is on shore leave.'

'Sorry, Captain Lascalle. There's no time to wait for them. A State of Emergency has been declared. My wife would have explained.'

'Your wife did. Commandeering my boat, she said. This is right? This is allowed?' Lascalle mimicked the word 'commandeering'. He folded fleshy arms over his stomach emphasising his near-nakedness.

Mark ignored the challenge. 'Yes, that's it. There's a revolution going on. People being killed.'

'So I must save you and your children?'

'Yes. I must go into the harbour. To that ship over there.'

Mark pointed to the north where they could see the *Salama* moored a little way offshore. As they watched, a motor launch set off from the wharf and headed for the steamer.

'And what is that ship?'

'It belongs to the government. Where they go now for safety, with the Sultan and his family.'

'So. That ship. Is it safe?'

'Yes, at the moment. What are you doing here in Zanzibar, Captain Lascalle?'

'Doing? I travel where I want. I am fishing sometimes,' Lascalle paused. 'Trading too. I am a free man, a businessman.'

Mark regarded Lascalle as the captain looked past him to the shore. The man's launch did not appear to be set up for deep sea fishing. Where were the fishing rod holders at the stern? The boat smelt sour, a mixture of old curry, burnt oil and unwashed bodies.

Heidi had found towels and he and Jack dried themselves. The captain had not moved. A black man with a grey *kikoi* wound around his waist appeared from the cabin below. He paused in the shadow, glanced at Lascalle and greeted them. The captain turned to him.

'Here is Chega, my first mate. Chega, we move now. We have a new captain. *Bwana* Mark. For the moment.'

The deep throb of the motor started up, the anchor was raised, and the launch turned and headed for the harbour. Behind them, they towed Mark's black Zodiac dinghy and Lascalle's wooden runabout with its outboard motor.

It did not take long to cover half the distance, then the pulse of the motor dropped to idling and the launch lost way, rocking gently sideways. Lascalle appeared above them and slid down the ladder. A pair of black binoculars now rested on his stomach.

'I am thinking,' he said folding his arms over the binoculars, 'up there. Looking at your position, I am thinking. Maybe it is dangerous to go close. You have your wives, your children. Girls. All those black men. Maybe it is better if you husbands go to that ship, first. I wait here. Then you tell me it is safe. Or it is not safe.' He pointed to his wooden runabout behind the boat. 'Maybe this is too far to row. You take my boat? We wait here. Out of trouble.'

'That makes sense,' said Jack.

'Can I see?' said Mark, pointing to Lascalle's chest. Through the binoculars, he could make out little. The *Salama* was offshore; the side facing the harbour was obscured. On the wharf, men were standing above a launch moored to the quay. They were not behaving like the rebels they'd seen previously.

'Fine,' said Mark. 'Jack, you with me? Let's go. It won't take long.'

They pulled the runabout to the launch and climbed in. The outboard was a single horsepower Seagull and it started at first pull. The captain held the rope to cast them off.

'I'll send you a message from the *Salama*,' Mark said. 'Then you come in and drop off our families.'

Without answering, the captain tossed Jack the rope and turned to Angela and Heidi.

'Ladies, I am captain again. Now, we wait.'

As they slowly pulled away, Mark and Jack watched Lascalle talking to Chega on the bridge.

'What do you make of him?' Jack asked.

'Not sure,' said Mark. 'Unattractive sort. Wouldn't trust him an inch actually.'

'His story?'

'Not a fisherman. Probably a smuggler. Of what? Who knows?'

'I imagine whoever pays,' said Jack.

'Are the kids safe? Angela and Heidi?'

'They should join us soon,' said Jack. 'I didn't tell you but Heidi has a revolver in her bag and she knows how to use it.'

Mark was not surprised. That he could have guessed.

09.45. The sea was choppier now, a few white caps further out. The tide was in flood and they were taking waves full on the bow, the runabout banging down on each crest.

'I'll go in, closer to shore,' he shouted to Jack. 'Be calmer water. We can check out Forodhani seafront.'

Inshore, the water was smooth. Jack raised his arm. 'Over there.' Ahead on the upper beach, short of the sea wall in front of the Beit-el-Ajaib, the House of Wonders, a lone black man was running north in short bursts.

'He's in uniform,' Jack called back.

Mark slowed the motor. Jack cupped his hands and shouted. The man turned and watched them for a moment before raising both arms, waving as he approached the water.

'Looks like the Residency Guard,' said Mark. 'He's a marked man in that uniform. We'll pick him up. Can you see any rebels?'

'No.'

As they approached, they made out the guard's formal khaki uniform with red epaulettes. He continued to wave at them until they were right at the beach. Mark steered the boat parallel to the shore line and idled the motor. He did not want to switch off. Jack beckoned; the guard rushed into the water, grabbed the gunwales and tried to jump in. He fell back and Jack seized one arm, Mark the other, and they hauled him on board. He appeared to be in a state of shock.

'*Asante, bwana. Asante,* thank you, sir.' He crouched in the bottom and looked back at the shore. Mark put the outboard into gear and headed for the *Salama*. The man told his story. He was the night guard at the British Residency, now called State House. Since the British Resident had left a month ago, he had little to do. The Prime Minister had not moved in and the Residency was unoccupied.

The first he knew about the insurrection was the sound of gunfire from the distant Ziwani Barracks. He had stayed in the guardhouse until he saw a bunch of rebels with rifles, creeping along the walls. They had seen him and, shouting to one another, two had dropped to their knees and shot at him but missed.

'I ran away, *bwana*. I ran like the wind into the gardens. I could hear those men shouting and calling. I got to the beach and hid till I saw no one was coming.'

From there, he had worked his way round past the hospital and Ras

Shangani, keeping always to the sea-side of the buildings. At one stage, he had tried to get back to his home in Ng'ambo past the High Court but he had seen a car being shot at and people dead on the street. He had run back to the beach near St Joseph's Convent.

'*Bwana*, who are these people? Are they *wabara* from over there?' He gesticulated towards the mainland.

'We don't know,' replied Jack as Mark accelerated out to sea. They passed round the black barges deeply laden with summer's clove harvest and emerged close to the *Salama*.

Jack and Mark could see the activity on the wharf. Several policemen were guarding the area while people were climbing down into a launch.

'Looks safe enough,' Jack said.

10.30. They pulled alongside the gangway of the inter-island steamer. The ship rose about fourteen feet from the water. It was a serviceable trader used for ferrying people and shipping cloves, copra and coconuts to the mainland. Mark could hear the deep chug of its motor on standby, and steam puffed from a pipe near the gangway. Here their families would be safe, he thought.

Various crewmen and some Arab men lent over the rails watching their arrival.

'We'll have to return this runabout to Lascalle,' Mark said.

He shouted up and a crewman threw him a rope. Jack secured it to the bow and the three of them disembarked. The State House guard became the centre of discussion amongst those who had watched him arrive.

The captain, smart in his whites, greeted them. Mark was aware of his own dishevelled appearance. The clothes he had hastily grabbed in the early hours were now creased and sticky with salt. Mark and Jack introduced themselves to the captain of the steamer, Captain Holliday.

'Has the Prime Minister arrived? Any Ministers?' Mark said.

'Not yet,' he replied. 'We're standing by. Several boatloads of Arabs have arrived. We have radio contact with Malindi Police Station, British High Commission and Aden, of course. The harbour is still secure.'

'So the Sultan, his family, they haven't arrived?'

'No.'

'I need to send a message to the launch we've come from. Tell them to come in.'

'Sure. We've been watching. A Morse code message?'

'Good. I'll come with you.'

Once on the bridge, Captain Holliday instructed an officer. 'Right away, send, "Safe. Come in".'

The officer stood outside turning the face of the communication light in the direction of Lascalle's launch.

'It should be obvious it's safe,' Mark said. 'No rebel would go flashing a message.'

They watched the motionless launch, less than a mile away. The captain was a dark figure on the bridge.

The officer re-entered the bridge. 'Sir, sent it twice,' he reported. They watched. Lascalle was not moving.

'Can I use your glasses?' Mark said.

Captain Holliday handed him binoculars.

Behind them, a phone rang and a crewman called the captain. 'Sir, Commissioner Sinclair for you.'

Using the binoculars, Mark could see Lascalle standing in the stern of his boat with Angela and Heidi. What was keeping them?

Captain Holliday returned. 'Sinclair's holding his ground. He is sending some police to the palace to escort the Sultan and his family. They're coming here.'

'That's good to hear. Better in the circumstances. What's your capacity?'

'In an emergency, maybe a hundred, plus perhaps another fifty if the journey's not long.'

'We must get the Sultan's bigger steamer, the *Seyyid Khalifa*. It's in Tanga. Can we request her immediate return to Zanzibar?'

'Sure, will do.'

'But where are the Ministers? What's keeping them?' Mark said.

'Sinclair asked me to tell you he's heard that the Pemba flight you organised was delayed in Tanga and will be here at midday but he thinks the airport is now overrun.'

'So reinforcements aren't likely.'

'Not unless Kenya comes to help.'

Jack put his head inside. 'Lascalle's not moving. Can you send the message again?'

Once more the officer moved outside, taking up the position behind the light. Mark could hear the clacking of the shutter flashing the Morse code.

'It's under way,' said Jack. 'They're coming.'

'Good,' said Mark. 'Captain, I need to communicate with Nairobi.'

'Back here,' said the captain.

10.50. Mark sat next to the radio operator and picked up a pencil. His forearms were salt-encrusted, his fingers stiff. Carefully he printed the message.

'Salama to Nairobi. Army HQ, Police HQ.

Urgent stop Rebels in control Zanzibar Town stop firing continues stop Cabinet at British HC stop Reinforcements urgently necessary prepared fight at airport stop. Rebels well armed and control all police stores and vehicles stop Commissioner and few men holding at Malindi Police Station stop.

He handed it to the operator. 'Urgent please.' As the man put on his radio headset, Jack appeared at the door of the radio room.

'Mark! Lascalle is taking off with them. Heading away.'

They rushed out of the bridge. Across the expanse of sea, they saw Lascalle's launch heading north-west across the harbour towards open sea. The white foam of his wake shimmered, an arrow leading away from them.

'What the heck is he up to?' Jack asked. They both knew.

Through the binoculars Mark could see little. In the haze, he could make out people in the stern but then no more.

'You were right to be suspicious of Lascalle,' said Jack.

'His launch is registered in Tanga,' said Mark, lowering the binoculars. 'Probably going back there. Heidi has your gun. Can she use it? Will she use it, if needs be?'

'Right, she's a fine shot, at targets of course.'

'Tanga's fourteen to sixteen hours away for that launch. We'll put out an alert for them when we have a chance.'

Captain Holiday came onto the deck. 'Phone for you, Mark. It's Commissioner Sinclair.'

Jack stayed outside watching the departing *Pluton*.

'Mark. They're taking potshots at us but it's poorly done,' said Sinclair. 'Thing is we don't have ammunition. If they attack seriously, we're finished. I sent some men to escort the Sultan. I reckon he has only ten minutes clear before a mob arrives. If the escort can't make it back here, keep them on the *Salama*. But Mark, it's looking desperate. No drinking water here either. We won't last the night, or sustained attacks.'

'We should know in a couple of hours about reinforcements.'

'Sure. Small's trying to contact the other side. We caught one of their ASP leaders and Small suggested we send him off with a message for negotiation. How can you negotiate with rebels at this stage?'

'And the Ministers? I'd hoped they would be here.'

'It's Small and Cross at the British HC, they're trying to set up a discussion with the rebels. Cross even said to me, I might have to surrender. I told them, I wasn't going to allow all these men with me to be butchered. Surrender, no way! Sorry, if that was their idea of diplomacy, it's not mine.'

'So they're hanging on to the Ministers there? Giving them hope?'

'Seems that way.'

'Well, our plan for a Cabinet meeting on the *Salama* is doomed.'

''Fraid so, it seems unlikely. I sent out a spy and he says that Darajani Market is in flames. Looting, drinking, the lot. This Okello chap has taken over the Central Prison, let out the inmates and given arms to them. Luckily they're hopeless shots. Mark, have you listened to him on the radio? I cannot let my troops hear it. This is the sort of thing I heard him say "... *the government is now run by us ... should you be stubborn and disobey orders, I will take measures eighty-eight times stronger than at present.*" And, "*If anyone fails to comply ... and locks himself in a house, as others have done ... I have no alternative but to use heavy weapons. We, the army have the strength of 99,099,000 ...*" The man is mad. Sorry, gotta go.'

Mark felt the situation slipping away. Options were closing. And yet if either Kenya or the British announced they were coming in, it could change in a flash. Locals remembered the Battalion of the King's African Rifles flying in when rioting broke out during the June 1961 election polling. The game could still be reversed.

'Sir?' It was the radio operator. 'We have a message from British HQ in the Middle East for Cross at British High Commission. Copy for us.'

Mark's heart leapt. Could this be it? He read the message.

Immediate from HQ Mideast. 12 Jan for High Commissioner. Have instructed HMS Owen a survey ship to stand by to look after British nationals should you require it. She could be with you in about 12 hours. Either come to Zanzibar or proceed to Mombasa to await orders whichever you prefer. Please inform me of your wishes.

Events were moving fast in the wrong direction. The British authorities in Aden were only worried about British nationals. No one else. The British would not help.

8. Fatima. The Darkness

Kuvumilia ni kukomaa   Forbearance is maturity

January 1964. Ngambo, Zanzibar

My childhood had ended. For many days, I did not move from the safety of Ali and Hala's house except for visits to the backyard where the chickens ran from me. All around us the madness of *Mapinduzi* raged. *Mapinduzi* means to turn everything upside down, and so it was. The mind is slow to believe, to understand horror. It sifted in through the walls of that simple house. We were close to Creek Road where gangs rushed up and down on their business of looting, burning and death. Shouting and crying entered our darkness.

Paka's brother was Baba Ali Bakary. He was a kind man who welcomed me into their home in this time of danger. He did not ask why, for, in his wisdom, he knew why and made it his duty to care for me with his family.

In the half-dark, I could see Ali's aged parents, his wife, Hala, and Ali's younger children sitting on two low beds. Mujab, their oldest boy, stood tall in a corner. They knew who I was and that, being of a Zanzibari Arab family, my presence could endanger them. All the adults would have been remembering the time before when violence swept our island.

I had time to think, and I wondered how you knew if a man or woman was African or Arab. It had not mattered to me before, for were we not all God's children, and most of the people of the island were followers of Islam? Was this hatred more a thing of poverty and wealth? Could you look at a man and say, this one is Arab and this one is African, this one wears a *kanzu* and this one does not, and in that moment decide on death or life?

No one moved from the house for hours that first day. At first I asked Paka, 'When will Baba come?' every few minutes but soon it was only a question in my head. After midday, someone came to the door and knocked and, after a pause, knocked again more loudly.

'*Hodi, Hodi!* Come, come, Brother Ali, do not be afraid. Come out and see these things your friend Nasri has brought to show you!'

Before Ali went out, he motioned to us all to be quiet and to stay. 'It is my neighbour, Nasri.'

We could hear men talking. Nasri greeted Ali. 'My friend Ali, my son and I have brought these presents for you and your family. Those Indians do not need them any more!' Nasri's laugh was harsh in our ears.

Hala whispered to Paka, 'He has been drinking alcohol.'

'But Nasri, what is this? We cannot take these goods!' Ali replied.

'Do not worry, my brother,' Nasri said. 'Field Marshall Okello is in command. He told us the time has come for us to take these things. We are chasing away the Arabs and those that work with them. The Sultan has gone and soon all his friends will be gone too. They are running so fast but not fast enough!'

Nasri laughed again.

I looked to Paka in amazement at these words. She put her head in her hands. Why had our Sultan Jamshid gone? Where had he gone? What did Nasri mean by 'running'?

Nasri did not wait for Ali's response.

'The Field Marshall is our new leader,' said Nasri. 'He stood up against the bullets of the imperial police and was victorious. He says that his magic makes him mightier than a thousand men! Raha Leo Centre is his headquarters and he is giving orders. Many times, he comes out and tells us the story of how he shot the police trumpeter at Ziwani Barracks and achieved victory. We are going into Stone Town soon. The police at Malindi Police Station are being chased away. The Field Marshall has a list of our enemies we must find.

'Come now, we need your help. There is much work to be done. Bring your strong son, Mujab. He can help my son and carry the goods we confiscate. Come, come, I will show you!'

Paka started crying softly and put her arms around me. I did not understand. How does one understand the unspeakable things men can do in such times? Only the thin wall divided us from the men as we sat in silence.

Ali's voice was low, even sad. 'No Nasri, this is not for us. Remember the time of stones and the bad things that happened? Who are these men who burn and kill and take things that do not belong to them? Think of what you do. I do not want these goods. Leave my son, this is not work we will do.'

Nasri was not put off easily.

'Ho! Ali, you will be sorry when you see what we get! Our leader has promised us the fine things the Arabs have stolen from us for many years. Houses and land will be ours. He says we will be the leaders. It is our time to be victorious! But first, the Field Marshall says we must find our enemies. Those Arabs who resist must be killed.

'We must hurry! Let me talk to Mujab. My son, Muti, his friend here, wants him to come. Otherwise what will his school friends say? That he supported the cockerel, the *jogo*? This cannot be! Where is he? I know he is with us in this work to take back our land.'

We all knew about the *jogo* and the *kisima*. The *jogo*, a cockerel, was the sign of the ZNP, the Zanzibar Nationalist Party. A village water well, a *kisima*, was the sign of the ASP, the Afro-Shirazi Party, which had lost the last election.

Nasri would not leave, and now we could hear him close to the door. He knocked again. We all looked at Mujab. Surely Nasri would not try to come into this house uninvited? Was it the drink making him demand entry? Paka put her arm around me. Mujab stood, putting on his cap.

'It is better I go, Mama,' he said, bending over her. 'Nasri must not come in.'

Hala cried out as he opened the door and left us. We heard the greetings of the men and more argument. Mujab said that he should stay to care for his Mama and sisters but Nasri laughed.

'You are old enough to leave your Mama's kitchen! Let your Baba stay. We will bring you back at the end of the day. I myself will care for you. Come now!'

Mujab left with Nasri and his son and when Ali came inside, Hala cried out to him.

'What could I do? He is an honourable boy,' said Ali.

I realised then that Mujab had left so Nasri would not discover that I was hidden in their house. It was Ali's kindness and their humble home that saved me from the bloodshed taking place in the streets of my town and the villages of my country.

At sunset, when the *muezzin's azan,* 'there is no god but God, and Muhammad is the Messenger of God,' drifted across our town, calling the faithful to prayer in the many mosques, we stayed inside waiting for news, waiting for Mujab's return, for my family to come to collect me. Ali had gone outside but never for long.

Hala asked many times. 'Where is Mujab?' She prayed and held her youngest child. The grandparents lay down on the mats. Paka told me to rest on the low bed with the other children for I could not sleep and she spoke quietly to Ali. She was hopeful all would be well. How could she think otherwise?

'Surely Ali, my brother, the British will send in their troops like they did last time. Remember? They were called the Coldstream Guards and, like before, this will be finished in a few hours. Soon they will come in by aeroplane from Kenya. Remember how they camped at Mnazi Mmoja and played their strange music? Surely they will come back. They cannot let us down. See, it is only a month since the British left us!'

No one answered her. We were hot, tired and hungry and that day stretched out as if it was ten days long. It seemed to be a lifetime of wondering what would happen.

As the light faded behind the shutters, Ali lit a kerosene lamp and went outside. We heard him call, 'Mujab!'

Hala shouted, 'My son, he is back!'

The door opened. What can I say? We all saw him standing in the light of the lamp. In that close space, Mujab smelt of smoke and something else. It looked as if he had dirt on his arms and legs. His cap was gone. Hala cried out and we all saw the darkness of blood on the front of his shirt.

This is what I remember.

9. Field Marshall John Okello. Surrender

17 January 1964. Zanzibar

Resistance in Zanzibar against my Revolutionary Government's forces continued for a few days. My enemies ran before me. As Field Marshall, I made radio broadcasts demanding surrender by the imperialists. I used my gift for making speeches. I told the imperialist Ministers they would be struck with bullets for their crimes. Later, I told them they were to be hung in two hours' time, at four o'clock.

I announced the names of men who were to receive fifty-five lashes and others that I would send to prison for seventy-five years. Education is important to me and I know my numbers well, so I let my army know I was in command.

Old men, women and children received quick training in the use of weapons so they could fight with us. I banned parties in opposition to me, the ZNP and the ZPPP, and told the people that anyone found with a photograph of the Sultan or membership cards of those banned organisations would be killed or detained indefinitely. Martial law was imposed and I was appointed President of the Court.

When I travelled with my soldiers, I heard about many offences committed against the Revolution. I stopped the car and tried these cases on the roadside and gave judgement immediately. If someone insulted my government, the sentence was one hundred and fifty-three years' imprisonment and fifty-five lashes. By the end of Tuesday the fourteenth of January, resistance was crushed. The American ships continued to patrol up and down but we were prepared to die if they tried to land.

I announced that I would inspect the shops in Stone Town and instructed the residents, men, women and children, to come out and kneel beside the road with folded arms as I passed by. Young men must be stripped to their underpants. I ordered them to sing this song: 'Mr Abeid Karume, father of the Africans, God bless him in his task and God bless the work of the Field Marshall.'

I found that most shops had been looted and many had been burnt. Figures on deaths and detentions reached my office. A total of thirteen thousand, six hundred and thirty-five had been killed. We did not know how many had been wounded. Over twenty thousand enemies and stooges had been detained. The battle had raged throughout Zanzibar Island, and because of strong Arab resistance, our guns roared like heavy rain. I told my men to shoot in all directions, and to kill whatever came before them, be it men, women, children, even disabled people, even chickens and goats.

After the fighting, I restored order. I heard that the people of Pemba were threatening resistance against me, so I told them I would bring my soldiers there with my guns and my whips, my *viboko,* and deal with them as I had dealt with the Arab people on Zanzibar Island.

I took it upon myself to draw up the new constitution. I was determined that the people of the islands would now be ruled fairly, and disunity would be no more. My main aim was to ensure economic freedom for the people. It was I who reformed the government as a Republic, and I was to be leader of the Revolutionary Government. It was I who named the provisional leaders and appointed their portfolios.

Abeid Karume was the man I made the new President. He had been sent to Dar-es-Salaam for safety. I instructed him to return to Zanzibar to begin Cabinet meetings. He returned the day after my victory and together we went to the broadcasting station where I introduced him as the new President, the President of the new Revolutionary Government. We had achieved this through our own sweat and blood.

I also contacted my brother African, President Nyerere of Tanganyika, and asked if he could help us with the supply of police and medical supplies. This he did. This same day, President Karume and Mohamed Babu of the UMMA Party arrived. Babu bowed down to me. In my private discussions with the new President, I told him I would serve under him in the new Revolutionary Government I had created.

President Karume commended my wisdom and courage. He said the new government would be the opposite of the old one under which the people had suffered.

10. Fatima. My Shangani Home

Call on me and I will answer you

13-18 January 1964. Ng'ambo, Zanzibar

We did not know what had happened to Mujab that day. On his return, Hala asked him, but he kept his eyes cast down.

'I hurt no one, Mama; I came back as quickly as I could escape. We must not go out. It is not safe.'

He would say no more, but went to remove his bloodstained clothes and wash. Many years would pass before I heard his story for he too was changed by these terrible events.

I was ignorant then of what took place during the *Mapinduzi*. Many times I asked Paka to take me to find Mama and Basilah in Stone Town, across Creek Road. I planned we would all go and welcome Baba and Taha from the *shamba*. I yearned to open the door of our town house and call out into its reception rooms and find my family there with their open arms.

The British let us down. Their troops did not come to help; neither did the troops of our neighbours, Tanganyika and Kenya. They deserted us, leaving Zanzibaris to kill and be killed.

It was Ali's baba, who surprised us. He sat on a low stool in the corner with his stick before him, resting his chin on his folded hands. In all our crying and talking, he said nothing for a long time.

One evening after our meal he said, 'The British, *Waingereza*, Bibi Paka why did you think they would help? They are gone and it is not a matter for them to worry about us. Always they did what they liked, what would make their country strong. The day their man in white, the Resident, left his palace on his navy ship was the day they forgot us. They will talk in their offices in London and do nothing. Yet they knew how it was with us. *Ajifanyiza chongo, angaona* (¹).' He stamped his stick on the ground as he spoke.

We waited there. More days passed. At night, I lay by Paka and I do not even know if I was awake or asleep for the nights were long. I heard Ali and Hala talking. Hala was speaking fast and asking questions and her husband's voice was low and calm. I feared then that maybe we could not stay with them. What would happen to us?

I remembered what Mama had told me about my childhood nightmares,

---

1   *Someone pretends to be blind in one eye, although seeing well* <swahiliprov-erbs.afrst.illinois.edu/index.htm>. (2014)

those dreams that come in the dark before dawn and I would wake up weeping. My Mama would come in and hold me tight. When I was in her arms, the terror shrank to a distant corner of my mind.

'There are things to fear beyond our control,' Mama said, 'but you can choose to be brave. It is true, fear is there, but you can overcome it. Remember with the strength of Allah, you can deny its power.' This memory brought me comfort.

Every night and morning, Ali would come and lead us in prayer in that tiny room and ask for His help and protection. I noticed that tears would come to his eyes. I knew then he was a devout man.

'In the name of Allah, the Compassionate, the Merciful.

[8.24]² O you who believe! Answer the call of Allah and His Apostle when He calls you to that which gives you life; and know that Allah intervenes between man and his heart, and that to Him you shall be gathered. [8.25] And fear an affliction which may not smite those of you in particular who are unjust; and know that Allah is severe in requiting evil. [8.26] And remember when you were few, deemed weak in the land, fearing lest people might carry you off by force, but He sheltered you and strengthened you with His aid and gave you of the good things that you may give thanks.'

Five days after that terrible first day, Ali said, 'Binti Fatima. Let us try now, my child. We will go and find your family. I have prayed for their safety. Abeid Karume has come back and he is now taking charge as the new President. The gangs of the Field Marshall have left our streets. Town is quiet. People are coming out and selling in Darajani Market. Cover yourself and we will all go together.'

Hala was frightened. 'Is is safe? This child looks like an Arab. What if you are arrested for helping her?'

'Be calm, my wife. If she is covered and with us, who will do this?'

We left the darkness of that humble house, to go on a journey where my fears would be realised. Paka came, both of us veiled but for our eyes. Mujab walked in front with his Baba. Creek Road, down which we had fled, was now quiet but shops were empty and broken: some had been burnt leaving nothing but black spikes. The rubbish that had covered the ground was now piled along the roadside, bits and pieces of people's lives. The smell

---

2   *The Qur'an - The Accessions.*

of smoke hung in the air.

Men were selling vegetables, piles of *muhogo*, our name for cassava, and oranges but people no longer stopped for long or to talk. We passed groups of men, dressed in army jackets and caps with pieces of green and yellow material tied round their arms. Over their shoulders hung guns and *pangas*. They laughed loudly and shouted at people. Some blocked the way and inspected the few vehicles. Cars and buses were carrying old branches tied to the bonnets and hanging from their windows. Fear was in my heart. Ali did not greet anyone.

Ali led us off Creek Road into the maze of narrow lanes that made up our *mjini* or downtown. He knew where our family house was. It had belonged to our family for many generations. It was a strange journey through almost silent streets. Every window was shuttered, every shop door was closed. White flags hung from doors and wilted branches stood against walls.

There were eyes watching and quiet voices behind the grey walls. No friends called to Ali in greeting as we hastened down the alleys. No bicycles rang their bells and no coffee sellers clinked their little china cups. The concrete benches, the *barazas*, outside every house were empty. Silence had fallen over our town.

We came to Shangani, not far from the Sultan's palace on the waterfront. There was our carved door, covered in brass studs and decorations, gleaming as if nothing had changed. Its great chain and padlock showed the importance of our family.

I used to laugh at Taha when he said, 'You must enter through the left door, it is the woman's door, and this is the man's door on the right for me!'

I would tease him and go out one door and in the other! And he would chase me up the stairs. Over the door was carved an inscription from the Qur'an. 'Enter peacefully, believers!'

When we arrived, I saw that our door was open. I thought: this is a good sign. Someone was at home! I entered first. But silence filled the whole house that once had been full of family and servants. First I ran to my Babu's room, my grandfather's bedroom, on the ground floor. He was not there. Papers were cast all over the floor and his furniture was knocked over. I ran from room to room calling for them, every name many, many times. No reply came back.

Paka was behind me crying my name, telling me to wait. I think she had been forewarned. Every room and every cupboard had been emptied. The kitchen floor was covered in broken plates and even the pots and pans had disappeared. I rushed up, up the stairs onto the flat rooftop hoping for someone to be there, maybe hiding like I had hid. Only the hot sun and sky greeted me.

I collapsed into Paka's arms burying my face into her kind body. 'Where can they all be, Paka? Where have they gone?'

She did not answer but Ali spoke to her. 'There are no bodies here, Paka. Maybe they have fled elsewhere.'

11. Field Marshall John Okello. In Charge

21 January 1964. Dar-es-Salaam and Pemba Island

I travelled to Dar-es-Salaam in Tanganyika for a short rest and for medical reasons as my throat was painful. I met with President Nyerere. I was in Dar-es-Salaam when the army mutiny against his government took place. The President asked the British for help and they sent in their army and stopped the rebellion.

When I returned to Zanzibar after my treatment, I was met by President Karume and taken to one of the Sultan's houses. The President and other Ministers were worried about a counter-attack from imperialists outside the country. They told me the bicycles, clothes and other goods which had been confiscated from looters and collected at my headquarters at Raha Leo had disappeared.

I travelled to Pemba Island with my men and inspected the island. I had my guns, one in each hand. People came out and shouted 'Freedom', and prostrated themselves before me. I had told them on the radio they had to do this, or fear my wrath. I made the Arab men sing the praises of the Revolution, *Uhuru na jamhuri,* and praises of their new President. I caused their beards to be shaved in public without water. I organised public floggings for those who did not accept the new regime.

This was the way to make people obey.

I believed that I would remain in Zanzibar only for a little while. I felt that I had a calling to liberate my brothers in other parts of Africa, in South Africa, Angola and Mozambique.

12. Returning to Salama Daima

Naught befalleth us save that which Allah hath decreed for us

22 January 1964. The shamba, Salama Daima

The days after the search of my deserted house in town were a time of torment. I was determined to find out where my Mama, sister and Babu were. Perhaps they were hiding as I was. No news came from our *shamba*. Ali and Paka were careful. They did not want to let anyone know who I was. We heard so many things, so many rumours about those arrested, those now called 'enemies of the Revolution'. We did not know who to believe, and the radio was full of angry words.

'We must wait, Ali. How can we trust these new leaders?' Paka said.

'Yes,' said Ali. 'See how many strangers there are in our streets now, people who do not wear the *kanzu*. I was told that everyone living along Hollis Road in Malindi and Darajani had to come out of their houses and bow down and touch their heads to the ground to pay respect to the Field Marshall as he drove past. They waited for hours on the road. When Okello came, he had two men in his Landrover pointing machine guns at them. They were so scared; they did not even look up when he passed.'

One evening Ali came home after evening prayers and told us he had walked past the Central Prison.

'A line of men, all Arab-looking, dressed in *kanzus* waited under guard. A policeman sat at a table, writing down names. Someone said all Arabs have to register and many are taken away to prison. The prisons are full.'

I wondered if Baba and my brother, Taha, might be held in prison. It was a strange hope.

Ali said it was too dangerous to leave town but, ten days after the Revolution, Ali, Paka, Mujab and I walked together back to my family's country *shamba*. Perhaps my Mama and Basilah were there waiting for me with Baba and Taha. It seemed possible.

We left early, before the sun rose. The shops that had once lined the road out of town were burnt or deserted. In the dirt, people had put up rough shelves and were selling vegetables.

'Where have the Indians gone?' I asked.

'Many have left the country,' Ali said. 'They were allowed to leave. People are saying that at the airport they were searched and their money and jewellery were taken from them. They could only take ten pounds in cash.'

Ali told us that he had heard that all farmland had been 'nationalised'. It now belonged to the farm workers and each family would get a bit of land. Was our farm, *Salama Daima*, no longer ours?

Near Marahubi Palace, a pole blocked the road and men with rifles watched us coming towards them. Two wore khaki uniforms and three others were dressed in bits and pieces of police clothing. A man stepped forward, raised his hand and asked Ali who we were and where we were going. Paka and I were covered so they could not see us except for our eyes. Ali replied that we were his family, calling me his daughter, and said we were going to pay respects to our cousins. They waved us through.

As we passed, a man called out to Mujab, 'Come, you are old enough! It is time to leave school and join the Revolutionary Army.' We walked on.

'The two khaki-uniformed men are army men that President Nyerere has sent in from Tanganyika to maintain peace,' said Ali. 'The others are revolutionaries.'

I wondered why President Nyerere had not sent his army straight away to stop the madness that befell us. Dar-es-Salaam is so close to us over the sea.

We came to our farm where a long road lined with mango trees led to our house. I wanted to run but Paka held me back. 'Careful, child, let Ali go and see if it is safe.'

Already I knew, for I could smell the same smell as Creek Road, the smell of burning. It seemed a long time before Ali came back. He wiped his hand over his face and shook his head. 'I am sorry, Fatima, there is nothing … a fire. No one is there.'

The house had been destroyed and only bits of stonework remained at one end. The fire had burnt the nearby trees and it was hard to imagine that here once stood our house filled with people. And where had Baba and Taha gone? Where were Mosi and Amina? There was only silence.

A little way from our house was the plant nursery where clove seedlings were cared for. Beyond that I could see the cement platforms for drying the cloves. How often I had sat there spreading out the fresh buds.

Ali spoke quietly to Paka and then to me, 'Binti Fatima, wait here with Paka. I will go and find out. Come Mujab.'

Around the burnt house, the sand was covered in footprints. Leaning against the fence by the vegetable garden were our garden tools. There was a seat in the shade where my Mama would sit watching Basilah and me. We would gather the yellow *shomari* mangoes we loved, and Amina showed me how to weed the vegetable beds.

I picked up her broom and started sweeping the earth, levelling the ground over the mess of footprints. My Mama would not like to see them, and it seemed right to smooth the earth as it was before.

'Fatima, my child,' said Paka. 'You do not need to do this. Come sit by me.' Gently she took the broom from my hands.

We sat in the shade and there was silence around me, and my heart was heavy. Yet even then I prayed for good news. The house was burnt but surely my family had escaped. Many people lived on our land, on our *shamba*. They grew their own crops and, when the clove harvest started, they worked for us. Perhaps my family were hiding in the villages or staying at our neighbours' farms. Maybe they were in prison or recovering in hospital.

Ali and Mujab returned. 'You must be strong, my child,' Ali said bowing his head. 'Your Baba and brother. May Allah have mercy on them! The people of the village buried them as is right and the *mzee* said the proper prayers for them.'

This was the fear that had walked beside me. These few words destroyed the world I had known till that moment.

We walked towards the sea on the path that so recently I had skipped along after my brother and sister without a care in the world. Oh, I wished that was me once more. From the huts by the *shamba* fields, men and women came out to watch us. We came to a place where the clove trees ended, and there beside them were three graves, new mounds, with the fresh sand of my island upon them.

I grew up then. It came to me that maybe I was the only one left. A terrible thing had happened. A horrible punishment had been inflicted upon us. What had we done to deserve this?

'Which is the grave of my Baba?' I said. 'My brother, Taha?'

Ali pointed to the first grave. 'That is the resting place of your Baba and your brother is next to him, and beside Taha is the grave of Amina.'

When I had last seen them, they were so full of life. Until that moment, I had known little of death. I looked around at the trees and at the sea for I wanted to remember this place. I prayed for forgiveness and mercy for them, for all those who died when I did not. And I thought what will Mama and Basilah do when they know this?

The *mzee* came up to Ali. '*As-salamu alaykum.* Please, we want you to know, this was not us. We did not do this terrible thing. We do not understand what happened. Men came in trucks with weapons, with stones, shouting and full of hate. We did not know them. Many did not speak like Zanzibar people.'

'Amina. Why old Amina?' Paka cried out. 'When we left, *Bwana* Ahmed sent them to the village. Where is Mosi?'

'Mosi is with us but he cannot walk,' the *mzee* said. 'He told us that Bibi Amina would not leave. She wanted to tell anyone who came to do violence that she was not an Arab and this family were good people who cared for all those on their land. Mosi said he wanted to stay but she was sure, as she was a woman and so old, they would not harm her. It was not to be. Please, forgive us for not helping. And now, who will help us now?'

13. Fatima. Zanzibar Hospital

Aloachwa kaachiwa mengi   *The people who are left find they are left*
                              with many burdens

23 January 1964. Stone Town, Zanzibar

We returned slowly to Ng'ambo. I hid inside their front room, not knowing what to think or do.

'Take courage, my child,' said Ali. 'You have a lot to bear. There is one more place we must look. Tomorrow let us visit the hospital to see if they know of your family from the Shangani house.'

The next morning, Ali came with Paka and me down Creek Road into Residency Road to the new hospital called the Hassanali Karimjee Jivanjee Hospital. Opposite it was the old cemetery.

A crowd of people at the gates were buying food from stalls or standing in line. Armed men ordered people this way and that. Ali, Paka and I waited for a long time against the high wall, for entry was controlled. Finally, it was our turn at the counter.

Two people were in the cubicle. A woman was seated and she answered our questions. A man stood directly behind her. With his arms folded, he was watching us.

'We are looking for family members. They are missing,' Ali said.

She did not look up. In her hands were papers with names in a column and marks against them.

'I handle admissions,' she said. 'What are their names?'

Ali gave the name of my Mama, Amal bint Yusuf, my sister, Basilah bint Ahmed al-Ibrahim, and my grandfather, Babu, Khaleed bin Hamdan al-Ibrahim. My eyes followed her finger as it ran down the names, turning page after page. Some names were crossed out. Had those people left because they were healed or had they died?

She reached the last page and returned to the beginning. I felt faint and the sounds around me went quiet. Did I want their names to be found? This hospital might be the only hope. Then the woman's finger stopped moving.

'Maybe,' she said and glanced at the man behind her. 'Here is the name of a man, Khaleed. I find only one name. He was brought in on the first day, the twelfth. He is still here. Our records are not perfect, you understand. The other two are not listed. Go and see if this is your relative.' She pointed behind her. 'The man is in Ward 12.' She passed Ali a piece of paper which we showed to the policeman at the gate.

Ward 12 was filled with men recovering from wounds and operations. There we found my grandfather, my Babu. At first I did not recognise him. His head was wrapped in a bandage and he lay staring at the ceiling. He was so still and so old. I kissed his hand and stroked his forehead, saying his name again and again. He looked at me, and his hands tightened on mine.

A nurse came over. 'Ah, you are his family?'

I nodded, hardly able to speak.

'I am sorry,' she said. 'He has suffered since his operation. He has had a stroke. We try to keep him comfortable. It is good you are here.'

Babu stared at Paka and Ali and then back at me as if he was looking for someone else. Was he hoping to see the faces of his son, my Baba, and Basilah? How long had he searched the faces around him wondering and fearing the worst? I realised that what had happened in the days of the Revolution had destroyed him.

My tears fell upon his hand and mine as they were clasped together. I would not let go, and I told him I loved him and I was well but I did not tell him more. Let him not know until he is strong like he was before, I thought. It is better this way. He smiled a little and we gave him water to drink and cared for him. His body was so thin; a few bumps under a white sheet with the hospital name printed in red around the border.

All around us men and women bent over the beds. Little room was left. Patients, the old and the young, lay on the floor and sat against the walls in the corridors. The nurses were running back and forth. I had been in the Karimjee Hospital before but I did not remember this strange smell hanging in the air.

'Paka,' I said. 'We must make Babu well. Can you go and find food, soft food, a plate and spoon? I will feed him. And some soap and cloths.'

Paka and I came every day staying until the nurses sent us away. Babu was peaceful when I was with him. We washed him, massaged his legs and fed him. I sang to him and told him the old stories that once he had told me. He had become as a child. My Babu was a devout man and we found an *imam* to come and comfort him and pray for him for Babu could not speak. The *imam* went from bed to bed talking to the injured and to the men on the floor with their crutches. No one in this ward had a normal sickness. They had terrible wounds from the *Mapinduzi* but they bore their pain and suffering without complaint.

The doctors and nurses worked day and night trying to save their patients. There were European doctors and also Zanzibari Arab doctors. I was with my Babu when a doctor came to see him. The *mzungu* was tall and had white hair and a high forehead with brown spots. He kept rubbing his hands together as he spoke to us. I could speak English but not well.

'*Habari*,' he said. 'I am Dr Hurley. Is this your Babu?' The nurse translated into KiSwahili.

'*Babu yango?*'

'Yes,' I replied in English. 'This is my grandfather.'

'I'm sorry,' he replied. 'Your Babu received a blow on the head. We did what we could but the next day he had a stroke. I don't think he is in pain.'

I could not look at the doctor at first but I heard kindness in his voice. Instead, I looked at his hands which were pink with long hairs on the back.

'Will my Babu get better?' I asked.

'I hope so,' he said. 'It's too early to say. I think it will take time. He needs rest.'

I had to ask. 'Did he come in with anyone else, my sister and Mama?'

The doctor looked at the nurse who shook her head. 'I was on duty when two men brought your Babu here. The first morning,' she said. 'They told me he was found in the street, in Shangani. He was alone.'

The doctor bent over so only the three of us could hear him.

'I'm sorry for your pain,' he said. 'I don't think your Babu is in danger now but men came into the hospital with guns. They were looking for someone. It might have been your Babu. They did not see him as we had taken him into surgery. I must tell you to be careful. Ask for me if you have any questions about your Babu. Stay well.'

As he was turning away, he stopped for I was rubbing at the bandage on my arm. 'What happened there?' he said. 'May I see?'

The nurse undid the wrapping Paka had bound over my wound. It surprised me to see how the swelling had spread. The doctor held my arm. 'This isn't good. We must treat it. You've been scratching your arm. Try to stop doing this. See, it's infected.'

He gave instructions and the nurse cleaned and bound the wound. She gave me pills to take. I had not noticed I had been irritating the wound.

I wondered about the nurse's words. If Babu was found in the street, what did that mean? Were my Mama and Basilah with him? If not, where were they? I did not even know if they had been warned about the violence.

How could they disappear?

I had to ask Paka. 'Do you think we should ask if Mama and Basilah were brought in but did not get to a ward?'

I could hardly bear to ask her to find out if they had died. Paka understood and nodded her head. 'I will go and ask this.'

Paka was gone a long time, and my heart hammered as I sat beside my Babu and held his hand. Paka came back. She was wiping her face.

'My child, they showed me a list of people brought in. Many are unnamed but there was no one that I can say would be them. They took me to a cold room where there were bodies, not yet buried. Your Mama and Basilah were not there.'

During the weeks that I cared for my Babu, I heard stories of what had happened during those terrible days. Trucks had arrived full of wounded and dying people, who had been dumped in the hospital courtyard. Bodies were thrown over the walls. Hospital workers had listened to the voice of the Field Marshall on *Sauti Ya Unguja*, and this had terrified them all.

Many who were arrested were taken to Raha Leo Centre, and kept there for questioning. They had to sit for days under the trees without food before they were 'processed'. Some were called 'enemies of the Revolution' and 'stooges', and were taken to Changuu Island not far from our harbour. Others disappeared into the Central Prison at *Kiinua Miguu*.

I wondered if Mama and Basilah had been arrested as the revolutionaries searched for my Baba. If this was so, I thought they might be detained somewhere. If Babu recovered, he might be able to give me news.

Babu tried to speak and I could see it was important for him to tell me something, ask me something, but he could not make words. He was able to eat slowly and swallow but forming words was too difficult. I believe his mind was sometimes clear and he would get upset and wave his right hand while holding me tight with the other. We fed him slowly but he ate little and got weaker.

When Babu died, I thought my heart would break once more. He looked at me and I held him. The nurse called the *imam* and they moved the bed so his feet were pointing at the *qibla*. We stood beside the bed and prayed with the *imam* as he said the *Surat il-Fatiha,* and asked for forgiveness for Babu's sins. I was glad I was with him at this time and could show him he was loved. I took comfort in remembering he was a man of charity, a man of learning who had been a leader in his community, and we would pray for him. He was kind to all people and he did not deserve the hatred that had taken his life from him.

The *imam* closed his eyes and I kissed his face. His body was taken to a room where he was washed and wrapped in a plain sheet, a *kafan*. The *imam* said the last *duas* for him while we prayed for mercy for his soul. I mourned for my Babu and I cried out for all I had lost.

The *imam* said, 'Do not cry, my child. You are being tested with suffering. Be patient, for this is what Allah decreed.'

Babu was buried that day. He was not put to rest in our family graveyard surrounded by mourners honouring him but we bowed ourselves to Allah's will.

Ali spoke kindly. 'Remember always,' he said, 'your Babu helped many people during his life and you were one of them.'

I could not speak for it came to me that I might be the only one left of my family. Afterwards, I thought that maybe it is better my Babu did not live to see and know what I have had to see and know. A week passed and then more weeks and still no news came of Mama and Basilah.

Truly! To Allah we belong and truly, to Him we shall return.

This is what I remember.

14. Field Marshall John Okello. An Undesirable Person

March-April 1964. Nairobi, Kenya and Kampala, Uganda

I am now in Nairobi. I have to leave Kenya by tomorrow. They are forcing me to leave. It is a most sad situation. I have to go to Uganda, where I was born but I have not lived there for a long time. Conspirators worked to undermine me. They plotted against me and I could not call on my freedom fighters in Zanzibar for help. My men, who formed my militia, are being disarmed.

When I met President Nyerere of Tanganyika and President Karume in Dar-es-Salaam, they said they did not like my radio broadcasts during the Revolution, and asked why I did not control my fighters. I think President Nyerere wished me to be gone so he might join Zanzibar and Tanganyika together.

I am dispossessed but not defeated. I will return to Uganda, and from there I will travel to other countries that need my services. For I am a Field Marshall. Have I not shown my mighty power and what I can do? I do not fear the night or the imperialists. My command will overwhelm them as it did in Zanzibar.

The new Revolutionary Government that I created in Zanzibar has declared that I am an undesirable person, an 'unwanted person'. I have been expelled by my brothers in East Africa without a shilling to my name. I have lost my clothes, my wages, my savings and the valuables I left in Zanzibar.

I, who understand African thinking, did not realise they would turn against me. I have telephoned President Karume eight times asking for my goods that I left behind, but nothing has come to me.

Kampala, Uganda

After I arrived in Uganda, I went to the embassies of Nigeria and Ghana offering my help but received nothing. Finally, as my black brothers would not help me, I have been forced to beg from Asians and Europeans in Kampala.

I fear my enemies will succeed in hiding the great things I have done. If I failed afterwards and was not a welcomed hero, it was because I was too trusting and did not see those conspiring behind my back.

15. Field Marshall John Okello. The Prison

January 1971. Makindye Prison, Kampala, Uganda

I have appealed again to President Idi Amin, President of Uganda, of my country, for his merciful consideration.

I think this is my last chance. I pray I will be spared. For I am unjustly imprisoned in Makindye Prison outside Kampala. There is nothing I have done against my President in any way, for it is not for me to try to overturn him.

When I met President Amin, I told him I was also a Field Marshall. I saw the President did not like this. I quickly asked him if I could help him in some way, as I had been a victorious warrior against imperialist Britain. Instead, I was locked up in this cell for years with many others. I sent a message to him asking for mercy. The reply came today.

A policeman came to my cell. 'Your President says there is no room for two Field Marshalls in Uganda,' he laughed. 'Now you ask for mercy. You did not show mercy to the Muslims of Zanzibar.'

I have suffered unspeakable acts of torture and I can no longer stand. Yet there is nothing I can confess to. Others in this cell have told me the East Germans have taught my Ugandan brothers how to control and terrify the people. They call this police unit the State Research Bureau, and they take pleasure in the horror of what they do here.

Another prisoner asked me if I knew that the East Germans were now doing the same in Zanzibar. 'How do you like the medicine you have brought upon yourself?' he said.

For sure, I should have stayed on Zanzibar Island and looked after my people there instead of believing my talents would be appreciated in other countries.

Now I can only remember the glorious Revolution where I triumphed.

Note: John Okello disappeared, presumed murdered, in Makindye Prison, Uganda in 1971.

Section 2. Fatima's Story. Survival

The struggle of man against power is the struggle of memory against forgetting. Milan Kundera

Until the lions have their own historians, the history of the hunt will always glorify the hunters ... It's not one person's job. But it is something we have to do, so that the story of the hunt will also reflect the agony, the travail—the bravery, even, of the lions. Chinua Achebe

16. Changes

Bahari haishi zingo   The ocean does not stop moving

January-April 1964

'I must go back to work at the harbour,' Ali said to Hala. 'The Revolutionary Government is shouting, "return to work or lose your job". Others are waiting, and they say we are just being lazy.'

Ali had been sitting outside with a neighbour, listening to his radio. He was a lorry driver for the British Government Clove Growers' Association which bought cloves from the *shambas* at harvest time to sell overseas. The British had said that if the farmers sold to them, they would get the best price.

I could see Hala was worried. Until Ali returned at sunset, she busied herself with her children, giving Paka loud instructions about slicing onions and picking the green pawpaws before the birds got them. She wanted Paka to take the dry children's clothes off the rope line in the courtyard and fold the clothes and put them away in the kitchen.

Hala was a nervous person and found it hard to bear the worry of this time. She was slim and seldom at peace. When she talked, she spoke fast, her large eyes blinking and darting away from the faces of those she addressed. Paka acted like a true sister to her, never complaining about the instructions, 'do this, don't do that,' but rather singing as they worked side by side.

When Ali returned and greeted us, we gathered near him. 'Most of the staff were there except for *Bwana* Michael, the Englishman,' said Ali. 'He has left for his home overseas. All the Indian office workers arrived, and two European secretaries, but some Arab workers did not come. I heard they are in prison. We waited for three hours without doing any work. Then two cars arrived.'

'Were they police?' interrupted Hala.

'No,' said Ali. 'They were black cars. One was filled with army men with rifles and the other was the big man in uniform with green and yellow on his cap. With him was Abeid Karume. He is our new President. That Field Marshall Okello has gone. My friend told me Karume got rid of him. The guards shouted, telling us to line up and be quiet. The Indians stood together.'

Ali paused, putting his hands on his knees and looking around at us.

'President Karume said, "We have a new Zanzibar! I have made changes and this place, the Clove Growers' Association, now belongs to the people. We do not need imperialist organisations in the new Zanzibar. The cloves you have in these sheds will belong to all of us. This money will bring wealth to our country and the farmers will get a fair share." He looked over all of us standing before him and said, "Why are there so many Indians, *wahindi*, in this place? I have travelled to India and Zanzibar is not India. I do not want to see *wahindi* here tomorrow." And he left.'

'What does he want the Indians to do?' said Paka.

'He wants them to leave Zanzibar,' Ali said. 'The other man with the President was Aboud Juma. I have seen him in Ng'ambo shouting for the Afro-Shirazi Party. Juma got out a paper and said the people whose names he read out must stand forward. The names he called were those of all the Indian staff, the Arab Zanzibaris at our work and anyone who was known to support the ZNP. Many Arabs were not there anyway. Juma laughed when he saw they did not come forward.

'He said, "We do not want them".'

'Afterwards, one of the senior staff told us they will close the Association as it is part of the British Government way of taking things from us. Everyone agreed this will happen. But it is a problem. We do not have money and we will not get the pay the Association owed us.'

Paka had no money either. She was part of our family, with us since before Basilah was a baby, almost twenty years. During the days I cared for Babu in hospital, I had not thought to worry about where the money came from for his food. Ali looked after his parents, his four children and his wife's Mama in the country. Now Paka and I were added to his family: I was worried, for we would be a burden to them.

'What shall we do?' I asked Paka. 'If there is no money, where will we go? Will Ali ask us to leave?'

'No, Fatima, we will stay together.'

I remembered. 'Do you have the packet Baba gave you? What was in it?'

'I have not looked. I kept it for you, my child.'

The days passed and still no news came of my family, so I opened the packet. Inside I found a bundle of shilling notes bound with string. A lot of money. I wept to see this. I handed it to Ali as he was head of the family. This last act of my Baba's was a gift to share with these kind people who had saved and cared for me as one of their own.

'Please take it,' I said. 'This will help us all. For you have saved my life even though it brought you danger. When Mama and Basilah are found, they will be happy about what you have done for me.'

Twenty thousand shillings! Paka thought it was the money from the last clove harvest that my Baba kept in the *shamba* to pay the workers. Paka did not work again; she cared for me and for Hala's children and all of us helped with this house that became my home.

I continued to sleep with Paka in the small room where Ali's elderly parents slept. Mujab and his brother and sisters slept in a corner of the main room, rolling out their mats every night. Ali and Hala had a lean-to out the back. There were chickens and pawpaw trees in an enclosed yard. When it rains in Zanzibar, our rain is strong: the water would flood under the door and Mujab would clear out a channel to direct the water elsewhere.

People were suffering. Stories went round and round. We would hear one story in the morning and another in the afternoon. We would hear that we would all be rich and the next day that no money for food was to come to Zanzibar. We heard the British were returning but then they were not. We watched and tried not to believe anything that we did not see with our own eyes.

Some things Ali saw and told us—just the good news. When we saw in the newspaper that our Revolutionary Government was recognised by the British and United States governments, everyone was pleased. Ali said the Zanzibar port was working once more: the steamers delivered goods and slowly our shops were beginning to open again. This did not last long.

Ali found a new job. He said he was lucky. Groups of men were standing at corners waiting for something to happen, waiting for the news of jobs, even a job for one day. A friend of Ali's had got a position as a driver for one of the new Ministers in the Revolutionary Government and told Ali to come with him quickly and together they ran to the Raha Leo Centre. Ali was interviewed and was given the job of driving for a Deputy Minister. He was pleased although the pay was not much.

'When I went to get my Deputy Minister's car for the first time,' Ali said, 'another driver told me the Austin was stolen from an Indian's showroom during the Revolution.'

It was cramped in our house in Ng'ambo and I was not used to being unable to wander around, to be without space and freedom. I stayed in the backyard for much of the time watching the children and listening to the sounds of the neighbours. In my old life, I did not think of where my food and clothes came from: if I was hungry, I went to the kitchen and Amina or Paka made food for me. Now I was learning how it was to wonder if there were enough rice and vegetables for us all.

At the end of April came surprising news. President Karume had met with President Nyerere and announced that our islands of Zanzibar and the country of Tanganyika were to become one country. Hala showed me a picture of the two Presidents mixing a bowl of earth from Zanzibar with earth from Tanganyika. Our *Uhuru* was no more.

'Why is this so?' asked Hala. 'Why do we need to join with Tanganyika? We are our own people.'

'They are saying in the streets that it is what Nyerere has always wanted,' said Baba Ali, 'also, they whisper another reason. President Karume is frightened of losing power.'

'Who could do that?' said Paka. She was frightened of more trouble.

'You have seen the Tanganyikan police?' said Baba Ali.

'Yes,' said Paka. 'They are the ones I trust.'

'The President needs those Tanganyikan police to help him against UMMA because the UMMA men are trained. Many whisper that they have hidden guns all over our island.

'Nasri told me President Nyerere would take those police away if President Karume did not agree to this joining of our two countries. Our President did not want it but his arm has been twisted.'

So we became the United Republic of Tanganyika and Zanzibar, and were no longer our own country. I thought of my brother, Taha, and how proud he had been that we became independent with our own flag and a seat in the United Nations.

Ali told us that hundreds of houses in Stone Town had been taken over by the government. The newspaper listed the owners' names and addresses with the properties they were to lose. No money was paid to the owners. The leaders in the Revolutionary Council took the best houses. They were also moving families from the countryside into houses where the owners had disappeared or fled.

'Paka, do you think we could go and ask for a place to live in Stone Town?' Ali said to his sister.

Paka was frightened but she went with Ali. I did not want to go back to my old home in Shangani; it would have made me too sad then. Paka and I had walked past it and knew strangers had moved in.

Shortly after Ali and Paka made their request, we were given two rooms on the second floor of a house in Stone Town. Ali left his parents in his Ng'ambo house. Our new home was near a major junction of five streets in the centre of Stone Town in the Sokomuhogo area. The rooms were large so they were subdivided into bedrooms for Ali and Hala and for their three younger children. Mujab had his own space as he was sixteen and taller than his Baba. Paka and I had our own area and to make it private, we hung up *kangas* on a string.

A verandah ran most of the way round the inside square of the house overlooking the ground floor courtyard. We did our cooking on this verandah outside our rooms. Everyone washed at the two taps in the courtyard. Our rooms looked out over a narrow street, so narrow we could look into the rooms on the other side and hear our neighbours' conversations. A staircase led to the third floor and then to the rooftop where we hung the washing and could enjoy the cooler air in the evening.

This house, once the home of one large family and their servants, now had eight families and an old woman living in it. The best front rooms on the first floor were taken by a man called Malik and his wife with their only child, a daughter called Zaniah. We had to call him '*Bwana*' Malik as he was in charge of our building. Ali said it was because he was a member of the UMMA Party. Malik would sit on the verandah and watch us. Sometimes he shouted at women if he felt they were using too much water.

'Keep out of his way, Fatima,' Ali said. And I knew why, so I always ran up the stairs past his rooms. Paka said Malik was watching me because I looked like an Arab.

Hala laughed. 'No, Paka, it is because Fatima is becoming beautiful, and their daughter is an unhappy child.'

'Be careful when you go out,' Ali told us. 'On the day of the Revolution, they opened the prisons, releasing all the convicts. Criminals have taken to their old ways. Now they are trying to find those prisoners.'

Once we stepped outside the door of our rooms, we walked with fear, looking behind us at every street corner. Stories passed from one to another and we did not know who to believe or who to trust. What we did know was that Arab-looking Zanzibaris had been detained and were forced to leave in dhows sent by the Omani Government.

Still I hoped for news of my missing Mama and Basilah but weeks and months passed and I heard nothing.

This was my new world. I discovered patience and to be satisfied with small things. Once I was always in a hurry, 'the impatient one,' Mama called me, and used to say, *Subira ni ufunguo wa faraja.* 'Patience is the key to tranquillity'. Slowly I got used to this life; slowly I realised Mama and Basilah were never coming back.

We had to help one another, and that is the way my new family survived.

17. The Books

Elimu ni kama bahari haina sahili　　*Knowledge is like an ocean without shores*

June 1964-February 1965

The Revolution took place during the school holidays. I was halfway through year six and the next year I was to begin high school. Most girls did not go on to high school. My sister, Basilah, had stopped schooling when she was twelve but I loved my school work and times were slowly changing, so learning for girls was not seen as valueless.

I could read and write in KiSwahili, our language at home, as well as English and I knew some Arabic. I had also attended Qur'an classes after school. Mathematics was one of my favourite subjects. We were doing long division and Taha would set sums for me to do to practise. I loved it when he gave me ten out of ten and did a big star in red.

In English, our teacher was a Miss Elliot and the set book for the year was *Anne of Green Gables*, a story about an orphan girl in Canada. Anne was so lonely she created imaginary friends. I thought then of the hardship that Anne had faced. My life had changed too but with Allah's help and mercy I would survive.

After the Revolution, nothing remained from my previous life. My schooling stopped. I did not even have my schoolbooks to read and study on my own. I was losing my chance to learn and losing my dream of becoming a teacher. I said nothing but Baba Ali and Paka knew this.

I had started to call Ali, Baba, 'father', out of respect. At first it was necessary to make people believe I was a relative but gradually I became part of this family. Baba Ali and his wife, Mama Hala, had four children. Mujab was the eldest, three years older than me, and Jannah and Subira were twin girls aged nine. The youngest was a boy of six, Munir. Later I found out that Ali and Hala had lost two babies, a boy and a girl, between the birth of Mujab and the twin girls.

Subira, Jannah and Munir returned to classes not long after the January Revolution when radio announcements ordered all children back to school. Ali and Hala's children could walk to their old classrooms in Ng'ambo from our Sokomuhogo area. They told me some of their teachers had fled and classes were now doubled in size. When they came home, I helped them with their homework. It was easy for me. I could forget my worries and laugh with their childhood delights.

One day Baba Ali came hurrying into our rooms.

'*Hodi*! Paka! Binti Fatima! I have seen schoolbooks for sale in Darajani Market. Come quickly and maybe we can find some for you.'

Paka and I followed Baba Ali to a *duka* down a side street behind Darajani Market. The shopkeeper did not allow us in at first but after Baba Ali spoke to him about me, 'his student', he showed us through to a back storage room. My heart beat with excitement when I saw what was there, for before us were hundreds of books packed round the walls. Many were in stacks, the spines showing they all had the same title.

I walked around taking one here and one there as quickly as possible. Soon Paka had to help me for my hands were busy. Baba Ali came in with two old baskets, *vikapu*, and we filled them. I realised I might not have a chance like this again.

'Look, Paka, this is one of the set books from my last year,' I said, 'and here are English and Mathematics for first year high school!'

Although some of these books were above my education level, I thought, I will learn again and become a teacher. I saw names of students were written inside the covers. I took blank exercise books, a poetry book in English and reference books that seemed to come from a library. Perhaps they were cast out by the teachers after the *Mapinduzi* because they belonged to the old colonial government and they were too scared to keep them.

'Look over there,' said Paka. In the back of the room were heaps of household things: rolled-up Persian carpets, copper trays, silver *jambiya*, long Arab swords in black coverings and the American wall clocks common in old homes. On the floor were piles of crockery, white with a red and gold border and Arabic writing. I picked up one plate and I knew this was the same design that was once on the Sultan's palace at Forodhani on the waterfront.

'See this,' I said. 'Can this be from the palace?'

Paka rushed to take it from my hands. 'Fatima! Shush! Put it back.'

Loud talking in the street disturbed us. I heard the shopkeeper greeting someone.

'Come, come, *Bwana* Hadir, I have the things ready for you. But one moment ...'

A stranger entered followed by the still-explaining shopkeeper. This man was tall, powerfully built, and his body filled the doorway. He was not old but older than my brother Taha. His cheeks had deep indentations giving him a sharp handsome look. My headdress was pushed back as I hunted for books, and I saw surprise and anger cross his face as he saw Paka and Ali with the *vikapu* of books and me with the plate in my hand.

'Who are these people?' He turned to the shopkeeper, who was waving at us to get out.

'I am sorry, *Bwana* Hadir. They are leaving.' The shopkeeper apologised. 'It is the schoolbooks. Only for a student. Forgive me, *Bwana*. I thought you were not interested in the books.'

This man called Hadir did not greet us or show any respect but stood waiting impatiently.

'Go now. Come back and pay later,' the shopkeeper said to Ali, pushing him towards the street.

With more books in my arms I was the last to leave. I would not leave the books behind. Hadir watched me and as I squeezed past him, he bowed his head and held my gaze and I was worried. I did not want this man to know and yet I saw knowledge in his eyes that frightened me. I pulled the *kanga* over my hair as I passed him. I could feel him watching as I walked out. This was the first time I saw Hadir.

'That shopkeeper is taking a risk,' said Baba Ali when we arrived home. 'We must tell no one what we saw. He knew those goods from the Sultan's palace were valuable but dangerous to have. He is greedy!'

'He will get money from the mainland dealers,' Paka agreed. 'That was why he was keeping stolen things. Why was he frightened by this *Bwana* Hadir?'

Baba Ali told us that after the Revolution, traders came by dhow from the mainland harbours of Mombasa and Tanga, and went from shop to shop and house to house buying up valuable things.

'They knew our shopkeepers could not escape with their valuables,' he said, 'so they got them cheaply. Families were forced to sell their precious things to the men who knocked on their doors holding out cash.'

I thought of all the stores in Main Street that once sold precious stones, gold and silver from Ceylon, Oman and Yemen. Stone Town was once famous for its shops selling jewellery to the tourists arriving on the ships. All had disappeared.

Baba Ali went to pay for the books but the *duka* owner would not take the money.

'He told me I was lucky,' Ali said. '*Bwana* Hadir has paid: he said we must tell the "student" the books were a gift for her.'

This worried Baba Ali. 'Fatima, do you know this *Bwana* Hadir?'

'No,' I replied. 'I have never seen him before.'

Baba Ali handed me a book. 'He told the shopkeeper to give you this from him.'

It was a large book with a hard cover and many coloured pictures. The title was *The World We Live In*. Baba Ali watched me opening the book. 'I do not like this. Why is this man giving gifts to Binti Fatima?'

'It will be all right,' said Paka. 'Those books cost us nothing and we will not see the big man again!'

But Paka was wrong.

I was happy with my piles of books. At home I sorted them carefully into subjects. So much knowledge was here! I thought of my grandfather, my Babu, who loved his library and who often read to me. With these books, I thought, I might learn about our world.

On the third floor of our new home, I found an old armchair in an empty room. I asked Baba Ali if I could have it, and he and Mujab carried it down and put it next to my sleeping area where the light fell from the window. The seat was made of woven palm leaves. Paka called it 'rattan'. I found a piece of wood to cover the hole and a pillow to make it comfortable. The rattan on the back had no holes and the arms of the chair were solid, a little worn from years of people holding them. This chair became my reading chair, my studying chair. I called it my 'teacher's chair'.

Many experienced teachers had left Zanzibar, so students who had a few years of high school now taught in the primary school.

'We do not all have desks any more,' said little Jannah. 'First they made two sit at each desk and now even that is not enough, so we sit on the floor. The books are one or two, so the teachers only talk to us and write on the blackboard.'

I liked to ask the children, 'What did you study today?'

One day, late in the year, Jannah said, 'Today we practised for the anniversary of the Revolution. We sang and marched up and down. We have coloured cards we must wave at the right time. We walked to Mnazi Mmoja sports ground. I was tired because it took all day.'

'It is more than two months to the twelfth of January,' I replied. So I understood schools were not what they once were.

I began to study my books while Jannah, Subira and Munir were at school and when they returned, I would read a story to them or make up a kind of lesson. One of my new books was an English novel called *The Secret Garden*. I started to read this aloud to the girls. I sat in my teacher's chair and, with my English dictionary at my side, I was like a real teacher. Sometimes I would ask them questions about what I had read to them. Munir did not come as he was too busy playing with his friends in the street but sometimes Hala and Paka sat with us and a few of the other children in our building.

Bwana Malik's daughter, Zaniah, started coming to listen to my stories and lessons in the afternoon but when her father found out, he stopped her. The next day Baba Ali came to me.

'*Bwana* Malik wants to see all the books you are reading to the children,' Ali said. 'He has found out that you read English sometimes and Zaniah speaks about a secret, a *siri*, and he asks, "What is this secret?"'

I did not want to give Malik any of my books for I knew they would not come back to me. I hid the books under my bed. Where would my books be safe? For the next two days, I stopped my lessons and hoped that Malik would forget.

I asked Baba Ali, 'How many must I show Malik? If I give him five, will he want more?'

Instead something else happened. Late at night, we heard people moving and in the morning, *Bwana* Malik and his family had disappeared, their rooms empty. Soon we found out why.

'President Karume was frightened of Mohammed Babu and his UMMA Party,' said Ali. 'Babu had to shut down his party last month, when all parties were banned, but UMMA people are powerful. Karume and his "Committee of Fourteen" have been chasing the UMMA people out. Some are in prison. *Bwana* Malik has run away.'

My books were safe. I started the afternoon lessons again.

Peace did not return after the Revolution. The people now in power had taken over using violence, and Baba Ali said they were worried the same might happen to them. East Germans arrived and they set up the prison system. The new government bought Chinese weapons and army jeeps and we saw them paraded on the anniversary of the Revolution followed by our new army and marching schoolchildren.

The Afro-Shirazi Party, which had now taken power, had a Youth

League and they selected young men to act as local policemen in every village and community.

One morning, pamphlets printed on yellow paper were put up in our street. It said that we should help the people who wanted to volunteer for the government, that they were here to help us. Baba Ali took one of them and brought it upstairs to read. Afterwards he and Hala spoke quietly in the night, and later I saw Hala used the paper to start the fire.

Kamil, who lived above the tailor's old *duka* in the next street, came to see us soon afterwards. His street had a 'Volunteer' who was demanding money from the families in the area. Kamil hoped to borrow some money to make him leave them alone. He said his children must be quiet because the Volunteer was watching them, to see if they did anything wrong. Baba Ali gave Kamil what little he could but it was not enough.

Four days later, after the full moon, a Volunteer was appointed for our street.

18. The Volunteer

Mnyamaa kadumbu   One who keeps silent, endures

1966-1967

A poor family lived in a single room on the ground floor of our house. Baba Sahir seldom had work. Hala shared food with them when our family had enough. They had only one child, a boy called Rasil. His Mama, Bibi Lama, had difficulty giving birth to him, and this struggle meant she did not conceive again.

'I give thanks to Allah that my only child is a son,' Lama said. She was proud of Rasil.

Rasil was a strange boy of about fifteen with a big head and skinny legs and arms. He giggled when he saw me, and we would find him waiting outside our rooms for no reason. He would laugh out loud behind my back and if I had not known his ways, it would have frightened me.

One day he stopped us as we made our way upstairs. Rasil was wearing a new green shirt. He spoke to Paka but kept glancing at me.

'I am a Volunteer,' he said slowly.

'Good, Rasil,' Paka replied. 'This is good news. What job will you do?'

'I must work in many ways,' Rasil said. 'The government needs me to help protect the Revolution. They will teach me. It is nation building.'

Two days later he again waited for us. It was as if he was repeating a speech, and his manner was forward for a young man talking to a woman, especially a young unmarried woman.

'Our leaders are teaching us this new thing called socialism. Today I must learn how to organise people at the meetings and rallies. I make sure people come to the meetings and do not hide behind the doors of their houses. People must not be lazy.'

For this is what we did. I hated going to the mass meetings to cheer slogans like *Zanzibar Mapinduzi daima*, 'Revolution forever', when the Revolution had destroyed my family. I was not alone in this dislike. Each January we were made to take part. We would stand in the sun for hours listening to President Karume talking and we would have to cheer each time he shouted what he was going to do for us: the roads and buildings he was planning.

The President told us we had to volunteer our labour and everyone waved their flags and shouted, 'Yes!' Once he talked for three hours and children and old people were fainting. We were all controlled by the fear of this man and his police.

The President shouted at the businessmen in our town. He said they were charging too much, and he made jokes about other countries, and we all laughed with him.

'I have stopped wasting money,' the President said, 'on buying tea for Zanzibar, for the sellers of this tea are sending us second-hand tea leaves. These leaves have already been used in the West. We shall grow our own.'

After some time, we heard on the radio that he had decided that only some people were true Zanzibaris. The Comorian and the Shirazi people would have to forget their community or leave the island. It was strange as he did not talk against the people from the mainland.

Rasil was keen to be a true Volunteer but he was not tough enough. His new position gave him pride and he took his role of social teacher and overseer seriously but making others suffer was not his way. He sat on the *baraza* outside our home watching the comings and goings of the street, greeting everyone politely. He was showing our community he knew what they were doing.

We realised the network of Volunteers were spies for the police and they could arrest people. Rasil never did but he would tell stories of young men being arrested for counter-revolutionary acts like having long hair or trying to be fashionable in new outfits. This is indeed what happened. At first we laughed and thought it was a joke that we had police to tell us what to wear.

A problem came over the long pants the young men wore.

Mujab said to Mama Hala one evening, 'Rasil told me this morning, I must not wear tight pants.'

'What does he mean?' said Hala. 'This boy must stop ordering us around.'

'Be careful Mama,' said Mujab. 'Rasil said his Volunteers are commanded to stop the bad influence from infidel countries. The President says growing long hair and wearing narrow-bottomed pants are signs that young men are following fashions from overseas. It is not the Zanzibari way.'

'But these are not new pants, you wear, my son,' said Hala. 'What must we do? Must we buy more? But where?'

'My friends say they are told to sew a piece of cloth into each leg, so it is wider.'

We could not help laughing but Mujab was right: the Volunteers made it their business to make sure young men did not wear what they called 'tight pants'.

Next day, Paka and I were walking down Sokomuhogo Street towards Darajani Market when we saw a group of boys stopped by two Volunteers.

'What are they doing, Paka?' I asked.

We stopped and watched. A Volunteer holding a piece of string made each boy stand on the *baraza* and measured the bottom of the boy's pants. The first boy was pushed off.

'Go. Your pants pass.'

The next boy was not so lucky. The string was longer than the pants. The Volunteer stood up and smacked him across the head.

'You are against the Revolution! Go home! If we catch you again, we will teach you a lesson.'

The Volunteer pulled out a razor and waved it around the young man's head.

When we went home, Hala said she was worried for Mujab, so she opened up the seams of his long pants and sewed a piece of green cloth into each leg. You could not use red cloth as that had been the colour of the Sultan's flag and so it was forbidden. Soon we saw boys walking around town with bright triangular pieces of material. Often the colours did not match so it was strange to look at and made us smile to see them.

Mujab's friend was not so lucky.

'They stopped him and shaved off one of his eyebrows,' Mujab said. 'He feels foolish and will not go outside until it grows back.'

Mujab and his friends learnt to spot the Volunteers from afar and they made up names for them. The ones who were trained by the East Germans were the most feared. They were the *panya* or 'rats'.

'Please be careful, my son,' said Hala. 'Do not play games with these men.'

'They are everywhere,' Mujab said. 'Some are like Rasil and are in charge of a street or village. We call them "ants". Others follow foreigners around and watch to make sure that no one speaks to them. They are the *mende* or "cockroaches". This way we can talk about them and they have no idea. We can laugh and they are ignorant.'

Baba Ali gave Mujab more advice. 'This is serious, Mujab, do not laugh. Look behind you when you are walking in the street. Always be careful who is watching. These men will see who you speak to, who your friends are. For these spies even the glances in the street mean something.'

I do not think Rasil was a wicked young man. The times we lived in changed people. Now we had to be careful with everything we said and only when the door was closed did we whisper our thoughts to one another. We noticed Rasil was always talking, telling stories, while we knew to be silent. His way of chatting to everyone was dangerous, and people in our street avoided him.

Rasil and his family now had more to eat. The shopkeepers would give him little things to keep themselves in favour. The young man got new clothes. He took to wearing a green and yellow peaked cap pushed back on his head. Paka told me to keep out of his way and not to talk to him but it was difficult with our shared washing place and staircases up to our rooms.

With these changes to our island came ill health and disease. I had malaria as a child. We knew what to do to avoid it, and we used to sleep under a net during the hot summer months and when the rains started. Now with water lying in the basements and blocked street drains, the malaria mosquitoes came back.

'President Karume does not like educated men,' Baba Ali said. 'Maybe he is jealous of them. At a Raha Leo rally he said, "Let us keep our distance from the educated by one hundred yards!" He has argued with the United Nations' health people. Now he calls them the *Ofisi ya Panya,* "the Rat Office", and they can no longer spray where the mosquitoes breed. He says we are naturally healthy, so we will not suffer.'

He was terribly wrong and children started falling ill. Their mamas took them to our hospital. Its name had been changed to the V.I. Lenin Hospital.

One day Bibi Lama came up to our rooms crying.

'Hodi, hodi,' she called. 'Bibi Paka, please can you help me? I need help! For two days Rasil is sick. My son said he is cold but he is hot, very hot and sweating. Now he is shouting strange things.'

Only Paka, Mujab and I were at home. We followed Lama down to their room that I had never been into before. Their sleeping space was dark, the air still. It was sad to see how little they had but I had come to know we make our homes where we can with what we can.

Rasil was lying on an old mattress wearing his beloved green cap. Stuck on the wall above his bed were coloured pictures from overseas magazines. Over the following days I came to know those pictures well. One was of snowy mountains. In another, a man in black was playing a guitar and a third was of a cowboy film star with a gun in each hand. I noticed that the cowboy wore his broad-brimmed hat pushed back in the same way that Rasil wore his cap.

Rasil did not seem to recognise us at first. He was talking nonsense and waving his arms around.

Paka felt his forehead. She had cared for our family during childhood illnesses and had watched when the doctor visited. 'Yes, he is burning,' she said.

'But he says he is cold!' Lama cried. 'What can I do?'

'Rasil has malaria. I am sure this is so,' Paka said. 'We must take him to the hospital.'

'No,' said Lama. 'They do nothing for you there with malaria. Too many people are suffering. They send you away.'

'Then we must help him,' said Paka. 'We must cool his fever down.'

For two days and nights we were there with him, taking damp cloths to reduce the fever. Lama went to the *imam* and he gave her pieces of paper on which some verses from the Qur'an were written. She put them in a dish and lit them, blowing the smoke over her son. These we call *mafusho*, and Lama prayed that they would drive evil spirits away.

Paka and I were with him during the day and Mujab stayed with him during the night. I saw how gentle Mujab was with Rasil. Sometimes Rasil shivered uncontrollably, and we could do nothing for him. Lama left us caring for her son while she ran to find a *mganga*, a traditional herbalist. She came back with a bottle filled with a dark green liquid made from pawpaw leaves and other spices. Rasil sipped this for two days, and he survived.

After he recovered, Rasil and his family moved across the street to empty rooms higher up, away from the damp of the ground floor. Rasil now took it upon himself to be our protector, and we did not have trouble from the Volunteers.

His story did not end happily. Shortly before President Karume was assassinated in 1972, Rasil's Baba, Sahir, spoke to Ali in the street.

Ali came upstairs. 'Sahir says Rasil has been missing for two nights; sometimes he does not come home but this is unusual. Sahir says Rasil returned with bruises and tiny burns on his arms last week and refused to speak about it. He and Lama are sick with worry.'

Two more days went by and we did not see Rasil sitting on the *baraza* in his favourite spot checking on our street life. Sahir took to sitting in his son's place, turning his head from side to side, watching and waiting. People spoke to him kindly as they knew of his fears. The following day we heard Lama had gone to the Volunteers' office at Raha Leo. Long after dark she came stumbling up the stairs. She was wailing and tearing at her hair. Hala sat her down holding her hands in hers. She told us what happened.

'Sahir said it might be safer for me to go,' Lama said. 'I went to the office and asked for my son, for Rasil. They told me to wait, and I did this for hours as the sun disappeared and the Maghrib prayers were finished. After a time, one of the Volunteers came outside. He shouted at me to go home, saying they had no one there called Rasil. I pretended to go away but I hid nearby where I could watch the young men arrive for their evening meeting. I saw a man I had once seen with Rasil. I followed him and caught his sleeve and begged mercy from him to tell me about Rasil, for he is my only child.'

She paused, her eyes full with tears. It was then I knew he was dead. Perhaps he had not been careful with his friends or what he said. Somewhere he had angered someone cruel.

Lama struggled to say these words. 'This man told me Rasil had an accident and was dead. I asked, please, could I see … could I have his body? But no, he said Rasil was already buried and he could not tell me where. I could not understand and I waited. I waited to see if I could find someone else to help, even to show me where his grave was, and that was when … when I saw more men arrive, and one was wearing my Rasil's green and yellow cap. You know the cap he loved? Then I knew these words were true. My son will never come home. Why have they done this? There is nothing for me now. Rasil was not a bad boy.'

That was so. There were so many caught up in this madness. Some were evil, some were only young and foolish, all suffered in the years to come.

19. Swallows

Kila ndege huruka na mbawa zake   Every bird flies with its own wings

1967-1968

I was learning about a different Zanzibar, one where there was never enough to eat, and our household lived in fear of what each day would bring. The freedom I once had was a dream of long ago.

One evening, I found a safe place and made a special friend. I had climbed up to our rooftop to say my evening prayers, and this is where I met Cecelia, the oldest resident of our building. In the corner of the rooftop was an old wooden storage shed which was her special place. The old lady was covered in a black *bui-bui*. The skin on her face was tight over her bones and her eyes were dark in wrinkled pits as if they had seen a lifetime of worry. I thought she was hiding away but the laughter in her face showed her pleasure in seeing me and her cheeks became round and full.

She waved me over to move beside her. 'Come beautiful child, I will show you something.'

Cecelia's head hardly reached my shoulder and I was just sixteen. She held my hand and used it to point under the rotting roof of the shed. I bent down. In the deep shadow, a nest made from lumps of mud was stuck on the wood. Three wobbling heads covered in wool were sticking out.

'See! Baby swallows,' Cecelia said. 'Every year the parents come back to the same place, build their nest on the side of our building away from the summer monsoon, and bring up their young. They know me and let me come close. At the beginning of the cool season, when the *kusi* monsoon starts to blow, they leave. When the monsoon changes again, they find their way back to this rooftop.'

'I wonder what they see as they fly over Africa. What people and lands do they pass?' I asked.

The old lady had a KiSwahili name but took the one given to her by the Indian family who once lived here, so we only knew her as Cecelia. Cecelia had worked for this family, the Goli family, who owned this house before it was taken by the government. Their clothing business was nationalised and they packed what they could and left. She did not know how old she was, but once told me she remembered the old Seyyid Sultan Khalifa when he was a young man, so I think she was maybe seventy. This old lady kept to herself, for you had to be careful where you put your trust, but she came to trust me.

Cecelia never told me if she had been married. She opened my eyes to a world I had never seen before. Despite our suffering, she gave me her understanding of beauty. She loved the birds of the sky. She said, 'Look up and see! All around you there is so much, and yet people stare at the ground.'

We sat on the rooftop looking across the red-grey corrugated iron and she told me stories and sayings of the old world. She would laugh and laugh until tears ran down her cheeks, for some proverbs carried hidden meanings. She loved riddles and would tease me with them, not telling me the answer until I had tried to solve them over several days. And when I heard the answer, it seemed so easy.

Her little bit of space, open to the weather, to the skies of dawn and dusk, became my place too, and others did not worry us there behind the old shed. She carried up a frayed Pemba straw mat with its woven colours, and we sat on this as the light left the sky.

Behind the shed, she tended her pots, a whole row of pots, big and small. The tops were covered in torn old mats.

'What are they for, Bibi Cecelia?' I asked.

'Look,' she said, and she lifted a mat. Inside was milky water. 'Taste it.' She laughed when I screwed up my face at the sharpness on my tongue. 'I am making *chumvi*, salt,' she said. Cecelia had old bottles and she would go to the sea and fill them, bringing them back to her rooftop pots. Gradually, as the water evaporated, time and time again, a layer of salt formed in the bottom. Finally, she boiled the mixture and ended up with a handful of salt. This she sold for a few shillings. We were all short of salt for our cooking.

From our rooftop, you could see down to the street level, to the passing life of Stone Town, as well as across to other balconies and rooftops. It was hard to keep secrets in our world, so many eyes peeping from behind the shutters. Our town did not have houses that stood alone. It seemed as if one house grew from another using the same wall to grow outwards, like mushrooms in wet weather. Each one was a little different, a room or verandah sticking out, but they shared the same understanding of how a home should be to survive. They were built to protect us, solid as the coral rock that formed the island itself.

Cecelia pointed to the sky and we looked at the clouds rolling in over our town with the monsoon wind behind them.

'Look how some grow tall and strong,' Cecelia said. 'They are the ones that will carry rain.'

Sometimes warm rain came like a curtain across the town, hitting the rooftops with a sound like drums while steam rose off the hot tin. It sent us hurrying below with our damp washing. Some calm evenings after sunset, Cecelia would come for me and we would climb up to the roof where the air was cool. We stared at the thousands of stars and the moon rising over the land.

'See that brighter one there? It is a planet, not a star.' Cecelia said.

'How can you tell?'

'Planets are closer to us and they look stronger.'

I took the book *Bwana* Hadir had sent to me, *The World We Live In,* and showed it to her. Together we looked at the pictures of our earth, of the undersea and its creatures, and the places I will never see. Cecelia asked me to read aloud as she said her eyes had seen too much and were tired. There were English words I did not understand so I would spell them for her and always she would know what they meant. This was another way I was to learn.

Cecelia opened my eyes to the little things around us. The way the geckoes on the wall would make little barks, how they hunted the mosquitoes that brought sickness into our houses. The way the shadows fell upon the walls of the house with a pattern like lace, and how delicate were the colours of the *kangas* drying on a clothes line.

We entered our house through an old Arab door. It was not as magnificent as the door of my family's house in Shangani but it was filled with ancient carving.

Cecelia explained the story she saw written there. 'See here at the bottom is a fish promising wealth from the sea. And here ... here is a long chain right round the door frame. It stops evil spirits from entering our home, and these are dates, fruit from Arabia. They give hope for plenty in this life.'

Food was always on our mind. When we had extra food, we would first give some to Cecelia. She survived on so little; it was no wonder she seemed to shrink with each passing year.

We hoped life would get better but, after three years, things got worse. At first, there were shops open, little *dukas* that bought and sold a few things. We Zanzibaris had always shopped each day for food. We did not need fridges. Most of these shops were previously owned by Indians. *Duka* owners with wealth or influence had managed to leave Zanzibar but the poorer ones did not have money for bribes. Unemployed young men were sent to labour camps and to avoid this, others left. They left with only the shirts on their backs.

'The wealthy pay the bribes and leave. I see many get ill-treated at the airport,' said Baba Ali. 'The government says that before they leave, they must pay for everything—the education and medical care they got by growing up here. Not many can pay, so they find other ways to escape.'

There were clever ways to get around the restrictions. Baba Ali told us how, soon after the Revolution, he had helped an Indian family.

'The Vohra family were Muslims and were given permission to take some of the money that was owed to them out of Zanzibar but it had to be as sacks of cloves. Karume does not like cloves; he says they are a colonial crop and we must grow our own food to eat, not cloves to sell. After the Revolution, *Bwana* Vohra came to the warehouse and I helped him choose sacks to be shipped to the mainland. But he was clever. He put his wife's gold jewellery into the middle of a sack, so it was not stolen at the airport. I looked the other way!'

The Deputy Minister for whom Baba Ali worked would talk to him in the car, although even this was dangerous in those times. In the quiet of the evening, Ali repeated what he had heard.

'My Deputy told me President Karume has decided to rid Zanzibar of the Indians, the Comorians and even the Shirazi people—anyone he thinks sounds foreign, even if they were born here and their parents were born here. He will make them give up their nationality and only be Zanzibaris. And yet *Bwana* D. says everyone knows Karume is not a Zanzibari himself. He came from Nyasaland on his mama's back but no one can say this out loud. They have invented a birthplace on Unguja for him.'

Baba Ali said, 'I am sad to tell you but they are going to nationalise the rest of the shops. All our *duka* owners will lose their businesses,' he said.

Paka wrung her hands. 'What more? How can President Karume do this? He said he would bring us freedom, not hunger. The factories and importing businesses have already been nationalised. Is that not enough?'

'Hush, my sister, Paka. You must be careful what you say,' said Baba Ali. 'Never ever repeat what I tell you. It could be dangerous for our family.

'Most of the men in the Revolutionary Council are from the mainland. The one most feared by everyone is B. And he is from there too. He is the wickedest of the racists. He is cruel and cares little for human life. My Deputy is frightened of him. If he comes knocking on your door saying he needs to talk to you, that is that; you are taken to prison. They send you to *Ba-Mkwe* where the Chief Security Officer is Hasan Mandera ... They call him,' and he paused, '*Ziraili*, the Angel of Death'.

Baba Ali spoke the truth. *Dukas* closed; their grey wooden shutters were pulled shut across the doors. Houses in Stone Town became empty as people left for the mainland or went to other countries. Other families moved away to live on *shambas* where they could grow food and keep goats.

When the rains came, parts of some houses collapsed and the remaining walls hung over the street. More people moved out and neighbours put wooden bars across entrances warning of the danger. Our town was dying as the people disappeared. Whole streets were silent. We became even more dependent on the ways of the government.

'They are saying Karume wants Stone Town to fall down,' Paka said. 'This was where most people voted against him before the Revolution, so he hates this place. The government is doing nothing for us.'

And it was true. Electricity was not common in our homes and the street lights hardly worked or were broken. There were too few working toilets and people lost their shame, using corners of the streets to relieve themselves. Drains were blocked and when the monsoon rains came, they flooded the ground floors of some houses. You could smell these places as you passed by. No one wanted to live there, and families found other houses in better condition to move into. Several houses around us were now empty, doors standing open with cats breeding inside.

One day, I met Cecelia at our front door. She had two *vikapu* filled with her bottles of sea water.

'My salt is almost ready,' Cecelia said as she put the bags down. 'This is the last lot.'

'Let me help you carry them,' I said.

'That would be good, child. You are young and your legs are strong. Let us sit here for a few moments.'

We sat together on the *baraza* and watched a family moving out of a house a few doors down. Their bits of furniture and boxes were tied with string. Pots and rolled-up mats filled the narrow street. A girl was carrying an orange and white kitten. Babies were crying.

'Soon only the old people and the cats will be left. It is so: Stone Town is dying,' Cecelia said to herself.

20. The Fish Head

Mtu ni Watu   *A person is people. No man is an island. Every person needs the company/help of others*

1968-1969

During those months of hunger, Hala and Paka were always worrying about food for the next day. We could not afford what once we had taken for granted.

Hala said, 'Maybe we have to sell Fatima's books?'

Before I could reply, Baba Ali said, 'No! They are her schooling and anyway they are worth little these days.'

Sometimes we gave away household things to get enough food for our family. Maybe it was to buy little dried fish, called *dagaa*. They were so tiny you ate the whole fish, bones and all. From them, we could make fish soup with some plants from the forest, like pumpkin leaves, *mboga ya tango,* and cassava plant leaves, *kisamvu*, and if we had flour, we made bread. That was a satisfying meal.

Paka taught me how to make *chapati* or *mkate wa kusukuma* and this became my special skill but often we could not get the ghee to make it. Baba Ali and Mujab tried to find what Hala would ask for to feed us all. Mostly they returned with vegetables. Meat was too expensive. Mujab found day jobs in Darajani Market and got handouts of food without money changing hands. Every night the children watched Hala cooking as they waited for their meal.

In 1968, the Revolutionary Government announced that the area of Ng'ambo, which was on the landward side of Stone Town, was to have new apartments designed by the East Germans. Ng'ambo was filled with hundreds of simple houses, most without water or electricity. The authorities announced this 'was the result of the poor state in which the colonials have left us'.

Those residents of Ng'ambo who lost their houses were told they would get the first choice of these new flats if they volunteered their labour for construction work. If you did not volunteer, you were accused of being one of the 'destroyers of national development'. Others volunteered because they were given extra sugar and flour on their ration cards.

One day, old Cecilia came back from the market most unhappy. 'I went to see the new flats the government is building,' she said. 'Do you know what they have done?'

'No,' said Hala. 'What now? Sit, take some water, and tell us slowly.'

'The graves,' she said, 'the old cemeteries of the Khojas Ithnashri. They are buried at Raha Leo. It was my people, the family who owned this house.'

'Khojas?' I asked. 'What has happened to the graves?' I knew Khojas were Muslims who had come from India. Two girls in my class at school were Khojas.

'They have destroyed them, concreted them for those new flats.' Cecelia clasped her face in her hands and wept. We could not comfort her.

Baba Ali was there when President Karume came to the construction site and left his footprints in the cement. Revolutionary Council members had their photographs taken holding spades as if they were working on the project. Everyone clapped and cheered. After two hours they disappeared and day after day it was prisoners and local people who worked there carrying the cement and the long steel reinforcing rods.

When the flats were finished, there were not enough for all those families who had lost their houses, because so many were given to government people.

We called these ugly buildings the 'trains' of Michenzani and only one thousand of the planned seven thousand were built. The old homes of Ng'ambo could house a big family and had a backyard for growing pawpaw trees and chickens but the new flats were like boxes and soon people called them 'containers'.

Mujab stayed away from Ng'ambo so he would not be caught and made to work for nothing. We needed his wages. If Hala managed to buy a *pishi* of rice, which is about seven pounds, it was a day when we were happy. Paka loved to complain, for she would remember the prices in the old market.

'Look! This *pishi* used to cost four or five shillings,' Paka said, 'and now we have paid twenty times more! Oranges are two hundred shillings for a little bag. How are people going to live? How can we feed the children?'

'I cannot go to Darajani any more,' replied Hala. 'I am too frightened I will be knocked over. It is a battlefield!'

Hala was wise to be frightened, for desperate people rushed to get food. Instead of going to school, some children were made to stand in those queues. Sometimes they were trampled in the rush. A pregnant woman was killed as a crowd went mad, pushing to grab a share of printed cloth.

Baba Ali came home one day carrying a large parcel wrapped in newspaper. He was barefoot as he rushed up the stairs, panting under its weight. He was smiling like a schoolboy and called us to gather round.

'Look,' he said. 'Look what I have got. We will eat well tonight!'

He unwrapped his prize. I stepped back in amazement. It was the head of a giant fish, its head bigger than that of a man. Blood was seeping onto the floor. Shining white eyes with round black centres stared at me: and instead of a nose it had an enormous spear. Its mouth was open as if it was gulping air. It was a terrible thing to see.

'What is it?' I asked.

'It is a swordfish, a *chuchunge*,' Baba Ali said. 'See! Much meat is left.'

And this was so, for where the body was cut off, there were two lumps of pink flesh either side of the backbone. Later we found it had chunks of meat in the cheeks that fed us all.

The huge fish head lasted us for three days. It was such a rich meat; a little bit filled you, and we made soup from the bones. But Ali had given his best shoes, his leather *makubadhi*, in exchange for this food, and he was left with old sandals as his only footwear.

21. Murder in the Mosque

Dunia huleta vyema na vimbi
The world brings good and bad things

April 1970

These were the worst times for survival in Zanzibar.

Many strangers had come to Unguja since the Revolution. Chinese people arrived and taught us their ways of farming. Our young men and even old people were taken to work with the Chinese in the rice fields without being paid. The East Germans set up prisons and the security system, and they were much feared.

Our President refused to allow sugar, rice and flour to be brought into Zanzibar from other countries. We heard that none of his advisors were brave enough to tell him the people were starving. Prices went up even further. The people who had farms could grow their bananas and cassava but for those of us living in town it was a difficult time. The queues grew longer and longer. If we heard from a passerby on the street that goods had arrived, maybe material for *kangas*, we would leave our work and hurry there hoping it would not all be sold.

Ali was sometimes given a present of food by his Deputy Minister. 'Those Ministers fly over to Dar-es-Salaam,' Ali said, 'and buy things there. When I collect them from the airport they fill the car with their bags of meat, medicine and clothing, even children's toys. Their families are never without as we are.'

When talking became dangerous and people would watch one another nervously in case a criticism slipped out, music became a safe haven for our thoughts. Our music is the *taarab* and, in the old days, the streets of Unguja would be filled with music. From one shop to the next as you walked past, *taarab* music would follow you along. Now we were told *taarab* was 'music of the Arabs' and anything Arab was now forbidden. It was foolish but what could we do?

Even the pictures and decorations of our private rooms were to be changed. People had framed prayers or quotes from the Qur'an hung up in their homes for religious guidance. These were in Arabic script as they must be if they are from our Holy Book. We heard they were not allowed as they were 'imperialist'.

'People are taking down the words of the Qur'an,' Paka said, 'even those little pieces of paper protecting us from the evil spirits, the *mashetani*.'

It was a serious offence, punishable by imprisonment, if you were found to have a picture of any of the Sultans, the old Zanzibar flag or even the old ZNP newspapers in your house. Women had been given *kangas* to celebrate our independence in December 1963. These *kangas* were in the colours of the ZNP and showed the rooster emblem. They had to be destroyed. Even the nurses' pink uniforms had to change as their colour was too close to the red of the Sultan's flag.

Before the Revolution a famous teacher called Sheikh Abdullah Saleh al-Farsy would speak on the radio. My Baba and Mama listened to him. Baba once told me this learned man had translated the Qur'an into KiSwahili. On *Sauti Ya Unguja,* Radio Zanzibar, he used to read passages first in Arabic and then in KiSwahili. It was a joy for the faithful. This program was prohibited after the Revolution.

In our mosque, the word of God is read aloud in Arabic and then explained in our language, for many do not understand Arabic. That is the way it is done. Yet one day innocent believers lost their lives due to the madness of an evil man and his hatred of the language of our Qur'an.

I was rinsing clothes on the ground floor when I heard men shouting in the street. I dried my hands and opened the main door a little, so I could peep out.

A grey-haired man in a white *kanzu* was beating his breast and wailing. 'A madman, in the mosque, he is shooting believers as they pray. Many are dead. A child is dead too. Allah have mercy on us all.'

Others came out. Soon a crowd gathered and together they ran back up the street. Paka and Hala came to the door and I told them what I had seen.

'Come my daughter, let us go upstairs and close these doors. We will hear soon enough.' Paka took me by the hand and we waited in fear of what we would hear.

Baba Ali came home and told us the story. 'They were holding *Maghrib* prayers in the Ithnasheri Mosque at Kiponda, and the *imam* was reading the Qur'an in Arabic, as we are taught. Mohamed Abdalla Kaujore, a Makonde man who is a chief lieutenant in the security police, was walking past with a friend. He rushed into the mosque. They say he was shouting, "Why are you using this foul language of the *Uarabu* people? It is the poison of imperialists. It is forbidden."

'He was waving a gun in the air and the *imam* thought Kaujore did not know the word of God, as we learn it in Arabic, so he tried to address him calmly. All those there could see the man was mad with hashish and he smelt of alcohol. Kaujore's friend pulled his arm to get him to leave but he stayed, shouting, "I must remove these wicked people, these Arab lovers". And he shot ... shot people as they prayed. A boy, called Abbas, only eight, at prayers with his Baba, was killed. The *imam*, Abdul Hashim, is badly injured too. What has come upon us?'

On the radio that night, Edington Kisasi, Commissioner of Police, called for calm. Five people died including the injured *imam*. Kisasi announced there would be an investigation, and 'we will take adequate measures regarding the crime that has been committed'.

But this killer, Kaujore, was powerful in the government. He was never arrested: instead he lives freely, walking around our town, unpunished in any way for his murderous crimes at the Ithnasheri Mosque.

Soon after this we heard the rumour that the Revolutionary Council was to make laws to control marriage between the different groups of the people of Zanzibar. Truly we knew we were living in evil times.

22. Forced Marriages

Nafusi na mali yasikukulie
Do not permit passion and wealth to rule you

Late 1970

The year I turned nineteen the Revolutionary Council changed our law of marriage.

Baba Ali told us. 'I hear a new law is coming. Unmarried girls, Arab, Asian or Comorian, must be prepared to accept African men, especially Revolutionary Council members, as husbands if they are asked. Our President says that in the old days the African slave women were forced to marry Arab men, and now he will make it the other way round.

'If the family refuse,' said Baba Ali, 'the parents can be caned with twenty-four strokes, fined fifteen thousand shillings or imprisoned for six months.'

This was indeed a shocking thing to do. And to make it a law! I always walked outside with my face unmasked. It was obvious I was an Arab girl and I heard women call me beautiful and men looked quickly at me. Recently a young man had asked Baba Ali if I would consider marriage. He had been respectful. Baba Ali asked me, in front of Paka, if I was ready for marriage and I said 'no'. Somehow I was still waiting, waiting for a miracle, for my family to come back.

The law, called Section 174, was published: it ruled that any of our revolutionary leaders, of whatever age, could choose a girl to marry and she could not refuse. Many families fled the country fearing for their daughters.

We did not know whether to believe they would do this bad thing. In our custom, marriages are family matters to be arranged after careful planning. The man will approach the family, often through an aunt or senior family member and if the parents approve, they will ask the girl if she is willing. She is not forced. It is better for your beliefs and customs to be shared in your new relationship. Now the Revolutionary Government was interfering in the most violent way against women.

Baba Ali said, 'The leaders are saying times have changed, and the Arab and Indian families must submit. The boot is now on the other foot.' He continued, 'I am worried. My Deputy has seen Binti Fatima and he made a comment that I had a beautiful daughter, and asked how old she was and whether she was married or promised to anyone. I told him she is my cousin's daughter but she is an orphan under my care. Those in power can now look for young girls and marry them against their wishes.'

'Does this mean the parents will be forced to agree?' I said.

I was amazed. Marriage for us was such a significant event. Most people on the island were followers of Islam. How could our leaders do such a terrible thing against our beliefs and custom? Had not the Prophet said a man should choose a religious woman? Yet religion was not discussed here. It seemed to be a way to take revenge on innocent people.

Baba Ali said, 'I am sad to say this. These men are old and desire a young wife.'

Two weeks later Hala came running into our rooms with our neighbour Zakia stumbling behind her.

'Come, come, Paka, Fatima, Zakia is visiting. She has news from her brother.'

Zakia lived in the house opposite ours: Hala often spoke to her across the narrow gap that was our street. They could easily throw things to one another—such as an onion Hala might need for the evening meal. Hala often sat at the window and together they listened to the radio music Zakia played, sharing stories of the day.

Zakia was a spinster, a large woman with bow legs, and she walked with a slow swaying of her hips. She had told Hala that this birth defect was why no one had offered her marriage. Now she lived with her brother and his wife, and helped care for their six children. Her brother had a job as a guard in the Revolutionary Council's meeting chamber. During the Council's gatherings, he and his group would control the movement of people around the building, for President Karume was careful who came close to him.

'Here is a stool, Zakia, please sit.'

Zakia's size made it difficult for her to rise from the floor. She sat panting and could not speak for a while. I wondered how she managed to be so large in spite of the food shortages. Her eyes were bright with the excitement of telling a story she knew would shock us.

'My brother has come back from the Revolutionary Council meeting. You will not believe what happened! He saw it all. What I tell you is true. My words are his words.'

Already Hala was blinking fast and wringing her hands.

'President Karume spoke about his decree, the Forced Marriage Act,' Zakia said. 'He said he wanted progress in this matter. He waved his hands and two guards opened the doors and in came four girls with six policemen. Behind them came the girls' families. They are unmarried Persian girls. One is only fourteen years old: her name is Nasren. The others are Badira, Fawzia and Wajiha. They were crying and so were their families. Some mamas were tearing at their hair. All of them stood there looking around, not knowing what was happening.'

Paka said, 'I am sorry for them. It would be better to die! This is a terrible thing.'

'Yes,' Zakia rushed on. 'President Karume said the girls must choose a husband from the men before them. Right then. He said groups like the Persians and Comorians must become part of the new Zanzibar, for now this island is for black Africans. A policeman walked up to the first girl and pointed to the Council member in the seat close by and said, "Will you take this man for your husband?"

'The girl waved her arms and shouted. "No! I am already engaged."

'The policeman did not listen to her and went from man to man, demanding she accept one of them, repeating: "Will you take this one? Or this one?" All the girls refused. My brother told me the noise was tremendous with the shouting and crying of the parents and their daughters.

'One of the Council members pushed forward and tried to say the words for a wedding ceremony, right there in that place! Nasren, the youngest girl, collapsed on the floor and families tried to push through to rescue their daughters. The police rushed into the chamber, holding the parents back and taking the girls away to prison. Karume said if the families continue with their refusals, the fathers would be imprisoned as well as their daughters.'

Hala was weeping. 'What will happen now?'

'I do not know,' Zakia said. 'Maybe if they continue to refuse they will be allowed back to their families. How can they force such a marriage? My brother said most of those men are fat and old and have several wives already.'

The following week, we found out Zakia was wrong. The girls were taken from prison: one by one, they were taken to houses belonging to senior army officers. Some of the houses were not in Stone Town but in the area called Migombani where the revolutionary leaders had built big homes. The officials left the girls and told them the men in those houses were now their husbands.

The remaining Persian families applied to leave. This was granted but only if they left all their possessions behind and would no longer be Zanzibari citizens. This was the way Karume chose to persecute and remove a group of our people he disliked. Yet we all knew these families had lived here for generations. Their ancestors had arrived on dhows from Persia.

A week later, Baba Ali spoke to me, 'You are nineteen, my daughter, for I see you as my daughter. Do you want me to look for a suitable husband for you?'

It was hard to answer this. It was not for me to find a suitable man to marry. It was *haram* for a man to show interest in a single woman and likewise for me to regard young men. If the Revolution had not happened, I might have been betrothed at this age, depending on my family circumstances. I had thought about it but it was against nature to be forward and, without my parents and their connections, how was I to find the right husband? I shuddered to think that it could be my lot to be one of the spoils of the Revolution, a gift to a middle-aged leader.

I had survived the destruction of my family. I was determined not to be cast into a forced marriage.

23. An Admirer

Mke mzuri halindwi   A beautiful woman is difficult to guard

April 1971

Bwana Hadir came into my life again. Since the time of buying the schoolbooks, I had seen him in the streets of Stone Town but I did not realise he had been watching me.

It was after the *kaskazi*, the north-east monsoon, had ended at the beginning of 1971, and we were waiting for the big rains to arrive. These ones we call the *masika* rains and they usually begin in March. This year they were late: every day we hoped this was the day the rain would come. People sat in the shade, or in dark rooms where it was a little cooler, and used fans made of leaves to move the air over their sweating bodies. Clouds would gather into great towers but the skies would slowly clear and the heat would return.

Finally one Friday, as I was waiting for the children to return from school and the men had gone to midday prayers, rain arrived. I remember it well. I was on the roof watching the storm approach over the sea. The clouds had built up in tumbling layers with the sun shining silver on the top. Around them remained the bluest of skies. A powerful force was driving the storm front towards Stone Town. The temperature dropped and the wind changed direction.

The washing on our clothes line started flapping and women and children came running upstairs to gather it in. A noise was in the air, like the howling of an animal. As the sea wind rushed through our narrow streets, it found paper and plastic and took them flying over the houses. The rooftops were bright against the darkness before us. The reds and yellows glowed and the edges of shadows were sharp on the buildings. The white tower of the Beit-el-Ajaib shone against the dark sky.

What a beautiful world it was! The sea was turning from blue to black: there was no longer a horizon but, across the sea, a line of black water was moving towards us. The blue spaces between the clouds had disappeared and grey tentacles of rain stretched towards the land. I saw Cecelia's swallows flying ahead of the storm and a fishing boat, its triangular sail tight with wind, racing for the harbour.

Electricity was in the air. I felt so alive, so full of energy. On every building, women were singing and dancing.

'It's coming!' They clapped their hands above their heads and swayed their hips.

The first raindrops stung my face and smacked like stones onto the tin roofs. I ran downstairs.

'Rain, rain is here!' I called out from the staircase before rushing to open the front door.

I waited on the *baraza*. Sheets of rain crashed down upon our street turning it into a river. I was protected by the overhanging roof and was above the rising water. People took shelter as best they could: the sound of the rain was like an aeroplane landing. The air was fresh and new.

I felt strangely happy and put my hand out into the curtain of water that fell before me. Further down the street, an old woman ran into the rain and was dancing and shouting, and, like a child, I felt it too—the joy of the rain falling and the arrival of the new season. I stepped out of my sandals, off the ledge into the ankle-deep water, and was instantly wet through.

I raised my face to the sky and the sweet rain and I danced. I felt no fear of the future or pain from the past. The rain wet my long hair and I drank from the sky. Two little girls joined me. We swung in a circle laughing and singing and stamping our feet in the rainwater as it collected in the street. It was so good and right to be there and to be alive as the rain fell, the rain that had been longed for day after day.

The first rain storm passed and I climbed back into our doorway wringing out my dripping *kanga* that had fallen round my neck. It was then that I saw him. A big man in dark trousers and a white shirt was watching me from the other side of the street by the barber shop. The barber had gone to prayers and, as was his habit, had left his shop open, pulling a chair across the doorway. The man did not avert his eyes. He smiled holding my gaze and bowed his head in greeting.

I recognised him as the man in the shop, it was Hadir, who years ago had sent me the present of a book. I went inside quickly, my heart hammering. The way he had stared at me had shaken and stirred me in some way. I wondered if this was dangerous. For certainly this was not acceptable behaviour.

24. Sweet Promises

Ahadi tamu tamu!   Sweet promises

April 1971

I was sitting outside on the *baraza* with Munir when a schoolboy I did not know came up to me.

'Binti. Is it you who is called Fatima?'

He was so serious, it was funny. 'Yes,' I replied. 'It is. Why do you ask?'

'*Bi mdogo*. For you.' He held up an envelope and when I took it, he hurried off. I looked beyond his running body. At the street corner I thought I saw Hadir walking away. I felt guilty and at the same time relieved that Munir was watching a game of *bao* being played and had not seen. Immediately I went upstairs to my bed. My name was written neatly on the front and underlined. Inside was a single sheet of cream paper. On it was written a poem, carefully presented in the centre of the sheet. It was unsigned.

In your light, I learn how to love.
In your beauty, how to make poems.
You dance inside my chest where no one sees you,
but sometimes I do,
and that sight becomes this art.

I was moved. My heart was beating fast. I read it several times before hiding the letter in a book. I knew it was from him. But what did it mean?

Now every time I went into the street I watched, but tried not to look as though I was watching, to see if Hadir was there. I sat with Hala's children on the *baraza* by our door as they played their favourite game of 'crocodile' where they pretended the narrow street was a river where a big crocodile lived and tried to catch them. Surrounded by their cries of fun, I glanced up and down to see who was around.

Three days later as I returned inside to help with the evening work, a boy followed me, for we did not lock the doors of our houses. This boy was not the same one as before and was quite serious about his task. He stood to attention before me holding out another envelope. 'Binti Fatima?'

'Yes,' I answered. 'Who gave this to you? Please tell me!'

He shrugged his shoulders and ran out the door. This new letter was heavy. I tucked it away as I ran up to my room. Inside was another poem: from the envelope, a slim gold necklace fell into my lap. I held the cold metal in my hand as I read the letter.

> *I want to see you.*
> *Know your voice.*
> *Recognise you when you*
> *first come round the corner.*
> *Sense your scent when I come*
> *into a room you've just left.*
> *Know the lift of your heel,*
> *the glide of your foot.*
> *Become familiar with the way*
> *you purse your lips*
> *then let them part,*
> *just the slightest bit,*
> *when I lean in to your space*
> *and kiss you.*
> *I want to know the joy*
> *of how you whisper*
> *'more'.*

I blushed when I read this. Never had I imagined such a poem could be sent to me. Written underneath were the words, 'I would humbly ask if you will allow me to address you. I have an honourable proposal to offer. My young friend will come for your reply tomorrow at midday,' and his signature, 'Respectfully yours, Salim Hadir'.

So it was him, Salim Hadir. I read the poem a second time. Ideas and emotions raced around my head and heart. What to do? I was totally confused by this offer. Was it a marriage proposal? If not, what was he offering me? I did not have a dowry, so what could I offer any marriage partner?

I did not sleep well that night as I thought again and again how to respond. At some time in the morning, it came to me: I had to seek help. Without my parents, I was not protected in such a decision. How I longed for them! I could not go to Paka for she would tell her brother. It was to Cecelia I turned.

Next morning, I found her on the roof. She was weaving, fixing a hole in a *kikapu*. Her fingers were flying over the thin strands of dried coconut leaves.

She greeted me. 'Come child, sit down next to me. You are frightening the swallows. Their babies are getting ready to leave the nest.'

I told her my story, of how I had first seen Salim Hadir, of how I had received two letters from him, and how I knew he was watching me. Cecelia listened until I had finished, her fingers weaving the fibres together.

'Can I see the letters?' she said.

I showed them to her with the gold filigree necklace. After reading them, she patted my arm and looked up to watch the birds.

'Do you see the young birds, Fatima? See they are on the edge of the nest, almost too big now to fit in. They are stretching their wings for their first flight. For them it is everything, that first flight. It has to be perfect. If it is not, they will die from a broken wing or be eaten by a hungry cat. After months of caring for them, the parents have to watch and hope they are strong enough for the long journey up the coast to their summer feeding grounds. Life goes on in their children.'

'But, Bibi Cecelia, what must I do?' I said. I was impatient and did not want to hear about her birds.

'What do you want to do, my child?' she said. 'Do you want to accept the advances of this man? What do you know of him?'

'Maybe ... can you find out more about him?'

'Do you see the wrinkles on my face?' she replied touching her face. 'I have seen a lot in this world and you must listen carefully. Those poems were not written by Hadir. They are the work of a famous Persian poet, a holy man who lived hundreds of years ago. His name is Mowlana. They call him "the knowledgeable one". Indeed these poems are beautiful but they are not being used in a holy way. Salim Hadir has seen your beauty and wants it. What does he know of you? Of who you are, my child? He lusts after you, wants to have you as a thing for himself. It is desire in his breast, not love. Who has seen these letters?'

I was crying. 'No one, Bibi Cecelia.'

'That is good,' Cecelia said. 'If Hadir was doing this the right way, he would not send you secret letters and gifts. He would find out who is Baba in this family and send someone to visit. Why has he not done this? I can tell you that. For you might have thought no one saw what was going on but people notice little things happening in our streets.'

I covered my face. I did not want to show Cecelia how ashamed I felt.

She put her arm round me and spoke gently. 'You are young, my child, and it is easy to be tempted by the admiration of a rich and powerful man, for that is what he is. People do not mind me asking questions and I see what is going on. Salim Hadir is married and has three children. He has a house in Stone Town and in Mombasa on the mainland, and he does business everywhere. The best he could offer would be to become his second wife but he might not even offer that. He will speak sweet promises only! *Ahadi tamu tamu!*'

'What shall I do with these?' I held out the letters and gold necklace.

'If you let me, I shall return the necklace to Hadir, and tell him that you are not available. It is better that you do not write to him, for a letter has legs. And these ... these we must destroy.'

Cecelia reached into her shirt and took out her matches. She looked at me, waiting to see if I stopped her, but I did not, although part of me yearned for something I was losing. There, on the rooftop, she burnt both letters, and I watched as the edges of the paper crumbled into black and drifted to the ground.

So it was that I did not go that way, but learnt that I still had to answer Baba Ali's question. Where would I find a suitable husband?

25. The Important Question

Kupoteya njia ndiyo kujua njia
To get lost is to learn the way

Later in 1971

One day, as I was collecting the food tray after the evening meal, Mujab said, 'Sister Fatima, I would be happy if you could lend me a book, a book about arithmetic.'

I had one textbook covering upper primary arithmetic which I had completed, and one for lower secondary which I had not. I also had a book, *Bookkeeping for Beginners*. For some reason, this came to mind. I had looked in the book and had seen that bookkeeping dealt with numbers. I gave these three books to Mujab. On such little things, your life can change.

For years I had helped Baba Ali's twin daughters, Jannah and Subira, with their school work. We worked next to our sleeping quarters. Six families remained in our house and there was little privacy.

I would give lessons before the evening meal, before light left our rooms. The girls were now seventeen and I was almost twenty. This was their last year at school. The youngest in the family, Munir, was fourteen and was not interested in his school work. At this time, Mujab was twenty-three years old, and had been working wherever he could. He had avoided going into the army and found work doing odd jobs at Darajani Market or at the Deputy Minister's office where his Baba was a driver.

Mujab would come home and have a rest before *Maghrib*, the sunset prayers. I had noticed he often stayed in during our lessons. I think he was listening. I came to expect him to be there and was conscious of him.

Mujab had grown into a tall man with strong eyebrows and dark eyes. He looked older than he was as he did not laugh much. Like his Baba, he took life seriously without his Mama's nervous ways. I felt he was at peace with himself. When he smiled, it was beautiful to see. He had well-formed hands with slender fingers and I would watch him fold one on the other in his lap when he was sitting with his family.

I had noticed how kind he was to his parents even when Mama Hala was unhappy with the world and shouting at everyone. Mujab had always played with his brother and sisters and they always ran to him when he came home. Although in the old days, I would have had little to do with men once I was a woman, in this new world, I often spoke to Mujab. For was I not part of his family?

What did I know of marriage? I knew my parents had loved one another as did Baba Ali and Mama Hala. I could see that but I knew some marriages were not happy. We lived so close together and I learnt it was most often the woman who suffered. A man could divorce his wife by saying the words, 'I divorce you'. She would have to return to her parents. For a woman alone in the world, it was not easy. If a man could afford a second wife, he was able to marry again. Although my Baba did not do this, it was not frowned upon in those times.

I said to myself, I must make this decision, this choice of a husband. Before the Revolution, my family would not have considered Mujab as a suitable partner. But those times were past and I did think about him. This seemed forward of me. In our religion, it is given to the woman to accept or refuse a suitor chosen by her family but it is not normal for a woman to take the first step.

I did not think I was 'in love' with Mujab: little did I know what that meant but I knew something had happened with those few contacts with Salim Hadir, and it was dangerous and frightening. Recovering from the attentions of Hadir had given me confidence. One morning I knew what I wanted to do.

I asked Paka, 'Do you think Mujab would want to marry me?'

You cannot imagine how Paka laughed and cried with joy. 'Are you sure?' Paka said. 'He is a good man and I know he admires you. He will work hard and do his best for you.'

How could Paka say, 'Make you happy'? Happiness was not something I could believe in. We did not marry for love in our culture but we all hoped for it. These were strange times to organise a marriage. Seven years had passed since I had lost my family. I could only think that my Mama and Basilah had died during the Revolution. I had given up hope. Surely if they were alive, they would have come looking for me. I now accepted I was the only one of my family to survive.

'Paka, will you be my voice in this for I do not have a man in my family? Will you be my *wali*?'

'How can I be?' Paka replied.

'Who else is there? Baba Ali cannot act for me as he is Mujab's father.'

'Fatima, to be a *wali* is a man's right,' she said. 'We will ask the *imam* for help. First, I can talk to my brother, Ali.'

Paka and Ali went onto the roof for privacy and I waited on my bed.

This would be the biggest step in my life and where was my family to guide and advise me? Jannah and Subira came home from school and I heard them jumping the missing step, taking off their shoes and entering the room.

'*Hodi, Dada* Fatima. Are you not well?'

'*Karibu.* Come in. I am well,' I said. They sat beside me and told me about their day. I was lucky to be part of this family and it would be right to marry Mujab but what did I know of his real wishes? For all I knew he was hoping for another wife, or did not want to marry until he was older. For men go far and wide and see much.

I wanted him to answer one important question before I would agree to marriage.

Paka came back. She was smiling and clapping her hands as she chased the girls out. As I watched her, I thought my Paka was once a beautiful woman, yet she had never married nor had children of her own. It was strange I had not seen this before. Was this because she was part of our family and did not want to leave? She took my hands.

'My brother Ali is going to talk to Mujab. He is so happy and said it would please him greatly to have you as his daughter. When he has spoken to Mujab and has come back to ask you, they will visit the *imam*. He is worried there is little to gift to you as *mahr*. But he says Mujab can promise to work hard. These times are difficult. We can but ask for guidance from Allah and pray for His grace in all that we do. We are His servants.'

Before I committed myself, I asked if I could talk directly to Mujab. Much was on my mind and this one matter needed dealing with before I could go further. It was the question of what had happened that first day of the Revolution when Mujab went with Nasri and his son and returned late in the day. With my eyes, I had seen him covered in blood. I had often wondered when he was playing with his brother and sisters if such a man could have done unspeakable things and still look so normal. Nasri had done bad things; of that I was sure. Could I marry a man who might have taken part in the *Mapinduzi*, who had blood on his hands, even if he had been ordered to do so by his elders? I did not think so.

Next afternoon as the sun was low over the sea and lighting up the clouds with colours, I went onto the rooftop and Mujab arrived. As is proper, Paka was there but she stood further away. I was nervous, but determined, standing with my back to the wall overlooking our street, my headdress down. Above was a pale evening sky with tall clouds floating past, a steady wind behind them. Mujab stopped a little way away, and did not look directly at me at first. I thought that, in the seven years since I had first met him, he had grown into a handsome man. A man many women would desire.

'Mujab, I would like to know something. I have to do a lot of thinking.'

'Yes, *Dada*, Sister Fatima, you may ask me anything.'

He was serious and I was too.

'Can you tell me what happened that day of the Revolution, when you ... when you, went with Nasri?'

Mujab looked surprised. His voice was calm. 'I told my family I was honourable.'

'Yes. It matters to me I should know more.'

'If that is so, I will tell you.'

He looked past me over the rooftops where black crows were twisting in the sky with their harsh cries.

'It is something I have tried to forget,' he said.

Mujab came to the stone wall near me and began to talk. 'You remember I left home with Nasri and Muti, his son?'

'Yes,' I said. 'I remember.'

'They took me to the Raha Leo Centre. On the way, I saw men pulling things out of houses and other houses burning. When we got to the Centre there were crowds, excited, shouting and running around this way and that. Trucks came with armed men, some bringing prisoners, others filled with goods. They carried things into the building and men were drinking alcohol.

'Nasri left us and said he was going inside for his "instructions". He returned with two boys, a little older than Muti. They had bottles with them. Nasri said he had been given a task. He was going up to Ras Nungwi to arrest some people for questioning. He said people there were resisting the Revolution and must be "dealt with".

'Nasri said they had other work for us to do as we were too young for men's work. The two boys with him had been ordered to go into Stone Town, to a house in Shangani, to search for weapons and Muti and I were to join them. The owners had fled but Field Marshall Okello suspected there were guns there that might be used by his enemies.

'We were told to search for things of value, hidden things. We were to confiscate them and bring them back to Raha Leo. Muti was excited. I think he felt important and was, I can say, keen to do something brave for the Revolution. We were given green material for armbands. Muti took me by the arm and we followed the other two into Stone Town. They did not have guns but one had a knife and the other a *panga*. I thought, in my foolishness, I could stop them doing anything bad but when I saw how keen they were to fight, to do violence, I was fearful.'

Mujab paused and looked at me without smiling. 'You know, Fatima, how you think of me is important, so I want you know the whole story, although it is a sad story.'

'Please go on,' I said. My heart was hammering, for I remembered that time. I remembered the burning.

Mujab started again. 'Muti said to me, "We will get you a weapon from the house where we are going. It is important to have a weapon, even a knife". It was silent in Stone Town, and the streets were empty. The boys leading us were frightened. We moved along slowly, as they checked around each corner and called back to us to "come on, it is safe" when they were sure.

'We came close to Main Street and I heard a woman weeping and, as we crept round the corner, I saw her collapsed in the middle of the street, her shawl over her head. Lying beside her on the concrete were two small bodies. Our two leaders ran forward with their weapons and the woman cried for help. She was not frightened of us. I think she thought we had come to help her. She said her son was wounded and could we save him? His head was in her lap and she was waving the flies away.

'We surrounded them. I could see the other boy was dead. He was on his back with blood covering his white shirt, his eyes open. Before this, I had never seen a child dead. The boy who was alive was called Ali. She cried out his name again and again, "In God's name, mercy on us. Save my Ali". The wounded child was looking at his Mama saying nothing. She told us Ali was shot for his bicycle, and no one would come out of the houses to help them or give them water.

'Our two leaders whispered together. Then they told Muti and me to follow them. "The boy will die. This is not our business," they said. They argued with me saying they had important work to do for the Revolution and the neighbours could help the woman.

'Muti was undecided as we all looked at this poor woman but they pulled him by his arm. I said, "I must help her". They ordered me to follow them. One took the *panga* off his arm. Muti begged me. But I said "Tell me where to go, and I will follow. First let me take this child to the hospital".

Eventually they accepted this and left.

'Ali kept asking for water but no one came out of their houses. I called out to the closed houses around us, "Water, we need water!" A door opened and a hand put out a tin of water before the door shut again. I think people were watching what was happening but were too full of fear. I took the water for the boy, and I lifted him and carried him to the hospital. We had to leave the body of her other child behind. It took me some time as I was not as strong as I am now.

'The Mama told me Ali and his brother were her comfort in her widowhood. She used to clean the Jamatkhana, the Ismailia mosque. They did not know about the Revolution that morning. She thought all would be well for Ali, her younger son, now we were going to the hospital but before we got there, he became still in my arms and I saw he was dead.

'We went there anyway. I could not tell her. I cannot tell you how terrible it was at our hospital with so many injured and dying. Young girls too. I will never forget. A nurse told us Ali was dead and I left his Mama with him, holding him and talking to him. How many tears can a Mama cry? And that is how I got the blood on my shirt and my arms. I did not go to the house in Shangani but came home to my family.'

Silence fell between us. I could hear the clicking of the swallows flying above me and women talking on the rooftops as on any normal day. I thought about the woman who had lost her two sons.

'Did you know her name?' I said. 'Did you find out what happened to her?'

'I asked about the Mama,' said Mujab. 'Her name was Aminabai and her neighbours told me she went mad. Aminabai sat on the street and wept and sang. People cared for her as much as they could. They said her life was finished.'

I thought, it is seven years since those times and our leaders talk about the Revolution as a happy event. Do they not remember nor mourn those who were killed? How long does it take you to forget? Where are the murderers? Are they going about their business as ordinary men, working in the fields, sitting on the barazas and eating mishkaki kebabs with their friends? Do they not remember every day, every hour? Do they lie awake in the dark and pray for forgiveness? Or do they sleep in comfort while the families of the victims suffer with a lifetime of loss?

We were quiet. Mujab had finished his story. I was waiting for my tears

2-116

to stop.

Mujab broke the silence but did not look at me. 'Binti Fatima, I did not want to tell you this story but it is better there are no secrets between us. I would like you to know it is an honour that you are considering we might marry. I respect you and know you are a good person, a follower of Islam. I would like you also to know that if you do consent, I will always care for you and protect you. I wait for your decision.'

He left me on that rooftop. Now I knew that Mujab had also been hurt by the *Mapinduzi*, had seen death and had tried to help a woman and her sons. He had carried the burden of that memory on his own.

I stayed there, watching over our town, at clouds racing towards me, as I had so many times. Such beauty was here beneath the sun and yet how sad our island had become. Our pain lay like these clouds over us all, our memories and our dreams. I wondered about our lives and why so many of us must suffer.

26. A Wedding

Arusi jambo la heri   A wedding is bliss

November 1971

'Why are you crying, Binti Fatima?' The *somo* asked. Her hand on my arm was plump, her wrist thick with silver bracelets. 'Many brides have fear of their wedding night. I am here to help and teach you so you will know about these things.'

I was not crying with fear of my wedding. I was crying with the memories of Basilah and her preparations to be a bride. Even now I did not know how she and my Mama had met their end. Now I was about to become a bride. Once my Mama had said, 'It will be your turn one day, do not be impatient.' My turn had come but I was without her, without my closest family who, at my side, would have shared the joy.

I was to hear those secrets of being a bride and wife that Basilah had heard, and my Mama before her. I was twenty, and I was preparing to marry Mujab, who was only twenty-three.

Hala and Paka had discussed who to ask to be my *somo*, my marriage counsellor. Together they came to me.

'We have chosen Hala's great-aunt Siti,' said Paka. 'She is an old woman. Very wise. We have spoken to her and she said she is honoured. Siti will visit tomorrow and stay for as long as you wish.'

'Here is my Holy Book. Take it,' said Hala handing me her Qur'an in its covering. 'Keep it by you while you prepare. It will protect you from evil spirits.'

Hala asked Baba Ali to find an astrologer to make sure our marriage day was favourable. He did not favour this idea but it was a time when we needed hope so he agreed.

It is not permitted for a betrothed couple to be alone together before they are married; always, there has to be a chaperone or *mahram* present. We did our best in the times in which we were living, and this is all Allah requires. We tried to be devout in our lives. I wanted to learn how to be a good wife and the *somo* would teach me. She would answer the questions that came into my head, for I did not know about relations between a man and a woman.

Siti arrived the next day, struggling to climb our stairs for she had swollen ankles. She lay on a bed as she gave me her advice. Hala put cushions under her legs and brought her a cup of chai. As soon as I met her, I was pleased with Paka and Hala's choice of my *somo*, for she was kind and the words she spoke were chosen with care. She did not waste her time.

'Your bedroom as a married woman is a special place,' said Siti as she sipped the sweet chai. 'From now on, it is not a place where other women may come. A private place for you and Mujab. Make it as nice looking as you can, with jasmine flowers, scents and pretty clothes for yourself. It is for you to please your husband, to keep him at home, not looking at other women. *Inshallah*, God willing. It is your responsibility. I will show you the ways this is done.'

Siti spoke of love and patience and the pleasure that would be ours. She gave me a lesson on the importance of showing Mujab that I found him attractive.

'For a man will not come home to his wife if he does not believe he is welcome in the bedroom,' said Siti. 'You are a beautiful woman and that beauty can be tempting to others, so you must guard it closely and show it only to your husband.'

Siti told me about how the Prophet had loved his wives. Of how he had first married Khadijah who was fifteen years older than he was. He had loved and trusted her, and she had advised him when he received the first revelation.

'The Prophet is an example to all men,' said Siti, 'of how to act as a husband, and we women as wives must follow the example of his household. Years will pass and the beauty you have, that now blinds the eyes of all who see you, will pass with those years. Your place as a wife and Mama must be built on these early years.'

There were ways to communicate about sexual matters without talking. Siti told me. 'Allah commands us to marry and tells us it is as if two halves of a whole are united in marriage. Always say *bismillah* before you make love with Mujab. And it is better to use a sign or wear a particular *kanga* when you are bleeding, to let him know you are not available.'

There were other more private things I was told and shown, some of which I did not understand until later. I was no longer a child, a girl. I was to become a woman, a wife and, one day, a mama.

Siti stayed with me during the days I was prepared as a bride. I sat on a cushion and Paka and Mujab's sisters brought me food and water. In the afternoon, neighbours came to visit, wanting to talk and sing wedding songs.

Cecelia found a lady called Faiza who did henna painting. She was business-like, arriving with her pots and brushes in a basket and papers with patterns. The henna dye was in a dark paste of lemon juice, sugar and oil. Faiza had brought two different colours, one a lighter golden-brown and the other a chocolate-brown. She painted sweeping curls and flower patterns on my body.

'Now Fatima, you must keep still. No wriggling with excitement while I do my designs,' said Faiza smiling. 'After you are married, do no housework until this fades. You are a bride, a *bibi harusi*, and these signs are only for your husband to see.'

The henna dye took some time to dry: I held out my arms and legs without moving until Faiza blew on them and said that the henna was set. Even the soles of my feet were decorated. Faiza washed off the brown paste revealing the stained patterns on my skin.

The women around me sat and watched Faiza as she painted and they praised her designs. Faiza was especially pleased with her work.

'When I have a bride such as Fatima to make even lovelier, I do my best,' she said to the women. To me, she said, 'I have given you this design on your hands for fertility, for healthy children, and this pattern on your feet is for wisdom and protection from evil spirits.'

I listened to the talk between the women about their marriages. I knew little of the ways of men. Most of what I knew came from this chattering at my wedding gathering and what Siti had told me. Some wives said it was never a pleasure to lie with their husbands. I heard men were demanding, needing sex more than a woman. I wondered why this was so. And some women never liked to be visited by their husbands: once they had children, they would chase their husbands away with excuses. The women teased one another as we sat together, and they collapsed onto the floor with laughter.

'He has no idea, for I have told him I have a medical condition where I bleed twice a month. It is so easy to fool him!'

Another said, 'I have told my husband—I have given you two sons and a daughter. It is enough. I am tired and busy, cooking and cleaning for you. I am forty years old. If you want to lie with me, now you must wait until I ask you. And he is too frightened!'

Yet another replied, 'He disgusts me and I have told my husband I don't care if he goes and finds a woman of the night. He must go elsewhere with his demands.'

Siti told these women off, clicking her tongue with displeasure at this idle chat, telling several women to keep their nonsense to themselves. Others told me quietly of the pleasure that would be ours.

Our family did what they could to celebrate our marriage. After the henna decoration was finished, I was given special oils to prepare myself. Paka had bought some oud wood and lit it on a burner. The sweet perfume scented the room and my clothes.

I was brought gifts from the families in our house and from our neighbours along the street. Everyone said, 'We must celebrate!'

So much happened. Cecelia gave me a beautiful silk sari that had been left to her by her Indian employers. It was not new, but she wanted me to make shirts out of it to wear with my *kanga*. And with both hands, she handed me a packet. 'This was given to me after the long years of my service.'

It was a delicate gold necklace with matching earrings.

'I have kept it for someone special,' Cecelia said, 'and you are the granddaughter I never had.'

Hala gifted me her best clothes and people in the street found little things to give me—a copper pot, old china decorated with blue and yellow flowers, a special cushion and a worn Persian carpet. A neighbour found an old American wooden wall clock for decoration.

The day before our promises were exchanged in the mosque, Baba Ali and *Mzee* Hamoud visited me when I was with Hala, Paka and Cecelia. I was veiled and covered with a *kitambi*, a bridal cloth; even my arms and hands were covered, so no man could see the henna painting.

'Binti Fatima, I ask you in front of these witnesses, do you agree to this marriage to Mujab Bakary?'

'Yes, *Mzee* Hamoud, I do.'

'Have you been given or promised *mahr*?'

'Yes, *Mzee* Hamoud, I have.'

'Please will you sign this document? I will take it to the *qadi* tomorrow and this will be proof of your consent.'

I signed. Prayers of supplication, or *duas* asking for Allah's blessing, were said by *Mzee* Hamoud.

The one I remember with joy is:

Oh Allah, bless our marriage and let it be a means for us to become closer to You in love and devotion. Let it be a source of untold blessings, happiness and joy.

The next day, the men of the family went to the *qadi* at the mosque. My signature was accepted. Then Mujab signed as did his Baba. My husband had promised to pay me a certain amount in shillings as soon as he was able. This was the *mahr*. After *kahawa* and sweet cake were shared by the men, they came back to our house. Mujab was dressed in a white *kanzu* with a long coat and, on his head, a new *kofia*, hand-stitched in blue thread. I saw him but for a few minutes, and he did not look at me directly. Cecelia gave him a garland of flowers which he presented to me, and my new family blessed us. We shared a glass of milk as the Prophet had done with Aisha.

The women gathered in one room and the men in another. Singing and dancing started around me. Trays of yellow rice, chicken and sweets were brought out, for everyone had found something to cook and share. Plates of coconut rice and fish, *machi bhat,* followed and everyone shared the feast. I was so happy through it all. It had been a long time since we had done such things.

I was now a married woman.

27. The Beach at Mangapwani

Allah bless you, and may He send blessings upon you, and may He unite you both in good

December 1971

'Brother Ali, it would be good to tell your Deputy about Fatima's marriage to Mujab. That way he will not think too much of it.'

Paka was worried about the forced marriages.

Baba Ali and Hala found us our own room. It was on the third floor under the roof of the house with a view east towards Ng'ambo. The sun shone in at daybreak, and Cecelia's swallows flew by catching food for their young. I came to love that room. Before us were Stone Town's jumble of houses and the green of the *shambas* was dark on the horizon. Mujab and I had little. Except for my books, my teacher's chair, our possessions were few. We moved my books out from under my old bed and Mujab made me a bookcase with planks. Now I could see them all. It was joy enough to have space and be together.

Mujab was also a virgin, so we explored one another as guides. I was not ashamed of my body but fearful of what hurt there would be. For Siti had told me it could be painful for a woman the first time; gentleness was needed. And it was so for us. I remember it well and shall do so until the end of my days.

A week after our wedding, Mujab said, 'Would you like to go Mangapwani beach? We can take food and spend the day there.'

I had told Mujab how I loved Mangapwani beach, how it was a favourite place for our family to visit, to play on the sand and splash one another in the waves, and to share a meal on the towels and *kangas* laid out on the grass by the coconut palms. Some say this was where slaves were taken secretly to the dhows waiting offshore but those days are long gone.

'My Amina at *Salama Daima* told me her Mama was a slave,' I said.

'Those caves at the end of the beach are too small for hiding people,' Mujab said. 'Come with me and I will show you a secret beach and another cave.'

We had this day to ourselves and Mujab led me beyond the main beach to a place of his childhood. A tiny island rose offshore with a dark topping of trees like a hat. As the tide was low, we could walk around the headland to the curving beach.

'If the tide comes in, we will have to wade back but I will be here to help you,' Mujab said.

Fishing boats avoided this bay for the white sand finished against a sharp coral rock face. Over the years, the waves had dug into the coral so it arched over the beach and, at one end, caves had formed. We stood before the entrance and I hesitated. Mujab took my hand.

'Do not be frightened. Follow me,' he said. 'Crawl for a little way and you will get a surprise!'

'Come in Fatima, it is safe!' Mujab called from inside, his voice an echo from the darkness.

The sand was cool. After several feet, I found I could stand up. The cave smelt of sea, salt and seaweed. I could see the space was big enough for maybe five people, not more. A narrow passage led towards the sea and through it, the gentle thud of the waves could be heard. We sat down together and it was so quiet and strange in that hidden place. The main beach with children swimming and fishermen mending their nets had disappeared. Mujab was excited and put his arm around me.

'We could stay here and be safe, just us two. No one will worry us!' I said.

'I came here as a child with my aunt,' he said. 'It is long ago. How much older I am now!'

We sat and talked, sharing the stories of our childhood before the Revolution. I thought that although his family had not been wealthy, we were alike in our memories of happiness.

'My Baba says his grandfather was a slave,' Mujab said. 'My Mama's family came from Persia a long time ago. A Prince of Persia was the first to come. They settled on Tumbatu Island and built a village of stone. Even now you can see the ruins. People there can tell you the names of their family going back over forty generations. They say that it was the *watumbatu* who asked the Sultan of Oman to come and save them from the Portuguese invaders.'

'My Mama's family came from Muscat in Oman,' I replied. 'They came with Sultan Said over a hundred years ago. My Baba's great-grandmother was a second wife. She came from Turkey. So we are a mix of many peoples.'

'We are now Zanzibaris. Different nationalities have come here and, God willing, if we have children, they will be the best of us,' Mujab said.

Pale crabs the size of my toes danced sideways on the sand, running from us as we lay there. I could hear their scratching on the walls and from the hollows came the beat of the waves on the shore. Mujab told me how he loved me, that his life had been blessed. He had never dreamed it was possible I would accept him, for he had admired me from the first moment, when he saw me in their house on the day of the Revolution.

'I hope I can make you laugh more, for it is lovely to see you happy. I will care for you until I die,' he said. I believed him.

He kissed the scar on my right arm and turned my face to his and we lay down together. I believe I conceived in that cave. It was the first time I had been naked in the open, and the sand on my back, the salt sea drops on my face and the pleasure my Mujab brought me that time shall be with me forever. I had not known a woman can know such delight from a man. No one had prepared me for this, for the way his body moved with mine and the colours I saw in my mind as my flesh welcomed him. How long we pleasured one another, I know not, only I would never be the same. There was no shame in this wonder of body on body, smooth and beautiful in our love. Truly it was a gift of life itself.

We said to one another we would stay as one, as we were that day.

Mimi na wewe pete na kidole. You and I are as a ring and a finger to one another.

:opard

u, mwenye kisutu   *I have seen the leopard but not the keeper*

Baba Ali returned home full of misery. 'I am sorry. I do not have a job any more. This is my final pay.' He held out a few hundred shilling notes. He hung his head as if it were his fault.

'Oh, my poor husband,' Hala said. 'What happened? Did you crash the car or displease someone? Why has the Deputy Minister sent you away?'

I knew how much we needed his income. I was thinking how much more difficult our lives would now become.

'No, no! His wife's sister's son has left school and needs work,' said Ali. 'He said he thought my eyesight might fail soon. He said he could not take a risk, as he might be a full Minister soon. I am afraid it is an excuse, and we both knew. Here is a letter to help me find other work.'

My Baba's money was long finished by this time, eight years after the Revolution. Our lives were more difficult than ever. People were starving. With the low wages and cost of food, even those with jobs found it hard to care for their children and old people. You could be put in prison if you were caught with smuggled goods, especially rice. We had to queue with ration cards for our allowance of flour, sugar and rice. It took hours in these lines before your family share was placed in your *kikapu*. The non-government shops had closed so town people were dependent on rations unless they also had a *shamba* in the country.

Nothing was thrown away. We used every scrap of food and clothing. Too many children had the shiny round stomachs of the starving. Our *kangas* became thin with washing. When they tore, we sewed them together again, overlapping the fragile cloth. Even the cats of our town were like walking skeletons.

Some evenings Hala said, 'I am not hungry tonight.'

I knew she said this because the meal was so small and she wanted her children to have enough. My heart was sore for her.

Mujab looked for work in Darajani Market. Some days he returned with nothing but he was strong and often found jobs lasting a day or two. Sometimes all the young men looking for work would be collected by the Youth League and made to work for nothing. They said he was volunteering for this work, calling it *kujitolea*, but there was no choice about it. He would come back hungry without any money.

'Some of my friends hide when they see a government truck,' Mujab said. 'We have a lookout to warn us but if they catch us, they take us out to the *shambas* or the rice fields where the Chinese people are, and we have to dig water channels or plant rice seedlings.'

One day Mujab came back and told us he and a few friends had been promised four days paid work.

'I will be away for three nights. It is for the government, for the National Hunters, *Wasasi wa Kitaifa*. We are to help with finding the animals they shoot.'

'Hunting what?' I asked.

'I do not know,' he replied. 'They used to hunt wild bush pigs.'

'But eating pigs is *haram*. Maybe these men hunt for sport.' I could not imagine people hunting for sport.

Mujab returned on the fourth day, his clothes tattered and carrying a bag of charcoal. We gathered round to hear his story, while Hala clicked her tongue looking at her son's clothes.

'We were taken far away in an old truck.' Mujab told us waving his arm. 'At the other side of the island, there is a forest, called Jozani, near Chwaka Bay. No *shambas* are there for the ground under the trees is often full of water.'

Hala clapped her hands forgetting about his torn clothes. 'See how old I am and I have never been there!' she said.

Mujab looked pleased. 'At sunset, we came to a village near the sea, called Charawe. Four hunters arrived carrying guns and ordered the headman, the *mzee*, to find us food and sleeping places. The villagers had little but we shared their meal of fish and rice. *Mzee* Kitanzi, the hunter's leader, told us they were hunting leopards but they would also shoot wild bush pig, deer and *duiker*. Our job was to hit the bush, shouting at the same time. This was to scare out the animals while the men with shotguns waited on the other side.

'We were scared but *Mzee* Kitanzi laughed at us calling us old women. He said the Revolutionary Government has declared war on the leopards and the witches who use them. The next day, we left before dawn, without time for prayers. We were given long sticks. The *mzee* came to show us the way, and with him came dogs and their handler, a local hunter. They told us they knew where the leopard had been seen.

'The hunters and dogs left to go to the far side of the forest. When we started walking into the bush before dawn, it was frightening. We beat the bush and trees, this way and that, to scare out the animals. I did not know where I was going. We shouted to one another, for the grass was high up to my shoulders and the trees shut out light from the sky. We were frightened of snakes. I fell over a lot—see how scratched I am!'

'Did you see any wild things?' Hala asked.

'Not at first, Mama, but we heard crashing in the bush and the calling of monkeys in the trees. Then we heard shots ahead of us. I was afraid they would shoot us!'

'What did they shoot?' Baba Ali asked.

'The first day they shot a leopard,' Mujab said, 'and *Mzee* Kitanzi told us no hunter was hurt because they had taken *waganga* medicine to protect them from the leopard. He was happy because it was a female and she appeared to be suckling young. He said the cubs would die without the mother.

'The leopard was smaller than I had imagined, like a big dog with yellow fur and dark spots. They cut off the skin and claws. The hunters cooked and ate some of the meat and some they gave to the dogs. They will get money for the skin and will sell bits of the body for magic, for *dawa*. A hunter offered me a paw without claws. He said it would sell well in the market but I did not want it.'

Hala reached out for Mujab's arm. 'I hope you did not touch the leopard?'

'No, I did not. The other young men were frightened to see it but I was not. One of the old village men was unhappy they killed the leopard. He shouted at *Mzee* Kitanzi and said, "You hunters should know, *chui kama mfalme*, the leopard is like a king!"

'*Mzee* Kitanzi took no notice of him. He told us he is looking for the witches, the *wachawi*. He says those witches keep leopards in caves and let them out at night to do wicked things.'

'What does he do when he finds a witch?' I asked.

'He told us he uses special oaths, a *yamini*, and the witches have to swear on the Holy Book to stop this thing they do with leopards.'

Hala was worried. 'And what else did they kill? Did you see any snakes?'

'They shot little *duiker* and two bush pigs. The pigs were cut up and the stomachs were thrown out for the dogs. They brought the meat back with us in the truck. The *duiker* is good to eat and five were given to the *mzee* in the village. During the day, we continued hunting and we saw snakes. The man near me killed a green mamba, *mtunguu*, with his stick. I could hear him screaming and shouting, "*nyoka!*" I thought he had been bitten. Big pythons live in the forest.'

Hala could not restrain herself. 'Allah was watching over you.'

Mujab nodded his head. 'That was so. On the last day I got lost in the forest for I was on the far edge of the beaters. I stopped hitting the bush and walked fast to catch the others. Water lies between the trees and I could not easily see the tree roots. It was then I saw another leopard. It was running for its life from the shouting men. It turned and saw me and stood without moving, and I watched it, and did not tell the others. I was glad this one was not killed, for it was most beautiful.'

Mujab said, 'I thought of the words of our Holy Book, Al-Isra, *"The seven heavens, the earth, and all who dwell in them give glory to Him. All creatures celebrate His praises. Yet you cannot understand their praises!"* How little we understand.'

I was proud of my husband for the way he showed us what was good in the world.

Mujab was paid well for his days of hunting and for a while we ate well. Soon, we struggled to feed our large family and to help Cecelia. Baba Ali's elder sister was a widow with a single child and had been given a *shamba*. After losing his job, Ali walked over eight miles each way to help care for her three acres. Baba Ali's parents moved out there as well. Luckily it was fertile ground, on the western side of the island and not too far away. In return, his sister shared the harvest of cassava, pawpaws, coconuts and greens from the forest. And we survived.

Late one night, Baba Ali told us how people were managing in the country. 'Farmers have been given land to work but they argue as some get more or are given the best land. It is better if I am there to protect her fields.'

Some villagers in the country suffered more than others. They were the ones who had been supporters of the ZNP Party that had been overthrown.

'They are suffering too,' Baba Ali said. 'The village councillors, the *sheha*, have all been dismissed and the Revolutionary Council has appointed its own men in each area.'

We knew young men with skills were leaving Zanzibar. They were here one day and gone the next. Escape was on their minds for we faced starvation and continual harassment by the Volunteers and Youth League Wing. However, you needed money or valuables to pay a dhow captain before he would collect you from a secret night-time meeting place along our shores. Such matters were only whispered about.

It was strange, but Ali losing his job might have saved him from death or lengthy imprisonment. On 7 April 1972, President Karume was assassinated. The news spread like the wind. I saw people running through the streets below us shouting.

Baba Ali called out as he ran up the stairs, 'President Karume has been shot, maybe killed. We must take care. Is everyone here? Quick! We must close the doors.'

Paka was out looking for crowds that might announce the arrival of a shipment of food or clothing. For this is how we lived. She arrived in haste. We gathered together and shut the front doors, waiting in our rooms looking through the shutters at the street below. We all remembered 1964 and knew that when leaders change, it is a time of danger.

A curfew was announced and the airport closed. Panic continued for some time. We heard that Karume had been shot while he was playing the board game called *bao* in the Afro-Shirazi Party headquarters at Kisiwandui. An army man called Colonel Humoud had done this.

'I am told by one who worked with me,' said Baba Ali, 'that those fearful of arrest are carrying their toothbrushes in their pockets so they are ready to be taken away!'

Sadly, one of those arrested was Baba Ali's previous employer, the Deputy Minister and, in such cases, Ali as his driver might also have been arrested. Hundreds of people disappeared into the prisons and were never heard of again. There were no independent law courts to protect you. Such was the state of our beautiful island.

It is true to say not many mourned President Karume's passing. Our new President was announced. It was Aboud Jumbe. Later we heard that this was fortunate, for the terrible Salim Bakari, who everyone feared, had expected to be Karume's successor. *Mzee* Jumbe was educated and some wondered how he had managed to survive Karume's presidency, for all knew how Karume hated and feared educated people.

'It is because Jumbe is a man who drinks alcohol all the time,' said Paka. 'Lama told me, and that is why Karume did not fear him.'

Afterwards Baba Ali told us that Karume had been worse than even we imagined.

'Binti Fatima, do you remember I asked you to go fully covered when you went into the streets during the last two years?'

'Yes,' I said, 'and I did.'

'I also asked you to avoid the street where the government cars went, did I not?

'Yes, we kept away from Vuga Road, Main Street, Creek Road and the Malindi area as you told us. Why was that?'

'I am sorry to say this but the President's driver travelled those streets in his black car and picked up young women.'

'What?' I was amazed. 'How could this be? What happened?'

'Even if they were married women or virgins, they were taken to Kibweni Palace, the Sultan's old palace that was President Karume's country estate. They were dishonoured.'

We were shocked at the depths to which our leader had fallen. Some people had hoped for a bright future after the Revolution. They believed that the deaths of 1964 were a brief event, and a fair society would come about, one better than under the Sultan or the British Government. Yet we now heard of the ways our leaders chose to behave.

It was a sad thing that most of us took comfort in the death of our President. Surely it was for Allah to judge him.

29. Early Marriage

Shukuru kwa uliyo nayo   Give thanks for what you have

1972

After the Revolution, many families were given three acres of land. This depended on which party you had supported and how powerful you were. The new farmers did not own the land outright so they could not sell or get a loan against it. Three acres of cassava were not enough to provide for a large family for the whole year as, in most cases, only part of the land was usable. It might have been sufficient in good seasons but not with the insects that came, the years of poor rains and the failure of seed. No one lived easily in those long years.

Finding food became a daily worry for each and every family in Stone Town and many moved to the country. Our family was now able to take over half of the top floor. This extra room became ours.

It was not hard to love Mujab. He said that he had always loved me but did not think I would consider him for a husband. Together we shared stories from our lives. I told him about each of my family members. Of what my sister Basilah meant to me and the kind of person my brother Taha was. To speak of them brought them into our new life together. I told him of my Baba and Mama and wept as I told him. There was so much to know about one another, and we would talk late into the night lying close together, our hands on each other's bodies.

We lay together in that room on the days Mujab did not work when he returned from *Fajr*, the dawn prayers. It was a safe place. We curled up saying little, listening to the sounds from the street below. Our houses did not have glass windows. When I opened the wooden shutters, the swallows with their white chests and shining blue backs flew past calling to one another and I felt a peace come over me. We were together and it seemed good that we had found one another. Truly it was a blessing from Allah.

I shared with my new husband the stories of my childhood. I feared that I would forget them for I had nothing left but a few precious memories. Sometimes I tried so hard to remember, and then I was not sure if what I saw in my mind was truly how it was, or was a creation of my desire. I wished I had listened more carefully to the stories my parents told me. Little had I known that my family would be destroyed before I was thirteen.

One morning we were lying together and the *masika* rains were beating on the tin rooftops and I remembered the story of the terrible hurricane.

'Mujab,' I said. 'Have you heard about the *kimbunga* of long ago?'

'No, please tell me.' He was kind and was patient with my memories.

'My Mama told me her grandmother was born in the year of the hurricane. It was during these same *masika* rains that a storm came from the south and destroyed the clove and coconut trees of the island. Sultan Barghash bin Said was Sultan at that time and his ships and his dhows sank in the harbour. My Mama said that her great-grandmother saw the wrecks on the seashore and the broken bodies of those who drowned.'

Mujab and I walked out to Baba, Taha and Amina's graves beyond the site of the old house. As Mujab was now my husband, I no longer needed to travel with Paka. We cleared the weeds and Mujab helped to put some stones around the three graves to show others to respect who was there. We did not have headstones as some do. And we prayed for mercy for their souls and the souls of those who had died during those terrible times.

We walked to the beach where *ngawala* were pulled up under the coconut palms and we sat in the shade. My husband smoothed the sand for me and wrote our names there. Children were playing in the shallow water where it shone blue and green in the bright sun. It was what I had done as a child. They came to greet us, and one I recognised from my childhood. Mujab asked them for a drink and they returned with two coconuts cut across the top. We call this sweet milk, *dafu*.

The *mzee* of the village arrived. He wore a *kikoi* around his waist and a torn grey shirt, and he was thin with more than just age. We stood up and exchanged greetings. He bowed with folded hands.

'This is Mujab, my husband,' I explained.

'You are welcome here, Bibi Fatima. Please excuse my dress,' he replied. 'We are working every day.'

I asked after his family and he looked at us and nodded his head.

'Times are hard,' is all he would say at first. With one hand, he shooed the children away.

'We have Volunteers in our village now. It is not easy for us but we have the sea and our *shambas*. Our young men have no jobs. You have come to pay respects?' He nodded in the direction of the graves. 'Your Baba was a just man; we respected one another and we pray for him.'

I knew he wanted to express his sorrow and I knew it was not his people who had murdered my family. Mujab and I stayed awhile near my old home, and we talked of what we might do, what our future held. When we were alone, he kissed my hands and held them in his and that day seemed sweet to me.

30. Hard Times

Pain you can endure, but the death of your child is a pain for which there is no word

1972-1973

During those last years of Karume's presidency and the start of Jumbe's rule, we felt as if the world had forgotten us in our struggle for survival. Perhaps the misery of our country was considered of little matter to others. President Nyerere on the mainland did nothing to help us although we were meant to be one country.

Baba Ali did not have a job and Mujab's earnings were little. We spent much time waiting for food to be available in the government shops run by the Women's Union. So much time was wasted. I can laugh now: how if we heard someone running down the street, Mujab or Baba Ali would go outside quickly and call out, 'Why are you running? What has come in?' And they would be off in a hurry to find the queue in case it was cloth or food that we could get with our ration cards.

How low had the country come! Our town was quiet with so few people living there. The fear of the unexpected made us careful: fear of what we said, who we talked to and where we went.

I was newly married and my life was changed by having a companion with whom to share my deepest fears and thoughts. I needed to be strong for I lost my first baby from an attack of malaria early in my pregnancy. The high fever caused me to abort. We had known I was pregnant but we had not yet told the family so it was not as painful as the second one. But I cried for the loss of that precious life.

Late in the same year that Karume was assassinated, I fell pregnant again. I was now twenty-one years of age and excited and nervous with the prospect of being a Mama. Our family shared the joy and Paka and Cecilia both helped me. They gave me extra food from their share and started thinking about how this would change their lives. We thought of names and how to make clothes for the baby. But, at about thirty weeks, I started to bleed and I was in such a state, falling in and out of consciousness, that Mujab and Paka rushed me to the hospital. They found a handcart and used it to get me there through the narrow streets. I lay in the cart looking at the sky and holding my stomach asking Allah to have mercy on me. I did not want to die and I dearly wanted this baby.

I was dealt with quickly at emergency for the nurse saw the blood. My baby was born without life. The doctor said it was too soon. My child was tiny, about the size of my foot, red and wrinkled with an old face and perfect little hands that would be closed forever. They let me hold him for a little while before they took him away. I saw that my baby was a boy and a nurse tried to comfort me.

'Do not worry. You will have more children, more boys,' she said.

It was not what I wanted to hear, for I dearly wanted our child to live and I thought of the hospital and losing my Babu, my parents, my whole family. I wept and for a week would not move from my bed nor eat anything. Life seemed without hope. I had been chosen to live a life of loss and suffering.

This is what I remember.

31. The Invoice Clerk

Ajifunzaye haachi kujua   No learning is a waste of effort

1973-1974

'Will you help me with this subject?' Mujab was holding the book, *Bookkeeping for Beginners,* which I had given him over two years ago. 'I have read it carefully but it is difficult to understand on my own. I asked an old shopkeeper for help. He showed me how they wrote ledger entries but their way is different. He said they follow the Gujarati way.'

Together we read the book trying to understand how it was that sales and expenses are recorded in a business. Mujab loved to work with numbers. There were exercises at the end of each section and we did these time and time again. It was difficult to know why you did these things, especially how the balance sheet and the day-to-day sales worked together in a business. And the English text had words unknown to me.

We wondered if our government offices used the same rules as this book but we did not know and did not know who to ask. Baba Ali was still friends with some workers in his previous Deputy Minister's office and he said he would find out. Baba Ali and Mujab found a cousin's friend who worked in the Finance Department. They had offices in Mambo Msiige, on the seafront at Ras Shangani.

One day, in the first year of Jumbe's presidency, Baba Ali and Mujab waited outside under the red flowering trees in Kelele Square. Mujab did not expect a job but Baba Ali was going to ask how to get the skills.

'You have to start somewhere, my son,' said Baba Ali. 'You are only twenty-five; you are not too old to learn.' Baba Ali was proud of Mujab.

So it was that Mujab was employed as an assistant invoice clerk in the Finance Department. President Jumbe's administration was spending more money and letting more imports enter Zanzibar. The Finance Department needed extra staff. Mujab was lucky he had asked at this time and, perhaps too, that he had asked the right person. He worked hard and tried to learn quickly. He knew that he had to be careful with what he said, to be a hard worker and not get politically involved.

Not long after this, President Jumbe brought in a new rule for anyone wanting a job in the government. Workers had to go through weeks of military training and work in the *shambas*. These workers were called the JKU, the Zanzibar Youth Service, and fell directly under President Jumbe. Luckily for Mujab he had been appointed before the JKU was established.

'They are like an extra police force for the President,' said Mujab. 'Why are our Presidents so fearful?'

We would sit on the roof after the sun set, with the cool evening breeze and he would tell me about the world at his work. President Jumbe liked to live on the mainland near Dar-es-Salaam so his Ministers would go there to talk to him. There they would buy food and goods for their families. Our shops were empty but our new leaders did not want for medicine, food and clothing. Later President Jumbe bought his own jet plane although Zanzibar could not afford this. In his plane, he travelled around Tanzania and spent even more time in Dar-es-Salaam.

Mujab, who was such a calm man, was angry. 'I see the cost of these things,' he said. 'People whisper and say our reserves are disappearing. President Jumbe wants to spend money on a fun fair for the people. He wants to call it the Uhuru Recreation Park and the cost will be five hundred thousand pounds! So much money! Cannot he see his people are hungry and have no work? It makes me sad to see our leaders living in luxury when we look at the poor families around us. Do our leaders not see what we see?'

'Be careful and repeat nothing!' I said. 'It is better not to even hear such things for it might be dangerous.'

After President Karume's death, the Youth League remained strong and the old guard in the government was still active. They were called the 'Liberators' by some and they were the ones we feared most.

The old Beit-el-Ajaib Palace, which was used by the British for their administration, was turned into a museum for the Afro-Shirazi Party to create a story about the late President Karume. Schoolchildren were taken there by the Youth League to see murals the North Koreans had painted of the progress they said had taken place in the years since the Afro-Shirazi Party was founded.

Mujab said that more money was gradually being spent on education. Everyone knew that our schools had become worse since the Revolution.

Life improved for us now Mujab had a regular job and, in the next year, Allah blessed us with a healthy baby boy and we named him Taha after my brother. As is right, he also took the name of his Baba, Mujab. Bibi Hala asked that we gave our child Mujab's Baba's name as well. So our first child was Taha Mujab Ali Bakary.

I did not have my Mama to help me but I had three women who I loved and who knew how to care for a baby. My husband was with me shortly after the birth and had given the *adhan*, the call to prayer, into Taha Mujab's right ear and the second call to prayer, the *iqama*, into his left ear. We committed ourselves to bringing up our son in the ways of Islam and righteousness despite the hard times in which we lived.

I was now twenty-three years old and the mama of a son.

32. The Sewing Machine

Kila mtu na mtuwe   Every human being needs a helper, a friend or confidant

1974-1975

'Old people beg at the mosque every Friday,' said Mujab, 'waiting for prayers to end. The *imam* told us that they have no one to care for them. Some are blind and frail and led by little children. What are we to do?'

Hungry people sat on the *baraza*, curled up against the wall. Hala told us one evening that the children of Baba Ali's younger sister had found a new way to earn money. It was from two elephants. We laughed. How could this be?

'What I say is true,' she replied. 'The new ship our President has bought, the *Mapinduzi*, came from India. You have seen it?'

'Yes,' we replied, for we had all gone down to the beach to watch this ship arrive. It was a sign—we hoped that our government would now allow more food to arrive.

Hala continued. 'Did you know that two elephants came in the ship as a present from India? They are keeping them in the gardens of the Marahubi Palace, and every day they walk to that new Barwani Hotel by the swamp. People say they are gentle. They listen to you.'

'Well, you know Saleh Madawa?' Hala asked.

We all knew Saleh Madawa. He was the most famous traditional healer or *mganga* in our town. And *dawa* is our word for medicine.

Hala smiled. She knew she was amusing us. 'Saleh Madawa wants the dung, the *choo*, from the elephants,' Hala said. 'Yes, it is so! He pays the children for the dung they collect. Now they follow the elephants every day from the palace to the hotel and fight over the *choo* dropping behind!'

'What does he do with the *choo*?' I asked. This was hard to believe.

'Baba Ali's sister says Saleh Madawa dries it in the sun. Then he mixes it with herbs and sells it to families with sick children or old people. They put a match to this *dawa*. You breathe in its smoke and it heals the chest.'

I thought it was a terrible thing in old age when every move was difficult, and the simplest things that once you did without a thought now cause pain. It was worse if you did not have family to care for you. My old friend, Bibi Cecelia, was spared this loneliness and struggle for we were there to help her.

Cecelia was like the grandmother I did not have. When I married, she had given me her most prized possession. This treasure of hers had been kept under a cover in her room for a long time.

'Come,' she said. 'Come, precious one, I have a gift for you.'

Cecelia threw off the *kanga* covering. It was not a box but a treadle sewing machine, black with a gold and silver swirling decoration, and the word *Singer* across the shaft and in the pattern of the cast iron base. I had seen these machines in the Indian shops before the Revolution. Those *dukas* had names like 'High Class Tailors'. The tailors sat outside the shops working with both feet on the treadle, moving back and forth in a steady flow. A belt round a large wheel drove the machine so they could move the cloth swiftly under the flying needle.

I hugged Cecelia until she cried for me to stop.

'It was given to me by the Goli family,' she said, 'and they taught me how to use it. My eyes have lost their strength. Now it is your turn. See the two drawers on each side. Here are the spare needles, scissors and a bag of cotton reels. I even have some oil for you must take care of the machine's moving parts. I have the instruction book to guide you. It has been eaten a bit by cockroaches.'

'In this drawer are the patterns.' Cecelia pulled out a wad of brown paper unwrapping neatly folded sheets. 'You see, this is for a shirt to wear with your *kanga* with seam allowances and sewing lines. This will be too big for you so I will show you how to cut one for yourself. We can practise on old cloth.'

I could not thank her enough. Now I was a student again, learning to sew.

'It is a beautiful thing, Cecelia.' I passed my hand over the cold metal with the shining design.

'It is, and may Allah bless you with many children, and with this you will make their clothes!'

I wish Cecelia could see us now. She was to hold our son, Taha Mujab, but she died before my daughter, Akila, was born. We decided to give Akila the third name of Cecelia, so she became Akila Mujab Cecelia.

Cecelia fell down the old wooden stairs when Taha Mujab was not even a year old and I was pregnant again. The broken step had been there since we first moved in and we had become used to it. No one had repaired it. I heard her cry out, but I was too late to stop her headlong fall onto the stone floor of our cooking area. The Chinese doctor at the hospital shook his head, and a woman translated for him saying that they could do nothing.

A nurse said, 'Take her home with these pills; it is better to die there with those who love you.'

Outside the hospital walls, young men were selling empty bottles for families to fill with traditional medicines, for little was dispensed to patients by the doctors. Mujab wheeled Cecelia back in the same handcart that had taken me to hospital when I lost my second baby, and we carried her upstairs to her room. Mujab said it was not hard for she weighed so little. She could not speak but would smile at us and squeeze our hands. We said the *Al Fatihah*.

In the name of Allah, the Merciful, the Compassionate
Praise be to God, Lord of the Universe,
the Compassionate, the Merciful,
Sovereign of the Day of Judgement!
You alone we worship, and to You alone we turn for help.
Guide us to the straight path.
The path of those whom You have favoured,
Not of those who have incurred Your wrath,
Nor of those who have gone astray.

Early on the third morning, she cried out in a strange language. We told her that we loved her and I thanked her for her goodness to me. We said the *shahada* for her, holding her hand and wiping her sweating face. *There is no god but God, Muhammad is the messenger of God.*

These were the last words she heard. After her death, the women in the household performed the rites of washing her body, wrapping her, anointing her with scented oils and saying prayers for her soul before she was buried.

Cecilia had opened my eyes and showed me that it was possible to laugh again, to look at the world without sorrow. Every year I wait for her swallows to arrive, watch as they build their mud nests on our roof and raise their young, and I remember her.

I sing to my children a lullaby that Cecilia taught me.
Grow my child, grow, grow big.
Grow like the banana tree, the coconut is too slow.
Grow like the coconut tree, the banana withers away.
Ooh, my child, ooh. Ooh, my child, ooh.

I thought of my second child, my sweet daughter, Akila, who is sleeping near us, and how life begins with such hope, and what difficulties await us. Only with Allah's help can we find the strength to survive.

Surely we come from God and surely we return to Him.

33. Baba Ali Arrested

Ajali haikimbiliki   There is no escape from fate

1981

One morning my body felt so heavy and I could not rise.

Taha Mujab was seven and kept pleading, 'Mama, please get up, don't be sick.' He sat next to the bed and held the cup for me to take sips of water. I felt every movement was a struggle, as if stones were upon my legs and arms. Soon I was sweating and feverish, and Mujab called his Mama.

'It is malaria, my son,' said Hala. 'Take this money, run to the hospital and buy the pills.'

It was the wet season when at sunset mosquitoes rose in clouds over our town. Drains were blocked and flies bred in the stagnant water. In daylight, they hid in the dark corners of our rooms, behind the hanging clothes. Hundreds would fly out when you shook out the shirts and *kangas*.

I was afraid our two children would get the fever. We only had one mosquito net between us, and I made sure Taha Mujab and Akila slept together under this protection. When they were little, this was possible. It was all I could do. Every night, I arranged the children head to tail and tucked the net under the mats and checked that no mosquitoes had got inside. But for Mujab and me, there was no protection.

Hala sat with me for three days as I wandered in darkness. Sometimes I was hot and other times shivered with a deep coldness that was impossible to escape. My body was so full with aching I felt I might sink into the earth.

I dreamt of the past, of the family I had lost and I cried out for them. I did not know where I was. The years dropped away and my childhood came back to me. I was lying on Basilah's bed and she was brushing her hair and singing. She turned and stood up but she could not see me or hear me as I called to her. Why did she not come to me? It was as if I was under the sea, everything moved slowly. Then it was not my sister any more but Hala comforting me. She wiped me with a cloth and gave me the pills Mujab had bought.

I awoke one morning to the sound of Cecelia's swallows outside my window. My children were sleeping by me and Hala held my hand, smiling.

'My daughter, you are better. It has been five days. Allah has answered our prayers.'

I was weak but I had survived. Malaria took many lives on our islands that year. Now I was determined we should get mosquito nets. It was the only way to protect my family.

At the evening meal I asked, 'Mujab, please, you must find a way to buy nets for the whole family. The children should have one each; your parents and Paka need their own, so do your sisters and brother and one for us. The only one we have is falling to pieces. I have mended it too often. We need nine nets for our family.'

'Fatima, you know I have tried,' said Mujab. 'The government shops are empty. I have asked at work and they cannot help. The only way is the illegal market. Men bring in goods by dhow at night. They demand three or four times the mainland price, dealing in hidden rooms, moving every time. But it is dangerous. If I am caught, I will end up in prison and lose my job!'

Next day it was not Mujab who was imprisoned, it was Baba Ali.

Hala came to our room late in the afternoon. 'Have you seen Baba Ali? He went out with a *kikapu* early this morning. He said he was going to wait for food at the government *dukas*. Where is he?'

She waited, standing on the *baraza* downstairs looking up and down the street. I remembered Rasil's Baba, Sahir, how he had waited for his son to appear, and I was fearful.

It was not long before one of Mujab's friends came running into our house followed by Hala.

'Mujab, your Baba Ali has been arrested. I was there. I saw it happen. Men were fighting for sugar and soap. A government official was walking past. He was suspicious and called the police who surrounded the room. Some of the buyers ran and escaped but Baba Ali was taken away.'

Baba Ali was caught with mosquito nets and some blocks of Lux soap he was buying for us. Mujab hurried to the Central Prison, *Kiinua Miguu*, but was told to come back the next day. It was because I had cried for those nets and now Baba Ali, who was the kindest of men, was in prison.

I fetched the gold necklace that Cecelia had given me and took it to Mujab.

'We must get Baba out of prison before he is hurt. Please, take this. With it you might persuade them to release him.'

'Do not weep,' said Mujab as he took my necklace. 'We will get him out tomorrow.'

Next day Hala gave Mujab some food and clothes to take to the prison in case they detained Baba Ali. As the sun was setting, Mujab returned, his

Baba close behind him. Baba Ali was smiling to see us all but I could see he was limping. He showed us bruises on his legs.

'The warders hit me with a cane when I said I did not know the name of the smuggler of the goods,' he said. 'They took away the nets and soap for themselves. "Confiscated," they said.'

Hala fetched water and soap to clean the cuts on his legs while Mujab told us how he had rescued his Baba.

'First, I went to work and asked to speak to my section director. I told him what had happened and asked if he could help us. I hoped we could pay a fine instead of Baba having a prison sentence. I was worried for I remembered smugglers were treated cruelly under President Karume. If you were caught smuggling cloves to Tanga or Mombasa, it was a death penalty!'

'What happened then, my son?' Hala said.

'I waited for two hours before *Bwana* M. called me back. He had written a letter and had it signed by his chief. He asked me what I was taking to pay as a fine and I showed him Fatima's gold necklace.

'He said, "This belongs to your wife? It is too valuable. I will advance you part of your salary. Six hundred shillings should be enough."

'I went to the prison and asked to see the warden, saying I had a letter to deliver. There were so many men in there, standing around waiting. They are so thin. It is a crime to criticise the government so the prison is full. But we can give thanks, for they let Baba out. I could see the warden was not pleased with my letter from the Finance Department. He put the shillings in his pocket and said, "Next time the fine will be double. I will remember you! The Revolutionary Council will punish those who cheat by buying imported goods." But he let Baba go.'

'Huh,' said Hala, 'and was he not cheating keeping the goods and the money?'

Baba said, 'Prisoners spoke to me. Some do not know why they are imprisoned. They are made to work all day with little food. They are only given bitter cassava roots and leaves to eat. This is food for goats. They said they are treated like slaves.'

What would have happened to Baba if we had not been able to get help?

34. A New Home, an Old Home

Shukuru kwa uliyo nayo   *Give thanks for what you have*

1984-1985

We waited for our lives to get better. It was now twenty years since the Revolution, and the young people could not even remember how good it was before 1964. Each time a new President came to power in Zanzibar, we hoped for more food and clothing and for less fear. So much depended on one man.

In 1984, Ali Hassan Mwinyi came to power. President Mwinyi promised much and tried hard to improve our lives.

Mujab was excited. 'Our new President is a good man. He has set up a constitution and a bill of rights. We have been told at work that more goods are being allowed in and he will bring the tourists back!'

There were not many things a woman could do to earn money in those days, but Cecelia had showed me a way. Over the years I got better and better at making clothes. For although on our islands women wear *kangas*, we need shirts to wear with them. The little children need everyday dresses and pants, as well as new clothes for *Eid Al-Fitr* when we break the fast and celebrate with a special day we call *siku kuu*.

At first getting cloth was hard but after President Jumbe was deposed in 1984, government shops had more essential food. Shutters that had been closed for years were pulled back and *dukas* opened along our streets.

Cecelia had shown me how to copy a pattern from an existing shirt or long pants using sheets of newspaper. Often I used old *kangas*, laying them out and cutting on the floor. Soon women came to ask me to make things for them. These mamas could only pay me a handful of shillings or give me some food or unworked cloth in exchange but that was enough to make life easier for our family.

One day Mujab came running home. I was scared when people were running. Usually it was not good news but he was smiling and could hardly speak at first.

'Y-y-y-ou know,' he was panting hard, 'I always walk past your family house on the way to Mambo Msiige?'

Mujab went to the mosque for dawn prayers and from there went straight to work.

'Yes,' I said, hushing the crying Akila. 'What has happened?'

'Well, there were three families living there, and when I went past, I saw one of them moving out. I asked what was happening. The baba said that he had inherited some land, enough for them to live on and feed his family. I asked if my family could move into his old rooms. He said I would have to talk to the resident on the floor above him who manages the house. On the way home I did this and after much talk of how good it was, he said if we could pay him one thousand shillings, we could have it. I asked if we could pay fifty a month from my salary and he has agreed. I do not think he has the right to charge us but it might be better that way.'

So our family and Paka moved into my old home, twenty-one years after the Revolution. We had three rooms. Later we took over another two rooms and Baba Ali and Hala joined us with Mujab's sisters who were now married. I felt that I was coming home. Something in my heart was calmed. I would look out on the world from the same rooms from which my sister, Mama and Baba's parents had looked. I would pray for them from their house. It was easier to remember my old life and give thanks for what we now had.

It was here in my family house that our third child, a daughter, was born when I was thirty-three years old and Akila was already ten and Taha Mujab was twelve. We called her Jamila, for she was beautiful and a blessing to us. I gave thanks to Allah for His grace and mercy and prayed for His guidance for my child.

I made little toys for my new baby girl and for Jannah's babies by sewing material scraps together and stuffing scraps into them. I hung some bright shapes from an old coathanger to make a decoration above their beds. Out of nothing we made things and it was satisfying. Part of one room became my workroom and Paka helped me with cutting and making children's clothes.

When we walked along Forodhani as a family during the cool of the evening, other women saw my baby clothes and toys. They came and ordered clothes from me and I bought kapok for stuffing the toys which made them even softer.

I learnt to cut the *kangas* to make use of the bright pattern on the cloth. Each *kanga* has a KiSwahili proverb or *jina* along the bottom. Some were not suitable for children's clothes but I worked patterns into the skirt or shirt bottom along with the border or *pindo*. The centre of the *kanga* is called *mji* and shows the main design, and this would form the main part of the child's dress. My customers had particular designs they fancied: often a duck or a bird would be on the ones for children. I did not put political proverbs on the clothing, only educational sayings.

Mujab was promoted at the Finance Department. Sometimes when a more senior clerk was ill, he was given the job of entering the invoices into an index and deciding which ledger account they would be charged against. He said he always asked for help and people liked that. His first meal of the day was at about ten, and he would sit watching the boats from the steps in front of Mambo Msiige, by Ras Shangani. Another clerk would join him there, an older man who had been in this department for twenty years. He started to teach Mujab more advanced techniques of bookkeeping.

'He said that I must be careful and not ask too many questions about some of the invoices.' Mujab said

'Why?' I asked. For so little did I know of the ways of corruption.

'It is quite easy. People create invoices for goods that are never delivered, or services never provided. The invoice is signed off and we pay it! So they get money for doing nothing. Or they invoice at twice the amount it actually costs.'

Mujab had to be careful.

35. Telling my Story

Mtoto umleyavyo ndivyo akuavyo   As you bring up a child, so he will be

1987

'Where are your Mama and Baba?' my older children asked.

I would say that they died of a sickness when I was young, and Paka was now my Mama and she was their Bibi, and Mujab's parents were there to love them too.

We had hoped for a better life after the death of President Karume but it was not to be. Fifteen years had passed since his assassination and even now we lived without freedom. As time passed and Taha Mujab and Akila went to school, we realised two things: the schooling was poor and it was twisted.

In many ways, the education became worse as the years passed. When Taha Mujab and Akila went to school during the years of President Jumbe, much time was spent on organising political rallies. Some said it was the Chinese people who gave the President this idea of masses of people performing together, for it was not something we understood from our culture. We called this new thing, *halaiki*.

For months before the annual celebration of the Revolution in January, the students would be trained for shows where they waved different coloured cards or held up revolutionary slogans, and wore uniforms as if they were young soldiers.

I asked Taha Mujab when he returned from school, 'What did you do today?'

'Mama, we went to the stadium to practise with the cards and our marching,' he replied. 'Our teacher says we make too many mistakes. Even the girls must march wearing caps like the boys and carry wooden rifles.'

When we sat on the roof in the evening, I said to Mujab, 'These *halaiki* are to show off their power over us. What does it teach the children? Nothing! It is a waste of time. They are growing up with empty heads!'

'It is true. We are forgetting how to think for ourselves. Such demonstrations make the children perform like ants,' Mujab said.

'It is not once a year that they make our children march. Every month there seems to be another student demonstration of *halaiki*,' I replied.

Mujab raised his fingers. 'January, the schoolchildren march for our Revolution; February, they march for the anniversary of the founding of the

Afro-Shirazi Party; then the celebration of the union with Tanganyika is in April. That is three. Four is in May; May Day for the workers. Five is *Saba Saba* Day to remember when the Tanganyikan African National Union was founded. I have run out of fingers and there are still two more. Six is in September and that is a strange one—Free Education Day. The last is in December; that one is to remember the independence of Tanganyika from the British.'

'Is it not strange that we do not remember the independence of Zanzibar in December? We were independent for so little time.'

Most of the teachers were poorly trained; some had only completed primary school. The classrooms had few desks: usually over forty children were in each class and each year the numbers were growing. No books from the old days were allowed, and the teacher taught from the chalkboard and the children shared slates. They were short of books, paper and pencils.

While I believed we were in the hands of Allah, it was hard not to wish for a better life.

Mujab agreed, 'What you say is so but be careful about showing our children how you feel. I think you should keep up the extra lessons for them. It would be better that way.'

That is what I had always done and although my education had stopped in 1964 when I was twelve, I remembered my early schooling and I had my pile of old books which I had read and re-read. These books were now twenty years old. They were my education. The knowledge was valuable and did not change with the passing of time.

It became my desire to give my children extra understanding. I read to them about the world in which we live although I had seen so little of it. I taught them the English that I knew. I did not trust the kind of education that this government would give my children. I had become a teacher.

It was especially hard to hear the lies the authorities and teachers told of the Arab people and the history of my people. It was as if they were trying to put a knife between me and my husband. Was he not a Zanzibari as I was? Yet they were describing one of us as an African and the other as an Arab, as if we were enemies and always would be.

'It is this thinking that killed my family,' I said. 'It is madness to continue this way. Who can choose without pain and suffering? Why do we have to choose? We are one people here, and only if we realise that can we have peace.'

'That is so,' Mujab agreed, 'but the hardliners in the government see it another way. They tell the story of how their Revolution is in danger. They say we must stick with this Revolution for it is who we are. They did not want our new constitution or for there to be restriction on the power of the President.'

Taha Mujab was thirteen and at secondary school, and Akila was twelve and about to leave primary school when she came home with a history book called *Zanzibar, the 1964 Revolution: Achievements and Prospects*. All primary school children were given a free copy and they were told to read it. I wanted to know how after twenty-three years the story would be told.

From cover to cover, the book was lies and hatred. This book caused me to tell my children the true story. Books have great value but I now realised that they did not all speak the truth.

Mujab and I called them together and I asked Paka to come too. She was an old lady now but still at my right hand.

'I have something important to tell you,' I said. 'We have not told you before in order to protect you but the time has come to know the truth. You must not repeat what we tell you, not yet. Allah willing that day will come. Paka can speak as well.'

I told them this story, of how their grandfather, great-grandfather, uncle and others were murdered and how Mama and my sister were never found. I wept to tell these secrets that had been hidden for so long in my heart. Now, with my husband at my side, I passed the story on to my children: as they wept with Paka and me to hear it, I knew that it would become part of their story and their lives. Those of my family who had died lived on in them.

'If my Baba had not sent me away with Paka on that morning of the Revolution, we would both have been killed. Many many innocent people died and their graves are not known.'

I told them that this house where we lived in Shangani was their family house that had belonged to my family for generations.

'This room looking over the square was your grandparents' room,' I said. 'Their names are Ahmed bin Khaleed al-Ibrahim and Amal bint Yusuf. As a child, I loved to visit Mama in this room. Basilah and I would watch Mama brushing her hair and putting on her jewellery on special occasions.'

'Why do you not know what happened to aunt Basilah and my Bibi?' Akila asked. 'Surely someone must know? Even now we must ask.'

'Do not be angry, Akila,' I said. 'It is hard for me to tell you what those times were like. I tried to find out but they disappeared and no one could tell me. You know my Babu died in the hospital. All my life I have wondered what happened and I have prayed for them.'

'It makes me cross, Mama,' Taha Mujab said. 'You have suffered so much and lost so much! Is that how you got the scar on your arm?'

I looked at the line that ran from my wrist nearly to my elbow, the scar that every January caused me to remember.

'Yes, my arm was injured as we fled that day. It is true I have suffered, my child, but look how Allah has blessed me with your Baba and with you, my children. And when I was a child, I was loved and cared for. Other children suffered more than I did. Much has happened that we do not know.'

Jamila was but three and too young to understand but Taha Mujab and Akila asked me many questions about my family and my childhood. Many of these I could not answer, for I had been but twelve and so much I did not know. My past had been taken away from me before I understood it.

I took my children upstairs to show them the room that was once Basilah's and mine. Next to it was my brother Taha's room that was now unoccupied. The roof had rusted through above this room: the damp had turned the lime plaster grey and the ripe smell of mould hung in the air. Recently Mujab and Taha Mujab had repaired the corrugated iron.

I held little Jamila's hand and we all climbed up onto the roof.

'As a child this is where I loved to sit after school,' I said. 'I would find shade behind this wall and read my schoolbooks and do my homework in the cool times of the day. See here.'

I showed them where my brother had scratched his initials into the soft coral stone on the wall. My initials were next to his: TH and FA. They were faded now, for it was over twenty-three years since I had sat in that corner and read my books. Now I would hardly recognise that child.

36. House with the Pale-blue Door

Ametubwikia kisimani   *A person has fallen into the well, he has got into a plight and help is needed*

1992

My house, for now I regarded it once more as my family house, was close to the beach at Ras Shangani, the beach we called *Forodha Mchanga*, or Sandy Harbour. As Stone Town pointed like a triangle into the sea, one beach was usually out of the wind. If the *kaskazi* was blowing, I could take the children further round the corner to the German steps and, if the *kusi* was blowing, Sandy Harbour in front of Mambo Msiige was protected.

After school, I would take my daughters, Akila and young Jamila, down the road and sit by the sea. It was there that I had once watched over my baby daughter playing in the shallows and Taha Mujab learning to swim. He was now almost a man, having finished high school. He met his friends at Sandy Harbour and if the tide was high, breaking over the steps between Mambo Msiige and the old English Sailing Club, they would jump and dive into the crashing waves.

Taha Mujab was eighteen, tall and slim. Sometimes his expressions were those of the young Mujab who I had married nearly twenty-one years ago. And other times, when Taha Mujab's face was thoughtful, it seemed as if my brother, who had died at almost the same age twenty-eight years ago, was still with me.

Akila was my clever child with a quick wit. She asked questions and loved her books. As she grew older, I could no longer answer her questions for she did not think as I did: her mind went far and wide wondering about why things were so.

Our house had three floors and many rooms. Over the years, more rooms became vacant and we took them over. On the ground floor, I had a workroom and showroom for my growing business. Only two rooms on the top floor were unoccupied.

We were now allowed to leave the islands. Some families moved to Dar-es-Salaam or Mombasa for our island could not provide enough jobs for the young people. This was before tourists came back. I can remember the first time I saw Europeans with cameras near the post office. Until recent times, we were not allowed to take pictures of public buildings, nor were we allowed to talk to foreigners. Times were changing and tourist hotels were being built along our north coast.

Living with our family were Mujab's parents, Baba Ali and Bibi Hala, and Paka. Mujab's sister, Jannah, her husband and two sons lived with us as well. His other sister, Subira, had travelled away to Dar-es-Salaam to marry.

Our bedroom window looked out over a narrow street. As a child I had watched people wandering along this street and I knew how the light and shadow played across the houses opposite, lighting up the doors and their carving. One of the houses was showing signs of collapse. We saw no one attended to its maintenance. This house had a traditional front door that a long time ago had been painted a pale sky blue. At the top was the 'W' sign that showed it was a charitable trust property.

We were determined that our home would not suffer the same way. Mujab, Taha Mujab and Baba Ali worked together to fix the plaster on the walls and they painted it over with lime wash. Mujab rescued sheets of galvanised iron from collapsed houses, and these we used to fix our own house.

At first the house across the road was fully occupied but over time, residents of the building became fearful and started moving out. I greeted a young woman as she was waiting with her children in the street. Around her were bags of possessions.

'This house is ready to fall down.' She waved her arms up at the cracks. 'Look at it. A disgrace! Water is coming in through the roof and the wood is rotten. I cannot stay here. I don't want my family to be killed.'

'Bibi, why don't the men fix the leaks so you can stay?' I asked.

'We pay rent. It is not much,' she said. 'It is a *wakf* property. Everyone says the government *wakf* officials must fix the roof with the rent money. We have complained but nothing happens. They are lazy. The stairs are rotten and dangerous for our children and old people.'

Cracks started to grow from the ground floor and zigzags travelled from the corner of the door. They were so wide you could put your hand into the gaps. We had seen these signs before. The walls above the first floor bulged outwards. The whole building was no longer square. The windows sagged and pieces of the lime plaster covering the walls fell into the street revealing yellow coral blocks like old men's teeth.

Mujab and I watched from our window as men wedged planks against the front wall. 'Those workers say the poles supporting the upper floors are rotten,' he said. 'Be careful when you walk past.'

More residents left. The front of the building finally collapsed in the middle of the day after a storm during the *masika* rains. It was by the grace of Allah that no one was hurt or killed. The walls fell into the street with a crash like thunder but the pale-blue door remained upright. Mujab rushed down to see if he could help, and a group of men gathered around. The house was now a pile of rubble, stones and dust: the mangrove poles were like the building's broken bones. You would never imagine that this heap of rubbish had once been a house in which people had lived for over a hundred years.

The police arrived and held back the shouting men who were trying to climb over the pile of stones to see if anyone remained in the building's back section. From my upstairs window over the settling dust, I could see two women were crying out and waving from floors that had overlooked the central rooms. These few rooms had not fallen down as neighbouring houses had supported the back of the building. The police helped the trapped women over the crushed stones.

Later, I walked out with Paka and little Jamila. The police had put yellow tape across the stones. I wondered, what would happen to the door? Surely it would be preserved. I thought of Cecelia and remembered how she had taught me to read a door.

'See, Jamila, this chain round the frame of the door is to keep out evil spirits. And here are pineapples, one on each side of the door, and these are dates from Arabia. All are signs of hope for a good life without hunger. Look how people's feet have worn down this step over the years. Once brass knobs would have been in these holes and the owners would have polished them till they shone. People unscrew the knobs and sell them for a few shillings. This sign shows it was a *wakf* property.'

For some days, I watched that door standing there with no house behind it, and then workmen came and started chipping at the remaining stone on either side of the door.

I called Mujab, 'Please, can you go down and ask where they are taking it?'

'Why, Fatima?'

'Please, I want it saved.'

Mujab came back a little later. 'Fatima, the door is sold. It is going overseas. They say that there is no use for it in Zanzibar any more.'

So my pale-blue door, with its protection from evil spirits, left our island. It had not been able to keep the house from destruction. This made me more and more determined to protect my house.

After the front door had gone, the house was forgotten. Children would jump on the stones and pawpaw trees sprouted and grew in the corners. Women hung their washing out to dry over the larger stones. The house was one of many that had crashed down during the twenty-eight years since the Revolution. I thought, this is what Karume wished for.

One day looking out from my bedroom window, I saw a young woman, carrying a girl child on her hip and a *kikapu* in her other hand, climb through the stones of the collapsed house to the back where the few rooms remained. Was she going to live there? It seemed so, as each day I saw her coming and going, making her pathway through the ruins.

I asked Paka to come and see. 'Do you know who this mama is? How can she live there?'

'I've seen her by the beach with the little girl. Where are her family? Maybe she will go away after a few days,' Paka said.

Paka and I were busy making and selling clothes from the front rooms and every day I saw this woman walking past. She was thin and short, almost a child herself, with a pretty round face and dark eyes. One afternoon, Jamila and I took Jannah's two boys to the beach and I saw the young mama on the beach playing with her little girl.

I greeted her. 'Are you visiting us from the country?'

She was shy and would not look at me. 'Bibi, I am looking for work. I come from Pemba Island where my son stays. We cannot find work at home. Forgive me, my name is Sara, and this is my daughter, Faida.'

I did not want to show her that I knew she was living alone in rooms with no water or toilet.

'What is your story, Sara? What has happened to your family?'

We sat on the beach and, as the children played, Sara told me about her life. She was from a Shirazi family living in a village near Wete on Pemba, our sister island to the north of Zanzibar. Her husband, Malik, had been a fisherman and, although life was difficult, they had survived as he caught fish and octopus and sold or exchanged his catch for things they needed. They had two children, a boy called Naufal and then Faida was born. But as time passed, it became harder to pay for clothes for the children and medicines for Naufal, who was constantly sick.

'The villagers talked about the old times,' Sara said. 'Before I was born, there was a time they called, *wakati wa neema*, "a season of abundance" but now came a time of suffering.'

Malik started to smuggle cloves. He would ferry the bags from their harbour out to larger boats waiting offshore. This was a dangerous business. They knew about the heavy punishment for this crime. You could be beaten and thrown into prison or put to death but the pay for the trade was good. As the clove farmers received little from the Revolutionary Government for their harvest, they hid sacks of cloves and sold them to smugglers who shipped the sacks to the mainland.

'The farmers were angry,' she said. 'They told us the world price was ten times what the government was paying them. They could not survive. Then the world price went down and they were paid even less.'

Soon Malik did more. He would collect household items from the smugglers to sell in Pemba, for shops there were almost empty and what was on their shelves was too expensive. In the hull of his *ngalawa*, he brought back packets of soap and beans, tins of oil and even rolls of cloth. He handed them to dealers who traded at night-time in the forest. Malik was now earning more money.

'I was frightened day and night,' Sara said, 'for I feared the government spies would find out what Malik was doing. At first, he only took a few things in his *ngalawa* but, as time went on, his loads became bigger.'

She was fearful every time Malik went out, although she was happy that they now had the money for medicines and Naufal got better. They could help their family. She wanted Malik to stop smuggling as she worried the neighbours would talk and, sooner or later, he would be found out. But her husband liked the excitement and the money he was making.

'Malik told me it was only for a few months, and he would stop after the next harvest.'

Malik would go out at night to meet the boats from Tanga and Mombasa in the deeper water off a tiny offshore island. He knew the sea and its ways but the night journeys were dangerous. He did not have a outboard motor relying only on the wooden *ngalawa's* single sail.

One night, he planned to go out with a full load of cloves. The wind was strong. Sara, fearing a storm, tried to persuade him to stay but he sailed out into the foaming sea. He never came back. Next day, they found his boat wrecked and his body washed ashore.

Alone, she could not survive. An abusive old man offered to marry her but she refused. In the village, she heard that life was easier on Zanzibar

Island and she decided she had to leave Pemba. It was better to take this chance.

'It is hard to see your children hungry. They did not even play games any more. We have suffered for so long,' Sara said.

Sara's mother-in-law, her *mama mkwe*, said she would care for Naufal as long as Sara sent money back for their upkeep, but she would not take the girl child. So Sara brought four-year-old Faida to Zanzibar Island and was hiding in this collapsed Shangani house while she looked for work. She had no money for rent.

I told Mujab about Sara's story

'I have heard that the people of Pemba have suffered,' he said. 'They had a regional commissioner who was called *Mamba*, or "Crocodile", as he was feared so much. Sometimes he would punish a whole village for a little mistake. If you did not stand up when his car passed, you would be flogged in public. People were so frightened that they jumped to attention whenever a government car passed. Pemba people speak about that time and call it *siku za bakora*, "days of the cane".'

'Oh, that is bad,' I said. 'When you are struggling, it is easy to forget that others may be worse off. Have times not improved in Pemba like they have here?'

'Perhaps, but our current President, Salmin Amour, does not like Pemba people because they voted against him. He is sacking or demoting people in government who are from Pemba, and he is stopping further education for their students. I am told everything is worse on Pemba, the roads, the power shortages, the schools. Through my Finance Department, I see the payments made for such services. It is not fair.'

'Is your job in danger?'

'I have to be careful,' said Mujab. 'President Amour hates the opposition and has imprisoned many of their leaders. They call him "Commando" because he will not allow anyone to stand up to him.'

After a moment he said, 'Allah requires us to help people in need. Can you find some way to help Sara and her child? We must have courage to change things little by little. She has shown bravery coming here with her daughter.'

I agreed. 'You have a good job and my work is bringing in more business. Let me find out what work Sara is able to do.'

But before I could speak to her, I was shocked by what I discovered.

That evening, after our meal was over, I was watching the sunset from my window when I saw Sara walking in the street below. Her child was not with her. She paused at the start of the pathway into the fallen building and looked behind her, as if she was waiting for someone. I looked down the street and saw a big man following her. Sara walked quickly across the rubble into the back rooms and the man turned in after her.

With the building now collapsed, no one else would be able to easily see what she had done. Only my window overlooked that spot. I was shocked. What was she doing? Could she be taking money from men? For that is what it seemed to me. I waited: after a while, the man came out alone.

After looking up and down the street, he walked swiftly away, his head down. I recognised him. In those brief moments, it came to me that it was Salim Hadir. His sharp face and the commanding manner in which he walked were the ways that I remembered him.

I sat down to consider what to do and found I was trembling. This information I could not share. It was too terrible. It seemed as if a veil had been taken from my eyes. Was I blind to the suffering of others? Had I been so caught up in my own story I was unable to help? I did not want anyone to know what Sara was doing to survive but before long everyone would know. Then I wondered, how did you know if your own husband was tempted in this way?

The light by our bed was a pressure lamp because most evenings the power failed. That night, before turning the lamp down so the flame over the wick died, I sat by the light and thought about these questions troubling me. My husband and I did not talk openly about sexual matters. They were private. I had been taught that a woman may enjoy sex with her husband but it was not discussed, not even in the privacy of her bedroom.

But that night I had to know something. 'Forgive me if I am forward, Mujab, but can you tell me something?'

'What is it Fatima? You are most serious,' Mujab said.

'Do you have a girlfriend?'

'No! Of course not! Surely you know that. Why do you ask?'

'Some men do. How would I know?'

'You would know,' he replied. 'You are my wife and every day that is a wonder and pleasure for me. You would not ask this unless you were unhappy about something,' Mujab sat up and faced me. 'Please tell me what has happened.'

His face was in the light and I could tell that what he had said was true. We had been together for many years and in that time you learn the face of your husband. I did trust him but also I was lost in confusion.

'I want to know more about such things. About girlfriends. Married men and girlfriends.'

'Something has happened. I hope you will tell me but I can answer your question first. Yes, men I know have girlfriends, and sometimes their wives know; sometimes they do not. Some men at work boast about it; others are quiet yet do the same thing.'

'Why do they not divorce, and then go with the other woman?'

'I cannot answer that. One man I know has one girlfriend after another. Maybe he wants to keep his house with his wife and children but wants pleasure with girls as well.'

'They talk about this at work?'

It was a world that I knew nothing about, and it surprised me that my husband knew all this while I was ignorant.

'Some do, and sometimes we all know what is going on.'

'What do you mean?'

'Well,' Mujab said, 'one girlfriend comes to the office sometimes. As I arrive in the morning, I see her waiting for her boyfriend in Kelele Square under the trees. One day, he saw me walk past, and later he told me they were making plans.'

'Making plans?'

'Fatima, it is all about secrecy but, in Zanzibar, it is hard to keep a secret for long! This man has a flat in the Michenzani blocks—those they call *Jumba la Miguu*, the house with legs. That is where he meets her after work. Tells his wife he has a meeting, or something. We hear it all. He is not ashamed, he laughs. He offers the flat to other men to meet their girlfriends and charges them rent. But he is my superior, what can I say? Each person must live with his actions. Is that not so?'

I was silent, thinking about this. How little did I know of the ways of men, yet we had been married for over twenty years.

'Now tell me, why does this worry you?' Mujab took my hand.

How could I tell him about Sara and what I had seen? It was private between me and her. Mujab knew almost everything about me but one thing he knew nothing of was the time when Salim Hadir had sent me the letters and the gold necklace.

'I saw a man I thought I knew following a girl into a house and I realised they were lovers.'

I had told a half-truth and felt bad that I had done so, for he waited and I think he knew more lay behind my story.

'Well,' Mujab said, 'let us turn out this light and lie down. You must not worry about such things and, please, let us share your troubles. For your troubles are my troubles.'

That night I thought about how the kindness of Baba Ali and Hala's family had saved me and how they had gathered me into their lives without a thought for the dangers of caring for an Arab child during the *Mapinduzi*.

I wondered what I was risking if I invited Sara and her daughter into our house.

37. Two Women, Two Friends

Njaa haina huruma japokuwa kitu huna   *Hunger has no mercy, even when you have nothing*

1992

At first light, the call to prayer sounded and I rose to watch from my window. Sara had not left her rooms in the collapsed house. I dressed and went out. Rain had fallen and the street was cool in the shadows. I made my way along her path through the tumble of stones. As I came closer, I could hear weeping. I waited in the opening, for the door was gone, and called out.

'*Hodi, hodi*, Sara? Can I come in? It is me, Bibi Fatima.'

The crying stopped and I climbed through the opening into the first room where the floor was covered with a scattering of stones. This space led through to a back room that was in darkness. A *kanga* hung across the doorway. The smell in the room was not pleasant.

'Fatima?' Sara pulled aside the curtain. She looked terrible, clutching a *kanga* round her thin body. Her uncovered hair was a mess. She wiped tears from her face. She looked so young and helpless, a child herself. Little Faida peeped out from behind her Mama. Her face lit up when she saw me and she gave a shy wave.

'Come, Sara, let us get you out. You cannot live here.'

The condition of the room where they had slept was even worse. I helped her get dressed so she could go out into the street. We packed the clothes, mats and pots that she owned into two *vikapu*. She had so little, and I could see that she was ashamed.

Only Paka was at home sitting in the shop downstairs.

'Paka, I have Sara and Faida here; I will be upstairs with them. Can you manage the shop?'

Sara and Faida followed me into our kitchen and I began heating water for washing.

'Faida, would you like something to eat?'

'Yes please, Bibi Fatima, please.'

The child was hungry and she ate all our leftover *chapatis*. I gave Sara some *kisheti*, or sugared doughnuts, with her tea. She ate carefully as if each mouthful was special. Faida was looking at the doughnuts.

'Faida, you can eat.'

'Thank you, Bibi,' she replied.

Sara watched Faida eating and told me about the hunger they had suffered in Pemba.

'I was Faida's age when the famine of 1971 came to our island. I think that is why I am small. After the rains failed, the fields were empty. Shops were empty too but anyway we had no money. Mama and Baba fought for food. In the forest, they searched for roots, poisonous roots. They washed them in the stream, boiled them twice, the second time in coconut milk and salt, before pounding them for porridge. If you did this wrong, the food would pierce your throat and you vomited. Some people died.'

I poured the sweet spiced tea, *chai*, into two mugs. Faida was picking up the doughnut crumbs from the plate and watching her Mama.

'Go on,' I said. 'I have never heard of this famine.'

'It is hard to believe the kinds of things we ate,' Sara said. 'Some fishermen ate the worms they collected for bait. Baba picked the wild pineapples and tiny bananas but they were soon gone. We collected taro and cassava leaves and we pulled the green mangoes off the tree and cooked them.

'Others searched the streams for turtles and climbed up the palm trees and killed the big bats that slept there. Still we went hungry, and all the time Mama would cry asking why no one from the government was coming to help. When I think of Mama, all I can see is her crying.'

I took the hot water and poured it into a bucket, mixing it with cold water until it was warm. Sara and Faida followed me up to the second floor to an empty room.

'You can wash and clean up here,' I said. 'First I must ask you, what can you do?'

Sara looked frightened. 'Do? Bibi Fatima, what do you mean?'

'Can you cook, or sew or do henna painting? That is what I mean.'

'I can cook but cannot sew or paint henna. But I can weave mats and make fish traps,' she said. 'You know the Pemba mats are the most beautiful. Also, my Bibi taught me how to do the massages for a girl before she is married.'

I went down to talk to Paka and Hala, and then to Baba Ali sitting on the *baraza* with his friends. Later, I spoke to my husband. I could not invite Sara into our home without talking to my family.

'I am glad you are helping her,' said Mujab. 'She is young without family to help. Jamila and Akila can help her and Faida.'

This is how Sara and her daughter came to live with us. Paka was the one most reluctant to accept them. She followed Sara around and watched her, and I realised that she knew what I knew.

'Fatima, is it right to take this strange girl into our home?' said Paka.

Paka knew me well. 'Give her a chance, let us wait and see.' I replied.

Paka was not relaxed and was not happy unless Sara was out of the house on an errand or playing with Faida on the beach.

It was Hala who became close to Sara. Hala was poorly, losing weight and energy. She struggled to get upstairs and do the simplest of work. Sara took to caring for her and I would hear them laughing together. Hala became weaker and we found out that she had cancer of her bones and the hospital gave her nothing but pills for pain. It was to Sara that Hala would call out for help. Sara would make her comfortable on our *baraza* so she could watch the comings and goings in the square and be distracted. Sara would massage Hala gently with cream when her legs ached and Faida would play games while the two women talked. In this way, Sara's kindness came out and I felt it was Allah's blessing she had come to us at that time.

Hala knew she was dying. She was in her mid-sixties but now looked like a tiny old woman. Baba Ali tried to help, taking her for slow walks around the square.

We gave Sara money to send to Pemba for her son's food and uniforms.

A month later, Mujab said, 'How do you feel about Sara staying with us? If you are happy with her, why don't we get her son to come from Pemba?'

This is what we did. I asked Paka to go with her and to take some money for Sara's mother-in-law, her *mama mkwe*. Paka was not pleased.

'Why should I go with that woman? She will be trouble for us. Wait and see.'

'Paka, I cannot go,' I said. 'Faida can stay with us. I want you to buy some Pemba mats and some of the leaves that they use to weave. I have an idea for Sara.'

When they came back with Sara's son, Naufal, Paka had changed. She was no longer cross.

'They have so little,' Paka said. 'Look how thin this boy is. He cried when we arrived, and Sara told me we have saved their lives. Let us put Naufal in school here. The schools in Pemba are even worse.'

Sara started weaving mats using the dyed palm leaves from Pemba. Her hands worked swiftly in the nest of colours, and Hala sat next to her on the *baraza* watching her and passing fresh strands. Pemba mats are known throughout our islands as the best for high quality weaving and for their blue, purple and green colours. Tourists stopped to watch her at work and saw how she stitched the long woven strips into the oval shape for a mat. They would come inside asking to buy one and then look at our clothes.

Our business was growing. Hotels were being built north of Stone Town and on the eastern coast where Europeans loved the long beaches. Italians were the first to arrive in large numbers. Hotels wanted the clothes we made for children in their shops but many did not want to pay for them until they were sold.

'You will have to invoice them. It is called "consignment". When they are sold, you will be paid,' said Mujab.

How good it was that Mujab could teach me how to run this business as it grew. Previously, I had put the money from my sales into a tin box, and when I needed some for buying *kangas* or paying our workers or even for food for the house, I would take the cash from this box.

'This is not the right way,' said Mujab. 'You must write it all down, where the money goes, and what you spend on our food should be separate.'

'Why is that?' I asked.

'You need to know if you are making money in this business: this way you know if you are charging enough for the clothes.'

Mujab bought me a cash book and an invoice book, and each night he checked where the money had gone. The consignment business was a problem. The new hotels were keen to take the clothes but not so quick to pay me when they were sold. I would wait until they came for more clothes and then ask for the money but often they were sorry—they had left their money behind, they would send it the next day or someone else had to authorise it.

When a new hotel up the coast was months behind in their payments, Sara and I visited them taking a *dala-dala* bus beyond Bububu where my family *shamba* had been. The hotel had purple bougainvilleas on either side of an old door that must have come from a Stone Town house. It opened to views over a swimming pool to the beach. White people lay on low beds round the pool.

'Look Bibi Fatima, they are naked,' Sara said.

We were both surprised to see a young white woman in a two-piece bikini. It was the first time I had seen such a thing. We were able to watch for a long time as we were told to wait by the office worker. A woman kindly indicated some chairs by reception so we settled down. Sara picked up the fashion magazines that lay there.

'Those are in Italian, Sara,' I said. She could not read or speak English. After some time, Sara became excited.

'Look, Bibi, these are children's clothes from that country. See how they are making the skirts.'

Sara showed me pictures of European children in red and yellow summer dresses in a playground. She had noticed how the bright patterned skirts were edged with plain colours which then matched the tops.

'We could do this. How pretty they are,' Sara said.

A young white man came to speak to us. He was about Taha's age and, although he was polite, I could see he was annoyed. Mujab had told me what to say, so when this young accountant gave the excuse that the clothes were not all sold, I had an answer.

'Thank you, sir, we will take them back as they will sell in town,' I said and stood up.

Then he paid me and kept the clothes.

Sara loved playing with the materials in our workshop. She would take down *kangas* and hang them against little Faida. She had a way of matching colours and patterns: our children's clothes looked even better with her help.

As the hot season arrived, words began to fail Hala, and the doctor said the disease had entered her brain. More pills were needed for the pain and she slept a lot, eating even less. When she did wake, Sara would be there talking to her or singing gently, and Mujab would read the Qur'an in KiSwahili to his Mama.

Hala died at the end of the year. She had been part of my life for almost thirty years. We gave thanks for her life and prayed for mercy for her soul.

38. Granted Such a Day

Radhi ni bora kuliko mali   Blessings are better than wealth

1995

I was forty-four in 1995. I say this because I want to remember this time all over again. It was thirty-one years since the Revolution, and often I see my family in my dreams. They are with me. I am older than Mama was when I lost her but, in my mind, Mama is still young and Basilah is waiting to get married. And the child of 1964 lives on in me.

Every January, the scar on my arm swells and aches. I bind it to stop myself scratching and opening up the old wound. It is the time when we take the children to visit the graves of Baba, Taha and Amina, to remember and to pray for their souls. I have made a seat between the coconut palms where I place pretty things. The village people of the *shamba* honour the grave sites. Others leave shells and flowers by the seat. The mango trees with the *shomari* mangoes that we loved to eat with salt still line the avenue to where the house once stood. We talk about the family we will never see. I say the same things to my children, tell the same stories every year, but it brings comfort.

'Basilah's wedding was to be a month after Ramadan. She was tall like you, Jamila, and her eyebrows were strong as yours are. She loved to sing and would play hide and seek with me in the house that was once here. There was a vegetable garden where we helped by collecting herbs for the evening meal.'

This day started as an ordinary day during our calm season after the rains, before the *kusi* starting blowing from the south. My daughters, Akila and little Jamila, were opening up the shop, sweeping the lane outside and making sure that our children's clothes were hanging by size and style on the racks beside the door.

The shop occupied a single front room with the office beside it. The front of the house had been lime-washed and flower pots stood either side of the steps. The name of the shop, *Kombe Clothing*, and the image of a seashell hung over the door. Visitors from the Arabian Gulf and Europe had arrived, filling the hotels. These tourists liked our cooler weather.

Akila was as lovely as I had once been, for hard work and having children changes a woman's body. She had won a place at the university in Dar-es-Salaam where she was studying law. Her sister, Jamila, the naughty one, loved teasing Akila and Taha Mujab. She was only ten but already said she wanted to be a teacher. My daughters when they were together were as I had been with Basilah, and it was a joy to see them.

Our house and shop were behind the main tourist road so we did not have many passersby but we had enough custom to keep us busy and we employed more women to sew for us. Akila did the sales work when she was at home and helped place stock in hotels.

On this day, two young people came into the shop and I could hear them talking in KiSwahili. It was KiSwahili with our local accent, what we call *Kiunguja*, not the accent of the mainland. We learn to hear the ways of our language, for it is a beautiful language, a language of song and poetry. I heard something different about the words and I listened carefully. The young man and the girl were talking. I thought they sounded a little older than my children, more self-assured.

'*Hodi*, are you open? Yes. Good morning. Come, Fatima, the shop is open, come, let us call Mama quickly.'

Curious, I came out of my office holding a child's dress that I was making. For some strange reason, my heart was thumping against my ribs, telling me something before my mind could believe it. Something about them had awoken cherished memories. It was the way they spoke and when I saw them, I knew. The girl was dressed in a bright yellow and black dress over trousers with a shawl covering her hair. She was tall and smiling up at the young man's round excited face. My heart stopped. Only one family looked like that. It was my family.

Yet nothing had prepared me for the certainty that now came. My mind was slow to follow the reaction of my heart. The girl was on the steps waving to someone and calling out.

'Mama, come. See this shop in your old home. We saw it yesterday. Come inside.'

Akila came to stand beside me. She looked at me in surprise for I was waiting for the woman to come through the doorway. Already I knew who it was. I dropped to my knees and praised Allah for His mercy.

When Basilah walked in, my mind had the memory of the young woman she was in 1964 but the woman who entered slowly, leaning on a walking stick, looked like my Mama. For us, thirty-one years had passed without each other. A lifetime. A lifetime of surviving for that is what we had done. How to describe our happiness and our tears at that time of discovery? She stood in the doorway and what did she see? How did she know, so surely, as I had known so absolutely?

Basilah kept hold of me, touching my face and stroking my hair and, when she could, she called to her children. 'Look this is your aunt, my little sister, Fatima. Fatima, it is she who you are named after.'

In one hand, I still held the child's dress.

In my dreams, I would sometimes see my family as if it were reality. But when I woke up, they had gone, and I wondered how the mind holds this other precious world to torment me. The loss of my family came upon me yet again. A cycle of loss. But now, Allah in His mercy had granted us both a special blessing. We were together again: our children would know one another, and I could share with my sister all the things that had happened to us in those missing years. She alone in all the world would know how to comfort me.

Basilah had two children; Fatima, her daughter, was almost the same age as my Akila. Her son, Ahmed Jasmir, at twenty-three, was the oldest of the cousins. Ahmed was named after our Baba. They now lived in Muscat in Oman but, for the first years of her marriage, she had lived in Cairo. Some families who had fled Zanzibar during the *Mapinduzi* were now visiting to show their children their homeland. Many would never come back. The loss and pain could not be faced. But for us, we had so much to tell one another. Thirty-one years to discover.

You can wait your whole life to have such a day. It might never happen. You cannot imagine the joy I was granted this day.

39. Thirty-one Years

*Maovu mengi huwa huru zaidi usiku wa kiza   Many bad things are set
free at the darkness of night*

1995

Basilah wanted to live in the joy of our meeting and finding one another,
so she did not tell me her story of survival until later. Over the next week, I
learnt what happened to them in that terrible time of January 1964, and why
I did not find them at home in Shangani.

Mama and Basilah were in our Stone Town house with grandfather,
Babu Khaleed. Before dawn, Babu heard fighting had started around two
police stations. He had listened to the radio but, with no news there, he
phoned friends. He only managed to get through once to Ahmed Khaleed,
his son, my Baba, at our *shamba*.

Babu told Mama and Basilah he was going to a white friend, a *mzungu*,
for help and to find out what was happening. This *mzungu* worked in the
government and would know what to do.

'Lock the door after me. Do not open for anyone except me. I will not
be long.'

Babu told them to pray, and she remembered him saying, 'If it is Allah's
will, we will survive.'

He slipped out of the house carrying a large package. Basilah said
they waited, expecting him back within an hour, but one hour passed, then
another and he did not return. They did not know where he had gone as
he was friends with several European people. She and Mama went to the
rooftop to see if they could hear or discover anything. From there, they
heard gunfire and shouting.

Basilah phoned Baba at the *shamba* but there was no answer. She
called to her friends across the street. They knew nothing but the rumours
were terrifying.

They turned on the radio and heard this man called John Okello
declaring that Mohammed Shamte's government was 'finished' and black
men must take up arms against the 'imperialists'. He called himself 'Field
Marshall'. His voice was strange. His KiSwahili accent showed he was from
the mainland, and his words of hate were those of a madman. Mama cried
with fear for her family, for Babu who had not returned. It was approaching
midday and still they could not get through to the *shamba*, although they

tried time and time again.

By this time, Basilah knew my story so she did not have to remind me of those days of madness. At some time in the afternoon, men hammered on the street door demanding entrance on the authority of the new Revolutionary Government—or they would burn down the door. They wanted our Baba and Babu, for 'they are imperialists of the ZNP'. These men would not accept the women's protestations that the men were not there, that only women remained in the house. Eventually, Mama felt compelled to open the door.

Several men rushed in. Running through the house, they threw furniture and papers around, and emptied all the cupboards while Basilah and Mama huddled with the servants. The portrait of the Sultan maddened the rebels. They tore it from the wall and smashed it: copies of the ZNP newspaper, *Mwongozi* or "*Guide*", were torn to shreds. They demanded that Mama tell them where the guns and weapons were. Although she said there were none, they did not believe her. They found an ancient ornamental sword belonging to Babu and took that. When they could not find the men of the house, they were even angrier, shouting and spitting in their faces.

'Where are they hiding? We will find them. Tell them Field Marshall Okello is coming. It is the end for you imperialists.'

These thugs told our servants to go home to their families and chased them from the house. They posted a guard on the street and ordered Basilah and Mama to leave the door open. Babu did not return: all day, they looked through the shuttered windows and worried as they feared for him.

Their phone calls brought no news of the family at the *shamba*: other news on the radio was terrible. They heard the Sultan had escaped and were saddened that he was forced to flee. Through it all, they did not know what to believe or what to do.

Worse awaited them. After dark, several men forced their way into our house. Of what happened then, Basilah could not speak, for the horror and shame were still with her. I held her hands as she wept uncontrollably as she must have wept countless times. The next morning, they were taken in by the Saeed family, their terrified neighbours, who had heard their screams. These kind people tended to them as best they could. Mama did not want to go to the hospital for they all knew by then what was happening in their country.

No news came of anyone else in the family: Mama could not speak about the attack on Basilah and herself and wanted to rush out to our *shamba.* But the Saeeds had heard Okello talking crazily on the radio telling his followers to take vengeance on people he called the Arabs. House-to-house searches, robbery and arrests took place over the next few days. Our house was stripped of its valuables: even furniture was stolen, leaving it in the condition that Baba Ali, Paka and I found days later.

After a few days with no news, only rumours of destruction and murder, Basilah, Mama and the neighbours believed there was little hope of finding Babu, Baba, Taha or me alive. In desperation, a son of the Saeed family offered to help although to do so was most dangerous. A week after the Revolution, he walked out to our old *shamba, Salama Daima,* to see what he could find.

'He saw the burnt ruins of our house and then he knew and was ready to run away,' Basilah said. 'A young boy came past and he asked the child what had happened. This child was also frightened but said the family of that house was killed during the *Mapinduzi.* He pointed towards the sea, said three people were buried there and that he would show him. The Saeed son followed and saw the three graves. When he came back and told Mama and me what he had seen, we were certain you had all died, that Baba, Taha and you were buried in those graves.'

'It was the grave of Amina,' I said.

'Yes. We could not imagine you had escaped,' said Basilah. 'Then the Saeed family decided they must leave. They had a share in a trading dhow which was in Mombasa Harbour. They contacted the captain and persuaded him to bring the boat to a beach south of Stone Town. One night, we all fled to Mombasa. What else could we do but go with them? The rest of our family had surely perished. The Saeeds were kind and cared for us.'

Basilah's dishonouring meant that contacting her betrothed was out of the question. In Mombasa, our family had remote cousins with whom they stayed hoping for news of Babu. Many Zanzibari people were already there, and a steady stream of families fled our islands as the violent ways of the Revolutionary Government were revealed.

In 1975, Mama passed away from a sudden heart attack. By that time, I was married with our first child. It pained me to think that she had been so close across the sea.

'Mama never was herself again: she had lost too much, and the shame and shock of the r-r-a-attack on me was too much for her,' Basilah said. 'She would weep constantly, refusing to get out of bed. At times, she was better and would play with the children in the house but those times were few and she never went out. Caring for her helped me survive through those early weeks and months. Mama had lost too much.'

This was how I learnt about my Mama's death. It was like a second death now I knew of its certainty, and I wept for the sadness of her lost life and the pain she had endured. It was a mercy Basilah had not fallen pregnant from the rape, as had happened to others.

After Mama's death, Basilah married a widower living in Mombasa, Jasmir Rashid. A man of kindness, she said. They left East Africa and moved to Egypt to live in Cairo, where her two children were born. Later, they moved again, to Muscat in Oman, and she had been there for fifteen years.

For two weeks, we spent the hours sharing the stories of our missing years. Basilah met my husband, Mujab, who was amazed that we had found each other and delighted with our happiness. Basilah then returned to Muscat but we had made plans for our future meetings.

40. House Troubles

Kwenda nawakati   To go with the times

2010

I arrived downstairs to find Paka dancing around in a pair of maroon slippers with shining sequins. She lifted her feet like a child overcome with joy.

'Fatima, see what I have found. These new shoes in the *dukas*. Different colours, like the rainbow. Come with me and I will show you.'

Paka had been out shopping, looking at the goods arriving in Stone Town. Even though she was over eighty she loved working in our clothing shop and having money to spare.

'How beautiful these are!'

'Yes, Paka, they look good on your little feet.'

We had become used to the shortages of the forty years that followed the Revolution and now we were amazed to see the shops full of clothes, shoes and food.

I could trust Paka and she was kind to people. However, she could not speak English, so when a European visited our shop, she would call up the stairs and I would come down from our workroom which had been moved upstairs. Mujab also now worked from our home. He had left the government Ministry of Finance and Economic Affairs and started his own bookkeeping business, calling it Assured Accounting.

One day early in 2010, Paka called me. I could hear urgency in her voice. 'Bibi Fatima, can you come? We have a visitor.'

In our front room by the racks of children's clothes, an elegant woman of Arab appearance was standing with her back to the window. I could not see her face properly. When I greeted her and moved closer, I noticed thick gold bracelets around both her fat wrists.

'Bibi, welcome to our shop. How can I help you?'

She turned towards me and I could see shock on her face. The woman was younger than I was but was so overweight that coils of fat lay like necklaces under her chin. Her pale face was carefully made up with bright lipstick: hoops of gold hung from her ears. Under her black shawl she wore a green silver-flecked silk shirt, tightly stretched across her body.

'You are ...?' She stopped and seemed surprised. Who was she expecting?

'Bibi Fatima. Welcome. Are you looking for children's clothes? I have new designs,' I said.

'No, Bibi Fatima,' she said. 'I am Bibi Zuha. I have business to discuss. Is this your *duka*?' The way Bibi Zuha had said *duka* was rude. She had not smiled and I was immediately concerned. I showed her to a chair and sat before her. Paka came to stand behind me. Bibi Zuha sat on the edge of her chair as if she did not want to stay long. I knew then this visitor was here to bring trouble.

'Bibi, your servant here says that this is your shop. Who do you pay rent to?'

I ignored her abrupt manner and rudeness to Paka. This woman showed us no respect or what we call *heshima*. *Heshima* is taught to us from childhood, and we say *Heshima kuheshimiana*. 'Courtesy is to respect each other'.

'Bibi Zuha, let me explain. I do not pay rent. My family lives here,' I replied. 'We have been here for over twenty years. And Bibi Paka is not a servant. She is a member of my family.'

I did not say it was my family house for that was my business, not hers.

'But, Bibi,' Zuha looked around, as if she was working it all out and did not believe me, 'this house belongs to the government.' She paused and placed her hands with gold rings and red nails on her knees. 'My husband and I have the authority to buy it.'

'That cannot be so,' I said, and anger flooded through me but I held my hands at rest in my lap. We had suffered much and it was time that it stopped. 'This house has belonged to my family for generations. It is the house of my Baba, my Babu and those before. How can it not belong to us?'

Bibi Zuha did not reply. She unzipped her black sling bag and took out a sheet of paper. This she thrust at me. I would have to get up to take it. I did not move and neither did she. She lowered the paper.

'That is not what the government papers show,' Bibi Zuha replied. 'This house was deserted by the owners at the time of the *Mapinduzi*. We have money and the government is allowing us to buy it. The shop can stay for a while but you cannot live here. I have come to tell you this.'

'No,' I said. 'How can we have deserted it? For I am here; I was born here and I have never left this island. My Baba was murdered, my brother was murdered but you can see me here. The government cannot steal it from us.'

'Times have changed,' she replied standing up and putting her paper back into her bag. 'Other rules are in place now. Why do you say it is stealing? It is the law.'

Bibi Zuha flung her shawl over her arm and I stood before her, preventing her from leaving.

'Bibi, let me tell you. Robbers came before and stole my family's possessions from this house,' I said. 'Is the government now going to be the new robber and steal the house itself? Is that what you have come to tell me?'

When she left without a word, I was shaking. 'Who are these people? How rude they are!'

'Sit, my child. I will call Mujab,' Paka said. 'What can we do if the government wants to take their money? The houses in Shangani are wanted now. The tourists are coming. Businessmen are opening shops and hotels. You can see all the building going on, new people arriving.'

'Paka, we will not let this happen. Bibi Zuha must go elsewhere and find a house that is falling down and fix it. She has come here because she can see we have kept this place well; it is painted and the roof is fixed. It is truly the best house in the square.'

Paka fetched Mujab from his office. My legs felt weak. I told him what had happened.

'Truly it is a problem. How can we prove this is your family house?' he said. 'I will go and speak to people I know in the Finance Department. Maybe they can advise us. Let us ask around to find out who this Bibi Zuha is.'

The next day Mujab went to discuss this matter with others. While he was gone, I was in the shop with Akila who was visiting from Oman with her two children. Akila lived in Muscat, not far from Basilah, with her husband, her son and daughter, my oldest grandchildren. She was qualified as a lawyer.

Someone knocked briefly and walked in. It was Bibi Zuha and behind her was a tall man. With amazement, I recognised Salim Hadir. He was older, but still carried himself with grace and a commanding air.

Bibi Zuha greeted me briefly, ignoring Akila who had come to stand beside me.

'Bibi Fatima, I have brought my husband, *Bwana* Hadir, to discuss these matters with you. He will tell you your position so you can understand the truth of what I told you yesterday. You must listen to him.' She stood aside and waved her husband over.

I turned to face Salim Hadir. He was not dressed in a traditional *kanzu* but wore European black trousers and an open-necked white shirt. I realised he was now a businessman coming to support his wife in their property dealings. At first, he looked around the shop and started to speak without really taking in those before him.

'I am sorry, Bibi, but it is as my wife ...' Then his eyes met mine and he stopped.

Although he bore himself as a man of power and position, I thought then that he had a sadness about him. He had become thickset, a big man. How had he lived since my life had so briefly crossed paths with his over forty-five years ago?

Salim Hadir struggled to find words. He looked at Bibi Zuha and back at me but she had not noticed his amazement, only his slowness in speaking.

'My husband, please tell these shopkeepers what is to happen,' she said. 'We are to buy this house. It is the law.'

'You are Bibi Fatima?' Hadir asked. He looked at me and our eyes met for a longer time. I could see the recognition and the memories in his face: the struggle there told of other things.

'Yes,' I said. 'My husband, Mujab, is not here. Would you like to wait for his return?'

Ignoring this, Hadir said, 'You told my wife this was your family house. Who were your family?'

'*Bwana* Hadir, my Baba was Ahmed bin Khaleed al-Ibrahim and my Mama, Amal bint Yusuf. My Baba and brother were killed during the *Mapinduzi* and my Mama and sister disappeared. My Babu lived here in this house, his house, our family house. He was attacked in the *Mapinduzi* and passed away in the hospital shortly afterwards. I was twelve. I was the only one to survive.'

If they were to steal this house from us, they would not do so without knowing the full story.

Bibi Zuha started to speak but, without looking at her, Hadir raised his hand. 'I was not living here then; I was in Mombasa with my family,' he said, 'but we knew about the killings. Why was this house declared abandoned?'

'It was dangerous. I was in hiding and a child. What could I do?'

'And now,' he said, waving his hand at the racks of children's clothes, 'this is your business?'

'Yes. My husband runs his business from here as well. He is an accountant.'

I was proud to say this. We had achieved much.

Bibi Zuha could not understand. She realised she had missed something. 'Anyway,' she said, 'we are sorry, but the records show ...'

'It is better,' interrupted Hadir, 'Bibi Zuha, for you to go now, go home. I will speak to Bibi Fatima and her husband. To you I will explain later. There has been a mistake with this property.'

Bibi Zuha could do nothing as we waited in silence. So she left but not before she gave her husband a fierce look. Akila, who had said nothing during this conversation, now spoke. 'Please, *Bwana* Hadir, will you sit? Would you like some coffee?'

'Please,' he said. 'Thank you. This is your daughter? She is like you.'

I knew there was a great difference between us, and that was right, for Akila had grown up in a different world. Akila left to make coffee. I was glad to hear Mujab arriving outside, and greeting his Baba who was sitting on the shady side of the *baraza*.

'I see that you still collect books.' Hadir pointed at the long shelves of books behind the counter.

'Yes, they have always given me pleasure.'

And as Mujab entered, he said so quietly only I heard, 'And so might I have.'

I could not reply and luckily for me, Mujab entered so my confusion was not noticed. Akila arrived with coffee. Salim Hadir introduced himself as a 'businessman from Mombasa'.

He apologised, looking at Mujab, 'There has been a misunderstanding. Now I know how it is, what happened to you and your family, I would like to help you.'

How times had changed. I could see that Mujab was a little surprised. Akila handed Hadir his coffee. We waited as he sipped his *kahawa* from the tiny white and blue china cup.

'Let me go back and explain the situation,' Hadir said. 'Shortly after the *Mapinduzi*, the Revolutionary Council appointed a committee to take charge of nationalising houses. It was not done in an ordered fashion. If a family owned a few homes, all but one might be nationalised. If the owners had fled, all the properties were taken. Each one was meant to be listed in the government gazette but some were not.'

'Was compensation paid to the owners?' asked Mujab.

'No,' said Hadir. 'They got nothing. It was regarded as the confiscation of the property of the wealthy and those in opposition to the Afro-Shirazi Party. Papers were sometimes signed, sometimes not. Few dared complain. You will know how families from *shambas* were then moved into these houses. Most of those families were poor and over the years no maintenance was done.'

I remembered hearing how President Karume hated Stone Town and the years when our houses were empty and no one wanted to live there.

'What about *wakf* or charity properties?' I asked. 'Were they left alone?'

'No,' replied Hadir. 'I am afraid most were taken over as well. Some were left for housing for the poor. The problem is they also have not been looked after.'

Hadir spoke slowly and firmly. He was a man used to others listening to him.

'It is more than forty-five years. A long time. I was a young man, on the mainland. It was a shock to all of us to see this happen,' Hadir continued. 'Now, the world has changed, business is back and people are forgetting they wanted socialism. The young people want education, work, to be able to travel. All these things. It is natural. Zanzibar has been discovered again. You will know how the tourists have arrived.'

'And Stone Town houses are seen as valuable for hotels and businesses,' said Mujab.

'Yes, that is so. Only some, for others are filled with poor people and the houses are slowly collapsing. The ones wanted are those with a view, or in a good position for shopping, on a busy street.'

Akila had been listening to our discussion. 'Excuse me, sir, can you tell me why the *wakf* property endowments were not honoured?'

I smiled for I could see that Hadir was surprised by Akila's question.

'Bibi Akila, I cannot answer that. It was a time of change. I was a young man then and everything was turned upside down. Nothing was valued; nothing was preserved,' Hadir said. 'You will know how the truth of that time has been changed as well.'

It went without saying that our house was desirable for its location and fine condition. Where did that leave us? Hadir was coming to this.

'I myself am looking for a property to expand my businesses in

Zanzibar,' Hadir said. 'I have a business in fishing as well as importing electrical products. So I went to the State Department and that was how I was told about this house.

'I think you must act before someone else tries to buy your house. Look at the original confiscation—was it because the house was empty, or because it was specifically expropriated? I would like to help you if I can. I know people in that department. The word *maendeleo* is everywhere now. All want progress; they are tired of being poor compared to the coast.'

'Thank you for your words,' said Mujab. 'This is a shock. This house means a lot to us, to my wife. It gives her comfort in her memories of the time before the *Mapinduzi*.'

He was right. This house was my centre, our family's safe place where we came home and felt contented. After all these years, the Revolution continued to cloud our lives and injustice was carved into our town. We would fight to stay here. It represented our survival as a family. I wondered if Salim Hadir was suggesting that bribery was the way to secure the house from business development and tourism.

Salim Hadir and Mujab arranged that they would go and see if the State Planning Office would change the status of our house once they heard that Mujab had married the original owner and we lived here. But how could we prove that the house was in fact my family house? I had no title to prove anything.

That evening, I went alone to say my prayers. I prayed for forgiveness, *astaghfirullah*. Afterwards, I felt peace come upon me. I knew what I had to do. I asked Mujab to join me on the rooftop after sunset.

'You have planned to go with Salim Hadir to the State Planning Office?' I asked.

'Yes,' he said. 'I will request a change in the status of our house. The sooner we do this the better.'

'There is something I need to tell you.' I told him what had happened before I married him. I told him about my dancing in the rain, the two letters that came from Hadir and the gift of the necklace, and the advice Cecilia gave me. 'I have not seen Hadir since that day the rain came. Not till today have I ever spoken to him.'

It was right for him to know: it was strange how I felt guilty although I had done nothing wrong—unless it was a mistake to not tell Mujab until now. It seemed such a little thing and yet now it was complicated.

'It does not surprise me,' Mujab said, 'for you were and are a beautiful woman, and some might wonder why you married me.' He was thoughtful, I could see that. What man wants to hear that another desired his wife and possibly still does? 'Let us think about this,' he continued. 'Maybe it is better I go alone, for now I do not want to go with *Bwana* Hadir. I have some advice from the Finance Department and that might help.'

Mujab was saddened. But what could I do to make it right again? It was never going to be easy. In silence, we watched the bats wheeling in the sky as dark shadows above our home.

'I have been told that in 1964, they had two presidential decrees,' Mujab said. 'The first one was in March and allowed confiscation of property on the order of President Abeid Karume. Compensation was only payable if "undue hardship" would be caused thereby. Later that year, another decree was announced. This added the clause that any Minister could sign property confiscation orders. Any Minister. You can imagine what happened then.'

'They took what they wanted?'

'Yes. They enriched themselves,' said Mujab. 'My old friend at the Finance Department told me two other things. One is by way of background. Before the Revolution, in 1963, the British organised a gathering in London under their guidance. All our political parties, the ASP, the ZNP and the ZPPP attended. They were to agree on the new constitution for independent Zanzibar. During the discussions, Abeid Karume, leader of the ASP, insisted on protecting private property. My friend gave me a copy of the old text. How he had it, I do not know. It says that there will be "prompt payment of compensation in the case of property which has to be nationalised for the public interest".'

'Yet he totally disregarded this when he came to power,' I said.

'Yes. That constitution was thrown away by the revolutionaries. Zanzibar did not have another constitution till 1979.'

'And the second thing you were told?'

'This is interesting. Our new constitution of 1984 included a Human Rights Charter. This lists our rights, and one of them protects private property. Compensation is payable if property is taken from you for the good of the people. Families who had houses and farms taken from them in 1964 now thought it meant compensation would be paid, or they would get their properties back. But no! The government said it was from 1984 onwards. It did not change the past.'

'So what can we do now?'

'I do not know,' said Mujab. 'Surely we can say you were left an orphan in 1964. It would be "undue hardship" to have taken your home from you, since the *shamba* was taken as well. We have not been paying rent here for many years which might be an argument that we did not pay because it was your home anyway. On the other hand, we need to get records, of your birth, your Baba's birth. Any family records we can find. If we can. I think that is what we must do.'

'Maybe Akila can represent us?' I said.

'Of course, our daughter is a lawyer! We must tell her this story but let us wait before asking her.'

'I agree,' I said. 'She has been in her new job as a junior lawyer only four months.'

'Yes, we will do this because it is right,' said Mujab. 'There has been too much stealing and taking of houses. It must stop.'

And so we were together and we would not give up easily.

Five months later, Mujab and I were struggling in our efforts. We sent a message to Akila in Muscat asking her to phone us in the evening.

'I was worried when I got your message, Mama,' she said. 'I thought Baba or Babu Ali was ill.'

'We are all well, my daughter. We need your advice, your legal advice.' I explained the situation with our home. 'We have tried to get records but there are none. All I have is my birth certificate listing the hospital, my Mama and Baba. Thankfully your Baba got that many years ago. There are no other records in Mambo Msiige.'

'Why? What about Basilah and your Baba, your Mama.' Akila asked.

'Nothing. They say they are all lost.'

'And the house record? There could be records of services provided such as telephone and electricity.'

'Again nothing. They say it is a long time ago and since there have been many Presidents, they don't have proper records.'

'So there is no record of the al-Ibrahim family owning your house?'

'There is nothing, Akila, nothing.'

There was a pause on the phone line and I thought of how far away she was and how I missed my child even though she was a grown woman.

'This is what you must do, Mama,' said Akila. 'You must get affidavits from everyone who knew it was our family house: Baba, Bibi Paka, Aunt

Basilah and yourself. The affidavit must say as much as possible and you must get it drawn up by a lawyer and witnessed. I will send you an example of the things you must say.'

'And what do we do with them?'

'Once they are lodged with the police, you take copies to the department concerned.'

'That is the Department of Planning,' I said.

'Make an appointment with the head of the department.' Akila said, 'and get receipts for all the documents you give them. I think I should come home and help.'

'No, you have only been there a little while. Come and visit when you have holidays. Let us see how we go. Maybe with the affidavits they will be satisfied.'

But somehow I knew they would not be satisfied with our statements. I walked through the rooms of my home until I came to the rooftop overlooking the sea. Each room spoke to me of my life, my childhood before the Revolution and then my time as a mama and businesswoman. It was home to Mujab and our children, to Baba Ali, Paka and Baba Ali's children—Jannah, her husband and sons, and Subira when she came back to Stone Town. We were fighting for all of them, for our family.

Section 3. Elizabeth. The Search

41. Memories

January 2010. Liverpool, UK

Greenhaven Residential Home, on the western green fringe of Liverpool, had been rated for the services and standard of care provided. It was purportedly amongst the best, yet to Elizabeth Hamilton it appeared a place of the barest survival, a waiting room until life had finished. This was where her father was now living.

Elizabeth booked into a traditional British pub for her ten-day visit to Liverpool. The Rising Sun had four en-suite bedrooms under the low eaves of its eighteenth century roof. She was the only guest. The pub was next door to Greenhaven and catered for its visitors. An iron-grey gravel pathway led across the lawn through a leafless avenue of oaks to a door with a brass plaque marked 'Reception'. Light rain was falling from the leaden sky as she walked there to visit her father.

The reception area had a low ceiling; the room was airless and over-warm, the walls painted lavender lilac. A large bowl of pastel artificial roses sat on a lace doily by the office window. She had not realised that even plastic flowers could droop. On the wall, next to a white interior door was a framed Mission Statement. Elizabeth read the first line.

'Our mission at Greenhaven is to provide quality care for our residents in comfortable accommodation, through a commitment to central values of privacy, dignity, independence, choice, rights and fulfilment.'

A large white-coated woman looked up from behind a computer screen. Elizabeth asked for Mr Hamilton. It was obvious that she was interrupting something.

'I'm Miss Broad, Assistant Manager,' the woman said pointing to her chest and a red plastic name tag in large letters. 'Is he expecting you, dear?'

'I'm his daughter.'

'Oh, good. I've met your sister. She was here last month. Mary? Yes. She phones regularly. Mr Hamilton will be pleased you've come. He doesn't get many visitors. You won't have long today. Dinner's in an hour.'

She pushed a clipboard with a lined register form across the counter. She had written Hamilton in block letters in the Resident column.

'Please sign here, and make sure you fill in time of entry and don't forget to sign out when you leave.' Miss Broad tapped each column as she spoke.

Elizabeth wondered if working in such a home sucked the kindness out of you. Miss Broad disappeared for a moment and unlocked the white door from the inside. The glass in the door was opaque. Like a prison, she thought. Once in, you're on the list, and it's hard to escape. Elizabeth's heart ached recognising that here her father would end his life.

'Your father is settling in, Miss Hamilton,' Miss Broad said over her shoulder as they walked. 'Takes a while for the old dears to get used to our routine. He's travelled, has he not? Loves to tell stories about faraway places.'

Elizabeth said nothing and Miss Broad continued without encouragement. The corridor was lined with waist-high rails, and as they passed by the numbered doors, she caught glimpses of inmates watching their passage.

Her father had been waiting. He struggled to stand, and the delight on his face wrenched her heart. She hugged him and his arms came round her, and she felt his spine and ribs, his head against her shoulder. He did not let go first. She had visited him two years ago and he had not changed much: his face still pitted and creased, his frame slightly more bent, his nose more beak-like. Our bodies hold us upright for but a little while, she thought.

She scanned the room. It was not much bigger than a large closet. An iron-framed single bed with a plain red quilt was set up along most of one wall. On the opposite side was an opening to a tiny bathroom. A flat-screen TV faced the bed and next to it was a two-tiered pine bookcase and a small wardrobe. A bedside table and two chairs facing away from the door completed the furnishings. A dim light entered from double windows. The view was over a low hedge down into a field where a herd of cows stood solidly in a line, their backs to the rain.

'I'll ask the kitchen to bring you both a cuppa, my dear,' said Miss Broad as she closed the door.

They sat side-by-side and talked of inconsequential stuff: the minutiae of travelling and arriving. Tea arrived in two thick white mugs, a single ginger biscuit on each saucer.

'In the cupboard, Elizabeth,' he said, 'there are chocolate biscuits. My secret stash. Better than these teeth breakers. Chuck 'em in the bin.' He smiled with glee.

'I'm lucky,' said her father as he dunked his biscuit and sucked at it noisily.

'Lucky?' she was caught out.

'To have a view from my room,' he replied. 'On the other side, those oldies face into the quadrangle. It depends what becomes available. A waiting list.'

Elizabeth stared out the window. Her father had always faced life head-on, uncompromising, even here.

'What can you see?' he said.

The scene had barely changed.

'Can you describe it?' He reached out to her. His hand was skeletal, the taut skin translucent, lumpy blue veins traced between his knuckles.

'The rain's stopping,' she said. 'It's getting dark. The trees across the meadow are misting over. Cows, those black and white ones, Frieslands I think, are moving, heads down, all in a bunch. It must be milking time. Can you hear the birdsong?'

It was so sweet to see it and to think how the wet grass would feel on her bare feet, and how the heaviness of the cows' bodies would be in the green, how they would watch her with those soft trusting eyes. There was more to life in that field than in her father's room.

A clink of crockery came from the corridor. Dinner was scheduled for a quarter past five; the smell of boiled cauliflower and brisket permeated through the ventilation system. Except under special circumstances the residential home was closed to visitors from the evening meal onwards. One part of her already longed to escape.

'No, not with the window closed and double glazing. They don't like us to open them but, if I'm taken outside, I can hear crows. Maybe, can you open it a little?'

Elizabeth slid the window back, standing beside the curtain and taking deep breaths. The staleness in the room was released, sucked out by the winter air.

'Your crows are marching behind the herd of cows and there's a flock of magpies flying across, seven I think. What's that saying about magpies?' she said.

The saying came to her: one for sorrow, two for joy, three for a girl, four for a boy, five for silver, six for gold and seven for a secret never to be told. *A secret never to be told*. That was so, that is so.

'That's better. Smells fresh. My sight,' he said. He rubbed his eyes. 'When I look, there's a shadow. I only see blurred shapes around the edges.'

Which was better if you had a choice, she wondered, your mind going or your body collapsing in slow degrees? Both ways of sliding towards death seemed miserable. She recalled lines from Dylan Thomas, *'Old age should burn and rage at close of day./Rage, rage, against the dying of the light ...'* Once they had meant little but now that she was approaching sixty, they were a painful reminder.

'You see that picture on the wall?' He indicated behind her chair. 'I want you to take it with you when you go. Take it tonight.'

It was a small oil painting glowing with colour in the dim light. It was the seafront of Zanzibar's Stone Town viewed from offshore. White stone buildings and red roofs were reflected in the ripples of a calm sea. To the right, stood the distinctive clock tower of the House of Wonders, the Beit-el-Ajaib, on the upper floors of which her father had had his office. The sun was bright over it all. She knew it so well. It was etched into her memory. That was how it was on that last terrible day, Revolution day, over forty-five years ago.

'Thank you. Will it be OK with Cynthia?'

'It's mine to give.'

A ball of pain sat like bile in her throat. She lifted the picture off the wall.

'Can I have a last look?' he said.

Her father held it close to his face and he appeared to look to one side and she realised he was using his peripheral vision. He lowered it to his lap and placed his fingers on the picture.

'I can see the blue of the sea! Remember how warm it was?'

Elizabeth noticed only one picture was left. No sign of photos of Mary or herself, only the large photo of the handsome head and bare shoulders of Cynthia smiled down on them. It was taken when she looked thirty, years before meeting her father. It depicted a sensual woman assured of her attractiveness to men. Other attributes that Elizabeth read into the image were overlaid by her own experience of her stepmother.

'We have a few days,' her father said. 'Come early. I don't sleep much, off and on. Morning time, I'm at my best. I need to ask you something, to do something for me.'

A carer entered without knocking. She had rolled-up sleeves revealing powerful arms, a polka-dot cap over her hair, and with her came the smell of boiled vegetables.

'Dinner time, Mister Mark. It's ready now. I've come to take you.

Bathroom first. Oh, we mustn't open windows, dear. I'll shut it right away.'

Her father turned to Elizabeth as the carer squeezed past them and pushed the window until it clicked closed.

'Elizabeth, please, take the picture now. For you, to remember.'

She pressed her hand over his. 'Thank you. I'll take good care of it.'

The carer turned to lead her father to dinner. Elizabeth waited, watching his skeletal form move slowly down the corridor until they turned into the residents' dining room and vanished. A hand seemed to squeeze her heart.

Elizabeth pulled on her winter coat and went out into the January gloom holding the picture tight against her body under her breasts. The avenue of dripping oaks was a tunnel of cool dampness. The residential home was worse than she had imagined. Where now was her father's escape route, the 'Plan B' he had always advised? His military view of the world required you to consider all possible methods of escape from your situation.

She had come for a visit from her home in Sydney, Australia, a final request from her father. Cynthia, her stepmother, had rung her. She had instantly recognised the imperious, dispassionate voice.

'Darling, we haven't spoken for a while. I hope you're well?' Not pausing for an answer. 'Your father is waiting to talk to you. Speak louder, dear, his hearing is a little poor.'

She had made a few visits to them over the last years. Cynthia didn't make an effort to keep up contact. In fact, sabotage might be closer to the description of her attitude.

'Elizabeth, is it you Elizabeth?' Her father's familiar voice. It had surprised her how tears had leapt into her eyes.

'Yes, Dad, it's me.'

He wanted to see her. Cynthia could no longer care for him and had arranged for him to move into a residential home. It was time. They both knew what he meant.

42. The Safe Box

January 2010. Liverpool, UK

'You'll want the full breakfast?' said the rotund proprietor of the Rising Sun when Elizabeth came down next morning into the empty pub. The room was permeated with the sour-sweet smell of spilt alcohol which no amount of mopping and lemon-scented oil would remove. 'It's included: bacon, fried eggs, sausages, the lot.'

She was about to demur when his wife came through. 'There's a call for you, Ms Hamilton. It's Greenhaven. Your father. He's agitated. They say, can you come over as soon as possible?'

The rain was steady with the wind behind it: by the time she arrived at reception, her coat was soaked. Unsmiling, Miss Broad was waiting for her in the foyer, and immediately started unlocking the interior door, talking over her shoulder.

'He won't listen. We found him on the floor, hardly a thing on. He's tearing papers up. Keeps asking for you. Shouting at us. It's upsetting our other residents.' She waved Elizabeth on when she paused by the register. 'Oh, you can sign in later.'

Once more Miss Broad led her but this time it was at a run. Several residents were holding onto their door frames, peering up and down the corridor. At the entrance to her father's room, a white-clad woman was waiting. She turned towards them.

'You his daughter? Elizabeth? Thank the Lord. He's shouting for you. Quite unreasonable this morning. Won't calm down. We were going to call the doctor.' The nurse stood aside.

Her father was sitting on the floor between his two chairs, his back to the window. Around his bare shoulders was a tartan rug; his skull shone tender-white in the pale light. He looked like a Hindu sage, removed from all dealing with life and death, but his demeanour was anything but calm. He was surrounded by a muddle of paper—lined pages covered in his fine scrawl, photographs glued on pages torn from an old scrapbook and paper-clipped sheaves of old newspapers. He looked up at her.

'Elizabeth,' he cried. 'Elizabeth. It is you. I thought you'd gone. I thought you'd left.'

'No, Dad, I'm here, staying next door. What's wrong? What happened?'

'Come here. I need you to see. I can't see.'

She crouched down next to him, making space amongst the papers. 'Calm down, Dad.'

'Yes, yes,' he said. 'I need you to help. Only you can help me with this. I have this dream, I saw him. I saw him in his *kanzu*.'

From the doorway, the nurse said, 'I'll bring you both some tea.'

'What is it, Dad? What's this about? Who did you see?'

'Look at this,' he said, 'all this. I wanted to see if he was in any of these pictures.'

Her father pushed the scrapbook towards her. Newspapers and photographs were stuck onto its torn pages, yellow with age.

'Zanzibar Revolution,' she said.

'Yes, Angela put this together. All the press reports.'

Elizabeth looked at the press headings: 'Armed Uprising in Zanzibar— British, US Warships at the Ready as Rebels Take Over Govt'; 'Bloodbath in Zanzibar: At Least 80 Killed'; 'Sultan Never to be Allowed Back'; 'This Troubled Island'.

The nurse knocked gently and brought in a tray with two mugs of tea.

'This will make you feel better, Mr Hamilton,' she said. 'Let's get you up and into something warm.'

Her father was lifted into his chair and allowed himself to be dressed. He sipped the pale tea.

'Sorry about that,' he said. 'I couldn't sleep till early this morning and then I had this ... dream. I'm not sure ... Strange, I could see ... see. I was there, through it all. And I thought I saw him, my friend, in this room, standing here, smiling at me, so calm, like it was *that* day again, and I knew I had to make it right.

'I need your help. Will you help me?' He leant towards her, and she took his hand. His fingers were trembling.

Elizabeth had no idea what was worrying him but she murmured 'of course'. Perhaps his night-time vision was a reaction to giving her the picture the evening before. She should bring it back.

'Close the door, please.' His hand was fluttering in hers. 'On the shelf by the TV,' he said, 'there's a book about Zanzibar. Can you give it to me?' She found it, a book covered in brown linen, *Zanzibar: Background to Revolution* written in gold on the spine. She laid it on the tartan rug, now covering his lap. He turned it around before opening it and took out papers slotted in between the pages. Without comment, he handed her two photographs.

One was a colour image taken from the sea off the Zanzibar seafront, not of the famous public buildings shown in the oil painting, but of the area she knew that extended to the right, south of the House of Wonders. It depicted the long house called Mambo Msiige and the beach at Ras Shangani. Blue sky above matched the blue sea below, and the buildings floated in the middle. The colour was faded. It was taken either from a coloured slide or using one of the first colour cameras.

Involuntarily she said, 'It's Mambo Msiige and our house.'

A moment of silence followed as she remembered the squeaky white sand, sprinting to the waves with the sun on her back, the cold rush of diving and the silence beneath the translucent waters. She was brought back to the present by the clatter of something metal being dropped in the corridor outside.

'Ah, yes,' he said, and handed her the second photo. It was a black and white formal photo of her parents. Her father stood behind her mother and had a hand on her shoulder. It seemed as if they had shared a joke, for unforced smiles were captured on their faces.

'I should have acted years ago,' her father said. 'I'm sorry to land my weakness on you but you're young and have courage. As the years passed, I knew it was important to try and do something about this matter. I felt there would be time. Life was busy, then I became tired and even then I might have done it, but then this.'

He gestured to his eyes. 'I thought it was enough to forget. To grow old and forget in the routine of living. But this dream, seeing him! The *mganga* would say it was his message, reminding me. Now, I have to ask if you will take my responsibility into your hands. If you can, go, see if it is possible, resolve it one way or the other. Please try. If not, that is my guilt.' He patted the scrapbook with this hand, head bowed. 'My guilt.'

It was his unfinished business. For some years, he'd hinted about an outstanding issue relating to their departure from Zanzibar. She was aware she'd glossed over those hints. What was he asking? God forbid, she had enough guilt to deal with. Maybe, she thought, there is a coming to account at the end of life, if you have time.

'I gave myself an excuse. I might have acted earlier but until about 1995 and the opening up of the island, it would have been hard to get a visa,' he said. 'They had listed me as "undesirable", due to my support of the old government, and we were Westerners. Your mother's death and then Cynthia stopped me too. Cynthia was always jealous of Zanzibar, even my stories, even my furniture. It was your mother's time. She didn't want to visit Zanzibar any more than she wanted to get my carpets out of storage. I left it all locked away. Now it comes back.'

'What are you asking me, exactly?' Elizabeth asked, hoping it was a simple act of nostalgia. A casting of ashes, or a visit to a grave.

He sighed. 'On the day of the Revolution, I hid things in our house by the sea; a box. Some were our things; others belonged to a local family. Valuables.'

She considered this: it seemed illogical. 'Why didn't Mum collect the box when she went back to pack up?' Elizabeth said. 'You weren't allowed to go back but Mum did. She rescued our clothes, furniture, even my kiddy toys.'

'It wasn't that simple. I wasn't sure what was in the box and we weren't allowed to take valuables. If she was found with something sensitive, there would have been trouble. I only guessed what my friend had left with me— now those are the guesses of an old man alone. Then, I was in the middle of things and every day the rules changed.

'When your mother was leaving through Zanzibar airport, all her bags were turned upside down and emptied out in the departure hall. The place was bristling with men who'd been given their first gun the week before. Told to seize what they wanted. They were in charge. I might have taken the risk but I couldn't saddle her with it. When she was there packing up, the house phone was cut off, so although I never forgot, I did nothing.'

'And what is in this box?' Elizabeth said.

'I don't know,' he said. 'Did you ever ask yourself what you would try to save from your burning house? My Arab friend brought me this package, prized things. He trusted me. He would've come for them if he could. Maybe he did and found no one there. Maybe he came after your mother left and found the house empty, deserted. Either way, I had the feeling they were his most precious possessions.'

43. A Request

January, 2010. Liverpool, UK

Her father was calmer next day. The nurse met her outside his room.

'I should have introduced myself yesterday, Miss Hamilton. I'm Mrs Henderson,' she pointed to the badge on her lapel. 'Mr Hamilton is better today, calmer. We are keeping an eye on him. The doctor is coming to assess his needs for further medication.'

'He won't want to be subdued,' said Elizabeth. Her father had heard her voice and was calling out. 'Mrs Henderson, may I speak to you later?'

Her father wanted to take a walk. 'When it rains like this, I have a route through the sitting rooms. I've got up to four times around, morning and afternoon; soon I'll make it five times. Let me take your arm and this stick and we can do the circuit. Talk as we go.'

Her father was eighty-eight, and he was still a good walker. Holding her arm tight, with a stick in his other hand, he led her slowly through two sitting rooms that flanked an internal courtyard. At the end, they could turn back through the dining room past the kitchen. The lounge rooms were lined with armchairs covered in grey and black brocade. In one corner, an immense TV broadcast a cooking demonstration to the half-empty rows of chairs and wheelchairs lined up in front of it. The residents were predominantly women. A few looked up but no one greeted them.

'It won't be so bad in summer,' he said. 'I can walk outside then. There's a rose garden and I'm told they let us walk down the driveway.

'Zanzibar,' he said. 'It's time to talk about Zanzibar. Finally you get a perspective. I realise Britain, impoverished by the war, wanted out of her Empire. She no longer had the will to rule and also the USA put pressure on her to get out.'

'Dad, you don't have to speak so loud, I can hear you.' Elizabeth noticed conversation had stopped in the sitting rooms. They were being watched. But her father was not concerned.

'Well, to begin with, we were thinking twenty-five years at least before handover. We knew it was coming but expected we'd have time to establish a framework for democracy and to work towards it with the locals. And then, suddenly, bingo! We were told, as soon as possible, hand over!

'Duncan Sandys, the British Foreign Minister, came to Zanzibar in '62 and we expected a fiery meeting with local political leaders. A man called

Mohamed Babu, intelligent, very angry, led the charge for freedom.'

Her father tapped on the window as if calling to attention an invisible audience and then turned to face the room. He raised his fist making an effort to stand tall. Then he stabbed the air with his stick, swaying slightly.

'"*Uhuru* NOW," he shouted. '*Uhuru* was the local cry. No waiting! But a surprise—Sandys stopped them in their tracks. He put up his hands and said, "All right, you can have *Uhuru*. Right now, we'll work out steps towards independence." I was there, I saw it all.'

All eyes were on them. A carer appeared at the lounge room door and waited.

'Shall we go through and sit in the dining room for a moment and then walk on?' Elizabeth said. Her father didn't pause in his recollections as they took their seats.

'So, instead of twenty-five years, we had eighteen months to get out! Ghana had been one of the first to gain independence, '57 I think, and their President, Kwame Nkrumah, was an instant hero across Africa. The rush was on!

'In all these political machinations, as a local official, you know but little of what is going on at head office. We were on the front line getting Zanzibar ready for democracy. And we tried, honestly tried. Frankly, you can read all the books and get a doctorate trying to understand what happened. Bottom line is, of course, we failed, and failed badly. It's hard to face, and I have contemplated this for over forty-five years.'

It was hard to see her father regarding the most important job of his life as a failure. She had been proud of him, of his promotion to the position as top political advisor leading up to the day of independence. Independent Zanzibar was launched with much fanfare. She had seen the pictures. Standing beside the young Sultan were rows of visiting dignitaries. Planes clogged the one-runway airport. Even Prince Philip had attended, representing the handover by Britain. The Union Jack had been lowered at midnight, and the new flag raised. Next day after much handshaking, the British Resident sailed away on the Royal Navy's *HMS Ark Royal*.

Those had been heady times and yet only a month later it all unravelled in an orgy of violence.

'So much against us,' her father continued. 'One side against the other: mainlander and Zanzibari, African and Arab, landowner and peasant, wealthy and poor. The critical thing was that the two main parties were divided almost fifty-fifty. The winning party in Zanzibar narrowly won several constituencies giving them more seats but they polled fewer votes in total than the losing party. Same thing happened in the USA in 2000. The Afro-Shirazi Party called "foul" and accused us of conspiracy. It became their main excuse for violence. They were not prepared to wait. Winner takes all!'

A bright-faced young woman entered the dining room carrying a tray. 'This is where you are, Mr Hamilton. I could hear you. You look happy having your daughter here. Here's your morning pills and water and I brought you both a cuppa tea.'

Her father's face lit up. 'Yes, Tamara, this is Elizabeth. Tamara is a ray of sunshine here. Looks after me. Always kind.'

They sipped their tea in silence. She could hear the TV, now on a quiz show with bursts of clapping, and the clink of crockery. We cannot change the past, she thought. How we long to sometimes, trying to work out how horror might have been averted by a fluke of fortune, a kind intercession, wisdom not yet granted. Yet nowadays who cared about what happened in 1964 on a small African island?

The story was etched in her father's mind as if it had happened the day before. He must have thought about it for years, trying to rework events, to understand, to change the outcome. He could parcel out his life leading up to this event and the time afterwards. Revolution day lasted more than any other day.

Her father seemed to be watching her. His blue eyes were rimmed in red with large black pupils.

'Can you see me at all?'

'Sort of,' he said. 'If I look to the right, I can see you on the side, but I can't make out details. Can't read, of course but can write in a fashion.

'Let me go on. I want you to hear this again, to know it all. It will be the last time. We, the administrators, tried to find this common understanding shortly after the final election. We had meetings to form a government of unity between the main parties. I remember we were even in the process of allocating out political prizes—various top jobs. Our plans failed. Why? A major fault line. They couldn't agree on the flag. The opposition didn't want red, or images of the clove buds that had once made Zanzibar so wealthy. Why not red? It reminded them of the Sultan's flag. History was their weapon. I remember one of the negotiating team was so overcome with anger, he was incoherent when speaking. We stumbled at the first negotiating hurdle.

'Do you remember any of this, my dear? Do you think about it?'

'Bits and pieces,' she said. 'Some events stand out clearly.' Elizabeth had her own reasons for forgetting. She was not going to burden him with Mary's and her story. In terms of murder and genocide it was of little consequence and yet it had changed her life, and it had been hidden too long.

'We had no army in Zanzibar and I am sorry to say this, the British failed us. I suppose, what was Zanzibar? An insignificant player on the world stage. The Cold War, Suez Crisis and concern about President Abdel Nasser and the rise of Arab nationalism were issues. The British Government had refused to sign a mutual defence pact with the independent Zanzibar Government— the one they had helped create! Secondly, and most tragically, on the day of the Revolution, when we appealed to them for help, they refused. The new government of Zanzibar really believed Britain would help. A bitter blow.

'Later, I found out that British HQ in Aden contacted our High Commissioner and asked if British subjects were being attacked or threatened. He said, "No!" That decided them. Who knows what conversations went on behind closed doors?'

'I suppose,' she said, 'that decision is responsible for the deaths of thousands.'

'Yes. It was. In such times, things unravel fast. People get killed for being in the wrong place at the wrong time. Often just luck. Go this way, not that. It's Sunday, so you decide to go to church and find yourself at a crossroads in Stone Town at daybreak. A rebel gang is there. Your car is shot up and your son is killed.'

Bending forward, he rubbed his hands together. 'I don't like to dwell on such memories now. I am old and it's painful. But once I start, it's a floodgate.'

'On the boat, the *Salama*,' she said, 'what happened there?'

'The *Salama* was too small. Desperate people kept arriving. So we arranged a transfer to the *Seyyid Khalifa*, a larger steamer. Revolutionaries started to fire at us. No one was hit but few locals escaped to us after that. It's hard to know exactly what happened but from the boat we were still calling for help from the mainland.

'In the afternoon, we got a message from Cross, the British High Commissioner, and Small, the British Permanent Secretary, that we shouldn't continue to ask for military help as they were helping the legitimate government to negotiate with Abeid Karume and the rebels. I was amazed!

This was barely twelve hours after it had started.'

Her father paused. 'Forgetting is hard. As I've aged, it's worried me more. There's been a long time in between but now these memories are strong.'

'If the Ministers had got to the *Salama*, would the outcome have been any different?' Elizabeth asked.

'Well, they wouldn't have had the humiliation of being paraded before John Okello and his thugs. They wouldn't have spent years and years in prison. Would they have been persuaded to resign in favour of the opposition? I wonder. Why did Henry Small, one of our British Permanent Secretaries, ask to work for Karume, a usurper, within hours of the Revolution? I fear something was going on there.

'I hand it to Karume. He did try to stop the killing unleashed by Okello and his gangs. It was too late. Most of those gangs were not Zanzibaris. People called them *wabara*, outsiders or mainlanders. Some called them 'Makonde'. In his book, Okello said he could not trust Zanzibaris to be part of his uprising.'

Elizabeth placed her hand on her father's right hand to quieten its fluttering.

'But it's over; it was a long time ago. You did your best. You could do no more. You were loyal to the government and your conscience. Now you must forgive yourself. With hindsight, we can all be wiser.'

'Maybe,' he said, 'but it has worried me. It's time to leave this matter. For long years, I've thought about these things. Lastly, I come to the box.'

He drank a little, using his left hand to steady his glass.

'Yes, the box. During that terrible morning, after you left for the launch, a neighbour came to our door. He was a Zanzibari Arab friend of mine, about your age now, around sixty. He'd tried to get through on the phone. He was running a risk. Gangs had started coming into Stone Town. He knew about the fighting and had two requests. Could I give him a gun to protect his family, and would I look after his family's precious things? I didn't have a gun. I offered to look after his belongings. They were wrapped up, and I put them in our own hiding place with our passports and stuff. I didn't look at what he left with me.'

'And afterwards?'

'I tried to get messages to him as I knew his phone number. I was in Dar then. We'd had frequent discussions about politics, about where

Zanzibar was going, what its future would be, Khaleed and I. That was his name, Khaleed. A wise man, a good man. He was one of the old Zanzibari families. I can't recall his surname. It might come to me yet.'

'Was Khaleed the person you dreamt of?' Elizabeth asked.

'Yes! Strange, it was so real,' he said. 'Khaleed was in the ZNP. They won the election. The revolutionaries would have targeted him. I asked others to find out what happened to his family. Weeks later, they went to his house in Shangani and said it was empty, everyone gone, the house ransacked. Maybe he had fled to the mainland. I understand a flood of people left. I hope they escaped.'

'So you want me to check if this box is still there, hidden, after over forty years?' Elizabeth tried to keep amazement and disbelief out of her tone.

'Yes.'

'It's a long shot. Very long.'

'I know. But you've never been back. Why not visit? Such a wonderful island. A paradise it was. And maybe, you can see what's happened.'

'What about Mary? Why can't she go?' Her bitterness showed.

He turned away from her and it seemed as if he was fighting back tears. 'I don't understand this. Why? You two were so close. I asked her when she came here. She has a big family and asked if you would go.'

'A big family?'

'Yes. Her three daughters are all married now. Mary has four grandchildren. You must know this?'

Her heart stopped. She did not know.

Her father stood. 'I'm tired now. Maybe I can tell Khaleed when I see him in my dreams that you will try. It will be a comfort for me. Let's walk to my room.'

Once in his room, he seemed about to collapse. He reached for the book on the Revolution she'd seen the previous day.

'Take this book, Elizabeth. My writing is hopeless now, like a child's. Inside is a description of where the box is hidden, was hidden. I've tried to draw it. And I've saved this money for your trip. The envelope is there.'

'You don't need to do that.'

'It's a gift from me, my blessings go with it, and I like to think I've paid for your trip back. Life is out there.'

'What do you mean?'

'Well,' he smiled, and patted her hand. 'Forgive me for saying this, but you don't seem entirely happy. I remember you were happy there.' He shrugged. 'Perhaps it's the melancholy of an old man but I was thinking that a journey to your childhood home might bring happiness back to you.'

44. Shetani

January 2010, Liverpool, UK and January 1964, Mambo Msiige, Stone Town, Zanzibar

Alone in the queen bed, under the low eaves of the pub's bedroom, cold seeped into her bones. How old she felt! She resisted sleep, fearing the dreams that hovered. Did she have the strength to take this on, to visit Zanzibar with her traumatic memories of departure? After all, what was so important about a box of things that in all likelihood had been discovered and disposed of long ago? Had she not relegated those memories to a remote corner of her mind?

Lying there in the stuffy ornate room, maroon drapes pulled shut against the winter rain, her body a thin thing under the covers, she recalled her bedroom in Mambo Msiige.

Their allocated colonial lodging was at the end of the historic building, the bulk of which was used for government record-keeping: births, marriages and deaths. Locals called the residential section in which they lived 'Stranger House'. Her high-ceilinged room opened onto a narrow verandah and looked inland over Kelele Square. In the December holidays, the flamboyant trees swung heavy with sprays of iridescent red flowers. At night, she saw bush babies leaping across the branches searching for nectar.

She remembered the *shetani* and her childhood dreams.

During the Christmas holidays shortly before the Revolution, she had nightmares. Perhaps they had been a premonition. The air barely moved in her room, the sea sounds a distant background to the clacking of the palm trees, restless in the monsoon winds. The house had no glass windows, only open casements with wooden louvres. The building had its own special sounds—the creaking of its shutters, the clicking of geckoes hunting mosquitoes, and when the wind rose, a low groaning that seemed to come from the roof timbers. Sometimes she thought she could hear the moment when the tide turned, the pause, its breath in the night air, and the release as the waves drove landward.

Her father dismissed her nightmares saying it was all part of growing up, something to do with puberty. Her mother would wake her and hug her close. 'You're shouting, Elizabeth. What's wrong? It's safe, my darling, there's nothing to worry about!'

Someone or something had been chasing her. She could not see them clearly but, in the dream's darkness, the threat was close, and her legs would not work. Nor did she know in which direction to escape and her heart thudded against her ribs. Elizabeth sensed a deep and cavernous noise beyond her knowledge of the world, and she tried to protect herself from this thing, this shapeless threat welling up, all powerful before her. It was strong and she was but a girl. When dawn broke, the memory of the terror would be only a faint trace.

A week before the Revolution, she woke in the early hours and saw something in her room, in shadow by the casement window, standing tall and thin without moving, as if waiting for her acknowledgement. She lay motionless under the mosquito net, listening to the sea's faint whoosh, the house creaking, and she prayed it would go away, for surely it was not human. And in the waiting, she slept again but this memory was with her next morning.

At breakfast, she asked her mother. 'I thought someone was in my room last night. Someone tall.'

'No,' replied her mother. 'That couldn't be. I always check on you both before we go to bed.'

Nadia, their housemaid, was collecting the plates. She paused and said one word, '*Shetani*.'

'Nonsense, Nadia,' said her mother. 'Don't fill Elizabeth's head with those stories. Please!'

Nadia was her mother's age, a stout woman with a round face and plump mobile features. She dressed in bright matching *kangas* and seldom wore shoes. Elizabeth never knew Nadia's surname and knew little about her. Nadia was indispensable, doing their laundry, sweeping sea sand from the verandahs, and helping in the kitchen.

There was a relaxed air between her mother and Nadia, for she was a trusted part of the family. Nadia had authority too. She would admonish Elizabeth for dropping her clothes where she undressed. 'Memsahib! Do you want scorpions to get into your clothes?' and clicked her tongue in disapproval as she chased their dog off the bed. She was always there when Elizabeth woke. Her mother said Nadia lived in the Ng'ambo area, the other side of Stone Town. Before siesta, she would walk home holding a parcel of food from their kitchen.

Elizabeth remembered the word *shetani* and next day she came across Nadia working outside in the sun, polishing brass trays. She sat down on the concrete wall overlooking the beach. Nadia was bent over, rubbing half a lime on the brass surface. Her breasts swayed rhythmically. The trays, with their twirling patterns of flowers and Arabic inscriptions, gleamed and flashed as they caught the light.

'*Jambo*, Nadia. *Habari yako?*' Elizabeth greeted her.

'*Mzuri sana.* Very well, Memsahib,' Nadia replied. 'Where is your sister who follows you everywhere?'

'Mary is drawing a picture for a birthday card.'

'Yes, she will be the artist. And how is your holiday, young mistress?'

'Good, thank you. But I go back to school in a week.'

'Yes, your Mama will miss you,' Nadia paused her stroke as if she was considering whether to continue. 'She cries a lot when you are gone.'

That shook Elizabeth. She did not think of her mother crying. At the airport, she was stoic, repeating travelling instructions until the last painful moment. It made Elizabeth feel guilty.

'Nadia, can you tell me? What is a *shetani*?'

'Ah, my child, I do not think your mama wants me to speak of this.' Nadia looked around.

'Mother is at choir practice. Please.'

Nadia lay the tray down and stood up, rubbing her back and looking out across the sea. '*Mashetani* are spirits that come out at night. We fear them, for most are bad spirits. When we see them, we are afraid.'

'What do they look like? Have you seen one?'

'No, I have not seen one, but I know people who have. Their shapes are many. Like animals, maybe half-donkey or dog, half-man, with big mouths.' Nadia grimaced as she gesticulated, her hands like claws.

Elizabeth tried to recall. What had she seen? Surely it was not a monster creature.

'Why do they come?'

'No one knows; some *waganga*, you know, where we get medicine, can use them. Powerful people can use them too, to attack their enemies.'

'Could there be one in this house?'

Nadia looked up at the streaky walls of Mambo Msiige. 'My child, this is an old house. We know not what its story is. Maybe it was not a *shetani* but a peaceful spirit from the old days coming back for its memory, a warning for us for these times. What did you see? Did you smell anything?'

'No, no smell. I thought there was something by the window, maybe it was looking out, and when I woke it moved into the shadow. Something tall and skinny.'

Yet, as she said this, was it true? Was the memory becoming a sure fact, the slight shadow taking bodily shape?

'It is good there was no smell and no wings but tall and thin, that is … I could give you a charm to keep you safe,' Nadia said, 'but maybe Mama would not like that!'

'What kind of charm?'

Elizabeth reached up to feel her own necklace, a silver chain with a golden-spotted cowrie shell she had found on the reef. She imagined a hairy thing that you would have to hang around your neck but Nadia had nothing around her neck and, if she was scared, why didn't she?

Nadia noticed her reaction and smiled. 'No, for protection, we hang special words from the Qur'an in our house to protect us from *Shaitan*, the evil one, in all his shapes.'

'Are *mashetani* like witches?'

Elizabeth thought of Grimm's fairy tale, a tale of children lost in a wood who are captured by a witch and locked in a cage to fatten up before she devours them. Why had she been told this as a bedtime story? Was it to put into words her dreams and fears?

'No, bad witches use magic or *uchawi*,' Nadia said. 'Most *waganga* are like doctors using herbs. Both can use a *shetani* to do their work. Remember, there are good *mganga* who help you when you have a sickness. But then, if you want to do something bad to another person, you would go to the *mganga* who knows magic.'

'Bad? Like what?'

'Child, why do you want to know such things?' Nadia said, and smiled indulgently. 'I can say, maybe if you are jealous of a girlfriend your husband is looking at. You want to teach her a lesson. There are lots of problems in our lives.' And, as an afterthought: 'They can use leopards.'

'Leopards? What can a leopard do?'

'Some *waganga* keep leopards. They train them to go and do their work at night. I do not believe this but others do. For when a person dies, and he had been walking around the day before, talking and looking as he always did, people say, "this must be *uchawi*".'

'Is that why people have killed leopards on Zanzibar? My father says it's illegal.'

'It may be but still there is fear. If you see a leopard, you can get sick. And some people use bits of leopard for *dawa*, for medicine.'

'That's horrible, poor animals.'

Nadia smiled, picked up the lime and resumed her vigorous rubbing.

So the past become real again. Part of her life that she had closed was opening up. Over it all loomed that great house by the sea where, perhaps for the last time, she had felt safe in the protection of her family.

Now her father had asked her to return to Zanzibar, to the place where she had lived before it all happened.

45. A Secret Never to be Told

January 2010, Liverpool, UK and 12 January 1964, Zanzibar Harbour

There are deaths before dying, Elizabeth thought, and that night of the Revolution was one of them.

At what stage did she realise an ordinary life was no longer hers to have? Maybe on board the stinking launch leaving Zanzibar Harbour for the mainland, or early next day when they arrived as refugees in Tanga Harbour, and people came to stare at them sleeping on rows of mouldy mattresses in the wharf shed, Mary lying crying next to her with memories neither of them wanted. Either way, an ordinary life did not long survive the twelfth of January 1964.

The vision had passed. 'Trailing clouds of glory do we come', wrote William Wordsworth. Children glow with the joy of it. It was the early bloom of childhood that parents watch with indulgence, their own memories caught up in their gaze. That January, the vision faded and the separation from Eden was complete.

*****

Off the Zanzibar waterfront, they waited in the *Pluton*, listening to intermittent gunfire and watching her father and Jack move further into the distance in Captain Lascalle's runabout.

Heidi pointed. 'Look.'

They could see smoke rising behind Stone Town. On the bridge, Lascalle saw it too. They watched him, his eyes going all over the place.

'What are they doing?' Her mother asked when Jack and Mark turned their boat towards the beach near Forodhani.

Captain Lascalle called down. 'I tell you. They pick up a man in uniform.'

They all followed the runabout as it approached the steamer, *Salama*, and disappeared behind the hull. A few minutes later, they saw a burst of Morse code flashing from the bridge.

'Thank God. That's the signal,' her mother called out. 'They're safe. We can go in.'

'Wait,' said Lascalle. 'I check.' He raised his binoculars and scanned the harbour. 'How do I know?'

'Know what?' said Heidi.

'It's safe? Could be the enemy. Could be a trap.'

'Why would the enemy send a Morse code signal?' her mother replied.

'I don't know,' he said looking down at them and resting his naked stomach on the guard rail. 'Morse, I don't use. Your *bwana* did not say what signal he sends. I am unsure. I am thinking. I am captain now. With women and young girls, pretty girls, on board, can I take a risky journey over there?'

'But you promised.'

'Better I take you to my home town, Tanga,' Lascalle said. 'The mainland is far from this fighting. My boat will be safe and husbands will find their wives there. Now I am in charge of my own boat. Captain *Bwana* Lascalle again.'

Her mother fell into silence in the face of his laughter. They watched the *Salama* from where a second series of flashes had begun. Captain Lascalle would not change his mind. Her mother wept in frustration as Heidi tried to comfort her. Afterwards, Elizabeth realised that Lascalle was never going to take them to the *Salama*, regardless of what happened.

The game had changed. The captain and his single crew member stayed on the bridge and his passengers remained in the back, from where they watched the seafront of Zanzibar getting smaller and smaller. Ahead was the passage between Prison and Grave Islands to the open sea and the route to the East African mainland.

Captain Lascalle made a speech. He was now in command and put on a generous air.

'Please, ladies, daughters, be comfortable. Help yourselves. Food and water are down below and the 'head', the toilet, is starboard side. It is better you rest up here. It is not so nice for'ard where my crew sleeps. Ladies can get seasick once we leave the harbour. I set course for Tanga. We should arrive early morning.'

Elizabeth's mother and Heidi sat discussing how events might unfold. Wondering who would come to help. If anyone would come to help. Her mother was a worrier and Elizabeth heard this confirmed as they motored along the palm-fringed coast.

Their course was north along Zanzibar's western coast and then across the channel to Tanga on the mainland. Two hours into the journey, before they left the island's coastline, they saw ahead of them a large grey ship approaching at speed.

Captain Lascalle came sliding nimbly down the ladder from the bridge.

'Ladies, you can see a British Navy boat, *HMS Ryall*. It is going to Zanzibar. Maybe they will shoot the bad people, raise your Union Jack, play

"God Save the Queen", and knock the rest of those black heads together and you can go home.' His laugh was scornful.

The ship sped past them, its black identification numbers prominent on the hull and the British ensign flying behind. A powerful bow wave rocked the *Pluton*.

Elizabeth and Mary waved and shouted at it with delight. 'Hurray! Hurray!'

Certainly the ship's arrival seemed to promise resolution: Elizabeth felt she and Mary could now take pleasure in this sea journey. It was an adventure they could share with their school friends next term. They sat on the foredeck holding onto the wire railing, their legs dangling over the hull. Laughing they dabbled their bare feet in the spray.

Elizabeth loved the sea: the wind in her face, the flying fish flashing out of the bow wave, their silver bodies glinting as they disappeared downwind, barely above the water, and the sleek dolphins springing out of the deep to travel with them.

The shoreline slipped past. Everything seemed so normal, the bays and gleaming beaches, the palm trees on the fringe and the clove trees beyond, the iridescent sea with the foam hissing behind them. Bubbles rose, suspended over the water before popping in the long wake. Surely all would be well. But as the line of the land shimmered like a mirage on the horizon, how was she to know it would be well over forty years before she would return?

'Let's play "somewhere",' Mary said.

'That's Dad's game.'

'Somewhere' was their family's game that had grown out of the launch of the Russian Sputnik in 1957. Elizabeth was seven and, with her family, she had searched the night skies in vain trying to locate the orbiting satellite.

'It's up there somewhere,' her Dad had said as they wondered which of the millions of tiny pinpricks it could be.

And their mother had sung gently, '*Somewhere over the rainbow, way up high, there's a land that I heard of, once in a lullaby ...*'

They had all joined in to sing Judy Garland's song from the *Wizard of Oz*, and that had evolved into a game of imagining a romantic world in distant lands. When bored in the car, or sad, or sometimes even when her father was tucking in her mosquito net at bedtime, they would imagine a faraway world. She would choose names of countries from the colonial postage stamps her father brought home: the Cayman Islands, the Gold Coast, the Bahamas.

'Yes, I'll start. Somewhere in Ireland, a baby girl is picking strawberries from her garden in the snow,' Mary said. Mary loved strawberries and they never had them in Zanzibar. It was a peaceful image.

'You don't get snow strawberries!' Elizabeth said. 'But it's nice! Somewhere in Swaziland, they are showing the film, *Cleopatra*. I want to see Elizabeth Taylor.'

'Mum said you are too young! It's naughty!' Mary laughed, 'Somewhere ...,' she continued.

Elizabeth was not listening: instead, she was wondering what her friend, Nataline, was doing somewhere in Stone Town. Nataline was Goan and lived close to them in the Shangani area. Would someone have rescued their family, her gentle mother, Rakel? They were not 'Europeans'. Would they be safe away from the gangs Heidi said would be let loose? What about their servant, Nadia? Nadia did not work on Sundays but if she had come to Mambo Msiige she would have been in the streets when the mobs came into Stone Town.

The girls made their way to the stern. 'Mum, what will happen to Nataline and her family? And Nadia? Who will rescue them?' Elizabeth said.

Her mother seemed to find it hard to concentrate. 'Nadia?'

It was Heidi who answered. 'Nadia lives in Ng'ambo with her family. They will be safe there. They are Africans, Elizabeth. I don't think they will be hurt.'

Elizabeth was not sure what difference that would make but Heidi's words carried authority. 'And Mum, what about Rakel, Nataline and her family?'

Her question hung in the air. Again it was Heidi who answered. 'Let's hope the British are on their way to sort out this rebellion. You saw their ship.'

'Maybe we can go home soon,' Elizabeth said. No one answered.

She and Mary decided to explore. Hand-in-hand, they walked on the deck in front of the bridge. The captain was watching them clambering over his boat and he called out to them. 'Explore it, kids. Have fun! Hey, come up and help your captain steer!'

Before they could reply, Heidi shouted from the stern. 'No. Not on the bridge. Elizabeth, Mary, come back down where we can see you.'

They visited the cabins down below where a clammy smell of unwashed bodies and stale food hung in the enclosed space. They opened every door finding only one cabin locked.

The head was a narrow space with a toilet, hand pump, miniscule basin and a hand shower at the other end. Filth was evident in the layers of brown scum, so Elizabeth peed suspended over the pan, not wanting to touch the toilet seat. She had to wedge her feet against the walls and hang onto the porthole to steady herself.

She noticed a picture behind the door. A topless woman was photographed from behind as she bent over a chair, smiling at the viewer as she looked back over her shoulder. Elizabeth had never seen a pin-up, and the woman's stance disturbed her. Enormous breasts hung down, red nipples erect, and the woman's scant bikini was a thin line of crimson between her buttocks. With the foreshortening, her bottom looked strange, as if it belonged to an animal. Elizabeth was mesmerised but vacated the room as soon as she had pumped and refilled the cistern. She thought if anything was going to make her seasick, that space would do it.

She pulled a face at Mary. 'It's horrible in there. Be as quick as you can!'

When Heidi went downstairs, she reappeared almost immediately. In her hand, she brandished the pin-up. She stood at the bottom of the ladder to the bridge and shouted. 'Captain Lascalle! It's none of my business what you do in your own time but I am not having this. There are young girls here.'

Heidi marched to the stern and threw the paper high above her. The girls watched as it danced in the wind before falling flat onto their wake where it was engulfed. The captain made no reply.

As time passed, the long swells of the passage to the mainland made Heidi seasick and she moaned and groaned. The two women huddled together in the stern as the north-east monsoon was steady on the bow giving their area a little protection.

'I'm feeling a bit sickie too,' Mary complained. 'My tummy's going round and round.'

Her mother found a blanket and arranged it on the slatted floor for them. Night descended. Elizabeth never remembered that sunset. Mary lay down with her, cuddling together as they once had. Their dog stretched down at her back. Elizabeth lay there praying her father would be safe now that the British Navy had arrived, that peace would return, that their summer holiday would continue. Under her body, the regular thump of the engine lulled her to sleep.

It was pitch-dark when she woke and silent but for the swish of the waves passing along the hull and the strike of the engine. Mary was gone from her arms. She wondered if her sister was being sick below decks or was visiting the head. Elizabeth rose to find her. The adults did not stir; Heidi, a large shadowy lump next to her mother. The upper deck swung black against the paler night sky. The bridge was dimly lit but she could not see the captain or his crewman.

Elizabeth went down below. The main cabin was empty. A night light over the galley showed her the way. She went forward holding onto a table as the boat swayed unevenly. The bow had been divided into two cabins. The head was located between the main galley cabin and the bedroom cabins where the passage narrowed with a gear storage area on the port side. The portside bedroom remained locked. She was nervous now and, steadying herself on the bulkhead, she looked into the for'ard starboard cabin. No one was there. She thought, surely Mary would not have gone up on deck on her own.

She heard a noise, between a gasp and a cry. Someone bumped the door of the head. She turned towards it.

'Mary, are you all right? Are you being sick? Can I help? Let me in.'

Keeping her voice low, Elizabeth leant her head against the panels. The door opened outwards and there stood Captain Lascalle in the dim light. For a moment, she felt embarrassed: she had barged in while he was busy on the toilet, for with one hand he was holding his shorts. But he did not appear disconcerted. He reached out, grabbed her arm and pulled her into the narrow space.

'Well, well, it's big sister,' he said. 'We would like your company.' She stumbled into the head wincing as he roughly pulled her arm.

'Where ...,' she started to say but then turned and saw Mary. She was in the shadow of the corner, half standing against the shower wall. Her shirt was open, pulled off her shoulders, her arms crossed over her bare chest and her pants pulled down. Mary's pink scarf lay discarded at her feet. Elizabeth saw the shock on her sister's face, her eyes large as she whimpered.

The captain tightened his grip on her arm as she tried to move to Mary.

'Keep quiet 'n still, sweetness. You don't want to get into real trouble out here.'

He pulled her to his hairy chest. He felt greasy against her. With his left hand, he reached down and shoved down his shorts, at the same time twisting her round to face him. His face was flushed as he grinned at her.

'See this,' he said looking down. 'You girls gotta see a good one before you grow up. Look at it, pretty miss, that's a real man's gear. They're gonna fuck you real hard one day.' Between them, he held up his thick penis and waved it like a torch.

Elizabeth couldn't stop staring at it. She had never seen a man's penis before. The captain kept her pushed against the wall while he pulled open her shirt front, shoved up her bra, and fondled her breasts. With his other hand, he jerked fiercely at his member, up and down, panting, mouth open with his effort and breathing more fucking words, watching her and making sure she was watching him. The pounding of the motor, thud, thud, thud was the background to the horror. From Mary's corner came a faint choking noise.

It was not long before he sank back on the toilet, his shorts hanging around his knees. With one hand, he kept hold of Elizabeth, and with the other wiped his crotch with Mary's pink scarf.

'Hey, no one's hurt, girlie. But you look cute enough to do more for your captain. I can steer you.' He chuckled at his joke and, with both hands, grabbed Elizabeth behind her head and started to force her face down towards his drooping sex.

At that moment, there was scratching and snuffling at the door followed by low whining.

'Shit,' he said. 'Shit. Bloody dog. Should've chucked it overboard.'

The captain released Elizabeth and she fell backwards against the porthole striking her head on the rim. Before he pushed the door open and left, he reached out and grabbed one of her breasts with his slimy hand and, squeezing hard, spoke close into her face. She smelt his fetid breath.

'Get out of here and shut up. It's like this for you two; say a word and it's real bad news for mumsie and her fancy friend. Easy for me and me mate in this big sea. Not a problem. Bit of boys' fun first and a long swim home. Understand?' He pushed his way out past her dog and disappeared.

Elizabeth felt sick with shame and shock. Mary had collapsed on all fours, dry retching.

'Did he hurt you?' she asked.

Mary shivered against her. 'Will ... will he kill us all?'

'No.' But she didn't know. That power was there.

'Look.' Mary raised her hand. It was black. You could not see the red. 'I came down 'cause I was bleeding. It's the curse, isn't it? Like Mum said.'

Then Elizabeth retched and vomited into the pan with a fear of things beyond her. She turned back and gathered up her sister in her arms, pulling her shirt over her tiny breasts and fixing her pants. She picked up Mary's scarf, lying in the waste, filthy and discarded and, balling it up, secreted it up on deck when they both crept back. She dropped it overboard and it slipped into the wake. Together, they lay sleepless on the shaking floor over the dark sea.

Dawn broke as they arrived in Tanga Harbour. The press was waiting, eager for firsthand news of the Zanzibar situation. Captain Lascalle acted like their rescuing angel. He told a story of how, while under fire, he had bravely plucked the family from the horrors of the Revolution, describing how the women had been distraught with fear when he had offered them an escape route on his launch. Neither Heidi nor her mother contradicted him.

Time and time again, in later years she wondered why she did nothing. Why was she locked into silence? She had felt guilty and soiled as if she had been complicit. Heidi would have done something if Elizabeth had spoken up. She could have shown them the bruises on her arm and her breast. Described it all. Or could she? She had felt doomed to carry this terrible secret that became harder and harder to talk about as each day passed.

Mary followed her as always, never leaving her side, looking at her, waiting for her sister to rescue her, to tell her everything was all right, and later to talk about how men could be and how they should be. Time existed before that day, and time after that day, and they could never be the same again.

Now the barriers she had created around her past were breached by her father's request. She knew as the hours passed and a greyish dawn filtered through the drapes in the Rising Sun that she must go back to Mambo Msiige, back to Zanzibar.

46. Return to Zanzibar

January 2012. Stone Town, Zanzibar

As the short-haul ATR aircraft took off from Dar-es-Salaam airport, a violent headache struck Elizabeth, creeping up from her neck to reside like a ball of fire behind her eyes. The grinding of the turbo-prop engines echoed in her head. She couldn't look out the window; the light generated a series of stabbing pains. When she turned her eyes inwards to the cabin, sharp radiance followed like stars in her sky. She had suffered only a few migraines, but when one came, it was intense and piercing. Medication was in her purse.

'Get in quick with these pills,' her doctor had told her. 'Early action is the answer, and rest.'

She slid her window shade to shut out the light, the blinding sea and sky, and rummaged in her bag for the two yellow pills, ignoring the stare from the safari-clad passenger in the aisle seat. Everyone else had their noses to their windows, waiting for the first sight of Zanzibar's palm-fringed shore. From the chatter around her, she realised her fellow passengers were mainly from a tourist group. She swallowed the pills without water and lay back, eyes closed, keeping as still as possible.

The woman passenger beside Elizabeth was shouting across the aisle, holding up a guide book, 'Any trip to Zanzibar should include a spice tour ... and here it says there's a Princess Salme tour, that Sultan's daughter who eloped. I've underlined that one. Slave chambers, of course, and I want to see Colobus monkeys. Monkeys are so *cute*. That's for day three. We'll cover the lot in four days.'

Elizabeth felt the engines ease back as they levelled out. She was hanging onto her armrests and trying to breathe slowly, to relax. She was not ready. The sense of passage, of leaving and arriving, was heavy upon her. What was lost to her was never more keenly felt than now. She did not need to see out the window for, in her mind, she saw the iridescent sea, the pearl-shaped islets heralding their approach to the mother island.

Her childhood journeys seemed so recent. Many times she had flown back from boarding school to Zanzibar, leaving behind the desperation of her school days. Time had stretched out before her then, full of possibilities.

The trouble was, Elizabeth thought, they did not tell the children of colonial families not to love these foreign lands, not to fall in love with their birthplaces. While parents dreamt of retiring in peace to another place called 'home', their children soaked up knowledge of the only world they knew: its different peoples, its spicy food, its birdsong, the way warm rain fell like a curtain through the palm trees. Their souls would be forever torn.

Eyes closed, a vision rose from her past: of coming out of their walled garden in Stone Town into a dappled square where a frangipani tree dropped its fragrant waxy flowers. An old man was bending to collect yellow-throated blooms into a *kikapu*. He was dressed in a white *kanzu*, a *kofia* cap embroidered in faded red on his bald head. Slowly he straightened to watch her. She knew he was collecting flowers for religious garlands and that she, a young white girl, in shorts and tee-shirt, was invading his spiritual space.

The plane was banking when the hostess, dressed in green and yellow, touched her shoulder. 'Madam, you must open your blind for landing.'

'Please, can I have some water?'

'Sorry, it's too late, we are preparing the cabin.'

Elizabeth raised the shade and glimpsed a flash of white: the triangle of Stone Town jutting into the sea at Ras Shangani. Still there. In a second, the white-walled city slipped away and they were descending over a pattern of rusty corrugated iron roofs interspersed with tropical green and bending palm trees. How big Zanzibar was now. At that moment, her task seemed ridiculous, the result of a momentary weakness, of believing in the impossible, that stories have a trajectory where we find things out, resolve things to our satisfaction and come out the other side, wiser and happier.

She was last to leave the plane and last to arrive at immigration. The sign above the entrance read 'Welcome! *Karibu* Zanzibar!' She wondered why Zanzibar had its own customs and immigration. Weren't they now part of Tanzania? The 1964 merger had been hastily engineered by Presidents Karume and Nyerere, and had become cause of bitterness ever since.

The female passenger who had sat next to Elizabeth during the flight and the woman's male partner were standing to one side. They held their documents tightly in front of them. Through the daze of her migraine, she realised they had been detained.

The middle-aged woman was dressed in shades of khaki, a black bumbag, festooned with multiple silver zips, was drawn tight round her waist constricting her stomach and bulging like a marsupial pouch. Her partner wore a bush-brown peaked cap adorned with a golden leaping leopard. They were clearly fed up.

The woman addressed Elizabeth in the conspiratorial voice that travellers adopt with one another. 'This man says we need yellow fever vaccinations. Travel agent never told us. Didn't need them for Tanzania, why here?'

Elizabeth didn't reply. She felt she was treading on broken glass and had to keep her head as level as possible. The pills were taking effect; she could sense a gathering flood of tiredness moving towards her.

'Madam, you have a three-month visa.' She took her yellow fever certificate and passport from the stony-faced official and walked on to collect her luggage. In the arrivals hall, the tourist group members were in a knot, all giving advice to their tour leader. They were arguing about the amount of US dollars in cash that would be needed to secure their travel companions' release from the prospect of on-the-spot vaccinations.

As she located her bag, a delicate-featured young Arab woman in jeans with a red scarf around her head touched her arm and spoke softly. 'Madam, I was behind you on the flight. You seem to be unwell. Can I help?'

Elizabeth turned. The young woman spoke English without much accent, or if she had to call it an accent, it was British. Elizabeth must have hesitated for she continued. 'I live here. My name is Jamila. Where are you going?'

'Hotel Starehe, in Stone Town. Can you help me with a taxi?' It was hard to respond. With each word, lines of pain grasped her head.

'You could come with us but there is no room. I'll organise a taxi,' Jamila said.

The young woman rolled both bags out of customs. Jamila walked into the throng with a confident air and crowds of porters and taxi drivers parted before her. An old lady with a stick and a couple who Elizabeth presumed were her parents greeted Jamila warmly.

After speaking to them briefly, she turned to Elizabeth. 'Follow me.' Outside, the air was thick with humidity, the smells of the sweating, jostling crowd and something else indescribably familiar. Jamila turned and, seeing that Elizabeth was struggling, took her arm. The sun's glare was electric and sharp, bouncing off the car bonnets. They arrived at a row of pastel-coloured cars decorated with bold taxi advertising. The young woman spoke to a driver in Swahili before opening the door and indicating she should get in.

'He will take you. Eight dollars. You are staying a few metres from our house. Come visit when you are better. It's called Kombe Clothing. I am a teacher in Dar and I'll be here for three weeks on holiday. By the way, I like your necklace. It's one of ours. Have a safe stay in Zanzibar.'

Elizabeth involuntarily touched the cowrie shell hanging from the chain around her neck. 'Thank you for your help, Jamila.' It was all she could say before she closed her eyes, welcoming the darkness. She was dimly aware that the taxi stopped a couple of times. Once she called out and the driver said, 'Police checkpoint.'

They came to Mnazi Mmoja, the Field of One Coconut. A raised avenue of casuarina trees marked the southern entrance to Stone Town. This she recognised, leaning forward as they drove past the hospital, the old Residency and entered the narrow roads between two to three-storey stone buildings.

It was as if she was floating now, floating into an old world where she knew every street, the shape of every building. They turned left towards the sea, past the old English Club and into Kelele Square where the flamboyant trees were still hung with crimson sprays. At the end, she expected to see the gleaming walls of Mambo Msiige and Stranger House. Instead, a barrier formed by a grey corrugated iron fence, two metres high, stretched across the road obscuring the ground floors of the two buildings.

'What's happening here?' she asked. 'What's happened to Mambo Msiige?'

'Mambo Msiige?' he replied. 'Hotel, they are going to build a new hotel.'

Hotel Starehe was three hundred metres beyond, and there she was greeted by a handsome man in an immaculate white *kanzu*, a traditional *kofia* on his head. He clasped his hands together and bowed.

'Welcome, Madam, my name is Abdullah. I am your Hotel Manager. I see you are booked to stay for a week. Madam, I have good news. We have upgraded you to a sea-facing room. Anything you need, please ask. Anything.'

Sleep was what she needed. Sleep and silence. After that, a week is what she had given herself. But first she had to sleep.

47. Mambo Msiige

She woke and slept again, dimly aware of the passage of light and the dark that came with noise, but the noise might have been in her head. After what seemed like a long journey through night, the light returned. When she woke, it was midday and it was as if her body was plunged into a deep lassitude devoid of pain. She lay and watched the folds of her mosquito net swaying gently. A light clicking noise began above her. Geckoes, she thought, the lizards are hunting now. They have been here all the time.

Later, she rose, showered and went downstairs. The hotel's entrance hall opened into an interior space filled with an open-air swimming pool. All the rooms had high ceilings with central fans. On the seaward side, a row of dense low-branching trees fringed the beach. The building appeared to have been a traditional Zanzibar home altered and extended for hotel use. The decorations were familiar, yet exaggerated: heavy ornate furniture, brass ornaments, black and white marble floors with scattered Persian rugs. Indian brass filigree lights hung in lime-plastered corridors. It was exotic and oriental in its mix of cultures.

What took her attention was the view from the hotel. It was so familiar, so little changed. It filled her with a rush of pleasure. The light brought a memory of pain but the view hurt her heart. She had not realised how much she had missed this, how important it was for her to be back here where a world of blues swept out to the fringing islands. Prison Island was on the horizon, a thin green line dividing sky and sea.

Abdullah greeted her, 'Madam, we are worried. Are you well? We did not see you.'

She was well but she was hungry. After a late lunch of chicken *biryani* with yellow rice, Elizabeth walked onto the beach, pausing by the deck chairs lined up inside a roped-off area. A woman in hotel uniform was rhythmically raking the sand. Nearby, elderly men in swimming shorts stretched their skinny legs and arms in uncoordinated tai chi movements. To the right, a bulky freighter was drawn up onto the beach. Heavily laden men were struggling up a ramp and disappearing into its cavernous hold.

Two men waited, a few steps from the barrier, watching her. One carried loops of colourful scarves over his arm. The other, dressed in a yellow Hawaiian-patterned shirt, approached the hotel's rope barrier.

'Madam, Prison Island trip for tomorrow? We have the best boat for you. And top spice tour. I can arrange, cheap-cheap with great guides.'

Elizabeth shook her head. The moment she stepped beyond the barrier, two more vendors appeared.

'Good day, Madam. Where you from Madam? America? Italy? London?'

The scarf man was painfully thin, dressed in ragged shorts and sneakers from which poked long brown toes. He said nothing but held out his arm while holding her gaze, his gesture willing her to admire his merchandise.

'I'm from Australia.'

'Ah! Australia,' the Hawaiian-shirt man answered. 'Kangaroo?'

'Yes,' she replied. 'Kangaroo.' He looked pleased at this exchange. A communication bridge had been established.

She turned and walked along the beach towards Ras Shangani. The sea was mirror-calm and so clear that boats moored offshore seemed suspended between sand and sky. Further out, the deeper water sparkled. A line of rough-hewn wooden motor boats, with outboard motors and thick forward-raked masts, were lined up on the gently sloping beach. Each had a tunnel-like canopy with a name and mobile number in large white letters: *Jambo*, *Karibu*, *Gladiator*.

The scarf man limped behind her for a short distance, his wares forming a fluttering rainbow.

South of the Hotel Starehe, the corrugated iron fence started and continued without interruption, curving with the beach until it joined the old stone sea wall, three metres high, parallel with the main building of Mambo Msiige. This side of the construction fence was gate-less. The proposed hotel site encompassed a huge seafront area: the open public space next to her hotel, the old English Sailing Club and Mambo Msiige. The low concrete buildings of the English Sailing Club had been demolished and it was this area and the public space that was now behind the fence. At the end, she could see the top two storeys of Mambo Msiige. For developers, it was a feature site, beyond price.

The forty-five years or so since she had left had taken their toll on Mambo Msiige. The building had a forlorn look. The top and third floors, where a screened protruding verandah ran for half the length of the building, were streaked grey and sections of balustrades were missing. Casement windows in the left half were broken, and lime plaster had peeled off in large sections. In a corner gutter, a fig tree had taken root.

Her old home, once called Stranger House, was at the furthest end, abutting the new five-star hotel, the Serena. Stranger House only had two storeys: these were built above a shallow basement and thus it was lower than the main Mambo Msiige buildings. Its raked roof faced the sea and was in contrast to the flat roof of the main building. Set in the roof's arch were three tall windows. Once, they had been the windows of her parents' bedroom.

Every house has its story and, in Stone Town, those secrets were tightly held. She knew then that she had loved this ancient house. It was a proud house that had endured. Its fringe of battlements proclaimed its role of protection. The sea wall protruded into the tidal zone and, in the spring high tides, the waves sprayed the lower windows. The sea smell was always there, fresh as the tide rose with the moon, a dankness with the ebb.

Cerise bougainvillea and frangipani trees with their delicate flowers grew between the walls and the façade of the main house, softening the frontal effect of the three storeys facing the sea and framing the gabled doors.

The house had once belonged to the British Government and was managed by the Public Works Department or PWD. Depending on your seniority in the Colonial Service, you were allocated, or could request, certain houses. It all depended on who you were, and your clout with those above you. When her father was appointed Permanent Secretary to the Prime Minister, he was delighted to announce that they could move there.

'We are going to Stranger House; it's right on the sea,' he said.

Sea views and ocean breezes were the prize. Each house was named after the previous British incumbent. Stranger had headed the Political Department, under the Resident, and had taken retirement with the approach of Zanzibar's independence. For those last years in Zanzibar, his house was theirs. The Resident was a 'Sir', born and bred into Britain's upper class, educated at private schools, finishing with a degree from Oxford or Cambridge. He lived in the palatial Residency.

Access from the beach to Mambo Msiige and Stranger House was up a flight of stone steps, the same flight she had last come down with Heidi, her mother and Mary on the night of the Revolution. Now a gate, two metres high, blocked the entrance. Two men in khaki uniforms, sitting on the crumbling steps, watched her approach. The building looked impenetrable: to gain access, it seemed she would have to approach from the inland side, from Kelele Square.

Elizabeth was not sure what she had been expecting but her idea of searching her old home now appeared stupid and dangerous. Anyway, it was most likely that the box had been discovered during the past forty years. It seemed sensible to go to the authorities and formally ask for permission to reclaim their family possessions even though she realised that this request might only lead to others joining the hunt.

She retraced her steps along firmer sand by the water. The scarf man was waiting for her, still despondent.

'How much for a scarf, this one?' she asked.

His face transformed as he drew forth a delicate red scarf, handling it as if it was his most precious possession. 'Thank you, madam. For you, it is only five thousand shillings.'

'Good, I will take it.' She converted the price to Australian dollars—less than four dollars, a cup of coffee.

Elizabeth draped it around her neck and walked back into Kelele Square, to the landward side of Mambo Msiige. Once out of the hotel's courtyard, another tout approached her.

'Madam, please, I can be your best guide to Zanzibar. I can show you much more: the palace, the slave market. Everything!'

He waved his arms in a circular fashion and half-blocked her way, smiling in encouragement. She smiled and shook her head. Disconsolate, he followed her into the square.

Above the fence, an information board in Swahili was headed with the word, *Tangazo*. That word she knew, 'Announcement' but the rest she could not follow, except that *Five Star Hotel* was written in English in the middle of the text. At the bottom was a date in italics, 'April 2011'. Nothing had progressed since then. Why not?

A dense mango tree shaded the façade of Mambo Msiige. She could not see into the area where the English Sailing Club had once stood. A gate with chains secured by a padlock was set into the corrugated iron fence. There were no guards but did there need to be? As she turned back, she noticed the corrugated iron was not flush with the ground for part of the way. Sheets of iron had been nailed to wooden uprights and the road was uneven. At its widest, the gap was about twenty centimetres and there the iron had been bent outwards. It seemed to had been pulled and then straightened. Someone else had got into Mambo Msiige.

The fence was opposite a building which housed a beauty parlour.

A woman wearing yellow and black matching *kangas* leant against the doorway watching her.

'Mambo Msiige,' she pointed, calling out in explanation before adding hopefully, 'Would madam like a facial, Zanzibar massage, *singo*?'

Elizabeth declined. She turned back to examine her options. It would be impossible to gain access from the road during daylight hours without being observed but, although it was small, the gap intrigued her. She realised she had not examined the sea-side fence closely, looking only at its height and the apparent lack of an entrance. What about under the fence? She hastened back through the hotel and along the upper beach.

The tide was now fully out and the exposed sand was not so pristine. Plastic rubbish floated in the shallows and a rank smell hung over the sea's edge. The sun was sinking, a moist warm wind whipping up white horses further out. It was a familiar sight.

Two outrigger fishing boats were sailing past, racing one another on their way to the night fishing grounds, their helmsmen shouting happily. Their triangular lateen sails, a dirty sandy colour, were tight with the evening breeze. A boy, as thin as the mast, was standing barefoot on one outrigger plank as it rose and dipped in the waves. He held a rope for balance, leaning back and waving, his body gleaming in the golden light, his shouts of greeting faint across the waves.

No vendors followed her this time. She realised most Muslims would shortly be summoned to their mosques for Maghrib, the evening prayer. This was a city of mosques. If the pattern of life had not changed, families would come out in the cool of the evening to walk and talk along the seafront. The quietest time for her to try to gain access would be at night or perhaps before sunrise when the *muezzin* once more called the faithful to prayer.

As the shoreline curved around towards the point of Ras Shangani, two guards came into sight. They appeared to be patrolling the access from the beach to the Serena Hotel, the only five-star hotel in Stone Town. The steps on which the two guards stood were directly below Mambo Msiige and slightly to one side of Stranger House. To the left, the long corrugated iron fence was bolted to wooden supports. Here, too, there was a gap between the lower edge of the fence and the sand. It was right in front of her but she had not noticed it before. The hole was small but with sand below, it could be enlarged enough for her to wriggle through. But what was behind it, and how difficult would it be to climb the old stone sea wall? Once she was up, what then?

She took a series of photos to examine later. The main building had two sections both three storeys high, one slightly smaller with a lower roof than the other. The effect was of layer upon layer of windows, balconies and steps. This close to Mambo Msiige, the arched door frames and fragile wooden balconies with recessed windows towered over her. Across the dirty lime-plastered walls great loops of black power cables hung like modern chains.

With her decision to try to gain access under the fence at night, Elizabeth realised she needed to know where her old house was in relation to the main Mambo Msiige buildings. She took up position on the beach opposite the first wall and paced it out.

The first section was slightly higher and had eight even-sized arches facing the sea. A flowery decorative pattern in stone filled the inside of these arches. This building was ninety-five steps long. The second lower section had a single door and various window openings. It measured seventy-eight of her steps. The problem was she would have to move along the wall directly behind the guards should they be on the steps. It would have to be done slowly.

The mystery of the box and the possibility it was still there kept her focused. The more she thought about it, the more it seemed unlikely. However, she was curious to visit her old home before it was changed into a five-star hotel. Considering the state of the building, it might even be demolished. In 1964, she had left without a goodbye, without a thought. It was time to say goodbye properly, on her own terms.

Elizabeth considered what she would need for breaking in. Black clothes would make sense, as she had worn over forty years ago on the night of the Revolution. She would buy a torch, screwdriver and wrench. The promise made to her father was that she would try. That was all. To try, and try she would. Once before, she had taken the easy path. Not this time.

48. No Entrance

The second night was a Saturday: now she realised why this front room, her upgrade, had been vacated. As the night wore on, singing and shouting intensified from the direction of the sea. She rose and looked out. There appeared to be a nightclub next door, and revellers had spilled onto the beach. The music and partying ended during the early hours when she had given up hope of sleep. Next morning, Abdullah frowned in sympathy.

'Madam, we have tried our best,' he said and pointed to a notice at reception. 'You see this? Alcohol is not served in this hotel. We are owned by Muslim people. We do not know what licence that restaurant has. Parties go on every weekend until so late. We have asked them, most respectfully, to be quieter for our guests. We have called the police. But nothing happens. I am most sorry. Would you like to move?'

'No, thank you,' Elizabeth replied. She would use ear plugs for the next night. She treasured the view too much.

'I forgot,' Abdullah said, 'this morning a woman called Jamila came to see you, asked how you were. She says she met you on the plane. I told her you were out and were feeling better. Is that so?'

'That is so,' Elizabeth replied and, on a whim, she asked, 'Can I talk to you for a moment?'

He frowned, looking instantly worried. 'Of course, Madam, please come to my office.'

She noticed he studiously left the door open. 'Are you comfortable? The room is clean?' he said. 'How can I help you? You have a problem?'

'Abdullah, I have looked at Mambo Msiige and I would like see it, to go inside,' she said. 'I am writing an article for a travel magazine. About Zanzibar history. The English press is interested. Sir John Kirk lived there and the explorers Stanley and Burton visited. I wondered if you could arrange this.'

As Elizabeth rushed through her explanation and revealed what she wanted, she sensed a problem. Those British explorers would mean nothing to him: in fact, her interest might make her appear to belong to the imperialist camp. Each generation would, in turn, rediscover that anger. A valid argument lay behind the resentment—weren't the explorers followed by colonialism and the grab for land?

She did feel that a lie about her motives was permissible. After all, she would only be taking what belonged to her family.

Abdullah's face, which had been wreathed in an expectant smile, fell into a visage of pain. 'Oh, Madam, Mambo Msiige! Not possible. No one is allowed. It is off limits, so to speak!'

'Why?' she replied.

'See how big it is and what a position! Everyone looks at this empty building,' Abdullah said waving his arms. 'Add on the space between it and this hotel, including the old Sailing Club, and you have something special. The United Nations brought a Swahili historian here. He said it should be converted into a museum. But think of the cost! Then someone said it had been promised to the Aga Khan for a hotel.'

The Aga Khan? She knew of him. Her father had spoken of him: he was the spiritual leader of the Shia Ismailis, and fabulously wealthy.

'He is a philanthropist, a good man, a big donor of funds to Muslim countries and communities,' Abdullah continued. 'It was the Aga Khan who created the Serena Hotel and has done work on our Forodhani Gardens. You have seen that? How beautiful they are now.'

She had. The open land in front of the palatial House of Wonders had been transformed. Every night, it was the meeting place for Zanzibaris and tourists to watch the sunset and eat from the snack stalls selling everything from sugar cane juice to grilled crayfish.

'Well, the Aga Khan came here. Much excitement, big presentation,' said Abdullah, 'and he opened the new Forodhani Gardens. The Aga Khan would have done a good job with Mambo Msiige but it would become another hotel. Then, a surprise announcement. The government said this property was now leased to a different hotel chain, the Q group, for ninety-nine years for one and a half million dollars and a yearly rental. The government offices moved out and Mambo Msiige was fenced off. The Stone Town Authority people were amazed and the Aga Khan, who had an office in Zanzibar, made an announcement that his charity was pulling out of Zanzibar.

'That's a pity,' Elizabeth said as she realised that Abdullah was excited by this issue.

'And worse,' Abdullah raised his arms again, 'now UNESCO says our World Heritage status is threatened. So, there is a problem. Still the old building needs fixing or it will fall down. Maybe corruption was involved. How does one know? You cannot say these things in public if you live here and run a business.'

He leant forward and returned his hands to his desk. 'So, it comes down to this; it is what you might call a "no-go zone"!' Abdullah's face expressed his dismay. 'It is sad for me to say I cannot help you further, for I wish to help you.'

'Thank you, Abdullah.' Elizabeth rose to go.

'But wait, Madam, I can recommend someone who knows about this building. Maybe he can tell you more. If you are happy, I will organise this on Monday.'

49. Stone Town Dilemma

The Stone Town Conservation and Development Authority was located in the Old Dispensary Building overlooking the harbour. The three-storey building had recently been renovated. With its complex ornamentation, fretwork and multicoloured windows, it gleamed amongst the weather-worn buildings.

Abdullah had organised an appointment with his friend who worked in the Conservation and Planning Division. Even so, she had to wait twenty minutes before Naji arrived, apologised and ushered her into his office. She thought he was only a little younger than her. Naji had a wide forehead, the protruding bumps prominent with sweat. A remnant circle of hair was slicked down over his scalp. He seemed to suck at the air through flaring nostrils.

Unlike Abdullah, Naji was dressed in Western clothing. He shook her hand with confidence and motioned to a single upright seat facing his desk before returning to his black leather armchair. His desk was neat with manila folders piled in one corner and a slim silver laptop in the centre. The spacious high-ceilinged office looked north over the Malindi area. A central fan created a gentle breeze.

Elizabeth thanked him for seeing her at such short notice.

'Not a problem,' he replied and pulled out a cigarette packet. 'Do you mind if I smoke?'

She nodded realising it was a rhetorical question. 'I hope you are having a pleasant stay on our island,' he continued. 'Abdullah told me you are a journalist and write travel articles. We are pleased to welcome tourists to Stone Town. How can I help you?'

'Thank you,' she said. 'I see development going on in your town. As you know, I am staying at the Hotel Starehe and my room overlooks Mambo Msiige. I was hoping to be able to see inside it for, as you will know, it has an interesting history. Oh, can I take notes on our discussion?'

Naji paused and looked out the open casement window, as cigarette smoke curled away from him. 'Sure. I ask you to send me your article when it is published. But Mambo Msiige? I am sorry. Entry is not allowed. For one reason, it is unsafe to enter and, furthermore, it is in the process of development. However, I can help you with other historic sites.'

She ignored his offer. 'Is the building in danger of collapse?'

'Parts are. Mambo Msiige was built about 1850,' Naji said. 'It is very old and, along with other houses in Stone Town, it has been neglected. You see we have this problem of maintenance.' He folded his hands beneath his chin as if he was preparing for a long speech. 'This is a special building and investors want it. Developers all want seafront buildings. Stone Town was studied by the United Nations and we gained World Heritage status soon afterwards. Now all development must be controlled, for each site has historic value. You cannot get permission to develop without complying with the rules, and these rules make it expensive, very expensive to fix such places.'

Naji paused, watching Elizabeth take notes. 'There are developers who believe it is easier to wait until their house falls down or becomes so dangerous that it is pulled down. Then you can quickly put up a cheap building, maybe of concrete blocks, and open your hotel. We must stop that.' Naji put his hands flat on the desk as if he was a headmaster admonishing his students for bad behaviour but could still smile indulgently. 'We know few have the money to do it the right way. Rains come and go with the monsoons and these old houses crumble a little more. You will see them all over town, piles of rubble, trees growing where there were once walls. We have countless problems.'

'And Mambo Msiige, what has happened there?'

'I can say no more. The decision is with the Authority. If you are interested, I can show you a few issues we deal with,' Naji said, and rose from his chair. 'See this map of Stone Town. We have over fifteen hundred old buildings and we believe around ten of them collapse every year. We are losing what we had and we need help. The Revolutionary Government simply does not have the resources to fix them. Mambo Msiige is just one of these buildings. Madam, you must realise we have come a long way. We are trying.'

Elizabeth rose to follow Naji's exposition. The wall was covered in documents and maps. A whole series was headed *Conservation and Design Guidelines for Zanzibar Stone Town*. Line drawings illustrated appropriate and inappropriate repair work. At the bottom of each page, she noticed, *The Aga Khan Trust for Culture*.

'The Aga Khan Trust has worked hard for Zanzibar,' Elizabeth said.

'Yes. It has. I can give you a copy of this. It is our guideline for best conservation practice. You can see it shows how lime is to be processed. We do not allow cement plaster.'

Naji detailed, in a long monologue, the international organisations involved, the conferences his Director attended, the 'stakeholders' to be considered. The UN's Commission for Housing and Shelter had helped produce a blueprint for Stone Town's conservation. Landmark buildings were identified. Elizabeth sensed Naji was now trotting out his stock speech, well-rehearsed, politically correct: she sat once more to take notes as a travel writer would.

'Thank you, Naji. One last question: I understand the issues facing reconstruction but why doesn't the government consider giving houses back to those families who had them confiscated after the Revolution? Their children might want their family houses back. They could fix them.'

Naji was startled. His voice raised a tone; he spoke faster. 'Nationalised. They were nationalised. People deserted their houses. Long ago now. It is not an option.'

'And if they did not desert?'

'Sometimes houses were still gazetted as nationalised.'

'Compensation for this?'

'No, no compensation.'

'And *wakf* charity buildings? Were they nationalised?'

Naji was not happy with this question. He sighed, his sigh expressing that this matter was beyond him, the question was unacceptable, raising unspeakable subjects.

'It is complex. I know nothing about such things from long ago. Today, we do what we can. I am sorry but I must hasten to my next meeting.'

Elizabeth thanked him and left feeling depressed. Perhaps there was a valid argument that the Development Authority should accept anyone who would proceed to save a historic building. So much was involved in restoration. How could it be expected that poor tenants, allocated rooms in the buildings after the Revolution, undertake expensive repairs? Much injustice had been done. But how could it be sorted out now?

Elizabeth paused under the flamboyant trees in front of the House of Wonders where women in bright *kangas* were sweeping up the detritus from the evening's food stalls. Their rhythmic movements and the slap of the waves against the old wharf added to the peaceful scene. A pair of skinny marmalade cats foraging in the rubbish bins watched her.

She had a vision of Stone Town. Season by season, the old town was disintegrating, its soul going as boutique hotels proliferated. New buildings would creep in with their concrete blocks, textured finishes, artificial mouldings and balconies with pre-cast balustrades. More tourists would arrive seeking the quaintness of its streets lined by houses slowly deteriorating beyond repair. Yet those same tourists wanted luxury too, so they would retire to their five hundred dollar a night, air-conditioned hotels overlooking the sea.

Now she was on her own. No way into Mambo Msiige existed but through her own enterprise.

Next day, Elizabeth took a bag of beach things and her red scarf and headed up the beach. Her trusty scarf man greeted her like a long-lost friend. A smile lit up his otherwise perpetually downcast face. On an impulse, she asked him, 'Do you have a black scarf?'

He limped beside her trying to interest her in every other shade, for black he did not have.

'But, Madam, I promise I get it. It is me! No one else. I must tell you my name for now you are my customer. I am Hamisi. I am *Mzanzibari*. This is my home.' He patted his chest happily.

'Good,' she said. 'Hamisi, that will be good.'

Elizabeth walked past the boat boys, the children leaping and diving in the shallows, sleek and gleaming as dolphins, and approached the guards on the steps of Ras Shangani. Thirty metres short of the guards, she turned and, as if she was finding a place to relax, spread her *kanga* out against the iron fence where the gap between sand and fence was widest, to the left of the bulk of Mambo Msiige. The guards watched her approach but they had to turn their heads to do so. After she had settled and started to pretend to read, they turned to face the sea once more. She became an unremarkable part of the beach scene.

Elizabeth gave herself to the view, and what a view it was. A light north-east monsoon was blowing in her face. From here, Sir John Kirk had watched slave dhows arriving from the mainland, and Henry Morton Stanley had waited while organising his clandestine expedition in search of Livingstone, lost in the interior. Richard Burton would have walked this beach as he had explored Zanzibar prior to his journey in search of the origins of the Nile. Here too, on a warm August night, *Seyyid* Salme, Princess of Zanzibar, pregnant daughter of the great Sultan Said, had escaped certain death to elope with her German lover.

Elizabeth observed the guards' movements. Every so often, they would leave their vantage point and disappear around the corner to the Serena Hotel. She timed them. About fifteen minutes later, they would appear again and glance at her once more.

During one of these absences, Elizabeth went to work. She dug a hole behind her, enlarging the gap below the fence just enough for her head and upper body. At first, the sand had been soft and easy to dig but, after several inches, it became much harder and gravelly. Her nails, being already ravaged, did not suffer further. She covered the hole with her *kanga*.

When the guards next wandered off, she lay down and, placing both hands on the sharp iron, pulled herself down backwards so her head was inside the fence. The edge of the corrugations pressed into her stomach. Above her, it was open to the sky and, looking to left and right, she saw, between the old wall and the fence, a gap more than a metre wide running for several metres before it narrowed. It was enough. She pulled herself out, shovelled sand, and sat up brushing sand out of her hair.

The guards were not back but two men were walking purposefully towards her. They were tall black men. Maasai! She recognised them immediately. Both men were swathed in red-checked cloth falling in folds to make a skirt ending halfway down their thighs, with one end of the cloth slung over their left shoulders. They held polished sticks at their sides and were festooned in bright woven beadwork, adding to their striking appearance. The man in front was heading directly for her while his companion hung back.

She sat up straight brushing her skirt free of sand, aware of her white naked legs, her dowdy appearance. The Maasai man who halted before her was impossibly tall and thin with handsome aquiline features over-shadowed by hooded eyes. His hair was tightly plaited and twisted across his head forming a peak over his ears. Beadwork ending in silver disks hung over his forehead and around his wrist was a bracelet of cowries. In this fabulous attire, he squatted down close to her, his hands clasping his staff, as if in supplication.

Removing his wraparound sunglasses, he spoke quietly, conspiratorially, 'Madam, my name is Sabore. I am Maasai. You are alone? I will be your guide and look after you in Zanzibar.'

He did not smile. His full lips covered gleaming white teeth. She looked beyond the two men and saw the boatboys were watching. Elizabeth stood up awkwardly and collected her things before answering firmly.

'Thank you, Sabore, I don't need a guide.' It seemed as if he was laughing at her, a certain disdain in his eyes, and she felt mildly angry.

Sabore stood up, towering over her, imperious, almost challenging. 'Madam, I know Stone Town, all places. It is better you do take me for a guide.' Sabore's pronunciation was good and she noticed the emphasis on 'better'. He turned and waved an arm encompassing his friend who was now talking loudly on his mobile phone. 'Or if you like Legishon, he is free to be your companion. Legishon gives you a good holiday time in Zanzibar.'

With a shock, she realised. Yes, of course, the *White Maasai*! The popular book and film about a white female tourist in Kenya who, after falling in love with a handsome Samburu warrior, had followed him home to his tribal lands in the arid north and married him. The book had chronicled the resulting clash of cultures and expectations.

She had never seen Maasai in Zanzibar during her childhood. She knew they were nomadic cattle-owning people of the hinterland, not the coast. But now, it appeared to her, the exotic African men were invited to lend atmosphere to the island's tourist experience. And it was not only as atmosphere. Lonely female tourists might consider a holiday fling.

'Thank you. No!' Elizabeth had to stop herself from running once she was past Sabore. She had a plan and there was shopping to do.

50. Behind the Iron Fence

The cries of the *muezzins* calling the faithful to prayer had faded long before Elizabeth, dressed in her black shirt, black pants and sandshoes, left the hotel. She wound the new black scarf around her shoulders. In a large sling bag, she packed her purchases: the screwdriver, torch and wrench. At the last moment, she took a couple of hotel pillowcases. She was determined. No turning back.

The beach was empty. Calm had settled across the seafront. The boats, secured for the night with front and stern anchors, were riding the offshore swell. Like a small flotilla, they faced the monsoon winds. The sea, a rolling oily darkness, had taken on the shades of approaching night.

Chatter, heralding the evening drinking, emanated from Livingstone's Bar behind her. Ahead was Ras Shangani and her chosen entry point to Mambo Msiige. At first, she thought there were no guards but, as she approached the steps, they appeared. Two men faced one another, silhouetted in the light streaming from the Serena Hotel. For a while, she would be out of sight at her proposed entry point. The guards began a slow walk away from her and she made her move.

Keeping close to the sea wall, she found the gap below the iron fence. A deeper shadow fell across its base. Quickly she dug the hole in the same spot. Without hesitating, she shoved her bag underneath to one side and lying on her back grabbed the sharp fence and heaved herself into the gap. She had to wriggle sideways to get her legs through as her body filled the space. She stood up slowly without banging the iron. A dim light came from above. Blood was pulsing in her chest. There is no rush, she told herself, go slow.

Reaching up and locating the top of the wall, she lifted her bag and pushed it onto the ledge. But how was she to hoist herself up? She shuffled along the wall. Where the gap between the fence and the wall became narrower, the wall was just as high. There was no way she would be strong enough to pull herself up; those days were gone. Then she remembered an old boarding school trick. Placing her back to the wall and her sandshoes on the fence close to a wooden upright, she pushed herself against the stones. By sliding her hands flat on the wall and slowly moving her feet up, one by one, she was able to shimmy up the space. The fence creaked with the pressure and the wall was rough on her supporting hands. Her legs trembled but it was surprisingly easy. She felt the edge of the last stone and pushed backwards to sit on the wall.

She was shaking, the muscles cramping in her right calf. Elizabeth grabbed her bag close to her chest. Rubbing her leg, she turned to look at the house. Light from the town shone on the upper floors; here, she remained in shadow. The huge bulk hung above her. At that moment, her search again seemed a ridiculous idea. What was she thinking? Surely a more sensible way could be found using authorised channels. And yet, why not? She was only going to fetch what was rightfully hers.

The pale walls of Mambo Msiige glowed with reflected light. Elizabeth's eyes adjusted. She could see the details of the Saracenic arches above the main entry doors facing Hotel Starehe. The arches were imposing—other worldly—presiding over the jagged pile of broken concrete that had once been the English Sailing Club. All that remains, she thought. This is where Abdullah says they plan to construct a huge hotel.

Elizabeth thought it unlikely that the main entry door would be open: anyway, she could not remember if a way existed through from the Government Records section to Stranger House. To her right, a narrow pathway ran between the front of the building and the sea wall. That space would lead to her old home. She took out her torch but resisted the urge to turn it on. If someone looked out from the neighbouring buildings, she would be clearly visible by the sea wall.

The cramp in her calf subsided as she relaxed. She stood up and, step by step, moved parallel to the sea wall. The building beside her seemed colossal: its walls taking on soft moving reflections from the sea and the light from the Serena Hotel. The steps where the guards usually sat were below the fifth archway and opposite a sea-facing entrance into Mambo Msiige. Although the guards might be out of sight, she knew they could be close to her, slightly below, on the other side of the wall. Keeping in the shadow, she started counting her steps.

Before she reached ninety-five steps, she arrived at the end of the larger building and the start of the smaller one. She started counting again. Seventy-eight steps to go. Here, the walkway between the house and the sea wall was narrower and the light was stronger from the sea side.

When she fell, it was so unexpected, she did not protect herself. Her right foot tripped against something on the concrete path and she fell sideways. Her upper arm hit the low wall as she collapsed against it. The pain was sharp and sudden. It was all she could do to not cry out. She lay down, rolling onto her back and rubbing her arm. It felt numb. Tingling ran down to her fingers. Was it broken? Would the guards have heard? Perhaps they were sitting on the wall below her. She listened. The pain receded and she breathed deeply. Above her, the night sky was cloudless, magnificent. She moved her fingers, stroked her arm and raised it up and down. No break, no blood, but she would have a significant bruise.

Elizabeth had forgotten where she was up to in her step counting. Halfway, she thought. As no noise had come from the guards' side of the wall, she continued on. She switched on the torch, shielding the beam with her hand. A low wall blocked her passage. This was familiar. A narrow alley to her left went part-way along the division between Stranger House and the main Mambo Msiige buildings. No light penetrated there but she knew it was the servants' entrance. A few more steps and she was next to the main door that led up into her house, that same door through which she had left during the Revolution.

Three large windows were on the upper ground floor. Below that, where she stood now, was the cellar level reserved for storage where they had kept their Zodiac dinghy. In the light from the shielded torch beam, Elizabeth examined the door. It was not a traditional Zanzibar door, studded and carved, but was darkly panelled with a modern handle. She depressed it and pushed. No give at all.

The sea sounds were stronger now: the wind had picked up and the rhythmic smack of the waves echoed in the beat of her blood. An ancient memory. Familiar music came from the verandah of the Serena Hotel: traditional Zanzibari music, *taarab*, the sound of the alleys and byways of Stone Town. It was haunting music, part-Arab, part-Indian, with *oud* and *tabla*, the quintessential Swahili coast music. Poetry set to music.

This time, with her whole body leaning against the door, Elizabeth pushed again. The top half yielded slightly. It felt as if something was barring the entrance, something solid and heavy. She shone her torch back to the alleyway and nearly dropped it as, with a sudden scuffle, two cats shot out. The short alley was filled with chunks of plaster and a dank putrid smell. Putting one hand on the wall, she worked her way along to the side door. It too seemed stuck until she shoved with her shoulder in a final desperate attempt. It gave a little and then a little more. Shining the torch inside, she saw a plank of wood that was standing behind the door. With another shove, the door was open, just enough, and she was able to squeeze sideways and step through the gap.

She remembered the room where she now stood as their storage area, where she and Mary kept their bicycles. Here, the ceiling was low, the air cooler, but permeated with a mouldy smell. The sounds of sea and *taarab* music no longer penetrated.

I'm in, she thought, I've made it this far.

Now, she boldly shone her torch around. The room was empty and she went through to where she knew the stairs led up to the first level, the public entertaining rooms and kitchen. The stairs were intact. The banister swayed when she put her hand on it, so she moved closer to the wall to avoid several broken steps. At the top, she expected to find a large living room facing the sea. Instead, the darkness continued and a wall stood before her. By torchlight, she saw there were two doors in front of her. She opened one, realising then that the traditional large room had been divided in two: offices or accommodation, she assumed. The narrow room looked out over the beach to the sea. A large shutter hung at an odd angle from the casement and reflections from the sea shone on the high ceiling. Irregular shapes on the wall showed where the lime plaster had collapsed.

She swung the torch beam low around the room. Papers littered the floor and, on the back wall, a large poster hung crookedly. She stared. It depicted the head and shoulders of a thickset, middle-aged black man, with strong heavy eyebrows over sunken eyes, his gaze averted. It was President Abeid Karume, the first President after the Revolution, assassinated in 1972 while playing a game of *bao* in the party headquarters. Karume was now watching over this room.

It was strange that his decaying image should be in the mausoleum of this house. Power and fear destroyed his goodness, she thought. Elizabeth's father had known Karume before the Revolution. Her father had told her at first Karume had not been a bad man but he changed later. He came to hate all educated people. Fear of others overwhelmed him. It was paranoia. Whatever Zanzibaris had wished for leading up to independence, they had not deserved this dictator.

This was not the room she was seeking. It had to be behind to the south and one level up.

She remembered her father's words. 'With your back to the sea on the left side high up, there used to be a connection through to the main rooms of Mambo Msiige. It's in the top floor storeroom. The Arab ladies could pass things to one another without going down to street level. It was eventually sealed up on both sides. We left space for hiding our things. That is where you will find it.' He had been confident, not 'may' but 'will' find, he had said.

In this changed house, it seemed unlikely. If people had added walls, surely they would have found the hiding place.

Elizabeth went back to the stairwell and climbed up the narrower stairs to the level where once there had been three bedrooms and a linen storeroom. Her parents' larger room faced the sea. The girls' bedrooms had faced inland over Kelele Square. Between them, on the northern side, was the storeroom where long ago her father had secreted Khaleed's valuables. The air on the second floor was stuffy with a musty fetid smell.

As these rooms had also been subdivided, she had to open unfamiliar doors. She turned back from the sea. The left back room, Mary's bedroom, had been converted into two tiny rooms, each about nine square metres. The storeroom door was ajar and she went in. This was it. It had to be. Before her was a narrow window, opening onto the alleyway above her entrance to the building. A dim light seeped into the room.

She shone the torch into the back corner. Here was the spot. But in the space was a cupboard, a large wooden cupboard with doors ajar. Her heart sank. Another obstacle. She pulled on the right-hand door and leapt back in shock. A furry animal shot past her onto the floor hissing as it went. It bounded out into the stairwell. It was not a cat, smaller than a cat, with grey fur and fluffy tail. Instinctively, she had recoiled in alarm but recovered immediately: a bushbaby, of course. Harmless, nocturnal. But why was it inside? She opened the door further: in the corner, in the glare of her torch, was a circle of twigs, leaves and paper enclosing a bundle of fur and three pairs of enormous red-rimmed eyes staring at her. She moved the beam of light away.

Elizabeth partially closed the door to protect the young bushbabies. She had a bigger problem. Leaning her shoulder against the back corner of the cupboard, she pushed. It rocked slightly but did not move. Crouching down and locking her feet against the wall behind her, she tried once more to shove the cupboard away from the wall. It would not budge. She was simply not strong enough.

She needed to think. She was so close; there was no going back. Stepping into the front room, Elizabeth looked out over the sea through the broken louvres of a casement shutter. The room had two external openings set into deep niches that revealed the width of the walls and curved around to form a seat underneath. Above each niche was an arched indentation for the display of an object of beauty. She sat down in the window seat and looked out. She had to settle herself, had to think.

A light breeze was blowing off the sea. Locals called the sea wind the 'health-giver'. The moon was past full, and falling towards the west. The sea glittered in the pale light and white horses rose and fell close to shore, appearing and disappearing in their ageless fashion. The beach was empty. It was past midnight and the *taarab* music could no longer be heard.

This had been her parents' room where, as a child, she had come for morning tea, had watched the fishing boats sailing out on the morning tide, had seen the tropical sunsets, each one exquisitely different. She felt like a ghost of herself staring out over a view as familiar to her as the shape of her own fingers. It was as if she could float out of that house and her life would be different, but the world had changed and nothing made it more apparent than the crumbling house in which she stood. Sitting there, she herself was the *shetani* she had once dreamt of in this very house, a ghost come back to remember and let others know of forgotten times.

Elizabeth had been part of this house: she had taken possession of its views, watched the days move across it, and known the creaking of its shutters and how the sea smelt when you opened the casement windows. She had played on these stairs, sat halfway up where they turned a corner and she could hide, holding the dog on her lap. Then she was gone and, where she once was, others came, others laughed, lived out part of their time. If had felt so substantial, her presence here, as if it would make some difference, mark her like an accent. For here, left behind, lay a clue to who she was.

What is a house, she thought, but a place of memories, of the days and nights of family life? Her mother had created a home in a land fundamentally foreign to her own cultural background. Only now, with her parents passed on and her own youth gone, did Elizabeth understand. And now the house, without people, had lost its soul. It was a place for haunting.

Her father had died a week after she left Liverpool for Australia. Peaceful, they said, in his sleep. Best way to go.

Cynthia had phoned. 'I didn't think you would come back so soon for the funeral. Mary can't come,' she said. 'It's all organised, a few of my friends only, for day after tomorrow. Oh, Tamara sent you her condolences. I told her I would pass them on.'

Elizabeth was told he hadn't suffered too much at the end. Not too much, Cynthia said. But how would you know? She had phoned Greenhaven Residential Home and spoken to the young girl who had lightened the pain of her father's last days. Tamara had cried and, all in a rush, had said, 'I wanted to tell you how wonderful Mr Hamilton was. So kind. He was happy after you left. Told me stories about Zanzibar. He gave me a bunch of cloves and Mrs Hamilton said I could keep it. Said I must go there one day and think of him. I'm going to do that.'

That was when Elizabeth knew for certain she would undertake her father's last request.

She retraced her steps to the basement looking for something to use as a lever: there she found the long plank half-barricading the side door. She hauled it up to the storeroom and returned to the first floor to collect discarded papers and bits of cardboard. She tore Karume's poster from the wall and folded it in four. Back in the storage room, she put the torch down so it shone over the floor.

Elizabeth rocked the cupboard backwards and forwards and wriggled a wad of papers under the front feet and then the rear feet. Next, she wedged the plank low down behind the cupboard and, sitting with her feet on the wall, heaved on the other end of the plank. The side near her slowly slid a few centimetres away from the wall. She secured the papers again, repeated her actions and the cupboard moved a little more. Eventually she could fit behind it.

She sank to the floor with her back to the rear of the cupboard and her feet against the wall. The floor was covered in a layer of fine sand. She pushed and the cupboard moved fairly easily. Now she could wriggle further into the gap and was able to push the far side of the cupboard away from the wall. All she could hear was her own panting and the scraping of the cupboard.

When the space was over a metre wide, Elizabeth stopped, gasping from the exertion. She was pleased the young bush babies had not deserted their nest. Retrieving the torch, she shone it into the gap. Loops of grey cobwebs caught the light, swaying, linking the cupboard to the wall. She did not want to think about what other creepy-crawlies lurked there. In the furthest corner built into the wall was a slatted wooden square flush with the floor. It appeared intact.

She retrieved her wrench and screwdriver, sat down and set to work levering from the edge. The clatter of the wooden slats coming away echoed through the room. To her heightened senses, it seemed an enormously loud noise. They were relatively easy to remove. The years of tropical dampness helped.

As Elizabeth pulled away the last planks a small door came into view. This was latched with a bolt and opened easily towards her. Behind it was darkness. Her hands were shaking. The torchlight revealed a narrow passage big enough for her to crawl forward. It was lined with a faded scrap of carpet. She tugged it up and threw the musty square behind her. Underneath lay a box. It was as her father had said.

She thought, it's still here, Dad. I've found it. And then she thought, you didn't warn me how big it is.

51. In the Dark

Her past was here in her hands. Her father's last gift to her, his last request. Accomplished. Yet here she was, crouched behind a cupboard in an abandoned house.

Elizabeth only had enough space to slip both arms around the box, lift it and shuffle backwards until she emerged from the gap behind the cupboard. She collapsed on the floor. The box was rectangular with brass corners and a simple centred triangular carving on the lid. The clasp was a brass loop with a rusty padlock. Her father had not mentioned a lock.

There was no possible way she could carry the whole box out of the house and back to the hotel. Unpacking it was the only option. Elizabeth took out the screwdriver and wedged it into the loop of the padlock. At first she tried to prise it open but there was not enough leverage. She hammered the handle of screwdriver with the wrench. The noise was deafening in the darkness but she was beyond worrying. She would be out soon.

The screws in the clasp pulled out. She tugged off the lock, opened the lid and shone the torch inside. A pale cloth lay on top and, below that, she saw envelopes, papers and packages. Some were heavy. Without examining anything, Elizabeth started unpacking the contents into her sling bag: when it was full, she put the remaining items into the doubled-up pillowcases. The box would have to be left behind: it was too heavy and cumbersome.

She slung the bag over her back and picked up the pillowcases, hugging the lump to her chest. All she wanted now was to get out. At first, she felt unstable but she re-balanced the bundles and, in this way, step by step, she negotiated both sets of stairs. On the bottom floor, it was easy to get to the side door but she took two trips to clamber over the debris. Out in the open, above the shining beach, the air was fresh. She felt exposed as she retraced her steps back along the front of Mambo Msiige.

The Serena Hotel's lights were dimmed, the guards nowhere in sight. The waves drummed louder: she could see the incoming tide had reclaimed half the beach, the waves sparkling in the moonlight. At the top of the wall, above her entrance under the fence, she stood close to the edge to see if the coast was clear. Once she was down behind the galvanised iron fence, she would have to move fast.

No one was in sight. Only one hurdle was left, to get out from behind the fence. Elizabeth was about to drop the first bag onto the sand when she heard voices approaching. That was a near thing, she thought. She crouched down and then flattened herself even further out of sight.

Two men, talking quietly, approached. They were walking close to the fence and stopped a few paces below her.

'Cigarette?'

'Thanks, *Bwana*. I like your Marlboro, better than Sportsman.'

One had a deeper voice, sounded older, commanding. The other was hesitant, nervous, a pronounced stutterer. Both spoke in English. She waited, hardly daring to breathe. The smell of cigarette smoke rose in the sea air.

'Sorry, my friend,' the older man said. 'It did not work out. I cannot proceed.'

'Good p-p-property, one of the best. L-l-looked at it myself,' the stammering man replied. 'Went to a lot of t-t-trouble for you, *bwana*. Here and there, records and things.'

'Well, yes. But wrong tenant there. It was theirs before the *Mapinduzi*. You did not tell me.'

'So? I removed those papers. Who w-w-worries about that now?'

'Maybe. I do not want it sold over her head.'

'Aha, *Bwana* Hadir. Is a woman involved?' a knowing laugh. The stutter gone.

'No, no. Listen, Yasar. Leave it alone. What else is around?'

'I told you, *Bwana*. Too many are looking for good properties: international investors with A-A-American dollars. Cash. They want good condition, few tenants, views, location. L-l-look around, lots are falling down. Too much money, red tape, too much time fixing those ones. They want land too, on the coast with a beach.'

A pause and she heard shuffling in the sand.

'It is worth your while.'

'Y-y-you have been g-g-good to me, *bwana*. A generous man. But it is getting more difficult.'

'Difficult? Even this one, Mambo Msiige, was sold. A special sale. Not so?' A deep chuckle.

'It has been officially investigated. Nothing to do with me.'

'Sure, my friend. Someone in your department must be worried.'

'No w-w-worries. Papers get lost, happens all the time!'

The older man replied in Swahili. It was odd: she found she understood the gist of the conversation. 'Shillings' and 'be careful' were terms that came directly to her understanding. A payment was required, and they discussed numbers before their voices trailed off along the beach.

Her right leg had gone to sleep under her. Rolling over, she rubbed her calf and it tingled back into life.

Elizabeth leant down and dropped her bags as gently as she could into the narrow gap between the wall and the fence. They hit the ground with a thump. She slithered down the same way she had come up, her hands raw from the rough surface. At the bottom, she positioned the bags near the depression in the sand. She then lay down using both hands to hold the edge of the sharp iron. She slid the front of her body under the fence and out onto the open beach. She ached to be gone.

As she pulled her legs out, she felt a stab of pain in her right shin as her long pants tore on the iron. She put pressure on the spot to dull the pain. Her fingers encountered wetness. Blood, there is blood. She could not think of this. It would have to wait.

Elizabeth scratched away the sand to enlarge the hole before she reached in and pulled her two bags through. Her heart was thudding in her chest and, despite the cool night breeze, she was sweating profusely. She shouldered the loads once more, pulling the black scarf over her shoulder. When she stood and took up the load, pain shot through her leg and her torn pants flapped around her shoes. She limped back across the beach.

The way back to the hotel was mercifully without incident. Although the hotel's main door was closed, the lights were on. She knocked, rang the bell and sank into a green plastic chair beside the door. A young man dressed in the blue hotel uniform opened the door and peered out. He looked as if he had been asleep.

He looked aghast at seeing her slumped in the chair, her injured leg stuck out. 'Madam. You are bleeding. Let me help you.'

He held out his hands to take the bags but, at first, she would not relinquish them. A thin stream of blood ran down her exposed shin over her sandshoes.

The porter rushed off and came back with a dishcloth. He seemed unsure what to deal with first, her wound or the mess of sand and blood on the entrance tiles.

'Madam. I must call my manager. Did someone hurt you?'

'No,' Elizabeth said. 'I fell. Do you have a first aid kit?' She hobbled into the hallway and the young man placed another chair before her. She could not look down at the blood. Bile was rising in her throat.

'Yes, Madam, it is behind, in the office. I shall fetch it.'

Armed with the first aid kit, the porter behind carrying her precious bundles, she hobbled up to her room. It felt a great distance but all the time she was smiling. She wanted to knock on every hotel door and shout, 'I've found it, I've found it!'

52. Revealed

Elizabeth sat slumped in the hotel room looking at the bags. She was reluctant. Was it possible that something might disturb the world she had constructed? On the other hand, she thought, what has this to do with me? It was almost fifty years ago and what could touch her now?

She attended to her leg which pulsed with pain. The blood had dried in thick mulberry-coloured lines beneath her shredded trouser leg. A long gash with jagged edges had been torn through the fragile skin of her shin. If there had been a nail she hadn't noticed it in her rush. She held her leg under the hot tap and tried to clean it while she bit a hand towel between her teeth forcing down the need to retch. In the steamy tropical climate, she knew her wound could fester fast. She covered it in antiseptic powder from the medical kit and bound it lightly.

As she hobbled to bed, she caught a glimpse of herself in the tall mirror. She saw a black figure with wayward grey hair lit up by the overhead light: indeed, she was like a grim wraith. Still in her cobweb-covered black clothes, she sank onto the bed, raised her leg on a pillow and fell into a deep sleep,

In the morning, the pillowcases and sling bag stood unopened by the bed. Pain throbbed through her leg when she lowered it. She would have to have the wound seen to. First, she needed breakfast.

Elizabeth hung the 'do not disturb' sign on the door, and limped downstairs with the first aid kit under her arm. It had rained in the early morning and heavy clouds rolled in from the north. The monsoon wind was showing its power: a dun-coloured sea was pounding the beach. From the breakfast room, she could see the morning exercise class was under way close to the hotel's barrier. A motley group of men were stretching and a lone woman in blue pantaloons and a red sweatshirt followed their movements.

Abdullah came to her table, concern heavy upon his brow. 'Madam, did you sleep well? I am sorry to hear you fell yesterday. Can I offer you fresh *dafu*, coconut milk?'

'Yes. Thank you. This was a great help.' She handed the first aid kit to him. 'Your night porter was most kind but I need to have the cut looked at by a doctor.'

'There is a private clinic near Darajani,' said Abdullah. 'Can I make an appointment for you? The doctor is a friend of mine.'

Upstairs, she spread a towel on the bed and heaved the bags on it. Her sheer determination alone must have made it possible to carry them. She made two piles. Her family belongings had been at the bottom of the box. Khaleed's things, brought to her father for safekeeping during the morning of the Revolution, were in a cream *kikoi*.

On her family's side were family passports; her father's will; a single page written to her mother; a packet of Zanzibar shilling notes that might have bought a tee-shirt if they were legal tender; and two presents wrapped in birthday paper. One of the presents was heavy and felt like a book.

On the other side were the valuables of a desperate man. Things Khaleed thought his British friend could protect during the possible disturbance. He had not thought of his own safety, wrapping these family belongings in a *kikoi* and going through the streets that Sunday morning. Her father had said he had asked for a gun to protect his family but had left without protection. If he had come across any revolutionary thugs, he could have been killed. What had happened to him on the way back to his family? Did he make it back?

From a linen sleeve, Elizabeth took out a heavy silver dagger, a *jambiya*, the traditional curved dagger worn by senior Arab men at their waists. She drew out the blade. Down its centre was a reinforcing ridge. The blade was tarnished, blunt. It lay heavy in her hands and, although it was for formal wear, it was a weapon. The scabbard was covered in intricate silver-threaded decoration and was attached to a wide silver belt by two rings. The belt was embellished with protruding whorls and bosses: its silver was backed by a strip of worn leather. It was a well-used heirloom.

Underneath was a heavy cloth bag from which tumbled seven heavily worked gold necklaces and various gold bangles and rings. The gold gleamed: it had held its beauty. The necklaces were in the ornate fashion that she remembered from the *dukas* in Stone Town's Main Street.

In a plain calico bag was a book in Arabic, bound in red leather, which she assumed was a Qur'an. Lastly, she drew out a foolscap envelope containing a single black and white photograph on cardboard, and two loose pages in Arabic.

The photograph was covered in a sheer film. It showed a group of six adults in a formal setting against a backdrop of pale full-length curtains. In the centre, a young couple was seated in two high-backed armchairs. On either side were two older couples. The three women were dressed in full-length dark gowns with delicate patterns woven into the fabric. Their heads were covered; the older two women were veiled but the young woman's face was not. The man on the left of the seated couple had his hand on the back of the chair. While no one was smiling, it struck her that this was the record of a wedding.

The two loose pages were different to each other. One appeared to be a poem with the black Arabic writing centred on the page so it formed a balanced design. It was not signed. The second page appeared to be even older. She took it to be a formal document; at the bottom the stamp reminded her of the Arabic calligraphy of the Sultans of Zanzibar.

It was not going to be simple. Now that she had found it, the box had created more challenges. How could she leave Zanzibar now and resume her life without resolving the ownership of these valuables and family documents?

She turned her attention to her parents' things. The four black UK passports were items frozen in time. After the Revolution, her family had obtained duplicate travel documents on the mainland. She looked at her parents' photographs. Her mother was beautiful. As a child you did not see that but now she could, and she felt a pang of sadness seeing the tiny formal black and white photo.

She picked up Mary's passport. The British lion and unicorn on the cover was a faded gold. *Dieu et mon Droit,* 'God and my right'. It was the divine right to rule. Mary's face had their mother's sweetness. She had also inherited her grace. The description; profession: student; Birthplace: Mtwara, Tanganyika; colour of eyes: Blue; hair: fair; special peculiarities: none. 'None' thought Elizabeth except goodness.

And how should my passport describe me, Elizabeth wondered?

She turned to the presents. The paper was decorated with a pattern of multicoloured balloons. She opened the heavier present first. It was for her fourteenth birthday, during the school term that would follow the Revolution. There was a cheerful card from her parents, her father's hand so steady then.

The large format book was titled *The World We Live In*. Elizabeth looked at the contents: 'The Earth is Born', 'The Miracle of the Sea' ... ending with 'The Starry Universe'. It was a guide to the physical world, its evolution and the wonders that were known in the late 1950s.

The second present was soft and came with a card tied on with blue ribbon. She recognised Mary's childish handwriting: 'To Lizzy.' She opened the present first. It was a golden teddy bear with a once-pink bow: Mary's best, dearest childhood bear. It seemed so insignificant, now squashed, its face filled with forlorn cuteness.

The card was home-made by twelve-year-old Mary. On the front was a drawing of the view from Stranger House and Mambo Msiige, from their old home: the yellow beach, passing *ngalawa*, the sea beyond.

Mary had drawn two girls standing by the low wall, holding hands. One was tall, the other shorter. Their dresses were bright against the blue sea. Everything was realistic except for the sky. For the sky was filled with stars, each one individual in colour and shape. A magic sky of rainbow stars. Inside the message was written using a different coloured pen for each line:

To my special Lizzy, the best big sister in the world, happy birthday.

My bear will look after you when I am not with you.

I will always love you to bits, Mary-Lou.

Underneath were two rows of red crosses and noughts: kisses and hugs.

Mary-Lou: Elizabeth's pet name for her sister. Louise was Mary's middle name. Only Elizabeth used it. That was then. Now she had lost it all.

*****

Mary-Lou

1975. Capetown, South Africa

Elizabeth was in love with the wrong man, Simon Venters, the Assistant Professor from the University of the Western Cape, who offered to help her with her doctoral dissertation. He was dark and wiry, wore black-rimmed scholarly glasses, had a lopsided smile and a way with words. Never, he said, had anyone understood him like she did. She had unlocked his poetic soul. At night, he took her outside Cape Town to the backstreet jazz clubs and showed her a world she had not known existed. Alone, they read to one another and shared stories of their childhoods. He had grown up in poverty. His family had been expelled to the Cape Flats to make a home amongst the wind-swept sand dunes far from the broad oak-shaded streets under Table Mountain.

It seemed so right except for a couple of issues. To begin with, he was married with two children, two babies. She didn't even know their names, only that one was a boy, one a girl. She didn't want to know more; it didn't matter. She argued to herself that this was his other, prosaic world, not theirs. And their world throbbed with a reality that made each day of that autumn seem beyond judgement.

He was all right with the deception for no one knew, no one was hurt. She was too, at first, but not later.

Those were the bad years in South Africa, the worst years when they believed nothing could topple the apartheid regime. It was another Thousand-Year Reich. Boys, white boys at the university, were conscripted to fight in Angola. That war was a secret, too. They called it the 'Bush War' except it was across the border in another country. Everyone had secrets. The country existed on secrets. Her affair was just another one, pretty exciting, and neither of them considered the future.

Until she became pregnant and everything became serious, the poetry forgotten.

At twenty-five, she had choices. It wasn't like she was a teenager. But she didn't want to face it alone. Simon was horrified when she told him. Now she wondered what kind of myopia he was dealing with: all he could talk about was his world of wife, babies, parents dependent on him and ambitions. He wept, said sorry, he would pay. Somehow sort it. Paying meant abortion. The way he assumed abortion was the only way angered her for she knew that way was his escape. Escape was foremost on his mind, not those steamy afternoons in his friend's flat when they lay entwined and her barriers disappeared.

For a little while, she didn't fully understand what was at stake. There was another issue, the complication of colonial worlds, of apartheid. She was 'white': he was 'coloured', the special name for the Cape people, who were of mixed descent of white, Malay, Hottentot and others over hundreds of years. This made it all more difficult; it made it her problem, not his. She was the one who had the choices, he said. And the child would be classified coloured if she was found out. So what to do?

She went to Mary, not to her father. Mary was a nurse in the seaside town of Knysna, seven hours drive east along the coastal road from Cape Town. Mary had made her choices, and had bought a house with her doctor girlfriend, Susan.

Mary was not horrified; she was even excited and didn't comment on the fact that Simon was coloured.

'You'll be safe. We'll help, Lizzy. Stay with us. Have the baby here, at home, and we can work it out. We can share.'

'I've got another year to do at 'varsity. My scholarship ...'

'You've got a few months to sort it out. But it'll be hard to finish. Can you postpone?'

'Not really.'

'You'll have time later. Pity Mum's not with us to help.'

Elizabeth wondered how her mother would have taken it. First grandchild born illegitimate and coloured in a country where race was taken so seriously, it dictated every move you made: where you lived, worked, ate, sat in the park and went to school. Parallel universes under the same sun.

She did not tell her father even though Mary tried to persuade her. Instead, from then on, she became good at lying. Evasions became her world; she built barriers around herself. Elizabeth explained it as a crisis in her life, a study crisis, and said she had to leave Cape Town to clear her head. Everyone said how thin and pale she was and commiserated over the stresses of academic deadlines and thesis writing.

Her father did not notice. He had moved to Johannesburg, taken a new job and was dating again. A handsome fifty-five year old widower had no shortage of available partners.

When she could no longer hide her swelling stomach, she packed her few possessions, her study books, and went to Knysna, to Mary and Susan's home behind the sea cliffs. For the last three months, she fretted, struggling to concentrate on her thesis. Words no longer had meaning.

Because her baby was in breech position, their plan did not work out, and she ended up having a caesarean in the local hospital.

Afterwards, Mary was bright with happiness, holding the baby for her to see. 'Look, she's so beautiful, Lizzy. What shall we call her?' But all Elizabeth could see was the end of her life as she knew it. Adding to her confusion was the fact that she had reacted so violently to the sight of blood, she needed to be given an anti-emetic injection to counter her nausea. Exhaustion set in.

It is hard to tell if a baby is 'coloured', because all babies are red and pink and messed up at first. There were tests for whiteness in South Africa, to establish the nuances of skin colour that dictated everything from birth to death. The 'Pencil Test' had been devised, where you stuck a pencil in a child's hair and if it stayed in place, because their hair was crinkly, the child was deemed to be coloured. But her baby girl had a shadow of straight thick hair like hers, and deep brown eyes that seemed to see Elizabeth and know.

The 'Fingernail Test' was the one her baby failed because her minute nails, like translucent raindrops, had darker moons, not pale moons like white people.

The hospital supervisor, a plump Afrikaner woman with shining red lipstick on her thin lips, came to her bed, slowly drew the curtain separating her from the next new mother, and sat down heavily. Elizabeth looked at her hair, a tight perm, dyed blonde with the roots a grey line in her parting. A clip on either side secured the crinkled waves.

'I'm Sister Jacobs. Mrs Hamilton, we have a problem,' she said with a slight emphasis on the 'Mrs'. 'Sorry. I think you know what it is,' she said in a whisper, and smiled a smile that said, 'You're caught, you've been found out'.

She went on in a matter-of-fact way. It was the Population Registration Act No 30 of 1950 that required all babies to be registered as White, Black/Native or Coloured. The baby would then be given an identity number that was logged into the apartheid system. In her case, the hospital couldn't register the baby as white. They observed the proper procedure. Hence the baby could not live in a white area, could not go to a white school. Should not, could not, be hers. Each time Sister Jacobs said white, her voice rose in what Elizabeth took to be an accusation.

'Where does baby's father live?' said Sister Jacobs, still smiling, still conspiratorial.

Elizabeth did not answer. Kept her hands under the stiff white sheets. It was there that she made the choice, lying there with her empty stomach and stitches where the baby had once been. Adoption. She would give the baby away. It was funny: until then, she had not felt guilty about having Simon's baby and now she did. She blushed with it.

'That's a good girl. We can organise it all,' said Sister Jacobs, straightening her blanket and patting the mattress, so that Elizabeth wanted to move away. 'Don't worry, we have done it before. Baby will have a good home. There are families. It's better if you don't see it again. We'll give you something to stop the milk. I will need you to sign a few forms. Tomorrow.'

As Sister Jacobs was about to pull back the curtain, Elizabeth said, 'Can I name her?' Sister Jacobs turned, hand firm on the curtain, lips tightening. 'You can and I can request it, that is all.' Elizabeth said a name, and the curtain was pulled shut.

Mary was horrified. 'You can't give her away. She'll end up in an orphanage. I've been there. There's no shortage of children in our coloured community. You can't do this. She's yours for life.'

'What choice do I have?'

'Don't sign a thing, Lizzy. Please. They can't force you. We can work something out. I'll talk to Susan. Get a lawyer. Wait, please wait for me.'

But she didn't wait: she signed that evening and gave away her baby. And so it happened that she lost her baby and her sister.

She never did get a doctorate. The price you pay. Elizabeth didn't realise she had one chance, and the choice she made was the parting of the ways.

53. Blood

'It's the blood. I can't stand the sight. Sorry, I faint or vomit.'

'Breathe deeply and look away.'

Elizabeth was sitting in Dr Hamid's surgery. The doctor pulled on milky-white disposable gloves and unwound the bandage round her shin. Dr Hamid had a moustache and a close-trimmed beard that followed his lean face and strong jaw line. She noticed flecks of grey in his hair. He smelt faintly of cinnamon, or was it cloves? She stared at the wall where the doctor's certificates were displayed in gold frames.

'You say a fence caused this? Maybe a nail?'

'Yes.'

'In the old days, we had to stitch.'

He gave instructions to his nurse in Swahili and she returned with two basins.

Elizabeth concentrated on the doctor's qualifications as she felt him swabbing the wound. Dr Hamid had a medical degree from Oman and two further certificates from London. She wondered what had brought him to Zanzibar to practise medicine. His clipped English showed total fluency.

'You say you've had a tetanus booster recently. That's good. I'll give you a course of antibiotics for possible infection as it's a rough cut. I can hold it together with a wound dressing. They are airtight but, of course, no swimming until it's healed. Keep it elevated as much as you can for a few days.'

'Thank you,' she said. 'Can I ask you something?'

'Sure.'

'Why Zanzibar? Sorry, I see you're from Oman.'

Dr Hamid paused. 'It's a long story. Oman has old ties with Zanzibar.'

'You speak Swahili.'

'Yes, many do in Oman. This might hurt a little. I must cut away this flap of skin.'

She felt her throat thicken and bile rising as the nurse passed and she caught a glimpse of the old dressing and bloody swabs.

She took slow deep breaths and balled her fists. 'Can I have a bucket?'

The nurse handed her an enamel basin. She needed distraction. 'I spoke it once,' she half gasped. 'I lived in Zanzibar as a child.'

The doctor stopped. 'Yes? Swahili? Sorry, this will hurt a little. A long time ago?'

'Before the Revolution.'

'Ah. So you have come back too.'

'Yes. Your family was here?'

'Yes. I was born in Unguja the year before the *Mapinduzi*,' Dr Hamid said. 'Luckily my family was visiting relatives in Mombasa for the holidays before Ramadan, so they missed the Revolution. They never came back.'

'Did most Zanzibari Arab families move to Oman?'

'Not at first. Many stayed on the mainland. They hoped they could come back to their homes. Later, families moved to Egypt, Yemen, Europe even Canada. After Sultan Qaboos came to power, Oman attracted our people. The Sultan encouraged this.'

He did not explain why he had decided to return to his birthplace.

'You have hemophobia?' he asked.

'I'm afraid so.'

'Too late to sort out?'

'I've tried; it's better than it was. Had it a long time.'

He stood up and opened the door. 'Well, you are all right to go. Come back in two days and my nurse can replace your dressing, so you don't have to. Call me if you have problems.'

She hesitated in the doorway before turning to him. It came out in a rush. 'Dr Hamid, thank you. A moment please. I need a favour. I have some things. Found recently. They belong to an Arab family who lived here before the Revolution. I don't know who they are.'

He motioned to her to come back into the surgery and closed the door. 'You want to find them? What are their names?'

'I only have a first name and a few papers, one photo.'

'A challenge. You are staying at the Hotel Starehe?'

'Yes.'

'I have a nephew living here,' Dr Hamid said. 'His name is Mubarak, Dr Mubarak Raisi. I will ask him to call you. He might be able to help. Sorry!' Opening the door once more, he indicated the full waiting room.

Elizabeth chose to walk back to the hotel through the centre of Stone Town. By the time she was halfway through the maze of streets, her leg ached and she was limping. At the beginning of Cathedral Street, she came to the junction where five narrow lanes met. A sea-blue shark was painted on the wall with a sign in red, 'Jaw's Corner'. It was a gathering place for men having coffee, playing *bao* and dominos, or watching the passing traffic and crowds of tourists. Opposite where she stood, she noticed someone had drawn an image of a clove on a black sign and written, *General Announcement. Freedom is coming to Zanzibar! Get Ready!*

A seller of mangoes sat next to his full *kikapu* doing a brisk trade.

Once there were only bicycles and carts in Stone Town, she thought, but now motor bikes were whizzing past at a dangerous rate. Elizabeth rested on the *baraza* next to the mango vendor and lifted her leg onto a step. The throbbing abated.

The mangoes smelt rich and ripe. She picked one up, holding it in both her hands. It was yellow, egg-shaped and firm. The skin was shaded in orange and yellow with a darker hue of crimson by the stalk. She knew it well. '*Shomari?*' The vendor nodded.

She bought a green coconut from another vendor. A bulging woven basket was tied to his bicycle. Resting on top was a *panga* with a silver blade. The old man deftly spun the coconut in his hand slicing off the top. She drank the pale milk, *dafu*. He watched her finish and then cut a spoon from the shell for her to scoop out the milky flesh.

Elizabeth felt a certain peace. There was nowhere else she would rather be.

54. Mubarak

Late afternoon, she was called downstairs for a visitor. It was Dr Hamid's nephew, Mubarak. Abdullah hurried out of his office, clearly delighted.

'*Habari*, Dr Raisi, you are welcome. I will order coffee for you and Bibi Elizabeth.'

Mubarak held out his business card which described him as an entrepreneur and facilitator with phone numbers for Zanzibar and Oman. He had 'PhD (Ohio)' after his name.

'Dr Hamid asked me to see you,' he said. 'I understand you are looking for an Arab family.'

'Yes, thank you for coming so quickly. Can we sit?' She indicated the bandage on her leg.

Mubarak was a slim young man, with an easy confident air, handsome in an aquiline way. He was wearing the traditional *kanzu* and *kofia*. She wondered if the visit was an onerous chore for him, commanded by his uncle.

'I know little about the family, only what my father told me. I am not here for long although I have extended my stay.'

'May I ask why has it taken so long?' Mubarak said. 'Times have changed in Zanzibar since 1964.'

'Well, it's better late than never. If you can direct me to where I can get advice, I would appreciate it. Otherwise, I'm not sure what to do.'

First, she placed the book on the table. It had a red leather cover: the ornate pattern in gold around the edge looked hand-painted. In the centre was a medallion with Arabic calligraphy that reminded her of a Persian carpet. The book was well used. She imagined the years and years during which it had been studied. Inside, the pages had neat border patterns. Next to the book, she placed the single sheet of Arabic calligraphy.

Mubarak leant forward and looked at the book carefully without touching it. He picked up two cloth napkins from the table. One he opened on his hand and with the other picked up the book. He handled the volume with great care, even reverence, before placing it down before him. Without the protection of the napkin, he picked up the single sheet and examined it.

'The book is our Qur'an,' he said, leaning back. 'It is old and well used. You do not write your own words or your name in the Holy Book. I assume this is the Qur'an of a devout man. This was a precious possession. You know we believe this is the word of God? Not the translation, but these exact words in Arabic are His words. That is all I can tell you about the owner. As a believer, I should not handle our Holy Book without first having performed ablutions.'

'Sorry,' Elizabeth said. 'I did not know.' She realised there might be issues with her, an unbeliever, a woman, handling this Qur'an. Unwashed and an infidel.

'You did not know. You found this sheet next to it?'

'Yes,' she said. 'It appeared to be with it.'

'It is a prayer, a *dua*, or supplication.' He looked up and she could see his questions gathering.

'And this.' She handed over the manila foolscap envelope.

With care, he extracted the page and spent time looking at it. She knew it was in Arabic, with a few Roman numerals and signatures.

Mubarak replaced the page on the table and sat back. 'May I ask, what is the exact origin of these items?'

'My father gave them to me. They belonged to a friend of his. All I know is his friend was called Khaleed, and he was about sixty years old in 1964.' It was a true description of its legal position but not its provenance.

'This page appears to be written in formal legal Arabic and again it is old,' said Mubarak. 'I would need to consult an expert to understand it fully. Perhaps my brother, who is a lawyer, could help us here. It looks as if it is a deed for a property in Unguja, which is the proper name for Zanzibar Island. It is signed and this would be the formal stamp of the Sultan of the time. I assume it is a grant of land. A precious document, I am sure. I cannot see any street names or numbers. You would have to research old property records, maybe of a hundred years ago or more.'

She handed him the photograph. Once more, he took his time, turning it over and looking on the back.

'An old photo,' he said. 'Look at the clothes and the setting. Of course, I do not recognise the family. I am too young and, anyway, I did not grow up here but in Oman.

'In the old days, there were eminent Arab Zanzibari families living here,' he paused, looking intently at the image. 'This is a formal family occasion. Maybe the family gathering for a wedding. The men are wearing the traditional Arab clothes. All three men are wearing their *jambiya*, these curved daggers. The young woman is showing her face, the older women are veiled. And look here, the photo is signed by Supreme Studio. They were the photographers in the old Zanzibar. The shop is still here on Kenyatta Road and is run by the grandson. You could try them.'

'How old do you think it is?'

'Hard to say. If Khaleed kept it as something special, maybe he is this man in the photo.'

Mubarak pointed to an older man in the image. Both the older adult men were wearing white *kanzus* covered by long cloaks. The oldest man stood tall, a serious man looking straight at the camera, his right hand on his belt where the dagger hung: a man of some standing, of authority.

'He looks in his late forties or early fifties. Maybe this is his son next to him. Maybe the son is getting married. You see they are both wearing the traditional *jokho*, the black coat for formal occasions. If I was to make a guess, I would think it is around the mid-1940s.'

He handed back the photo. 'What are you going to do with these things?'

Elizabeth now knew how she felt but not how far this commitment would take her. 'I will try to find the family.'

'It is sad to say but it may not be possible,' Mubarak said. 'There was turmoil during the Revolution. We call it genocide. Thousands died. Families left as soon as they could. Properties and farms were nationalised, people imprisoned. In the memory of our people, it is a time remembered with pain.'

'So this family may no longer be living here?' Elizabeth said.

'We call them the Zanzibar diaspora. There are old ties as this is where their ancestors are buried. There are dedicated family graveyards here. Others say they will never come back.' He paused as if debating the wisdom of his next remark. 'It is hard for them to see the state of Zanzibar. They come and they weep.'

'Yes,' she replied. 'Much has changed. Few now will know what it was like before the Revolution.'

'Ah,' he said and smiled fleetingly. 'You lived here then? You would have been a young child. And your father?' Mubarak did not seem to be a man who smiled often.

'He worked for the British Government,' she said, 'and then briefly for Mohammed Shamte's Government before it was overthrown.'

'So that is your interest in our island. It was your home and you will remember.'

He showed reserve in his attitude and she did not know why. How was she to know the politics of modern Zanzibar?

'I wonder,' she said, 'if you know someone who can help me with my search. It is the only way I can hope to solve this. I will pay them, of course.'

'I will try,' he replied. 'First, I would like to know the whole story, things you know about this family without realising it. Let us go over the details again. This is a mystery and it might be too late.'

So she went through the story. Most of it. She told him of her father's connection to the family but not how she had found the hidden valuables. It did not seem important to the issue at hand. Mubarak listened without interruption.

'What I learn from this is that Khaleed's family lived near Mambo Msiige,' said Mubarak, 'so most likely in the Shangani area. You see, in those times, Stone Town was inhabited by extended Arab families: most of them lived close to one another, in wards called *mtaa*. For example, the people living in Shangani would have different family connections to those living in Malindi. The second thing that I hear is he, or his son, was involved in the Zanzibar National Party. Their coalition won the 1963 election. If he was attacked that day, or during the following days, it could be for this reason.

'We each have our family stories of what happened. What you tell me would be of interest to the Zanzibaris who still ask questions about the days of the Revolution. There are different stories being told. Even now. You know what they say: a picture is worth a thousand words; the same is true with firsthand accounts. First, shall we visit Supreme Studio and see if they have any records of these photographs? Tomorrow at ten?'

55. Photographs

'Supreme Studio is one of the surviving businesses,' Mubarak explained as she limped along beside him towards Kenyatta Road. 'They kept going through the worst times. They served the new masters by taking publicity photos for the Revolutionary Government. Propaganda campaigns, you understand. So I fear it's likely they destroyed pre-1964 records. Let us see.'

Walking with Mubarak, she wasn't accosted by hawkers or guides. He seemed to know everyone, greeting the groups of men hanging around the entrance to Gizenga Street, the main tourist route into the narrowest streets of Stone Town.

Supreme Studio occupied a one-room shop near the post office. Two customers were being served ahead of them. Black and white pictures of Zanzibar covered the walls. At one end, two portraits, formal head and shoulders shots, were mounted side-by-side in pride of place. Two Presidents, one old, one current: two inheritors of power. She recognised the severe unsmiling face, matching bushy eyebrows and moustache, the bulky shoulders of the late President Abeid Karume, first President of the Republic. It was the same image she had seen in Stranger House.

She remembered his background. The British, committed to class structures and well-versed in putting other people down, used to call him the 'boat boy' before the Revolution. Abeid Karume had travelled the Indian Ocean as a seaman, returning to Zanzibar to work in the harbour, doing odd jobs, ferrying people to and from the mail ships. There he discovered he had a talent for leadership, an ability to stir people with his speeches. His emotional demands for political power for the poor were appreciated, and he rapidly rose in the ranks of the African-orientated party, the Afro-Shirazi Party. And after the Revolution, Abeid Karume inherited the mantle of power and, with it, the ability to send people to prison on a whim or, on a day when he was feeling magnanimous, to let them out.

Elizabeth's father had said Abeid Karume was likable, with a ready laugh and a mercurial temperament. They had been travelling together during the 1961 riots when Karume had leapt out of the car into a violent mob to rescue an Arab-looking man.

'Saved the man's life, he did,' her father said. 'The people listened to him. He was a natural leader, knew how to command a crowd—one of those speakers who pause for effect, who emphasise the words that matter. The people loved his speeches then. He could talk for hours. Yet he turned into a despot. He disliked educated men. I suppose he felt threatened.'

Next to President Karume's photo was the image of the current President, Dr Ali Mohamed Shein. She wondered what sort of leader he was. How did you avoid the corrupting influences while holding office in a country where wealth and poverty walked hand in hand?

Two young tourists, girls in bright shorts and sleeveless tops, were at the counter. 'Do you have any photos of the Sultans?' one asked.

'No,' the owner replied, without smiling and shaking his head. 'There are no photographs of Sultans here.'

Again Elizabeth feared the photographer's stock had been condemned as representative of the old regime. Yet, on the other hand, she knew that oil paintings of the Sultans of Zanzibar once more hung in the People's Palace and the House of Wonders. Maybe the Revolutionary Council no longer felt threatened by the possibility of the Sultan returning.

Mubarak spoke to the owner in Swahili and introduced her.

'Jamal will help us if he is able,' he explained. Jamal was short, middle-aged, his thin hair slicked down with what looked like a greasy hair product. He was sporting a grass-green shirt open at the neck to reveal a gold chain. Jamal carefully removed Khaleed's photograph and stared at it without comment. He turned it over and pointed to tiny writing.

'Yes, this is ours. You can see these are my grandfather's initials, our stamp. It is old, most likely taken when he first set up his studio. The studio was used when I was a child but it is gone now. See this number on the back, CB4287? It was his way of numbering for reorders, the sitting number. I know already it is from 1942. He was extremely organised, you understand. Let me check.'

Jamal pulled out a folding set of steps from under the counter. He opened them and, nimbly for his size, climbed up and handed down a cardboard box from the top shelf. Mubarak placed it on the counter. Jamal returned to face them. He took out a pile of black foolscap books in various state of decrepitude. Ignoring the top few, he found one near the bottom. He licked his finger and flipped the pages, slowed down and ran a long fingernail down a list.

'Here it is, job CB4287, May 1942.'

Mubarak asked in English. 'Does it say the customer's name as well?'

'Yes, there is a name but it is only a first name and second name, Ahmed

Khaleed. Khaleed would have been his father's name I think. In those days, everyone knew everyone. It was a small town; perhaps clan names were not needed. I think this is a wedding. There were many weddings when my grandfather used his studio.'

Elizabeth realised what he meant, for the piles of more recent photos she had been looking at were of a series of political meetings. The images showed President Karume in set promotional pictures in front of building sites and military parades surrounded by crowds waving flags.

'Thank you,' Elizabeth said. 'This is excellent. We have the son's name now. Ahmed. Would you have any more shots from this wedding, maybe negatives?' Surely a photographer would hate to throw negatives away. They were his livelihood.

'We keep negatives, of course, but this is long ago,' Jamal looked at Mubarak as if he was sizing him up. 'They are stored elsewhere.'

Mubarak took over. 'Can you look for them?'

Mubarak glanced at Elizabeth and she nodded. 'I will pay for your time.'

'Come back tomorrow,' Jamal said.

A box of old historical postcards was on the counter. She picked one out that depicted the old Main Street with the post office on the right and the rows of jewellery shops on the left. She recognised the name, *Ranti da Silva, Manufacturing Jewellers, Gem Merchants, Ivory Carvers*. A bearded Arab coffee seller with his conical copper urn and china cups in hand stood to the fore, drawing your gaze into the scene. At the bottom of the street, the houses opened to the sea. It was the Main Street as she remembered it from her childhood. She bought it.

They left the studio, avoiding the scooters and cars in the narrow road. There were no footpaths.

'You realise,' Mubarak said, 'he was probably in danger for even keeping the negatives. His father took that risk. The only way they kept their business was by being useful to the Presidents. When you are a dictator, you have to keep persuading the people you are doing the best for them. And,' he said with emphasis, 'telling us that the past, the time of our Sultans, was oppressive. So you re-write history, say it again and again until you believe it.'

'Maybe his father couldn't bear to throw away the negatives. They were his life's work.' Elizabeth said. She held up the postcard and showed Mubarak.

'Look. This is the same spot from which this was taken maybe sixty years ago'.

The post office was grey now, with black stripes. All the old trading shops were replaced by the generic tourist shops found throughout Africa. The road still dropped down towards the shining glimpse of the roiling dirty sea between low stone buildings. Always the sea.

'A lot has changed,' he said, 'and is still changing. But we need to know the past,' Mubarak said. He turned to her. 'Do you remember what it was like? How it was back then?'

'Yes, a little. Now I am here and thinking about it. The Europeans lived such a separate life, so cut off from the local ways. We saw it all from behind a wall, physical and mental. Mind you, my parents never liked the social stratifications ruling the lives of the British. But it was there, dominating everything. The colonials called Britain 'home' and had paid leave to go back there every three years. I like to think my father was different. He used to say he was an African. Of course he was not: it was more a statement of his independent mind.'

Mubarak persisted. 'There are few people around to tell the story of our history. Families left, and now they are spread across the world. We need to know what life was like. Why have our people suffered so much when this country has so much to offer? People are asking questions again, raising political issues about our country. Asking why has it gone wrong? Why has it not delivered the education our children need?'

Yes, she thought, if we do not speak, who will speak in our place and what will they say?

They started walking back to the hotel. She noticed an internet café had opened in the post office, its notice above the signs for Western Union and Bureau de Change. Once she had collected stamps and had loved the Zanzibar stamps with the Sultan's turbaned head and images of clove bunches or fishing boats. Half the world had appeared to be part of the British Empire.

At school, the world map on the wall had glowed pink with the network of the British colonies. To be part of that made you proud. Names like the Cayman Islands, Seychelles, Trinidad and Tobago. Where were these places that shared the connection to Britain? On reflection, she thought the pride was based on the belief that the British Empire was basically good and those under its care were well treated. She had been unaware she was living through the Empire's fast decline and, more to the point, that the British had not always been the heroes in the game.

Those heroes of the Empire after whom her school houses were named were but forerunners of imperial domination: Stanley, Burton, Rhodes, Speke and even Livingstone. The lands they traversed were to be marked out to satisfy Britain's colonial ambitions.

Mubarak was thinking aloud. 'Few people have told us what it was like, what happened. You know what they say about history? About the victors writing it? That is what has happened. In fact,' he laughed derisively, 'years ago, a history book about Zanzibar was given to every student here. Free. It was a ridiculous invention, a twisting of history and downright lies. But it was needed by the regime. Why? Because the worse that life is now, the more you have to tell your people how terrible was the past. How you rescued them from even worse despots.'

'But I suppose lies only last so long. Doesn't truth find a way? Eventually, people can come and go. Look at the flood now,' said Elizabeth indicating the groups of tourists, walking into Gizenga Street with their guides. 'Is this good?'

'Maybe, maybe not,' said Mubarak. 'I have to go now. I will meet you tomorrow to visit the photographic studio again.'

Over coffee on her own, facing the ever-moving seascape, she re-examined the photograph: the heavy drapes at the back, the table to one side with a formal flower arrangement. If it was 1942, the couple being married would now be around ninety and their children also would be old. If there were children of this marriage, they would recognise this picture, this happy gathering.

The next day, the seafront was under attack. A storm was imminent. A line of staff carried the hotel furniture, carpets and crockery from the beachfront lounge into the back of the hotel. Wooden shutters and doors were firmly shut against the rising wind.

Abdullah was running around, shouting instructions. He came over to her.

'Bibi Elizabeth, please be careful today. At high tide, the seas will be close to us. It is better to stay inside.'

Mubarak arrived early. He found Elizabeth in the lounge with the photo before her. 'This photo, Mubarak, it would be familiar to their children. You know how children like to see pictures of their parents, and these at the back would be their grandparents. If children were born of this marriage, they would have been young adults or teenagers at the time of the Revolution. And now? They would be around sixty. Old, maybe like me, but they could recognise this.'

They sipped dark sweet *kahawa* watching the grey foam swirling up the shore. The bright outlook was gone; the sea turning black. The tourist boats had been moved behind Ras Shangani for protection. Today, there would be no trips to Prison Island to see the giant tortoises.

'The monsoon is strong,' Mubarak said. 'In the old days, the dhow fleet would have been well on its way to Zanzibar. Imagine being in a dhow with such a storm behind you.'

'You would be too young to remember those days?'

'Yes! But my parents have told me. The dhow trade was the lifeblood of our island. The dhows brought much business. My parents dealt in carpets and other valuables from the Gulf and Shiraz in Persia. The carpets would arrive with the desert sand in them. Arab chests, copper trays and silver came in the hold. Our town was wealthy then: now we are poor and produce nothing. Even the cloves which were once of great value are worth little. All we have is tourists, hotels, NGOs and corruption.'

Mubarak got up. 'That is enough of the past,' he said. 'Let us go and find out about the photographs. Storm or no storm.'

56. The Storm

Jamal was alone in his shop and he greeted Elizabeth and Mubarak with delight. Before they reached the counter, he waved an envelope at them.

'Yes. I have something for you,' Jamal said. 'All night. It took me all night. I am like the detective in the movies. I found the negative of your photo from 1942. That was easy. And then I am thinking, maybe this family came back. I took down my books and boxes. I went through every entry. I did not give up. I found this! One negative with the same name. Ahmed Khaleed. If I hold it to the light, you can see three children around a chair. Also it is my grandfather's studio.'

Elizabeth held the square negative up to the light, keeping her fingers on the edges. The negative appeared to have a little foxing but there were clear outlines of three children, a boy and two girls. The boy, who looked the oldest, was sitting on an ornate armchair and a girl, about nine or ten, had her arm along the back of the chair. Another smaller girl was closer to the camera.

'Do you know the date of this second photo?' she asked.

'Yes, November 1955,' Jamal said.

'Mubarak, maybe these are the children of the couple in the wedding photo,' she said. 'Well done, Jamal, can you make us three copies of this and the original wedding photograph?'

'You will have them. Give me two days,' he said.

They walked outside where the sky was heavy and darkness lined the horizon.

'Have we time to walk back through the Shangani area?' she asked.

'Only if we are quick, Bibi Elizabeth,' Mubarak said. 'The storm will not wait for us. Come this way.'

Mubarak hastened down Kenyatta Road. All the tourist shops were taking their wares inside, folding their shutters. Opposite the entrance to Gizenga Street, they turned left and hurried on. The street they entered was so narrow the sky was a thin ribbon above them. Raindrops began pinging on the corrugated iron roofs over the *barazas*.

'We are too late. Let us take shelter. Come,' said Mubarak.

He led her to the right and then up steps to the front door of a small hotel. The air was heavy and a moist wind drove down the narrow street. The onslaught was immediate. One moment, there were a few drops and the next, the street was awash, a shallow river. They stood and watched. The noise of the deluge hammering on the galvanised iron roofs and the warm sweet smell of tropical rain brought Elizabeth a strange joy.

Others were watching. Two girls were peeping out of a doorway across the way, one face above the other. They waved shyly. We are all taking pleasure in the downpour, she thought. A man on a bicycle came down the water-filled street. He was laughing in spite of being soaked. Mubarak watched over her shoulder.

'Look at these houses,' he said. 'The building with the children is in good condition but the one next door is about to fall down. If maintenance was done, it could be saved. But they are not privately owned and where is the money for this?'

'It makes you cross?'

'Yes. Sad too,' he continued. 'The Aga Khan and the United Nations were doing up the most important buildings but there are hundreds that cannot be fixed by them. It's a losing battle. Come inside; they have a restaurant here and we can have lunch while the storm passes.'

Inside the thick coral walls of the old building, the sound of the thundering rain was subdued. She heard the plink-plonk of water. Hotel staff were placing buckets under drips coming down near the walls.

They were led upstairs to a dining area. It looked out over a courtyard where a single palm and several pawpaw trees were swaying under waves of rain. They were served coffee and a sweet bread.

'I have not eaten this morning, Bibi Elizabeth. They serve Zanzibari food here. Let me ask what they have. We are the only guests; they may feed us well.'

Mubarak disappeared for a few moments and came back with a man who was wiping his hands on an apron. Mubarak was smiling happily.

'Bibi Elizabeth. Good news. Majid here is cooking for tonight. He says he has enough for us too.' Majid was nodding his head.

'Chicken *pilau* with a side of *ndizi*—bananas in coconut milk,' said Mubarak, 'it is one of my favourites. I will order for both of us. My wife has no time to cook. For me, the rainstorm comes at a good time.'

Elizabeth had not seen this side of Mubarak. He obviously loved his food. Together, they watched the silver sheets of rain. The silence was comfortable.

'I have been thinking,' Mubarak said. 'Your father said Khaleed's family had a *shamba*, a clove farm, and he thought it was north of this town? We know the grandfather was Khaleed and he was in the ZNP, maybe holding a position, and his son was Ahmed, and it is most likely Ahmed had a son, two daughters. They had a house in the Shangani area'

'That's right. It's not a lot, is it?'

'Perhaps not but Zanzibar was much smaller then: in Stone Town, the families should have been well known. What I can do is ask at the mosque. The day after tomorrow is Friday, our special day of prayer we call *ijumaa*. I could put the word out, make an announcement, a summary of who we are looking for and say we want to speak to people. You could put it in the paper but you have to be careful. There are complications with discussing what happened in the Revolution. Leave Jamal's photo for a next appeal. Hold it in reserve.'

'I like that idea,' Elizabeth replied. 'I'm prepared to offer a reward.'

'Well, make it worthwhile. Get people talking and it will get around. A hundred dollars is a lot of money here. Remember the average wage is around two dollars a day. A vast gulf between rich and poor. But do not make it too much or else some will turn up telling stories.'

'Chancers, we would say, people taking advantage,' Elizabeth said.

'Oh, that's how you say it,' Mubarak laughed. 'Yes, too many chancers. You will have seen the chancers hanging around the ATMs off Main Street. What are you going to do if you find this family?'

'I don't know. A story will be put to rest. Give them the photos, the deed and,' she said, 'I have gold jewellery that belongs to them.'

Plates of steaming rice and chicken arrived, and Majid hovered nearby to hear their comments of appreciation.

When he left, Elizabeth asked, 'Mubarak, excuse my personal question. Can I ask you what you studied in Ohio for your doctorate?'

Mubarak put down his fork. 'Yes, sure. First, I did a Masters degree in African History. Ohio University has an African Studies Program.'

'And what was your specialisation for your doctorate?'

'The thesis was on Zanzibar, of course.'

'What aspect?'

He looked out at the rain which had subsided to a gentle shower. The courtyard was slowly transformed by sunlight.

'Slavery during the nineteenth century. Slavery and the economics of slavery,' Mubarak said. 'Sadly, my degree does not educate me for much in the way of earning a salary. I did not think of teaching. So I am here looking for business!'

'Slavery is a dirty word here, is it not? It was common centuries ago across the world,' Elizabeth said.

'Yes, it was,' said Mubarak. 'You learn the history your country wants you to hear. What do the Dutch remember about Jan Pieters Coen, the Portuguese about Alfonso de Albuquerque in the Spice Islands, the Belgians about King Leopold and the Congo? These were terrible leaders doing horrific things in their greed for spices, for rubber. Yet Westerners come here and judge the Arabs for the slave trade.'

Elizabeth was subdued in the face of Mubarak's outburst. 'I have heard of Leopold but not the others.'

'And in terms of economics, slavery is still providing earnings here in a twisted way.' he said.

'Surely, it is in the past.'

'Yes, owning slaves is in the past in Zanzibar, not elsewhere of course. Across the world there are millions living in slavery. Even now. Here, it informs the present. The anecdotes of slavery are the main stories the guides tell their clients. It adds to the excitement, the spiciness of our island.'

'They are not true?' Elizabeth asked.

'They call it the Arab slave trade and, yes, part of it is true but they leave out—because they do not know—the whole story. If you have time tomorrow, let me take you and show you something to explain my point. I can show you a different Zanzibar, a new Zanzibar. Look, the rain has stopped and sadly our plates are empty. I will walk you back to the hotel.'

The streets were washed clean by the storm, the air sweet as steam rose from squares of sunshine. Women were sweeping flood debris into brown piles and calling to one another. Staff from tourist shops were hanging out the bright *kangas*, tee-shirts and scarves. Wooden carvings were being carried out. Business was back to normal and her search was not without hope.

57. Slave Chambers

Mubarak collected Elizabeth in a grey Toyota that had seen better days and drove her around the north of Stone Town. At Darajani Market, they encountered a traffic jam of cars, taxis and *dala-dala*, horns honking and drivers shouting out their destination for passengers. Crowds at the roadside wore bright clothes and carried *vikapu* of vegetables, fish and live chickens. Turning right into Sultan Ahmed Mugheiri Road, he found a parking spot outside the forecourt barrier in front of the Anglican Cathedral. The building loomed above them. Even though the façade was in shadow she could see it had been painted and repaired and that there were new signs on the door.

'You recognise this place?' Mubarak said.

'Yes, of course. This was our church. My mother was a choir member.'

'The tourists come here now. Let's go.'

He opened the door for her and Elizabeth followed him towards the entrance. On the left was a sign for Monica's Guesthouse and Restaurant. A smaller sign advertised Paul's Art Gallery and beyond was another hand-written sign: *Welcome to Anglican Christ Church Cathedral, the former Slave Market Site.*

A group of youngsters waved them onward towards the ticket office.

'Go in and do the tour. Takes about fifteen minutes,' said Mubarak. 'I'll wait for you by the cathedral.'

A guide stepped forward claiming her. He wore a black, green and yellow shirt made from local *kanga* cloth, faded shorts and a white baseball cap with 'Espana 2010' in red letters.

'Saeed is my name. Welcome to the slave chambers and the cathedral,' he said. 'First I show you the slave cellars' and he pointed to a steep flight of stairs down into a basement. 'Then you see our art exhibition before I take you to our slave monument and cathedral. Please follow.'

Hanging from the wall, on the way down, was a rough notice, *Slave Chamber—A small hut was on top. Slaves were kept in terrible conditions, so many died of suffocation and starvation. The amount was terrible.*

Saeed led the way pointing out a sign to mind her head. At the bottom were two cellars, one to the right, one hard left. The ceilings were low: a few centimetres over her head—a grown man would have to bend. Elizabeth entered the larger cellar on the left. It was at least ten to fifteen degrees cooler than outside.

The cellar was five by five metres with a concrete ledge running hip-high halfway around and taking up three-quarters of the room. Two large concrete pillars rose from the ground to the roof and, from overhead beams, rusted chains hung down ending in curls on the ledge. The height from the raised ledge to the roof would only allow someone to sit, not stand. Two narrow slit openings provided a glimpse of the street at ground level and showed the thickness of the walls.

'These are the slave chambers,' Saeed announced dramatically. 'The slaves would be brought here by the Arab slave traders and imprisoned before being sold. The men were packed in here on the one side and the women on the other. Seventy-five men were forced in here and sixty women and children over there.'

He paused for effect. 'Many slaves did not survive due to the air. There was not enough air.'

It was not a horrible space as it was but, if people had been imprisoned there in any number, it would have been a hell hole. Elizabeth turned to him and, keeping her voice low, she asked. 'Was it built for slaves? Why would they have this ledge running around the edge?'

'Slaves,' he said, 'see these chains. The building was put up on top of the slave cellars and the cellars altered. From here, the slaves were taken to be sold.'

There was no denying the horror of the trade, that she knew having read widely on the colonial abuse of Africa. Every life was valuable, and the idea of buying and selling people with the purpose of exploiting them in every way possible filled her with revulsion.

Saeed interrupted her thoughts with a tap on the shoulder, indicating she should move along. 'I will now show our art exhibition,' he said.

She followed him back upstairs where the walls were covered in intense oil paintings of wild animals, of intricate Arab doors, of dhows under sail and of stylised contorted figures against lurid sunsets. After the gloom of the cellars, these images exploded with life and colour.

'If you like, you may buy,' said Saeed. When she demurred, he pointed outside. 'Come now and see our slave statues.'

As she walked out into the searing heat, her guide continued. 'You see, Madam, they lined the slaves up over there, tied them to trees according to their sizes. It was the time for selling.'

Under an immense cycad on the right of the Anglican Cathedral was a sunken monument. Five grey life-sized figures with bowed heads, arms at their sides, stood in the hollow space. They had wire round their necks and were joined by neck chains. It was simple and moving. The figures were roughly cast but their faces were fine, each one showing a distinct character, a resignation, desperation. By looking down on the figures, Elizabeth felt she was in a position of power, or authority. Or was it responsibility?

'Here was the Slave Market,' Saeed announced. 'The Arabs brought them from the mainland on the dhows. Hundreds died on the way. Here they were sold for Arabia, or for work in our island's clove plantations. This is where they were whipped. Some cried. If they did not cry, it was good. Those were strong and they got the best price.'

When the tour was over, she thanked Saeed, giving him a generous tip. Mubarak was waiting in the shade and suggested they sit in a row of wooden chairs in the Anglican Cathedral's foyer. The chair seats and backs were smooth and shiny from use and Elizabeth wondered if any Christian slave owners had sat here to pray. Before them was the pale golden-vaulted ceiling of the church.

'Yes. What you have seen is impressive and sad. Just so,' Mubarak said. 'Only a slight problem: the underground chambers were built by St Monica's for storing medicines, not for slaves. Construction was around 1900, long after the ending of the slave trade and closing of the market. You saw the ledge inside. The whole story of suffocation and starvation is fabricated. They have no historical basis, no sources to refer to. It sounds like the story from India—you know, the Black Hole of Calcutta. Someone has installed those chains in the basement and now there is a way of making money.'

'Oh,' said Elizabeth, feeling foolish. 'It was all made up? But slavery was pitiless, endemic in the system and was here.'

'Yes,' said Mubarak, 'but didn't they emphasise it was Arab slavery? East African slavery was driven by economics. Did you know the cloth sold here is called *Merikani*? "American" in KiSwahili. American cloth was traded for slaves in the interior. Unhappily for Zanzibar's Arab people, for a few decades, things combined to make slavery profitable on a large scale.'

'Ivory?'

'Yes. Increasing demand for ivory came from the Western world. The Chinese already used a lot of ivory. They all preferred African ivory because it is soft, better for carving. And who was to carry those heavy tusks down from the interior? Slaves. And for those years in the middle of the nineteenth century, slaves were needed for the clove plantations in Zanzibar.'

'That was before refrigeration, when spices were essential for cooking and perfumes,' Elizabeth said.

'Yes, cloves were being sold to Western countries, to Indonesia,' continued Mubarak. 'Slaves were in demand for the sugar plantations in the colonies: Mauritius, Réunion and Seychelles. The French had a base in Madagascar. They exchanged guns for slaves. Brazilian slave ships were in the Indian Ocean too, flying Portuguese flags. The slave trade was underpinned by Western demand and Indian financing.'

Mubarak paused as a tour group entered the cathedral. Their guide pointed to the tall wooden crucifix on the left of the nave. He announced it was made from the tree under which David Livingstone's heart was buried.

'See it is all about slavery,' said Mubarak. 'Tour guides across Stone Town take tourists from one site to another talking slavery. Few guides are trained in history or guiding. The thing is, what irks us and, I might add, all historians, is that the history of slavery was held to be a justification for the 1964 Revolution and genocide, as if we were responsible for what took place more than a hundred years previously. What is more, the Revolutionary Government now makes a mess of these islands and they tell their people, "times are bad but you don't want the Arabs back, do you?" Yet we all know it was better before 1964.'

'Politicians have always used "history" to manipulate people,' said Elizabeth.

They watched as the tourists followed their guide. Camera flashes lit up the ornaments. A couple posed in front of the altar and a young woman in the group took their phone and gestured to them to move closer together, bending slightly to get the angle right. The guide pointed at the stained glass windows over the font. The panels showed three figures. The central figure was brilliant white where the coloured glass had been broken and replaced with the regular transparent kind. From the right hand panel a saint in a crimson robe waved a blessing over the ghostly figure.

The guide's voice came over to her. 'This window was made for British sailors. They died chasing the Arab slave dhows.' He then turned and led his group behind past the altar rail. His casual entry into the sanctuary irked her. It was an area holy to Christians.

More for her mother than herself, she said a quick apology to God for the intrusion, and as an afterthought she added 'And if it is for the good, make *this* work out. Please.'

More flashes went off and she had to turn away from her growing irritation.

'I always thought of Zanzibar as a place of religious tolerance,' she said. 'I remember this cathedral was built with help from Sultan Barghash. He was a Muslim, but he allowed Christian missionaries to do their work with freed slaves. Zanzibaris used to be able to follow their beliefs without persecution.'

'Yes, true, but the issues dividing local people fifty years ago remain,' said Mubarak. 'That's the point. There has been little reconciliation. What does it mean to be a Zanzibari as opposed to someone from the mainland?'

His raised voice carried in the emptiness. Tourists were turning to watch them and the guide had paused in his exposition.

'Until the government opens up this conversation,' continued Mubarak, 'we are doomed to be divided. And one way to start is to return properties to those families whose land and houses were stolen after the Revolution. Apologise for past excesses, for the genocide. It would be a great act of goodwill.'

They faced the towering space of the nave. She remembered that upward pointing arches were meant to take your thoughts to heaven. It was a space for contemplation, for hope for better times. To listen to others.

There was silence between them: the pleasant settled silence of people comfortable with one another.

'What are you thinking?' Mubarak said.

'Actually, I was thinking, your mother must be proud of you.' It surprised her as it came out. She had not meant to say that but it felt right. 'I would be happy to have a son like you.'

He sat up, obviously pleased. 'Thank you. I think she loves me but always a Mama worries. Sometimes, I think her worry is more that she wants me to be something different, something better. You do not wear a wedding ring.' He held up his hand to show her a narrow band of silver on his left hand.

'No.' she said. 'It never quite happened.'

He did not pursue the issue. 'It is a big step, a risk. I was not sure. But I am now. My wife is the best. I cannot imagine life without Aziza. She is in practice here, you know. A doctor. She will specialise in paediatrics eventually. At the moment, she is supporting me.'

'Aren't you in the hotel business?'

'Sort of, that was the plan. But last week I was appointed as a visiting lecturer at the State University of Zanzibar. For a year, I am to teach a history module. But still, I should have time to help you with your mystery. Tomorrow, we'll collect the photographs from Supreme Studio. On Friday, I will make some announcements in our community and see where that takes us.'

The tourists had finished with their cathedral tour and they followed the group out into the sunshine. 'I'm feeling lucky,' said Elizabeth, touching the old wooden doors on the way out as she had done as a child. For some reason, it was true.

58. The Intersection

Elizabeth had several days alone before Mubarak would come back to her with the results of his inquiries. It was a wonder to her how he had come to her aid with a disarming generosity. To pass the time, she wandered in Stone Town, from one narrow winding alleyway to another. Looking for the familiar. Remembering.

She knew which side the sea was on by following the shadows on the buildings and the position of the sun, but, time and time again, she was uncertain which route to follow. There were squares busy with activity, wider roads filled with tourist shops where touts lay in wait. The smaller laneways were home to a rich and diverse private world. It was where children played and rode their bicycles. Mothers swept the roads, watched their children and spoke to neighbours, so many walking, greeting one another. Conversations filled the streets.

For some hours, she walked away from and towards Kelele Square in the Shangani area trying to work out the way that Khaleed might have come to see her father. Vehicles were allowed into Kelele Square and on the road past her hotel leading to Forodhani and the House of Wonders but no cars could enter the largest sections of the town.

The old American Consulate building was on the inland side of the square and four very narrow lanes led away from this area. She followed each laneway, looking at the houses. There were so many of them, all impenetrable. Each house had a few ground floor windows with bars and closed brown shutters. Their front doors opened directly onto the street. Along the walls of all the houses and across the intersections, great snaking loops of power cables made their way through the city.

One lane from Kelele led to a tiny square, the centre of which was filled with a pile of enormous coral stones, rubble which must once have been a home. Twisted corrugated iron stuck out and a nest of pawpaw trees had grown in the centre. It was as Naji had said, for on one side of the ancient stones a modern three-storey house of cement blocks was nearing completion. On the outside of the house, rows of fussy balustrades shone bright white.

There were innumerable houses along the many routes by which Khaleed could have made his way to Mambo Msiige that morning in January 1964. There would have been many witnesses that day. Someone would have seen him hurrying along with his burden. Those hours would have been seared into the memory of everyone in Zanzibar at the time. Surely someone remembered. How many stories were there? Told and re-told. She had been a witness too, her own story just one tiny part of the whole.

The friendship that had brought her father and Khaleed together was a thin skein across the years speaking of respect and compassion and, at the end of his life, her father had recognised this. Now it was her turn to learn compassion, be courageous before it was too late. This awareness filled her as she walked because, without quite realising it, she had made a decision and it was true and it was good.

Elizabeth's leg was stronger now and she walked with barely a limp. The uneven streets no longer challenged her. She examined the thread of her life. It was like the black lines she followed through the streets, turning and joining. Now she had something solid onto which she could hold. She was not sure where that would lead but its certainty gave her pleasure in all that she now saw as she turned this way and that, greeting people who greeted her, managing to smile and see the place for perhaps the first time. And a glow came over her for anything seemed possible at that moment.

Late one afternoon, she found a remote square in the Malindi area beyond the Sultan's palace. A few bicycles stood against the wall by an ancient door on which were scribbled layers of marks and messages, faded and half rubbed out. The door did not speak of prestige and wealth: it was a pedestrian door devoid of any brass bosses, its wooden panels dented and cracking. A blue 'W' above the door denoted that the building was once a charitable donation.

A red motorbike was resting against the *baraza*. She sat down beside it wanting to disappear into the background. Two schoolgirls in white headdresses skipped past. They glanced at her, giggled and ran away speaking quietly to each other and adjusting their scarves. Although the sea was not far off it could not be seen or heard from within the arms of the buildings. Stone Town was well named. Here, she had stepped into a place that felt as ancient as the earth, a place of memory. Her thoughts returned to the person she once was: to when she and her sister had parted.

*****

Mary. *Mary-Lou.* Elizabeth had left Knysna, left her sister's house without explanation. Put the birth, the baby and her fight with Mary behind her and gone to the UK. There she had lived for over a decade, qualifying as a high-school teacher of English and History. It was an easy way out. The cold and wet, the dismal surroundings, the relative poverty, a sort of passage of punishment for messing up.

She had various short-term relationships which drifted to a close without any particular upset. It was as if none mattered enough to cause her suffering. She found it easy to keep to herself, making polite excuses to avoid social events and not reciprocating with questions about people's lives. This helped keep colleagues at arm's length and gave her the space she needed as she endeavoured to forget.

Mary tried to contact her, wrote to her: 'Did Elizabeth want her to find her baby, her daughter?' And then it appeared that Susan and Mary had found her. Bitterness came to Elizabeth. What right did they have to interfere? At first, Elizabeth wrote back, short missives without offering anything. When Mary told her joyfully how they had seen the baby, Elizabeth felt a pain shoot through her heart. Then, she felt anger that Mary was doing this to her, emphasising Elizabeth's act of desertion.

Mary wrote, 'So sweet she is. And thank you for the name: Mary-Lou. She still has the name and we are making a plan. Shall I send you a picture? Come home and see her.'

No! It was not to be. Elizabeth felt it was a deep well into which she would not fall. She turned away, writing back that, 'She did not want to hear any more.' And then she returned the letters unopened. Why? She wondered later. Why had she lost the grace, the compassion that Mary had? On what day had that happened? Where had that anger come from? But, by then, it was too late.

From then on, she heard through her father. Bits and pieces. Susan and Mary opened a medical practice in Knysna and were doing well. Had adopted three children over the years. At the end of 1989 at the age of thirty-eight, Elizabeth escaped a depressing relationship by taking a teaching job in Sydney, Australia. By now, she felt that she was a confirmed spinster, set in her ways.

It was on TV in Sydney that she watched Nelson Mandela walk out of prison hand-in-hand with Winnie. Most of South Africa broke into a riot of celebration. It was February 1990.

Mary found out where she was and wrote. Elizabeth opened this one as she had not received a letter for many years. Once more, Mary pleaded for peace and reconciliation.

'Come home,' she wrote. 'Come home, Lizzy. Things will be different now. No more apartheid. Mary-Lou is home too.' And Mary had told her father. 'He needed to know, Lizzy, that he has a granddaughter. He's sixty-eight now. I cannot tell you how thrilled he was.'

Mary-Lou. Elizabeth knew each birthday. Counted the years, the birthdays. Fifteen then. A teenager at high school, almost a woman. All she could remember of her baby was the tiny hand that clung to her finger amid the stiff white sheets. But pride is a horrible thing. The sin of Lucifer sitting like a dark dam within her. So fixed and horrible she had not the power to breach it. And so the years of silence continued.

In that Stone Town square, it was as if she had held her breath and was weightless. She did not need to raise her chest one more time. Perhaps that was how you died. Lost the will to breath, the body said, enough. Disjointed memories flashed past for one last moment, a sense of regret before you lost all needs, and your time was passed.

*****

Time had passed, the shadows moving across the walls in that darkening space, and Elizabeth returned to the present. Someone was watching her from the shadow over the opposite *baraza*: a bent old man, his legs drawn up under him, his head half bowed. For a moment of shock, she thought it was her father: the skeletal head, the jutting jawline, the look was there. She thought the man was blind for he seemed to look through her, not at her: seeing something else, a *shetani?*

His presence seemed an acknowledgement of her situation, her sense that she had passed through to making a change, shedding a self she couldn't sustain any longer. She rose and stood before the *mzee*. He raised his head and touched his heart with his right hand and bowed slightly. She bowed, saying nothing and hobbled away, her legs slowly gathering strength.

She knew what she had to do. Had to undo. There was a past life she had not lived. But there was a future she could still live. It would start now.

59. Interviews

The large entrance hall was lined with wooden benches. Light entered intermittently as the door opened and closed behind them. Before her eyes had adjusted, she was aware of men and women waiting around the perimeter of the hall.

'This way, follow me,' murmured Mubarak. He opened a side door, nodding for her to enter. 'We will be using this room for our meeting.'

Here the light poured in through large casement windows facing the street. Vertical bars on the windows caused jail-like shadows on the black and white floor tiles. The high ceilings and cool space were more welcoming. Bright coir mats were scattered on the floor, chairs and stools arranged along the side. The walls had no decoration. It was a spartan place.

Two elderly men waited on benches. Before each of them was an old school desk with a slanted lid and an empty inkwell hole in one corner. Both men wore traditional clothing. As she and Mubarak entered, they rose and bowed briefly, touching their chests with their right hands before sitting once more, saying nothing.

Mubarak reciprocated and turned to her. 'These men are from my community. They will oversee these discussions.'

She realised she was asking them to delve into a past with a history that had been layered over with political fabrications for over forty-five years. The truth was a threat to those who had inherited power on the island. Different versions could be given of the same incident, further confused by years of propaganda. The misinformation continued. Who was to say what was true and what was not? Revisiting the past might be dangerous.

One by one, people entered. If she had expected this to be easy or quick, she was mistaken. When Mubarak was called on to translate, it took even more time. Many stories began in Swahili – and even though she could not understand the words she followed along, drawn by the intense emotion in the telling. Always Mubarak patiently encouraged the storytellers before filling her in with interpretation in English, the narrators watching her face as she listened as if hungry for a response. Three women of late middle age and a man came forward. One thought she remembered the family but had nothing concrete to offer. She could not recall where they had lived. They were recollecting a time when they were teenagers or even younger. The community had been considerably smaller in the 1960s and the web of communication, intermarriage and friendships had lasted in their minds.

'Near Bububu?' Mubarak said. He turned to Elizabeth. 'This woman says she thinks the family had a *shamba*, a farm, north of the town, about six miles, near Bububu.'

The next old woman asked for help in finding her missing uncle and to understand what had happened. She spoke of a lifetime of wondering where her father's only brother had gone. He was a teacher in the countryside near Ras Nungwi at the time. There had been chaos for weeks and families had dispersed. Some ran for safety into town, others fled north hoping to escape by boat, hundreds were interned for weeks.

The woman asked whether there were places overseas to which her uncle might have escaped. She said his name several times, pausing for answer. Finally she took out a tiny black and white photograph of a tall serious man with a girl standing next to him and showed it in turn to each of the men at the desk and then holding it in both hands brought it for Elizabeth to see. She pointed to the girl and then herself. She asked, 'Could anyone help with answers? Was it too late?'

One of the elderly men took down the woman's details and Mubarak spoke to her for a while.

Next a young man came forward. It was clear he was hopeful of taking advantage of their situation, saying he could definitely find this family but they must pay him for his help and information. He hinted at his connection to those in power, at secret knowledge. Mubarak was not intimidated and the man was dismissed.

Then silence, all waiting. She felt the anticlimax. There was a general shuffling of feet. She rose and limped up and down to alleviate the ache in her bandaged leg.

One of the onlookers stood up and came across to the desks. Elizabeth saw he held *bismillah* prayer beads in his right hand and was clicking through them even as he whispered to Mubarak.

Mubarak turned to her. 'One more is waiting outside, an old man who would like to speak. He is known to us and we are unsure but let us hear him out.'

She nodded and an aged man entered. He was so bowed she could not see his face at first. A young boy was at his side, his arm supporting and leading the bent figure. The old man raised his head slowly. Elizabeth watched his painful movements as he lowered himself. He looked only at

Mubarak. The boy sat cross-legged at his feet.

'Thank you for coming, old man, *mzee*. Let us hear you,' Mubarak said in English and Swahili.

The man sat up straighter and raised his face. Elizabeth was not sure how much he saw as his wandering gaze reminded her of her father trying to see with diminished sight. He was wizened; his eyes drooped within weeping sockets. He appeared to be close to ninety, his face deeply lined. On his head, his *kofia* was grey and frayed.

'My name is Omar Shambe and this boy is Salim, the son of my granddaughter. I have been told you are looking for someone from long ago.' He paused and laid his hand gently on the boy's head. To Elizabeth's surprise, Omar spoke in clear English.

'It is a long story I have to tell you. I am not a clever man, nor a young man, but if you will listen, I will tell you things I have told no one before,' Omar paused. 'I believe I can help you with your search.'

Mubarak nodded. 'We are here. Tell us your story, Omar Shambe.'

'Thank you. I was born in Makunduchi, over there, but I came to live in town, in Ng'ambo, what the English would call "the other side" of Stone Town. Workers and labourers lived there, over the creek before it was filled in. This was the time of the old Sultan, Seyyid Khalifa.

'I was not well educated although I could read, but I was a hard worker and tried several jobs before I worked as a boat boy at the English Sailing Club there by Ras Shangani. First, I helped with cleaning but, over the years, they gave me different jobs and I learnt to speak English. The *wazungu*, English people, most were good to me but some would call me "boy". I married young and my wife, Anisa, had a child, a son, and we called him Hasan, as he was special to us. For Anisa nearly died and doctors said she would not have another child.

'The *wazungu*, the men and the women, loved to sail their wooden boats in the harbour and race around the point. The boats were not like our dhows or *ngalawa*, they had no room for fish or passengers. They would chase one another, each boat trying to go faster in the monsoon winds. They would argue about who had come first.

'I learnt to clean their boats, scraping off weeds and shells, polishing and painting them to make them move swiftly through the water. I would be given extra money for this work.

'After the races, the men with their wives would get together in the club and drink alcohol. They would watch the sun setting over Prison Island and talk about what would happen to Unguja. They talked about elections, about our Sultan, about how the British colonials would leave one day and go home to England. They were not careful about what they said, and how loudly they said it. I would listen and remember. At night, I would tell my wife, Anisa, the stories I heard.

'My son, Hasan, grew to be a strong boy, taller than his friends. He brought great joy to us, his parents, and to his grandparents. His mama would cook him *ugali* and shop at Darajani Market for the best fish for him. It was my happiest day when he passed his exams and we were told he was accepted into Form 1 at the Aga Khan High School. Because we were poor, we were told it would cost us only five shillings a term.

'At that time, there was much trouble in Unguja because of the elections for independence. We called it the "time of politics". It did not worry me but I listened to the talk at the English Sailing Club. I told my family about how the English were troubled about the coming of freedom, of *Uhuru*. Some white people did not like the Afro-Shirazi Party and their leader, Abeid Karume. They said he was not a Zanzibari and was not an educated man. They laughed and said he had once been a boat boy, like me. Others did not like the other party, the ZNP, the party of the *jogo*, and their leaders, saying the Arab people should go back to Oman or to Egypt.

'I had reached forty years and Hasan was fifteen. Hasan started to listen to the talk of *uhuru* with other boys at school, and one day he told me he had joined the Afro-Shirazi Youth League. I was worried but it did not seem a matter for much concern. He would go to meetings after school and I would ask him what they did. He told me men came to teach them about how our country should be run. It was then I saw he was getting angry and excited. He told us terrible stories about the Arabs from long ago, about slavery. He shouted and listened to nothing from me any more.'

Omar told his story and no one interrupted. He paused to take deep breaths. His great-grandson would look up at him and massage his feet and hand him a glass of water. Elizabeth noticed Omar's ankles below his long white *kanzu* were swollen with black smudges like bruises. The soles of his bare feet were pale cream with deep cracks. They looked like ancient wood.

'The story of the Revolution is known, of how the police stations were overrun and how the Sultan escaped to the boat in the harbour, of John Okello and his men from the mainland, and the things he said on the radio that brought terror to all in Zanzibar. During that night, we were woken by shouts and strange noises but it was not until daybreak when we turned on our radio that we heard our new government was being attacked.

'Boys from Hasan's school arrived at our house, and they said he was needed to fight in the *Mapinduzi* and he must go with them. A few of them had sticks; others waved *pangas* in the air. They said the Youth League of the Afro-Shirazi Party had called their members to come, to stop the Arabs from taking over. They were shouting, going mad with excitement. Our son went with them; we could do nothing.

'Who was there to raise their voice against what was happening? No one. Those days were terrible for we lost the son we knew. But worse was to follow. We waited for Hasan to return, day after day. We prayed for his safety, listened for his homecoming, his voice calling out in greeting, his smile for his Mama.

'We ourselves were afraid. We listened to the radio and heard John Okello's voice. He called himself "Field Marshall" and his voice was strange to our ears. No one can forget that voice. He spoke of death—to the Sultan, his wives and his children. He told the Arab fathers to kill their families and then themselves before he came with his men to kill them all. He spoke of revenge. Houses were on fire. We could smell the smoke and hear the screams of terror. And to my shame, Anisa and I hid inside for two days: we did not try to help.'

At that moment, Elizabeth had a terrible sense that this story would end in nothing but sadness for her search and for the old man. What father deserved to see his son changed into something he could only fear? The love never died. She knew Islam taught you to accept your earthly lot but sometimes that would be hard. Omar's story had taken well over an hour. His voice was getting quieter. She wondered if this was with shame at what he had to tell, or with exhaustion.

Mubarak put his hand up. 'It is time for prayer. Let us come back when we have done our duty. We will eat and be rested. Come with us, *Mzee* Omar.'

Elizabeth was invited to eat with the women in a back room while the men went to the local mosque. Three women were in the room all sitting on oval Pemba mats. With a greeting, she joined them on the floor. They smiled and silently offered her the bowls of *pilau*, fried fish and *samoosas*. She was given a plate; the others shared from communal dishes. She had not realised how hungry she was. The *samoosas* were crunchy with light pastry. She showed her appreciation with her limited Swahili, '*Mzuri chakula. Asante.*' They replied in English.

60. Hasan's Story

Omar's story was a confession, a confession for his son who was not there to tell his story. Elizabeth realised Hasan was dead and the lifetime of Omar's suffering was being revealed.

After a week, Hasan returned to his parents. He was dressed in odd bits of combat wear with a revolver slung across his chest and an Arab sword. His father could tell his son had been drinking alcohol. Hasan deposited a bag of odd household things with them saying they were payment for his 'work'. Omar said he did not touch them. Hasan said he would not come back to live with them, for now he was in the new army created to protect the islands from invasion by imperialists.

Mubarak stopped translating the odd Swahili phrases. She realised it was too distracting to the flow of the story. Once more, Elizabeth found she could understand. It was as if her brain was catching up while she was remained unaware. She listened as Omar poured out his story to his silent audience in that austere room. At various points, there was a shuffling of feet or an 'ahem' in agreement. More people had gathered, standing as mute witnesses. The women who had shared their lunch with Elizabeth came to sit beside her.

Omar said that from time to time Hasan visited them. He had acquired a new persona, a swagger and a determination to show his authority. At first, he talked proudly about making sure the Revolution was here to stay and rounding up enemies but, when his Mama covered her face and wept and his father could only look at the floor, he came less and when he did, he was silent about his work. He would bring food and money and leave without saying anything or staying to share a meal. His parents did not know what to do. The English people had left, the Sailing Club was nationalised and, without Hasan's help, they would have starved.

They depended on Hasan and, as the years went by, they preferred to remain ignorant of how Hasan was living. Some things they knew. Hasan had access to food while the community struggled for survival and he boasted about his power to order people around. The detail of his life was hidden from them but there were rumours on the streets and they prayed that he was not involved.

'Zanzibar is an island; you cannot hide for long,' Mubarak said later in explanation.

Hasan married a woman of whom they had no knowledge. The formal marriage ceremony so important in their society was not performed. He occupied a house at Mazizini and now called himself a 'sergeant'. Omar had nothing to do with his new domestic life although Anisa would visit to see her baby granddaughter. Hasan put on weight and, more and more often, he smelt of alcohol whenever they did see him.

He started to shout at them. 'Why don't you thank me for what I do? Why do you look at me like that?' And on a quieter note, 'You must be careful not to criticise the Revolutionary Government.'

Omar found it easier to go out or feign sleep when his son came to visit. Sometimes Hasan brought his daughter and that was easier for Anisa as she could take delight in the innocent child. Anisa would tell Omar afterwards that Hasan was devoted to his only daughter, her only grandchild. She would cry. Anisa spent a lot of time crying.

After five years, Hasan informed them he had been promoted to be an assistant in the special prison for political prisoners. It was not the Central Prison of *Kiinua Miguu,* but the prison the East Germans had helped establish. It was called the 'Father-in-law's' Prison, or *Ba-Mkwe*, and run by a man called Mandera. Its purpose was to control the people through terror and they did this with torture. Omar and Anisa knew about this prison, how people were never seen again, how feared it was. Once more, Omar did not want to hear.

When Karume was assassinated in 1972, Hasan's life started to fall apart. His womanising and drinking finally became too much for his wife. She left with their daughter and returned to her parents in Wete on Pemba Island. Under the new President, the *Ba-Mkwe* Prison continued for a while. President Jumbe consolidated his hold on power with a flurry of arrests but gradually the reign of terror was scaled down.

In 1980, sixteen years after the Revolution, when Hasan was in his early thirties, he lost his job and was demoted to the regular army. He had access to as much alcohol as he wanted and his drinking worsened. Anisa developed high blood pressure and, fretting over the loss of contact with her grandchild, distraught over her son's condition, she had a stroke and died shortly thereafter. She had been Omar's connection with his son over the last years.

One evening, almost twenty years ago, before yet another anniversary of the Revolution, Omar had come home from evening prayers to find Hasan sitting on his doorstep. He had not seen his son for months. By now, Omar was struggling to survive on the meagre government handouts. In spite of everything, he was pleased to see Hasan and even more to see he was sober. Hasan said he wanted to talk to him.

Hasan had come to say 'sorry'. Sorry for hurting his father and dead Mama and failing them. He said he was finished. Omar did not know then what 'finished' meant. His son sat on the floor, his large bulk collapsing down. He told his father that he hated himself and Allah would not forgive him. He talked on and on into the night telling him things a father did not want to hear, that no human wants to hear, of torture beyond understanding. Tears flowed down his cheeks but Omar found it hard to show mercy.

Instead, horrified at the details of this confession, he had asked his son, 'How can a man do this to another and pray at day's end?' No answer came from Hasan.

The Prison Commandant, Mandera, and his team, including Hasan, extracted confessions from perceived enemies of the state. Some men were sixty years old. Hasan beat men on their backs and the soles of their feet with thin sticks made from the guava tree while Mandera demanded confessions. There was worse: they burnt men's private parts with cigarettes and put chillies on their wounds. Many men died in prison, some from their untreated wounds, others from sickness, and some were executed. Omar had been horrified and said he had tried to forget these things but he remembered some names of the victims of torture and he wanted to say these names today. There should be a record of this, he said.

Before Omar finished, he spoke of the start of this madness, of what Hasan had said happened the first day of the Revolution, the twelfth of January 1964. Hasan told his father, this day had 'changed his life to one of evil'.

His group of youngsters, gathered from here and there, had been given weapons, *pangas* and a couple of rifles, put into the back of a lorry and driven north to Bububu. The assigned destination had been given to their leader. The vehicle was festooned with tree branches, the sign of the rebel force. Green and yellow were their colours. After a short drive, they turned off and went through the forest to a *shamba*. He was told it belonged to a ZNP official, an enemy of the Revolution, and this man was planning to kill African men and enslave their women. The young men shouted slogans as they went and were mad with excitement.

They attacked and murdered all the people they found in the house, a man and his son, including a woman servant. Although she was old, and not an Arab, some men had raped her. They ransacked the house and set it on fire.

'The name of the Baba of that family was Ahmed bin Khaleed al-Ibrahim,' said Omar. 'Ahmed bin Khaleed al-Ibrahim. I remembered. My son did not know the name of the young man. He said there were no children in the house.'

This news had come with a horrendous story of lives destroyed. The next part of Omar's story was the key that gave Elizabeth hope. For the previous five years, Hasan had been visiting the site of this massacre to pray for forgiveness and mercy, for he said this first act troubled him greatly.

He said he had seen a woman and a man, with three children, coming to tend the graves and pay their respects. He asked the local villagers who they were and they told him the woman was the surviving daughter of the family who once lived there. Her name was Fatima.

Suicide is strongly condemned by Islam. It is strictly forbidden to take your own life. Next day as the sun rose, Hasan went to the beach near Ahmed bin Khaleed al-Ibrahim's house and shot himself in the head with his police revolver.

Omar said he found it hard to tell his story. It would be easier to push it away but he knew it was important.

'You see. It is true it is painful for me to remember and to tell you,' Omar said, 'but this is what I believe: even if it is a long long time ago, if a little healing, a little good could come of remembering the names of those killed, then it would give some comfort to me. For such is my life: *Kweli chungu si uwongo mtamu*. "Bitter truth is better than a sweet lie".'

Omar covered his face with both his hands.

'The only joy in my old age is my granddaughter,' said Omar, his voice fading, 'for she and her children, they care for me. I do not deserve it.'

His story was finished. There was silence. Elizabeth felt it was a form of respect, an appreciation of Omar's effort. Mubarak was first to speak and he thanked Omar and invited him to go to evening prayers with their community.

Elizabeth knew Omar's story was a breakthrough for her search. Omar left as he had entered, his great-grandson caring for him. A low buzz of discussion followed him out. Elizabeth was tired, her leg throbbing.

'That was hard, very hard to tell this story,' Mubarak said, 'to look back and relive such pain. Perhaps there are numerous such stories in our history but you live only one life and sometimes they are difficult journeys.'

Mubarak departed to attend *Maghrib* prayers with *Mzee* Omar. 'We will talk tomorrow, Bibi Elizabeth. I think the journey is nearly over.'

61. Old Questions

Mubarak was not alone when he arrived at the Hotel Starehe the next morning. Overnight rains had washed the air clean and the gathering of elderly men was starting their gentle stretches facing a silver calm sea. On this day, two women joined them but stood to one side, shoulder to shoulder. Their exercise was interspersed with laughter. Elizabeth thought fleetingly that she would like to join them.

There was no laughter on the face of the purposeful man accompanying Mubarak.

'Bibi Elizabeth, this is my brother, Saif,' said Mubarak. 'Let us find somewhere private to talk.' Saif was dressed in Western clothing, although he wore a blue embroidered *kofia*. He had the same lean handsome features of his brother but kindness was lacking in his face.

Manager Abdullah was profuse in his greetings and directed them to a quiet corner. 'Coffee? Can I bring you all coffee and something to eat?' He appeared pleased and curious about the meeting, hovering not far away.

Saif was a sterner man than his brother, without the effusive politeness she had come to expect in Zanzibar. At first, he would not look at her and she felt a latent distrust emanating from him.

'Bibi, Saif is a lawyer and I have told him about your case, about our interviews,' said Mubarak. 'He may be able to help. Last night, after prayers, I spoke. I asked about the name we now have, Ahmed bin Khaleed al-Ibrahim. Everyone shook their heads. You know a woman does not take her husband's name in our culture. She retains her birth name. So Fatima, daughter of Ahmed bin Khaleed al-Ibrahim would be called Fatima Ahmed al-Ibrahim or Fatima *bint* Ahmed al-Ibrahim, *bint* meaning "daughter of". Sometimes, a woman is called by her son's name, Fatima, Mama of Saif, for example. So ....'

Saif interrupted. 'So we may be able to trace her but, if we assume she grew up here during the despotic years of the first Presidents, she may have had to change her name. For safety.' Elizabeth could hear the lilt of an American accent. Had he also studied in the USA? 'However, there is another possible way forward. My brother says you have a property deed?'

'Yes, I do. Would you like to see it?' She had brought the photos and deed with her and laid them out.

'Saif is trying to help families from the Zanzibar diaspora claim back their houses,' said Mubarak. 'There may be a way forward if we can identify the house.'

Saif took the old document with reverence. Elizabeth has not seen this gentleness in him until this moment. 'Old, this is old.'

Mubarak smiled. 'You like old legal documents, do you not?'

'True. They tell a story. This one does. See here,' Saif said. He pointed to a black stamp at the bottom left. It was square with a peaked top containing flowing Arabic writing, and balanced left to right with dots and dashes. 'This is a royal insignia, the Sultan's monogram. I know this one. The insignia of Sayyid Barghash bin Said, Sultan of Zanzibar, of the Al-Busaidi clan. He ruled here for eighteen years, dying in 1888. The writing states, in the flowery legal terms of those times, the terms of a grant.'

'It is a grant of land?' Mubarak said.

'Land and house.'

'Does it indicate the location?'

'Yes. See this here.' Saif pointed to a line of Arabic writing. 'It is in the Shangani *mtaa* or neighbourhood. It also has the notation that it is in the square on the side of the sea. I do not think it would be Kelele Square so it must be the other square in Shangani.' Saif turned the paper over and held it closer. 'Look at this. Did you notice this before?' he said.

'What is it?' Elizabeth said.

Saif pointed to five tiny lines of Arabic script. He sat back with a satisfied air. 'We are lucky. These are the names of the descendants of the original owner, right down to the time before the Revolution. The last name is the one you were given.'

'Amazing,' said Mubarak, 'I did not look at the back. What are the names?'

'At the bottom the one we know, Ahmed bin Khaleed al-Ibrahim: the next would be his father, Khaleed bin Hamdan al-Ibrahim.'

'Khaleed, that's the name my father gave me. Khaleed was his friend who brought the box for safekeeping,' said Elizabeth.

'Then there are three more names, all ending in Ibrahim or al-Ibrahim.'

'So this proves the family's ownership?'

'Yes,' said Saif. 'A valuable document but, even if we find the daughter, she may not get the house back.'

'Why?'

'It is case by case,' said Saif. 'The authorities are not acknowledging the properties were taken illegally or unjustly. But there seems to be a little flexibility. We go from one department to another. It depends where the house is and who is now occupying it. If there are many residents paying rent, it is a problem as accommodation must be found for them. Compensation is often asked for. This can be difficult. My clients' families got nothing in compensation when the houses were nationalised in 1964. And then, consider the condition of these houses.'

'They are run down?' Elizabeth said.

'An understatement,' Saif replied. 'They are often occupied by over ten families and each room is full. Houses fall down every monsoon season.'

'Sometimes rooms with high ceilings have been subdivided by adding another floor,' said Mubarak with a cutting gesture of his hand. 'So the original owner or their children are faced with extensive maintenance costs.'

Saif leant forward, pushing the tray of coffee aside. 'There are many people I deal with and I have heard numerous stories of hardship and survival. You were here then and your father ... can I ask you something?'

'Yes. Go ahead, but I was only a child,' she said. She felt defensive.

'Our Sultan. Mubarak said your father was on the boat leaving Zanzibar with the Sultan.'

'That is so, and I should also have been on it.'

'People say he ran away, leaving his people. What do you know?'

She paused: so this was what was on his mind. The antagonism. The British to blame. Was she guilty by association? Close on fifty years ago and questions still unanswered.

'Saif, Mubarak, I can only tell you what I heard from my father. At the time, I hardly understood what was happening.'

'What did he say?' said Mubarak leaning forward, shoulder to shoulder with his brother. 'For us, this history is important, every part of it.' Abdullah, had crept closer and was obviously listening.

Elizabeth remembered the scene, her father leaving, the white *Salama* floating on the water, the sunny blue day turning horribly wrong.

'They were going to kill the Sultan and his family,' said Elizabeth. 'The one on the radio, Okello, warned the Sultan he was coming for him, said the Sultan should kill his family first before he and his mobs arrived. Sultan Jamshid wanted to stay, to fight. He had a few arms and men with him but he also had women and children. My father, the Police Commissioner and his own advisors begged him to go to the safety of the boat before the rebel thugs got into Stone Town. The Sultan was reluctant. He only left at the last moment.'

'And on board?'

'My father hoped, expected, Mohammed Shamte and his Cabinet members would come and they would have a government to be a voice in the negotiation. For an unknown reason, the Cabinet members were given different advice by the British High Commissioner—advice to stay and negotiate with Karume and Okello.'

'So they were all captured and imprisoned,' said Saif.

'First, they agreed to make a radio announcement resigning, stepping down,' said Elizabeth. 'They were told it was to stop the bloodshed.'

'But it didn't, did it?' said Saif. His voice was strong and again had an accusatory air.

'No,' she said. 'It did not. My father and the others waited on board until they had rescued the police contingent at Malindi Police Station. When they were being shot at from the shoreline and no more people were escaping, they left Zanzibar on the *Seyyid Khalifa*. Sultan Jamshid called a council. He wanted to go to Pemba Island where they had many supporters, wanted to fight from there. My father said the Sultan was a brave man.'

'He went to Mombasa instead,' said Saif.

'Yes. It was the *liwali* of Mombasa who invited them there for safety but they were refused entry by the Kenyan Government,' Elizabeth kept her voice level. 'Kenya had promptly recognised the revolutionary mob and perhaps President Kenyatta was worried the coastal people would welcome the Sultan with open arms. It was a bitter blow, my father said. If they had Shamte and his Cabinet on board, they had more options; instead they had few arms and even in Pemba there were not many arms.'

There was silence between them. Mubarak looked at his brother who hung his head.

The past, she thought, is twisted and changed by a hundred voices in the passage of time. Yet families were still looking for answers to make it understandable. Everyone has a story and the story gathers certainty as the years pass. What happened? There are those things known for sure, a shot fired, a death, a bloated body on the beach, a narrow escape. Other events are guessed at; the story told in many versions, like a rumour. Were they not all trying to steer a path through a turbulent history towards the hope for a better future?

It was Mubarak who spoke next, his voice calmer. 'What happened when they left Mombasa?'

'After they were denied entry, they sailed along the coast for a few days,' she said. 'The boat was overcrowded and they were running out of food. My father said they worried about a mutiny, about the police on board, worried if they were loyal. All this time, negotiations went on with the British. Finally, they organised safe passage through Dar-es-Salaam for the Sultan and his family.'

'Asylum in Britain?' Saif said.

'Yes. The British Government also gave him an allowance under travel restrictions.'

'It suited them, to get him out of the way,' Saif said.

'I suppose so,' Elizabeth said. 'You learn over the years. President Nyerere was close to the West. It was the time of the Cold War and the British were playing their own game. Many wonder about Nyerere's involvement. Oscar Kambona is a name that keeps coming up. He was Minister for Defence and Foreign Affairs in Tanganyika and was close to Zanzibar's Mohammed Babu and a man called Hanga.'

Saif leant forward. 'Have you seen the films of the Revolution?'

'Sorry?' she was thrown.

'On YouTube, the YouTube ones shot from the air.'

She had seen them and wept. Who would not weep? The old Italian films had been transferred onto the internet. They showed the slaughter that had taken place, the long rows of *kanzu*-clad men being herded by rifle-toting rebels along paths between the coconut palms, the open mass graves, the mudflats at low tide covered in bodies.

'Yes, Saif, I have seen them. They are terrible.'

'Do you think they are genuine?' Saif said.

'Yes, I do. I know they are controversial,' Elizabeth replied.

'Some like to believe those scenes are staged—for them, it is better to deny genocide.'

'I don't think you could ever have staged what I saw,' she said. 'I am sorry.'

'It is not a matter of blame,' said Mubarak. 'We are all responsible to try to make it a better world, to make sure it does not happen again, to stop the poison of hatred that you see in those films. There is something we believe in: it is *heshima,* which in English is "respect and honour", but more than that. We need to bring back *heshima* to our islands.'

'Not so easy,' Saif said.

'No,' said Mubarak, 'it will not be easy but it will be worth it. It is the only way to stop the cycle of anger and argument. Almost fifty years! We have to make a better future.'

They sat without speaking, all three dealing with memories. And it was in this space that Elizabeth remembered the conversation she had overheard on her way out of Mambo Msiige.

'I meant to ask you. Do either of you know a man called Hadir, *Bwana* Hadir, a developer, he buys houses?'

Mubarak, looking stunned, sat back. Saif looked at his brother and some understanding passed between them. 'If you are speaking about Salim Hadir, yes, we know him,' he said. 'Why do you ask?'

'Mubarak was telling me about properties in Stone Town,' Elizabeth said. 'I overheard a conversation, one night, early this week.' She told them about the discussion she overheard on the beach and, in doing so, she explained the full story of her search in Mambo Msiige.

Mubarak laughed. 'You are a brave woman, Bibi Elizabeth.'

'This is important,' said Saif, 'for me and my clients. We have problems with that government department. If they are corrupt, it explains a few things. You say his name is Yasar and he stutters? I know him. He is the head of the department.'

'You must be careful, Saif,' said Mubarak. 'Think of the consequences of making this public, for all of us.'

'No,' said Saif, 'I shall not make it public. There are ways to stop this wicked business without going public.'

'And now, let us take this document and go for a walk,' said Mubarak standing up. 'It is time.'

62. The Hidden and the Open

Elizabeth took her sling bag, heavy with Khaleed's possessions. It came to her that almost fifty years ago he had walked the same route she was taking. Now she was the bearer of his most precious things and, like him, she was trying to find a safe haven for them.

Mubarak led the way, turning right towards Kelele Square and then left down a narrow pedestrian alley. After fifty metres, they rounded a sharp corner into a square between old stone walls. On their right was a pile of rubble, the remains of a house long collapsed. Three pawpaw trees grew amongst the stones and plastic bags. Over the larger stones around the edge, *kangas* and shirts were draped creating a mosaic of colour.

Saif held the deed in his hand. He turned to them. 'This is where the document shows the house.' They all stared at the rubble. He smoothed the deed flat against a wall and looked at it, puzzled. 'No,' he said, turning around and squinting into the sunlight, 'not that corner. It should be on the sea-side. It has to be over there.'

There were nine remaining houses opening into the square. As with all Stone Town houses, the façades revealed little. Several had traditional wooden doors, some single-leaved without friezes or carved lintels. Two had grander entrances with brass fittings and intricate geometric patterns carved in their frames. Around the edge of the square, most houses had short *barazas*. Three elderly men watched them from the cool shadows.

Saif pointed to the western side of the square. 'There.'

Before them was a three-storey house with an impressive door and a long *baraza*. The face of the house was bright in the sunlight. Tubs of crimson geraniums flanked the entrance and above it hung two signs, 'Kombe Clothing' and 'Assured Accounting Services'.

The huge door was freshly oiled, its brass knobs shining against the dark wood. As Elizabeth approached, she heard raised voices so she hesitated in the doorway. Inside, a group of men and women were facing each other, deep in argument. She paused for a moment allowing her eyes to adjust. Behind her, Mubarak and Saif shuffled off their sandals by the mat. It was a large room with a high ceiling striped by dark wooden poles. On one side were low racks of children's clothes, on the other a counter with a till, a large armchair with rattan backing and a table draped with a *kanga*. Black and white photographs of Zanzibar covered the walls in what appeared to be an exhibition.

The group turned to watch them as they entered and a young woman detached herself from the group. 'I am sorry, we are not open at the moment. Please come back later.' She appeared distracted and hardly looked at them.

Elizabeth knew her. It was Jamila who had helped her on her arrival two weeks previously. Before she had time to speak, Jamila turned back to the group. Two men in formal attire were facing an older man and woman. Elizabeth assumed they were Jamila's parents, the ones who had met her at the airport. One of the officials, in a white shirt with black epaulettes, appeared to be a policeman. He was writing in a notebook.

The man Elizabeth assumed was Jamila's father said, 'Why bring a policeman? We are not robbers.'

The short man answered. 'Sergeant Lobo is here as w-w-witness. H-h-he is recording this meeting. I am t-t-telling you. We have tried to negotiate with you for two years. The time has come.'

With a shock, Elizabeth recognised the voice of the stuttering man she had overheard on the beach, the man called Yasar. She looked at Mubarak and Saif. Saif nodded. The arguing group took no notice of them.

The older man replied. 'What is it you want? Why must we move out? We have lived here for twenty-seven years. Twenty-seven years! Because we have cared for our house, it is valuable.'

'Maybe, but I have checked,' Yasar said. 'T-t-the *mzee* who allowed you to move into this house has been found. We have his testimony. You paid him rent for only a little while until he left for the countryside. To us that is acknowledgement you knew you were not the owner. Y-y-you knew and yet you stopped paying. Negligent, we call that n-n-negligence. You should have been evicted. S-s-so if we wanted to, we could charge you backpayment of rent for all those years.'

The older woman spoke. Elizabeth could see she had been crying. 'I have given you my birth certificate. You know I am Fatima bint Ahmed al-Ibrahim. We have given you affidavits from my sister, and from Bibi Paka who knows it all. I ...'

Elizabeth's heart clenched in her chest. All she heard was the name, *Fatima bint Ahmed al-Ibrahim*. It was her! They had found her. She turned to Mubarak. He smiled, gestured to her. Saif handed her the paper he had been carrying.

Yasar's voice was gathering in certainty and anger. The stutter left him.

He was wagging a finger at them. 'And what do they prove?' he said. 'Your names, maybe so, maybe you never left, but where is proof this al-Ibrahim family owned this house? There are no records of this in our department. If you move out quietly, I can help you. This is a favour to you because you have been here a long time. If you go quickly, I ...,' he gestured in the air, 'my department, is prepared to forget the rent you owe us. It would be a lot of money because we could charge interest.'

'Excuse me,' said Elizabeth. 'Sorry to interrupt. Fatima?' They all turned towards her.

Yasar turned his head towards them briefly. 'There will be no sales today. T-t-the shop is closed. It will have to move.'

'Your grandfather, Fatima,' Elizabeth said, ignoring Yasar. 'Khaleed al-Ibrahim?'

'Yes?' said Fatima. 'Why? What are you asking?'

Elizabeth wanted to weep, happiness was close behind. 'I have brought you something from him,' she said and held out the old document, the proof of ownership.

'W-w-what is this? Who are you?' said Yasar.

Fatima looked stricken. It was Jamila who, turning, recognised Elizabeth and came to her. 'You are the woman from the plane? Who are you? What is this?'

Elizabeth handed Jamila the document. 'I am Elizabeth Hamilton. My father was friends with your mother's Babu,' said Elizabeth. 'On the day of the Revolution. It is a long story. I thought your family was lost.'

'Lost?' Fatima had sat down. 'What is this? Jamila, do you know this woman? Who is this? We are not lost.'

'No, Mama, we are not lost. But Bibi Elizabeth has found us.' Jamila was looking at the paper. 'I cannot read this. What is it?'

'Excuse me, I am Dr Mubarak Raisi,' said Mubarak. 'That is the formal document of this property. It is signed by Sultan Barghash bin Sultan gifting it to the al-Ibrahim family. My brother here, Saif Raisi, is a lawyer, a specialist in such documents. You know one another?'

A barely polite nod was exchanged between Saif and Yasar. Fatima had sat down to examine the document. 'Where did you get this?' she said. Her face was beautiful to Elizabeth. For days, she had imagined what the three children in the photograph would look like. Here was one of them.

'It has been hidden,' said Elizabeth, 'for all this time.'

Yasar glanced at the paper. 'W-w-we will have to examine this. It does not c-c-change the fact it is time for your family to move out. You can submit an appeal to the authorities with this new thing you have found.'

'Mr Yasar?' Elizabeth said. 'Do you know *Bwana* Salim Hadir?' Yasar was startled. He said nothing. 'I understand you have a special arrangement with him. Is that so?'

'W-w-what is this? What right have you to come here and say these things?' Yasar said. Elizabeth could see his eyes darting from Mubarak to Saif and back to her.

'Yes,' Elizabeth said taking a step closer to Yasar. 'A special arrangement to do with bank accounts in US dollars for certain services, certain desirable properties. You spoke about valuable documents that go missing. I will make public these things I hear.'

Mubarak came to stand beside her. 'The Revolutionary Government says they are against corruption. Certainly they will not be pleased to have this made public. This is a policeman you have with you? That is good. We can make the necessary statements right now so we can help the government make sure that nothing is wrong. There is that department I know—the Zanzibar Anti-Corruption Authority. We only want to do our duty.'

'Of course, we must all do our duty,' said Yasar. 'I have only been working for the people to increase growth and end poverty.' He turned sharply and gestured to the policeman. 'He comes with me,' and using Swahili spoke sharply without a stammer to his colleague before he moved around Mubarak and Saif towards the door. 'A-a-and if th-th-there has been a m-mistake with this property, I must apologise and hope that you won't take it any further.'

He left and they heard him shouting back and forth with the men relaxing on the *baraza* as he crossed the square. Then they heard only silence and the cawing of crows circling overhead.

Mubarak and Saif introduced themselves. Mubarak said, 'Yasar will leave you in peace now. I have been helping Bibi Elizabeth. She has worked hard to find you. It is a long story and it is her story to tell.'

'My life has been full of surprises,' Fatima said. 'Many times I have been sad, maybe even lost. Now I have a story to hear and I give thanks once more.'

63. Time to Dream

Six months later

The sands of Zanzibar are white, so white that under the midday sun the glare hurts your eyes. At the old *shamba* of Salama Daima the beach is small, curved between two rocky headlands: a scoop of beach edged by deep rows of coconut palms giving welcome shade. The headlands offer protection from the main force of the seas driven by the *kaskazi* monsoon.

Today white-caps of the high seas can be seen further out where the sea is deep dark blue. There is no fishing on this day of strong winds. The *ngalawa* are pulled up on the shore and resting this way and that on their outriggers.

In the shade, four women sit side-by-side. Between Fatima and Akila, a two-year-old is digging in the sand. Fatima runs her hand through the pile of sand growing beside her. 'At first it looks white but, if you look closely, there are many colours, little shells and remains of sea things.'

Akila pulls the hat over her daughter's head. 'She is like you, Mama, she is my serious one. All day long she is asking questions!'

'We have a big question to answer,' says Fatima. 'Have you thought about it, Akila, Jamila, Elizabeth? Can we do this together? Is it possible?'

'I am committed,' Jamila says, 'We have the promise of a lease on this land from the government, and I have three teachers ready to join us. We can start small and grow with each year.'

Fatima turns to Elizabeth, shifting a little as the pile of sand grows beside her. 'And Elizabeth? Tomorrow we will come with you to the airport. Not to say goodbye but to welcome your sister, Mary, and your daughter to Zanzibar.'

Discussing her sister, her daughter, does not come easily to Elizabeth. She is learning how to find the words and stop the tears that come without reason. 'I can think of little else today,' she says, 'but I am with you too. I will help. Jamila must tell me how I can fit in.'

'You are a teacher,' Jamila replies. 'We will need all the support we can get, and you are re-learning your Swahili.'

'Aunt Basilah and I will help with the funding,' said Akila. 'You are unlikely to get any financial support from the Zanzibar Government. We must set up a charity. I can do the legal work for that.'

'The gifts from my Babu will be a start,' Fatima says. 'We have no need to keep the gold jewellery. Such gifts should not be wasted. Basilah agrees and will help to sell them.'

'I received a gift too,' says Elizabeth. 'My fourteenth birthday presents from my sister and my parents. That's how I recognised the book in your shop. It's the same book.'

'*The World We Live In*,' says Fatima. 'I know every picture, every word of that book. It was my schooling.'

'Did you translate the loose document from the box?' Elizabeth asks.

'Yes, the Arabic was difficult. Saif helped,' Fatima says. 'It is a *dua*, a prayer, a promise to Allah. I have a copy for you, Elizabeth, and I will tell you why it is special. Each thing you brought us was precious beyond words. It is our connection to the past. It has helped with our healing. Now there will be a tomorrow where there is less pain in our memories.'

They watch Akila's two older children dancing along the shoreline. A boy and a girl, their footprints are washed by the waves, their slim bodies outlined by the light from the sea, their high voices like distant birdsong.

'A long long time ago, I watched Taha and Basilah running there. Who could have imagined our lives? Now it is time for my grandchildren to run free,' Fatima says. 'I give thanks for the mercy of Allah.'

Translation of 'Ahd Namah'

(Promise to Allah)

In the Name of Allah, The Beneficent, The Merciful

O Allah! The Creator of the skies and the earth

The Knower of the hidden and the open

You are The Beneficent, The Merciful

O Allah! I promise you in this earthly life

and I bear witness that

there is no one worthy of worship except You

You are One and Only without any partner

and I bear witness that

Sayyidina Hadrat Muhammad Sallallahu alaihi wa Sallam

is Your servant and Your Messenger

(O Allah!) Please do not leave me to my own self

because if You abandon me to my own desires

I might be drawn towards evil and away from goodness

and I have no support except Your Mercy

So accept my promise with You

to be kept till the Day of Judgement

Truly, You never break a promise

And may the blessings of Allah, The Exalted

be on His best creation

Sayyidina Hadrat Muhammad Sallallahu alaihi wa Sallam

and on his family and all companions

(O Allah! Accept this prayer)

With Your Mercy, O The Most Merciful of those who show mercy.

Epilogue: Salama Daima

Saburi, heshima nusu ya hekima   *Patience and respect are half of wisdom*

Take the road north from Stone Town that follows the coastline all the way past Tumbatu Island to Ras Nungwi, the northern tip of Zanzibar Island. Nowadays, it is called Malawi Road. New development stretches along the road for a long way but eventually the dense housing disappears and the coconut and clove trees can be seen behind the *dukas* lining the road. Everywhere there are people: old ladies are tending their simple shops, young men ride by on bicycles and children watch the passing traffic. These people are not wealthy. Sometimes an old windowless *dala-dala* bus rushes past, its rooftop covered in baggage.

The road passes through Kibweni where the Sultan's palace is now a state house of the Revolutionary Government. Beyond Kibweni, you come to the village of Bububu and the road turns a little east inland. Less than a kilometre further on, beyond Chuini, you will see a road on the left with a neat sign, *Salama Daima School for Girls*. Take this turning. The road winds down towards the coast for over two kilometres. The last section is through an avenue of massive mango trees that bear the fruit called *shomari*. A long time ago, a house stood at the end of this avenue: today, this is commemorated by a simple notice.

Further on, you can see a collection of white-washed single-storey buildings arranged around a quadrangle. This is the school we have come to visit. The head teacher is Jamila al-Ibrahim. Currently, schooling is provided for the first three years of primary education: a kindergarten is also attached. Each year, another classroom for a more senior year of schooling is to be built. In three years' time, all primary years will be catered for. Fifty girls are in each year, in two classes. All the classrooms have desks and are fully fitted. To one side are the specialist rooms: a science room, nutrition centre, a library with computers and the teachers' offices.

The girls' uniform is simple: a deep blue dress with a white head covering. Not all the children wear the head covering when they are young. It is each family's decision. Schooling is free. The Revolutionary Government helped by releasing land for the school but is unable to fund schools to the level required for adequate education. Instead, each child is sponsored through appeals to the Zanzibar diaspora and through a room levy system to which several local hotels have elected to contribute.

The library is well stocked and is managed by Fatima, the mother of the head teacher Jamila al-Ibrahim. Fatima delights in reading to the younger girls. She says 'I teach them to love books, to love stories and, through listening, they learn.'

One corner of the library is called Cecelia's Corner. It is a space dedicated to study of the natural world. Children do projects related to the environment. On the walls, you can see their drawings of local birds and animals.

The language medium is KiSwahili. English is taught from the second year of schooling. Elizabeth Hamilton oversees this subject. She has recently moved to live in Stone Town.

The ongoing teacher education program is partly funded by an Omani charity. Teachers from Zanzibar can travel to Muscat and gain further experience. Jamila's Aunt Basilah who lives in Muscat organises this teacher exchange.

Beyond the school buildings is a playground, a single sports field and a short path leading to the sun-drenched beach. Just before you reach the last coconut palms, there are three graves on your right.

The sand around the graves is brushed smooth and there are no weeds. Many come here and remember those who died in 1964. And we remember too that one day we shall join them.

Jamila says, 'Long ago, my great-grandfather hid a box of treasure in an old house. The treasure slept there until our time of need. It saved us. Now we do not hide our treasure. We give it to our children and that learning is our gift for the future, for the world in which we live.'

Glossary

adhan (adhâh)	the Islamic call to prayer
Al Fatihah	from the Qur'an, the first seven verses often called 'The Opener', a prayer for God's guidance and help
askari	African policeman
ASP	Afro-Shirazi Party. Lost the 1963 election under the British Administration
astaghfirullah	prayer seeking forgiveness
ayah	nursemaid
baba	address: father
babu	address: grandfather
bao	game played on a wooden board with indentations using seeds or stones
baraza	a meeting or a meeting place—also refers to the concrete seating outside Swahili houses
bi mdogo	address: young woman (*mdogo (s)*—meaning small)
bibi harusi	a bride
bibi	address: for a married woman—also grandmother, can be shortened to 'bi'
bint-al-sahn	honey cake
binti	address: for an unmarried daughter
Bismillah	in the name of God
bui-bui	black shawl-like covering in silk or cotton for a Muslim woman
bwana	address: formal male address, like 'Mister' or 'sir'
chai	tea—scented with spices; also, any tea
chapati	unleavened round flat bread of Indian origin, also called *roti*
choo	toilet room; *mavi*—excrement
dada	address: sister
dafu	milk from a green coconut or an unripe coconut
dagaa	small fish like sardines
dala-dala	communal taxi buses
dawa	medicine, *madawa* (pl)
dua	a prayer
duiker	small antelope—in Zanzibar, it is Ader's *duiker* which is about thirty centimetres tall
duka	small shop
Eid Al-Fitr	holiday at the end of the month of Ramadan; breaking of the fast
Fajr	dawn prayers
G&T	gin and tonic (an alcoholic drink)
habari?	'How are you?' or 'Any news?'
halaiki	large crowd, politically inspired
hamali cart	a solid wooden handcart with car tyres used to

	transport goods to the harbour and to the market in the narrow streets of Stone Town
haram	a forbidden act, a sin that is punishable
hatari!	*Danger!*
heshima	respect or courtesy
HMG	Her Majesty's Government
hodi?	'Can I come in?' or 'Anyone home?'
Hujambo (Jambo)!	'Hello!'
ijumaa	Friday
Inshallah	Arabic: if God wills it
iqama	second call to prayer—given inside the mosque.
jambiya	Arabic curved dagger worn at the waist in Oman, Yemen and historic Zanzibar
jamhuri	republic
jina	Swahili: name or a proverb inscribed on a *kanga*
kahawa	coffee, often served in tiny china cups
kanga	traditional clothing for women: a rectangular piece of material wrapped around the body. Two identical pieces are usually used. (Named after the guinea fowl)
kanzu	traditional long white robe worn by Muslim men
karibu!	'Come in!' or 'Welcome!'
kaskazi	north-east monsoon (blows mid-November to early March in East Africa)
kiboko	whip (s), *viboko* (pl) traditionally made from hippopotamus hide
kikapu	basket woven from dried palm leaves or fibres, *vikapu* (pl)
kikoi	traditional rectangular cotton cloth worn by men
kimbunga	hurricane or storm
kisheti	sugared doughnuts
kitambi	bridal cloth to cover the bride
Kiunguja	Swahili dialect of Unguja/Zanzibar
kofia	embroidered prayer cap worn by Muslim men in East Africa, also any cap
kujitolea	volunteering (work)
kusi	south-west monsoon (from April to late October)
liwali	headman or governor appointed in colonial times
ma'salaam	'Goodbye': 'Farewell, go in peace'
maendeleo	progress or development
mafusho	charm: a Qur'anic verse written on paper and burnt. The smoke drives off evil spirits
Maghrib	Arabic for evening: the evening prayer
mahr	specific items promised or payable by the groom before marriage: dowry bride price
mahram	people you are not allowed to marry. Also means—

	acceptable male escorts for women
Makonde	Makonde tribe on the southern coast of mainland Tanganyika and in Mozambique
mama mkwe	mother-in-law
mapinduzi	revolution
masika	the long rains (mid-March to end of May in Zanzibar)
Merikani	American. The name given to the cheap white cloth imported into Zanzibar from America in the nineteenth century and worn by men and women
mganga	herbalist/witch, or a doctor, *waganga* (pl)
mishkaki	roasted meat on sticks, shish kebabs
mji	the central design on a *kanga*, the traditional cloth worn by women
mjini	downtown—sometimes a name for Stone Town
mtaa	ward or section of the town, neighbourhood, *mitaa* (pl)
mtunguu	snake—green mamba
muezzin	man appointed to issue the *adhan*, the call to prayer from the mosque
muhogo	cassava
mzanzibari	a person from Zanzibar, a local
mzee	address: older man, term of respect, *wazee* (pl)
mzungu	white person, *wazungu* (pl)
ngalawa	small wooden fishing boat/s with outriggers
NGO	non-governmental organisation
nikah	marriage agreement
nyoka	snake
nyumba kongwe	old houses—(sometimes the local name for Stone Town)
oud wood	wood, also called *udi* (incense) or agarwood, that emits a perfume when burnt
oud	ancient musical instrument like a mandolin used by *taarab* players
pakacha	fruit basket woven from a coconut leaf
panga	sharp steel blade for cutting bushes; a machete
panya	rat
pilau	rice cooked in stock with added spices and vegetables, meat or fish
pindo	the border pattern of a *kanga*, the traditional cloth worn by women
pishi	volume measure for grains, sugar and rice
qadi	a judge who applies Islamic law and presides over marriages
qibla	the direction which a Muslim faces in order to pray. It is the direction of Mecca

Ras	cape or promontory as in Ras Shangani or Ras Nungwi
salat	formal prayer
samoosas	triangles of pastry filled with curried vegetables or mince and deep fried
Sauti Ya Unguja	Voice of Zanzibar (or Radio Zanzibar) (a radio station)
shahada	Muslim prayer of faith
Shaitan	Arabic: Satan
shamba	farm
sheha	village councillor
shetani	spirit, also Satan, the devil (sometimes *sheitani*), *mashetani* (pl)
Shirazi	the Shirazi people of the coast have Persian connections from ancient times
shomari	a type of sucking mango—Zanzibar has many varieties of mangoes
siku kuu	celebration (big) day; such as the day after the end of Ramadan; a holiday
siri	a secret, *wingi* (pl)
somo	female counsellor for women before marriage; also namesake; companion
Surat il-Fatiha	first chapter of the Qur'an, consisting of seven verses
taarab	music of the Swahili coast using an *udi* (*oud*) and various instruments
tabla	Indian drums. Part of the *taarab* orchestra
uchawi	magic
ugali	maize flour cooked with water to a stiff porridge-like consistency
uhuru na jamhuri	freedom and republic
uhuru	freedom (political)
UMMA Party	the socialist party (Masses Party) formed in 1963 by Mohamed A B Babu as a breakaway from the ZNP. Forced to disband shortly after the 1964 Revolution
Unguja	local name of the main island in the Zanzibar archipelago, commonly called Zanzibar
vitumbua	small sweet hot rice cakes like doughnuts. Usually eaten with breakfast
vuli	short rains (mid-October to November in Zanzibar)
waarabu	Arabs (pl), also *mwarabu* (s), *ustaarabu* means civilised or well-mannered
wabara	mainlanders (pl)
wahindi	Indians (pl)
waingereza	English people (pl), *mwingereza* (s)
wakf	charity endowment, usually consisting of a property
wali	a mediator or guardian for a woman seeking

	marriage
watumbatu	people of Tumbatu Island—off Zanzibar Island's north-west coast
wazir	advisor or minister
yamini	an oath
ZNP	Zanzibar Nationalist Party, in coalition with the ZPPP
ZPPP	Zanzibar and Pemba People's Party

References—Chapter Quotes

Maps: Zanzibar. Land Survey Office, Zanzibar, 1961 from *A Guide to Zanzibar,* Zanzibar Tourist Information Bureau, East African Printers, Nairobi, Kenya, 1961

KiSwahili proverbs:

Chapters 1, 4, 8, 13, 16-39, epilogue, *Swahili Proverbs: KiSwahili Methali,* Centre for University Studies, University of Illinois, <swahiliproverbs.afrst.illinois.edu/> (October 2014)

Chapter 5, for further discussion on mainland invasion: Ghassany, H, *Kwaheri Ukoloni, Kwaheri Uhuru! Zanzibar na Mapinduzi ya Afrabia,* H Ghassany, USA, 2010

Chapters 16, 18, *Methali za Kiswahili – Swahili proverbs, <www. mwambao.com/methali.htm> (2014)*

Other quotes:

Chapter 10, *The Koran, The Believers, Al-Mu'min 40:60,* Penguin Classics, trans. Dawood, N J, p. 332, 1956

Chapter 12, *The Koran, Chapter (9) sūrat l-tawbah (The Repentance).* 9:51, Translated: *The Meaning of the Glorious Koran,* Pickthall, M, 1930

Chapter 16: Salah, M T, *Chinua Achebe: Teacher of Light, A Biography,* Africa World Press, 2003, p. 59

Chapter 27, *Haq Islam, Duas on Weddings, <www.haqislam.org/ dua-on-marriage-wedding/> (2013)*

Chapter 28, *The Koran, The Night Journey, Al-Isra 17:44,* Penguin Classics, trans. Dawood, N J, p. 200, 1956

Kundera, M, *Book of Laughter & Forgetting*, Harper Perennial Modern Classics, USA, 1999

Chapter 32, *The Koran, The Exordium, 1:1–1:7,* Penguin Classics, trans. Dawood, N J, p. 9, 1956

Communal—Nine Lullabies from Zanzibar, in *Women Writing Africa – the Eastern Region, Volume 3*, City University of New York, USA, p. 432, 2007

Further Reading

Books: Al Barwani, A M, *Conflicts and Harmony in Zanzibar – Memoirs,* Oman, 1992

Al Busaidi, Saud bin A, *Memoirs of an Omani Gentleman from Zanzibar,* Al Roya Press, Oman, 2012

Al Riyami, Nasser bin A, *Zanzibar – Personalities and Events (1828–1972),* Beirut Bookshop, Muscat, Oman, 2012

Barwani, N, *Gone is Yesterday—Imepita Jana,* Bright Pen, Bedfordshire, UK, 2010

Bennett, N R, *A History of the Arab State of Zanzibar,* Methuen & Co Ltd, UK, 1978

Burgess, G T, *Race, Revolution and the Struggle for Human Rights in Zanzibar,* Ohio University Press, Ohio, USA, 2009

Clayton, A, *The Zanzibar Revolution and its Aftermath,* C. Hurst & Co, London, 1981

Fairooz, A T, *The Truth – to refute Falsehood,* unpublished MS, Dubai, 1995

Ghassany, H, *Kwaheri Ukoloni, Kwaheri Uhuru! Zanzibar na Mapinduzi ya Afrabia,* H Ghassany, USA, 2010

Glassman, J, *War of Words, War of Stones,* Indiana University Press, Indiana, USA, 2011

Gurnah, A, *By the Sea,* Bloomsbury Publishing, London, 2001

Hall, R, *Empires of the Monsoon,* Harper Collins, London, UK, 1998

Hunter, H L, *Zanzibar – the Hundred Days Revolution,* ABC—CLIO, California, USA, 2010

Ingrams, W H, *Zanzibar – Its History and its People,* Routledge, Oxford, UK, Digital printing 2006 (1931)

Lebling, R, *Legends of the Fire Spirits – Jinn & Genies from Arabia to Zanzibar,* I B Tauris, UK, 2010

Lofchie, M F, *Zanzibar: Background to Revolution,* Princeton University Press, New Jersey, USA, 1965

Martin, E B, *Zanzibar – Tradition and Revolution,* Hamish Hamilton, London, 1978

Okello, J, *Revolution in Zanzibar,* East African Publishing House, Nairobi, Kenya, 1967

Peera, Z, *Memories of a Zanzibar Wedding,* 1995, in *Women Writing*

Africa – the Eastern Region, Volume 3, City Uni. of New York, USA, 2007

Petterson, D, *Revolution in Zanzibar*, Westview Press, Colorado, USA, 2002

Sheriff, A, *Dhow Cultures of the Indian Ocean*, C. Hurst & Co, London, UK, 1988

Sheriff, A, Ferguson, E, *Zanzibar under Colonial Rule*, Ohio University Press, Ohio, USA, 1991

The History & Conservation of Zanzibar Stone Town, ed. Prof Abdul Sheriff, Ohio University Press, Ohio, USA, 1995

Articles & Web Sites:

Cameron, G, *Zanzibar's Turbulent Transition*, Review of African Political Economy, N 0.92.313–330, ROAPE Publications Ltd., ISSN 0305–6244, 2002

Myers, G A, *Making the Socialist City of Zanzibar*, Geographical Review, Vol. 84, No. 4 (Oct., 1994), pp. 451–464, American Geographical Society, <www.jstor.org/stable/215759>, (2009)

Suhonen, R, *Mapinduzi Daima – Revolution Forever: Using the 1964 Revolution in Nationalistic Political Discourses in Zanzibar*, Master's thesis, Institute for Asian and African Studies, University of Helsinki, <helda.helsinki.fi/handle/10138/19217>, 2009

Triplett, G W, *Zanzibar: The Politics of Revolutionary Inequality*, The Journal of Modern African Studies, Vol. 9, No. 4 (Dec., 1971), pp. 612–617, Cambridge University Press Stable, <www.jstor.org/stable/160218>, (27 July 2009)

Walsh, M T, *Eating Bats on Pemba Island*, University of Sussex, UK, for Mvita: Newsletter of the Regional Centre for the Study of Archaeology in Eastern and Southern Africa, Vol. 6, pp. 15–18, (1995)

Walsh, M T, *The Use of Wild and Cultivated Plants as Famine Foods on Pemba Island, Zanzibar*, Etudes Océan Indien (Special issue: Plantes et Sociétés dans l'Océan Indien Occidental), Vol. 42/43: pp. 217–241, (2009, 2011)

Walsh, M T, Goldman, H, *Chasing imaginary leopards: science, witchcraft and the politics of conservation in Zanzibar*, Journal of Eastern African Studies, Vol 6, No. 4, 2012

Wilson, A, *The Threat of Liberation – Imperialism and Revolution in Zanzibar*, Pluto Press, London, UK, 2013

History of Zanzibar web site: <http://zanzibarhistory.org/ 2013>